C000063974

NO MORE DEEDS

THE DUNN FAMILY SERIES
BOOK 3

RICKY BLACK

CHAPTER ONE

SEPTEMBER 2021

NATTY DEEDS LAY IN BED, restless and unable to sleep. He couldn't turn off his thoughts, which seemed to be a regular occurrence these days. Lorraine was asleep next to him, and even as Natty lay there, he could hear her murmuring in her sleep, constantly moving and frowning, making little faces.

It had been a rough time for her as of late, and Natty was full of guilt over what had happened to her. His stubbornness and immaturity almost cost Lorraine her life.

When Natty thought about her dying, it made his whole body clench.

Hence, the insomnia.

Lorraine had been forced to take someone's life, and the experience had changed her, likely forever. Natty was doing his best to help her through it. He wanted them to move in together, but Lorraine didn't want to upheave her son, Jaden, by moving too quickly. While Natty understood her reasoning, it still disappointed him.

Unfortunately, Lorraine wasn't Natty's only concern right now.

Months ago, Natty had stepped up. He had returned to work for his uncle Mitch after a short period away, and was now the number two person in the organisation. An argument with his mum had revealed the twisted truth his family had kept from him: His uncle had ordered the murder of Natty's dad, Tyrone Dunn.

Since learning this, Natty hadn't spoken to his mum, and didn't plan to. The love remained, but was corrupted. He couldn't look past it.

He wouldn't look past it.

At the gravesite of his dad, Natty had made a vow. He would murder his uncle for what he had done.

Even as he made the vow, Natty knew it wouldn't be an easy task. Mitch Dunn had been a powerhouse in the Leeds crime game for decades. He had survived many wars and kingpins, and was still going strong as the dominant force on the streets of Leeds. He was wily, respected, and well-protected.

Natty didn't have a choice, though. He didn't know the full circumstances of why his dad had been murdered, and while it wouldn't change anything, it didn't deter his desire to know.

How could he find out, though?

Rudy Campbell, his father's old friend, and Mitch's former right-hand man, was dead. Natty himself had pulled the trigger.

At the time, Natty thought he was protecting his family. He hadn't known he was leaving a bigger monster behind.

It was scary just how twisted his family was. Natty was trying to plan his moves properly. He had been accused in the past of rushing in, losing his temper, and acting without thinking.

He was at a loss about what to do, though. Currently, he was at the mercy of his uncle. He worked for him, taking his money, running his business.

Recently, his uncle had even given him a bonus, with two hundred and fifty thousand pounds being paid into an account. It was more money than Natty had ever earned in a single sitting, and it spoke to the level his uncle was at. His wealth and power were unfathomable to Natty.

Yet, he still needed to die.

Realising sleep wasn't coming, Natty climbed from the bed, tiptoeing so as not to disturb Lorraine. He didn't expect he would. She was quite a heavy sleeper, whereas years of working in the Hood had taught Natty to get up and move at a moment's notice. You could never be caught slipping, and his training with Clarke had only exemplified that.

Natty headed downstairs, surprised to see the light on in the living room. Eleven-year-old Jaden Richards was on the sofa, watching television. He glanced up, freezing when he saw Natty.

'Little man, what are you doing up?' Natty asked. Jaden had gone to bed hours ago, so it was a surprise to find him still awake.

'I couldn't sleep,' said Jaden, looking sheepish. Natty sat next to him, letting out a grateful exhale. Lorraine's sofas were incredibly comfortable.

'Why? What's going through your mind?'

Jaden gave him a blank look, and Natty grinned. He'd forgotten he was talking to a child for a moment.

'Sorry. I just wondered why you couldn't sleep,' he said.

'I don't know,' said Jaden. He glanced at Natty, then back to the television. Natty sensed he had something on his mind; something he was unsure of how to bring up.

'Jay, if there's ever anything you want to tell me, you know you always can, right?'

Jaden looked at him again but didn't reply.

'I promise, I'll always try to listen,' Natty finished.

Jaden played with his fingers, unable to resist fidgeting. Natty faced the television now, trying to see if he recognised the old action film playing. It had Dolph Lundgren in, but the name escaped him.

'It's . . . it's my mum.'

Again, Natty faced Jaden.

'What about her?'

'I'm worried about her.'

Natty said nothing, silently imploring Jaden to continue.

'She's always upset, and I don't know why. Sometimes I see her crying, and then other times . . . she's staring into space, but when I ask her what's wrong, she just says she's fine.'

Natty was surprised Jaden had picked up on Lorraine's mood, but shouldn't have been. He was a sharp kid, who had his mum's brain.

'Sometimes it gets like that,' Natty started. 'Your mum has a lot on her mind, but she'll be fine.'

'I think it's to do with my dad,' said Jaden, his tone almost conspiratorial. Natty hid his surprise. Jaden knew his dad was dead. They had gone to his funeral, after all. Natty had accompanied Jaden and Lorraine, and the day had been tough.

No one knew who had killed Raider, and the story spreading around the streets was that he'd died in a gang war. That being said, when Lorraine arrived at the church with Natty, it sent tongues wagging. No one said anything directly to her, but the tension in the air was clear.

There had been little contact from Raider's family since that day.

'What makes you think that?'

'He always made my mum upset,' said Jaden. 'When he used to come and see me, sometimes they would shout at each other. After he left, she would cry. I saw her.'

Natty hesitated, then reached out and hugged Jaden, gratified when the boy didn't pull away.

'Your mum will be fine, Jay. Sometimes people just need time. Do you know what the good thing about all of this is?'

Jaden shook his head, waiting for the answer.

'Your mum has both of us. We can help her, no matter what the problem is. We're her guys. Right?'

Jaden nodded, smiling.

'Good. If we're going to help her, we need to be fresh. That means you going to bed and getting some sleep.'

'Okay, Nat. I'll see you in the morning.'

'Cool, kid. Goodnight.'

Jaden went upstairs, and Natty kept watching the film, wondering what he could do to help Lorraine. He still wished it had been him that had murdered Raider.

At least then, Lorraine wouldn't have to deal with the burden.

Natty stifled a yawn, debating going to make some coffee. It was two o'clock in the morning, and he woke up early most days. He had some errands to run tomorrow, but they were things he could push back if he needed to.

Perks of being the boss, he mused.

After glancing in the kitchen's direction, Natty turned off the television, clambered to his feet, then headed upstairs. He would try to go back to sleep and log a few more hours of rest. Brushing his teeth and washing his face, he slid back into bed, smiling when Lorraine instinctively cuddled up against him. With that, he closed his eyes.

CHAPTER TWO

SPENCE WAS DEEP IN THOUGHT, staring out of his living room window, thinking about life. He was in recovery from a gunshot wound to the arm, sustained when he'd foolishly ridden along with Natty on a mission. The mission was a success, but Spence took a hit and, without Natty's quick instincts, would have likely lost his life.

Thinking about that day was a regular pastime for Spence. He often cursed his lack of action and preparedness, despite being told otherwise by Natty, Clarke, and anyone else that listened to him.

With Natty in charge of the crew, Spence had a free role. Essentially, he oversaw their dealers and reported to Natty. Natty led the crew and had been doing exceptionally well for the past few months, but Spence could tell something was wrong with him. He was often distracted and looked like he had the weight of the world on his shoulders.

Spence knew it wasn't from work; he understood the rigours of the job. This was something different; something personal. Spence recognised that because he was going through the same thing.

A few months ago, his ex-girlfriend, Anika, had resurfaced shortly after his accident. She had left Spence over a year ago, writing him a letter where she had admitted being unfaithful, telling him she couldn't be with him anymore. Spence had been heartbroken but worked through it with the help of Natty and Rosie, his current girlfriend.

When Anika left, her business went kaput, and she'd burned through her meagre savings. When she first called Spence, he'd hung up on her, not wanting to speak. For the next month, she kept calling, trying to apologise, until finally, they met.

Spence entered the coffee shop, feeling foolish, wishing he had the forti-tude to turn around and leave. He knew nothing good would come from being here, but it was too late now.

The coffee shop was in the heart of the city centre, and being mid-morning, there was a small queue of people waiting to be served — several women in business dress and a more casually attired group of students.

Spence slipped past them, his heart hammering against his chest when he saw Anika. Her face brightened when she saw him, and she stood. She looked haggard compared to when he'd last seen her, her hair not as carefully coiffed, and her makeup less carefully applied. She was still beautiful, and he quashed that fact, vowing not to get caught up.

As he approached, Anika leaned in for a hug, but Spence shook his head. They sat down. Anika put her hands on the table, then put them back on her lap. She'd dressed in a pair of jeans and a vest top, her jacket splayed over the back of the chair. An empty cup of coffee rested in front of her, and her phone was next to it, face-down.

Spence noted how worn the phone cover looked, and kept his eyes on it, before chastising himself.

He wasn't the one that had done wrong. He could look into her eyes.

'It's really good to see you, Spence. You look great.'

'Thanks,' replied Spence, not returning the compliment.

'How have you been? How's Natty doing?'

Spence shook his head again. 'We're not doing this, Anika.'

'Doing what?'

'Small talk. Skip it, and tell me what you want.'

Anika's eyebrows rose.

'You sound like Natty,' she said, trying to make a joke. It fell flat.

'If I'd acted like Natty earlier, I might not have got my heart broken.'

Anika coughed into her fist, unable to meet his eyes for a moment. She seemed unable to sit still, glancing around the cafe, before taking a deep breath and looking at him again.

'I really am sorry, Spence.'

'Your letter said you were,' said Spence bluntly. 'Carmen passed on your message too, when I tried to ring her after you left without a word.'

'I know, Spence. You're not wrong, and I'd understand if you hated me and never wanted to speak to me again, but I need to explain.'

'No, you don't.'

'Yes, I do. I never wanted to hurt you, but I felt trapped in a life that I wasn't sure I deserved.' She paused, as if anticipating him speaking. Spence didn't, and she continued. 'You were always so positive . . . always working toward something, and it felt like I was just there. Tagging along.' She gave him a once-over. 'You're definitely dressing a lot better. The investments must be doing very well for you.'

'Again, what do you want, Anika?'

Anika wet her lips.

'Do you want a coffee?'

Spence's nostrils flared.

'Talk. If I wanted a drink, I would've got one.'

Anika nodded.

'I want us to try again. I don't deserve it, but I love you, and I want us to make a proper go of it.'

Spence would be lying if he hadn't felt a slight jolt when Anika said the words, but it wasn't enough. It would never be enough.

'I have a girlfriend,' he said. Anika visibly slumped before him, but quickly pulled herself together.

'Rosie?' she asked after a moment.

'Yes,' said Spence. Anika was quiet, looking at her hands. Spence considered leaving, but was curious about what she would say next. Finally, Anika blew out a breath and gave him a small smile.

'I don't really have a right to be angry.'

'You don't. I'm glad you recognise that.'

'Did you want Rosie all along?'

Spence shook his head. 'I wanted you. You were the one who cheated, remember?'

Anika nodded.

'I did, and I will always regret it. You were wonderful, and I hurt you.' She got to her feet, then paused again. 'I . . . I'm going to work on myself. I want to be able to look at myself without loathing the image. I hope to see you around, Spence . . . I'm glad you're doing well.'

Since that first meeting, Anika had contacted him a few times, but he hadn't responded. He'd told no one he'd met her, knowing Natty and Rosie wouldn't understand.

Still staring out of the window, Spence sighed to himself. Anika was a stress that he didn't need. Ever since the meeting, he'd felt guilty. Spence was a planner by nature. He took pride in having his life mapped out, and his investments were proof of that. It was clear living under those circumstances had negatively impacted Anika.

Was he the problem?

Spence hadn't changed. If anything, he had doubled down his organisation and planning. Rather than bringing Rosie down, it seemed to lift her. She was interested in investing before they became close, but working with Spence took her to a whole new level.

Spence wondered if he and Anika were never meant to be. The more he thought about it, the clearer it was that they weren't compatible. He was as bad for her as she was for him.

Spence stood up. He didn't want to think about his ex-girlfriend anymore. Grabbing his jacket and phones, he left the house, the bodyguard he'd been assigned following. It still irked Spence that he needed a bodyguard, but Natty wouldn't hear otherwise.

Climbing into his car, he waited for the guard to follow suit.

CHAPTER THREE

MITCH DUNN SAT in his house, looking at his phone. His call had just ended, and after a moment, he slid to his feet and made a cup of tea. He'd lived in his home for over twenty years and had developed the habit of listening out for familiar sounds; certain floorboards creaking, the sounds of neighbours hailing one another as they walked down the Moortown street, the wind whistling through the iron gate at the front of the house.

The familiarity brought him comfort.

Mitch knew that nobody would expect a man of his status to live in a *normal house*. Money was no object. If he wanted a mansion, he could have had one. He often imagined himself pottering around from empty room to empty room, fingering the dust settling on the various surfaces. It wasn't for him.

Not until he retired, anyway.

He would need a cleaner when he did. Possibly more than one. Inviting people into his home that he didn't know was a risk he was unwilling to take.

Mitch waited for the kettle to boil, making his drink and adding two spoonfuls of sugar. His doctor had recommended he make the switch to green tea, but Mitch had ignored him. He'd earned the right to his creature comforts.

The call Mitch had held was about his nephew, Nathaniel, who called himself *Natty Deeds*. Nathaniel had always had potential. With little family left, Mitch had been keen on nurturing him.

Tasking Rudy Campbell with overseeing his progress, Mitch had watched as his friend struggled to get a handle on the young man. Nathaniel had his dad's charisma, but also inherited his temperament. Trouble often followed him. Or he went looking for it. Mitch had wondered whether appointing Rudy to oversee his progress was a mistake. He was, after all, Nathaniel's stepdad. A complex relationship that threatened to bear no fruit.

Until it did.

When Nathaniel stumbled across Rudy's side venture, everything changed. Rudy had carefully constructed a group, intending to kill Mitch and take control of his organisation.

Nathaniel blew the whistle on their plans, finally showing the maturity Mitch had been looking for. When he followed orders and executed Rudy and Elijah, Mitch knew he was ready.

It was amusing, Mitch thought, that after all Rudy's efforts to help nurture Nathaniel, his pulling the trigger on his mentor had become his moment of graduation.

Mitch had been pleased enough to offer Nathaniel the keys to the kingdom, only for his offer to be turned down. Far from the status-hungry, designer-label-driven young man he'd once been, Nathaniel had even turned down half a million pounds to take on the role.

Due to this, Mitch had considered his angle. *If it wasn't money and respect that moved his nephew, then what was it?*

Mitch kept tabs on his nephew, as he engaged in a relationship and became a stepfather. He'd let it happen, but always intended to bring him back into the fold. Nathaniel was blood and, more importantly, was too skilled to be permanently out of the fold.

It didn't take long. Nathaniel's motivations had changed. That much was clear to Mitch. When Roman attacked his friend Spence, and Natty was compelled to help, Mitch knew he had him. The key wasn't money, clothes, cars, or jewellery. Not anymore. Loyalty and love were Nathaniel's motivations, and that was something Mitch could use.

Mitch sat at the kitchen table and sipped his drink, unsure why he even bothered with the table. He rarely had guests, and when he did, he always met them in the garage or in the office he'd had built. Ultimately, it just seemed proper, and was harmless.

Nathaniel was doing well in his role, but Roman was still out there. He was charismatic, seemingly skilled, and had flourished under the guidance of very skilled gangsters. More importantly, Mitch knew precisely who was backing Roman, and that was something that couldn't be allowed to fester.

When Mitch had finished his drink and washed the cup, he called Clarke.

'Everything good?' Clarke asked by way of greeting. As always, he sounded alert.

'I need to see you at my place, as soon as you can.'

'On my way.'

Clarke hung up, and Mitch went to freshen up. Clarke arrived twenty minutes later, and Mitch led him to his office. He sat in his luxury leather chair, but Clarke remained standing. Being used to it, Mitch didn't comment.

'Roman.'

Clarke didn't so much as flinch.

'Still in the wind. Has a few people on the street, but they're minors. He's mostly wholesaling, I imagine. He's stayed low-key since Natty dropped his friend.'

Mitch tapped his fingers on the desk, pursing his lips.

'Nathaniel should have taken him out by now. I was under the impression your training with him was going well.'

'My training probably kept him alive. Potential-wise, as I told you before, he's a marvel. He has great instincts.'

'Those instincts aren't aiding him in finishing a potential enemy. Roman may not be the same threat he was months ago, but he's still out there. I want him gone.'

Clarke nodded.

'Okay.'

Mitch rubbed his eyebrow.

'Why hasn't Lisa got to him yet?'

'Roman isn't Warren. He's not a horny idiot, and he doesn't let just anyone into his circle.'

Mitch waited a moment before he spoke again.

'When you've spoken with Nathaniel and Lisa, I need you on top of something else.'

'What do you need?'

'I want a full inventory of exactly how many crews are being supplied by Jakkar's lackeys.'

Clarke frowned, showing some reaction for the first time.

'Is there something going on that I need to know about?'

Mitch looked his most loyal subordinate in the eye before replying.

'Not yet.'

————

Detective Inspector Brown sauntered into Natty's ride with his usual swagger. He had an enormous grin on his face as he turned to Natty. Brown was shorter than Natty, with dark brown skin and light brown eyes. He'd had a shape-up since they'd last spoken, and his usually messy facial hair had been trimmed and neatened.

'You look good, Deeds. Real good. I'm surprised to hear from you, though. Usually, it's me running you down. It's not even pay day.'

Natty ignored the man's posturing. It was part of his act, he was fully aware, but he and Brown would never be friends, or anything resembling friends.

'That's why I'm here. What am I paying for?'

'We've already gone over the ground rules.' Brown rolled his eyes.

'We went over *your* ground rules, not mine. We can visit that another time, though,' said Natty. 'I've got a job for you.'

'Excuse me?' Brown's eyebrow rose.

'You heard. I pay you, and now I'm making use of that. I want to know everything you can find on my uncle.'

'Your uncle?' Brown's brow furrowed.

'I can tell you his name if you're not sure,' said Natty mockingly. Brown scowled at him.

'What are you trying to pull, Deeds? You trying to set me up?'

'Think about what you're asking . . . how would that even work?' Natty scoffed, liking that he had the cocky detective rattled. 'You don't need to worry about why I'm asking. Just do it, and get results. You do that . . . maybe you'll earn a bit extra on top,' he finished, sweetening the deal.

Brown glared at Natty as he stepped out of the car, slamming the door shut behind him.

Chuckling, Natty watched him leave, already mapping out the rest of his day. With Roman at least temporarily removed from the picture, things had only got better in the past few months. The money was up in all areas. The income from the drugs racket was still the most lucrative, but other areas, such as protections and loans, were also increasing. Jermaine had hit the ground running in Little London, and was doing well with their teams there.

A pang of sadness hit Natty then, and he felt his good mood shift, thinking of his protégé, Carlton, who had been murdered several months ago.

That reminded him of something he needed to do.

After making a quick stop at one of his spots, Natty drove through the Hood, pulling up at the top of Francis Street. He climbed from the ride, smiling at an older woman walking by with a dog. The dog barked and slobbered in Natty's direction, but he smiled at it and moved on. He glanced around, seeing nothing out of the ordinary.

Despite forcing Spence to travel with a bodyguard, Natty often skipped out on doing the same. He only did so for a short while. Roman and Keith attempting his life was a warning that he was a target. He liked the space and clarity being on his own provided him, but was aware of the risk he was taking.

Thinking of Spence made Natty remember he needed to run something by him.

Stopping in front of a fading red door, Natty firmly knocked, waiting for someone to respond. Thirty seconds later, the door was opened, and an elderly woman peered out at him. She had grey hair that was almost white, inviting brown eyes, and a stooped posture.

'Can I help you?' She asked in a stronger voice than Natty expected.

'My name is Nathaniel,' he replied. 'I knew your grandson, Carlton. I was wondering if you had a few minutes?'

Carlton's nana sagged when she heard her grandson's name, but after a moment, she nodded, and he followed her inside. They sat in the kitchen, and he turned down her offer of tea. She struggled to sit in her seat, taking several moments to do so, clearly in some difficulty.

Feeling pity for her, Natty averted his gaze, allowing her to settle without him watching. His eyes took in his surroundings as they flowed across the room. The kitchen was dated, but surprisingly clean. The dark brown varnished cupboards gleamed in the sunlight breaking through the window. A wooden stool stood on the floor before them, there to assist the old lady in finding those hard-to-reach spots. The floor was different. It was old and worn. Light-coloured polyvinyl flooring that had discoloured over the years.

Natty's eyes returned to Carlton's nana, who still shifted awkwardly, struggling to find comfort.

'Do you need some help?' Natty asked, feeling guilty for disturbing her.

'I'm fine,' she said. 'I have a woman that comes to see me. She will be here soon, and she can help. How did you know my grandson?'

'We were . . . friends,' said Natty. 'He was a good man, and he had a ton of potential.' Reaching into his jacket, Natty handed her a stack of money, tightly wrapped with two rubber bands. Carlton's nana took the money, shooting him a suspicious look.

'What is this for?'

'I just want to see you looked after,' said Natty, wishing there was more he could do. Seeing Carlton's nana made him think of Delores. He hadn't seen her since Rudy's death, and felt a fresh wave of guilt. He needed to rectify that as soon as he could.

'I've had money stuffed through my letter box a few times . . . at least once a month since my Carlton died. Were you behind that?'

Natty nodded. He'd left instructions for money to be delivered, and for their people to check on the old woman. It was clear people were cutting corners, and that didn't sit well with Natty. He had an obligation to the lady sitting before him. It was something he needed to address with his group.

'This is too much. I don't need it,' she protested.

Natty shook his head.

'Do whatever you need with it.' He placed a piece of card on the kitchen table, unsure if the woman had a mobile phone, unable to see one nearby. 'If you need anything else, ring that number, and you'll be taken care of.'

Seeing that there was no sense in arguing, the old woman nodded.

'I'm going to go. You don't need to see me out. Rest up,' said Natty, only to be ignored as she struggled to her feet. Ignoring her protests, Natty helped her this time, and was startled when she pulled him into a hug. He held her gently, feeling like he would break her if he squeezed too hard. Thankfully, she let him go rather quickly.

After she saw him to the door, Natty took a deep breath when he stepped outside. He was tempted to go and see Delores straight away, but decided to wait. Instead, as he walked to the car and climbed in, he called Spence.

'Nat? What's happening?' Spence asked.

'We're having dinner,' said Natty.

'Are we?' Spence replied, confused.

'Yeah. Tell Rosie. I'll text you with details, but the four of us are gonna catch up. I'm cooking,' said Natty. He'd mentioned it to Lorraine earlier, and felt they both needed it.

'Okay, bro. I'm looking forward to it. Let me know the details.'

'Cool.' Natty hung up, smiling.

———

ROMAN SAT in a safe house in Armley, sipping white rum from a bottle. He poured some on the floor in memory of Keith, his best friend. It was a ritual he had everyone once in a while, honouring his boy by drinking his favourite liquor. Keith had fallen foul of the Dunns in the middle of their war. Both he and Manson had been gunned down. Two soldiers with solid reputations gone.

Keith's death would always sting. Despite their differences, he was like family. When he learned what had transpired, he was ready to ride out on the Dunns. Still, he was smart enough to realise he was outgunned.

The Dunns had gone from strength to strength, recovering seamlessly from the hits they'd taken, and were sitting pretty, almost daring Roman to strike at them.

If Roman was going to win, he needed more capable personnel. He was low on resources, and that needed to change. Mitch Dunn and his nephew Natty would be difficult to get at. Roman had a score to settle with Natty. He'd learned that he was responsible for the deaths of his friends, and Roman vowed he would be the person to pay Natty back.

He needed to move carefully, however. He didn't have the war chest to compete with the Dunns on a day-to-day basis. Keith and Manson made that mistake, and paid the price with their lives. Roman had implored them to move slowly and consider their actions. He wished more than anything that they'd listened.

Roman's phone rang in the middle of his brooding, but he ignored it when he noticed it was Ahmed calling. The last people he needed to speak to were his drug suppliers. All they seemed to do nowadays was try to lecture him. It was his people opposing the Dunns, though. He would do things his way.

Placing the bottle on the coffee table, Roman lurched to his feet and headed to the bathroom. After using the toilet and washing his hands, he returned, seeing he had a text message on his phone. He frowned when he noted who it was from.

Danielle had been a fling of Keith's that Roman suspected he had deeper feelings for. She was younger than the pair, and stunning, but Roman had never been particularly enamoured with her. She had been present when Natty Deeds had murdered Keith, and he suspected she had inadvertently led them right to his friend. He couldn't prove it, though. Sighing, he rubbed his forehead, then looked at the text message again:

What are you doing?

Blowing out a breath, Roman typed out a reply, then took another sip of his drink and closed his eyes.

CHAPTER FOUR

NATTY WAS IN HIS ELEMENT, working his way around Lorraine's kitchen, in the middle of cooking dinner. It had taken a while to get used to the space, and even now, he still missed his own. His kitchen was bigger than Lorraine's and certainly tidier, but he'd enjoyed the solidarity that came with cooking his own food.

His dad had taught him how to cook, and his mum added to that. He had so many memories of cooking meals at his house, often cooking for Spence and Cameron — though sometimes they would just drink instead and order food instead.

Natty sighed. Life had seemed so simple. He often wondered if he was happier back then, but dismissed it. He'd come along by leaps and bounds, and he didn't regret his path.

Smiling, he continued cooking, wishing he'd thought to change his clothes before doing so. He wore a light blue shirt rolled at the sleeves, jeans and a pair of black shoes he'd bought years ago at a christening. He'd shown them to Jaden, who had giggled and mocked them as *church shoes*. Natty had retaliated by tickling him until he was crying. The memory made him smile again.

'Why are you just in here smiling to yourself?' Lorraine asked, observing him from the doorway. Her look turned sultry. 'You look good doing it, I must say.'

'You look good enough to eat,' said Natty. Lorraine wore a simple black dress that ended just above the knee, and black heels. Her hair was bedraggled, and she wore eyeliner, but no other makeup. Natty didn't think she needed it. In his view, she was the most beautiful woman in the world, and that feeling had only deepened. He was enamoured with her full lips and smooth features.

'Concentrate on your food,' she said, inhaling the smells. 'It looks good. I could do without the onions, but still.'

'Don't worry. You know I can throw down in the kitchen. I won't overdo it. How are you feeling?' He asked, returning his attention to the cooking. 'You've been a little quiet since you finished work.'

Lorraine shook her head. 'I'm fine, Nat.' Her gaze roved up his body. 'Rolled-up sleeves suit you.' Moving toward him as he stood over the cooker, she stroked his arms. Natty grinned.

'I'm glad you like it. I enjoy seeing you in little dresses a lot more.' Distracted, he reached out for her, but Lorraine stepped back, shaking her head again.

'You've been touching food, silly.' She motioned to his hands, covered in the seasoning he'd used on the meat. Natty chuckled as she left him and went to finish getting ready.

———

'I'M LOOKING FORWARD TO THIS,' said Rosie.

'Me too,' said Spence distractedly, his hand reaching down to the wine he had between his legs. It was in a fancy green bag that he'd paid a few quid extra for in the city centre. He hadn't lied. He was looking forward to the night and was counting on his best friend to distract him.

More often than not, his thoughts would stray to Anika, wondering if he could have done something different. It irritated him he couldn't shake it, but so much of his personality was hard-wired toward bettering himself.

If there was some flaw that had driven Anika away, the last thing he wanted was for that same flaw to ruin his relationship with Rosie. Things had been better for them lately after a time of stress and drama, and he wanted that to last.

Rosie watched Spence as he drove, knowing something was wrong. He drove without issue, seamlessly switching lanes, but his expression was guarded, and had been so for a while. Often he would come out of it and return to normal, but she didn't know what was going on, and that worried her. She'd only recently relaxed after ambushes, shootings and gunshot wounds.

Rosie had known what Spence did long before she got involved with him, yet she had convinced herself that he and Natty were small time, moving a few grams here and there. The reality had stunned her, and even now, she was still coming to terms with it.

Despite his mindset, it hadn't affected his wardrobe. Rosie knew Spence was good with his money and invested well, but his wardrobe definitely represented his status. He wore a black blazer over a crisp white shirt, trousers, and shoes. Rosie inhaled the *Armani Acqua di Gio* aftershave she'd recently bought him, pleased he'd worn it, even though it made her want to rip his clothes off.

'Are you okay?' She finally asked. Spence glanced at her, smiling.

'I'm fine, babe. It's just been a long day.'

'Okay. I'm here if you need to talk about anything at all,' she said, deciding not to pry. Spence nodded, and she stayed lost in her thoughts. She wished he would communicate with her. If she'd done something wrong, she wanted to know. If it was street-related, though, Spence knew how she could get. That would explain his reluctance to speak to her. For a while, she'd barely let him out of her sight, worrying he'd end up getting hurt, or worse.

Despite relaxing, she wondered if the tenseness was down to things escalating again. Her thoughts shifted to her friend. Lorraine had also been through a lot in the last few months, and Rosie hoped she was okay. She did her best to remain available to Lorraine, but sometimes they ended up missing one another.

She would enjoy this evening, and make the most of the time. If she could learn what was bothering Spence, she would see that as a bonus, she mused.

———

'YES, BRO!'

Natty opened the door to Spence, crushing his friend with a hug. Releasing him, he gave Rosie a quick hug and a kiss on the cheek. 'You look amazing, darling. Why don't we leave Spence in the car? Me, you, and Lorraine can have a party without him.'

Rosie giggled as Spence elbowed Natty. 'You couldn't handle us, Nat. Me and Lo would kill you.'

Natty laughed. 'You're probably right. I'm getting old. Lorraine's just finishing her hair, so that'll take either five minutes or five hours. Let's crack open some of Spence's sophisticated wine.'

Lorraine joined them a short while later. They had a drink, then Natty served the food. They kept the conversation light, complimenting Natty on the lamp chops he'd made.

'You got the flavour just right,' said Spence, with everyone agreeing.

'Obviously, I missed my calling as a chef,' chuckled Natty, sipping the wine. 'This is good stuff, Spence. I need to pick up a couple' bottles next time I'm in town.'

Spence mentioned the name of the shop, and Natty planned to visit next week. It was always nice to have a few bottles knocking around. He'd grown accustomed to having a glass or two with Lorraine at the end of particularly tiresome days. Hard liquor didn't relax him in the same way.

When they'd finished, Rosie and Lorraine stayed talking in the living room, and Natty and Spence retreated to the kitchen. They sat at the table Lorraine usually worked from, and Natty poured them both another drink.

'I've probably had enough,' said Spence, always the sensible one. Natty snorted.

'Get an Uber. You can pick your car up tomorrow or summat.'

Spence shrugged, accepting the glass.

'I'm sorry we haven't spent much proper time together. I'm glad we did this,' Natty continued. 'Getting the whole organisation into shape has been messy. Every time I think something's sorted, another thing pops up.'

'What sort of things?' Spence asked. He'd served for a time in an upper position in the crew, one he still kept, working alongside Natty. That being said, he'd only had his eyes on the drugs section. There were various other rackets the Dunns were involved in.

'Just a few areas slacking, thinking no one was paying attention to them. I got them back in line.'

Spence nodded. Natty was effective like that, and had a way of galvanising the surrounding people, making them work harder, knowing they couldn't take liberties.

'What's next?' He asked. Despite Natty's mood, there was a shadow in his eyes he'd seen a few times during the night.

'We keep building and keep stacking.' Natty sipped his wine, stifling a yawn. 'That reminds me. I'm gonna wanna sit down with you soon and think about diversifying. Need to keep making my money work for me, and I don't want to get caught with my trousers down.'

'I get you,' said Spence. 'We can sort it whenever you're ready. I've got a few ideas that might work.'

'Sounds good. How are you, though? Are you doing okay?'

'I'm fine,' said Spence. Natty watched him for a moment.

'Cool. If there's ever anything you need to discuss, or if anyone's ever troubling you, let me know. Cool?'

'You know that goes both ways, right?' Spence met Natty's eyes.

'I know.'

———

'HOW'S WORK?'

Lorraine and Rosie were savouring their drinks, *112* singing along in the background. It was one of their favourite groups, and the r&b tunes created a nice vibe.

Lorraine sighed, sipping her drink.

'Up and down, if I'm honest. I'm still making up for lost time,' she said.

'What do you mean?'

'I took some time off after Raider . . . well, you know,' she said awkwardly. 'Anyway, that stunted my development a little. I used to get along really well with management, but things are frostier now.'

'I'm sorry, Lo.'

'Don't be. It's a competitive industry, and you get left behind if you can't keep up. No way around that.'

'Does Natty know?'

Lorraine shook her head, sighing. 'I don't want him worrying more than he already does.'

'Natty's always going to worry regardless, babe. If things are happening personally, then tell him. He might be able to help, or offer some perspective.'

'When I need my manager's legs broken, he's the first person I'll call,' joked Lorraine, both women giggling despite the serious conversation.

———

SPENCE DID as Natty suggested and left his car. He and Rosie took an Uber, a weird thought hitting Spence that he hadn't had to take his bodyguard along.

The bodyguard he still resented being forced to have.

Spence respected the fact that people wanted to look after him. Decisions to run into shootouts aside, he was as conscious of his personal safety as the next man, but it was galling. Even tonight, Natty sounding so concerned about his welfare had irked him.

For a fleeting second, he wondered if that was why Anika had cheated on him: because he wasn't strong enough.

As Spence and Rosie entered the house, the thoughts stuck with him.

Natty wouldn't have been cheated on, Spence knew that for sure.

'Spence?'

He blinked. He'd stood in the hallway and hadn't realised he wasn't moving. Rosie stared at him, her concern palpable.

'Sorry about that,' he said, giving her a smile. She didn't buy it.

'Are you sure you're okay?'

'I probably drank more than I should have. I'm fine, though. Let's go get ready for bed.' He headed straight upstairs. Rosie followed, her expression unchanged as she studied her boyfriend.

Spence went to the bathroom, washing his face and brushing his teeth. One thing was clear: the dinner was supposed to make them feel better, but Spence felt worse.

CHAPTER FIVE

GRINNING, Natty reached down and lifted Clarke to his feet, the older man also smiling.

'You're getting good,' said Clarke, brushing himself off. 'I'll need to start taking you seriously.'

'Like you haven't already,' said Natty. The pair laughed and drank some water, leaving the training room; a converted cellar in a safe house in the Hood. It contained numerous mats, a free weights rack in the corner, skipping ropes and other bits of equipment.

'Seriously, you've come a long way, Natty. I always knew you had it in you, but you've taken to all this better than expected. You take everything in, and you learn from your mistakes. Don't lose that.'

'I appreciate that, Clarke,' said Natty, touched by his words. Clarke had done a lot for him since he'd rejoined the crew, and had been available for advice and support, as well as training him. He shook off the guilt he felt about his plans. Clarke was loyal to his uncle Mitch. Natty planned on killing uncle Mitch, but had given little thought to what came next, or how he would navigate it.

One thing was for sure: he needed to ensure Lorraine and Jaden were kept out of it.

Natty hoped Brown would give him something he could use —

ideally, something that kept his name out of it, but time would tell. When Rudy had attempted to move against Mitch, he'd learned of Rudy's coup with little effort. Natty needed to move smarter.

'Come on. You can drop me off at Paula's.'

Natty and Clarke drove to Paula's house. She was in the kitchen when they arrived, hugging both men.

'You two stink,' she said, making a face.

'That's the smell of men that conquered the world,' said Clarke, heading to the cupboard and grabbing a glass, then making himself a drink. He glanced at Natty, who shook his head, signalling that he didn't want anything.

'Are you staying for dinner, Nat?' Paula asked, smiling warmly at him. It still surprised Natty that Clarke had struck up a relationship with Paula. She had three children of varied ages from a previous relationship. Natty didn't know what had happened to the dad, or how Clarke had ended up on the scene, but the pair seemed to work. There was a nice, homely balance with them, something Natty hoped he and Lorraine were replicating.

'No thanks, Paula. I appreciate the offer, though, but I need to go and see someone.'

'It's not Lisa, is it?' Paula's eyes twinkled. 'She mentioned you a few times the last time she came by.'

Natty fought to control his expression, glancing at Clarke and noting the stony look on the older man's face. He understood the reaction. Clarke looked at Lisa like a daughter. Natty was with Lorraine, and Lisa was . . . complicated.

Clarke's apprehension made complete sense.

'Lisa's a chatty girl. I'm sure she talks about a lot of different people.'

'Are we talking about the same Lisa?' Paula laughed. 'She talks when she needs to, and rarely volunteers anything she doesn't. If you were to look up *guarded* in the dictionary, you'd see a picture of Lisa rolling her eyes at you.'

Natty chuckled, still trying to downplay it. He tried his hardest not to think about Lisa, and it was often a losing effort. He had known her for around seven months, being introduced to her upon returning to the crew, but there had been an instant chemistry between them, punctuated by a passionate kiss they'd shared a few months ago. That confusing encounter was almost always on his mind. Natty wished it hadn't happened, but also yearned for more.

She was a curious case, one Natty had given great thought to. She seemed to understand him in ways he feared Lorraine never would. Lisa was well and truly entrenched in the life, excelling in deep cover operations. It made it easy for her to relate to Natty's problems. As deadly and as dangerous as she was, Natty accepted that, if Lorraine wasn't in the picture, something significant would likely have happened between them.

'Anyway, I'll leave you both to it. Natty, if you change your mind, there's more than enough. Pete, shout me when the water starts to boil or better still, make yourself useful and turn it down.'

'Will do, don't worry about it,' said Clarke. Paula was at the door, when she paused, turning.

'Have you sorted out the parking situation for that event?'

'What event?' Natty asked.

'Danny's having a fight. I can't remember where, but Pete has all the details,' said Paula. 'You're welcome to come along? I don't think it's sold out yet. Want us to get you a ticket?'

Natty nodded. He hadn't been to a boxing event in years, and figured the change of scenery would do him good.

'If you can, that would be great.' He had an idea. 'In fact, can you get two if possible? I'll bring Jaden. I don't mind paying.'

Paula waved him off. 'It's our treat. Don't worry about it.'

When Paula went, Clarke stood and closed the door behind her, his demeanour seeming to shift.

'What's going on with you and your uncle?'

Of all the questions Natty expected, that one hadn't made the list. His heart pounded. *Had he been rumbled already?*

'What do you mean?'

'I spoke with him yesterday. He's annoyed that you haven't finished Roman.'

Natty didn't even bother hiding his annoyance.

'We've broken his back, Clarke. We eliminated key personnel,' he said. 'My job is to keep the money up and run the team, which I've done. My uncle has always liked things quiet, so what's changed?'

Clarke seemed surprised at Natty's passion, and Natty inwardly cursed his quick temper. He needed to keep calm, especially around Clarke. He was cagey, and would pick up on the vibe if it continued.

'Are you sure you're okay, Natty? It's okay to say if all of this is a bit too much,' said Clarke.

Natty's body tensed as he processed the unexpected information. 'Is it? I didn't think the way we do things left much room for choice.'

'You have choices, Natty. You have a lot of power. Your star is rising, and the crew members look up to you. That's reflected in the profits, but you're doing a lot. Add to that all the extra work you're doing with me . . . it's okay to say if you're overwhelmed.'

Natty wasn't sure what to say, but he was annoyed by the questioning. This was the streets. They were in the jungle, and he didn't want Clarke, or anyone else thinking he was weak, or overwhelmed.

Clarke was waiting for a response, though, so Natty relaxed and gave him one.

'I don't think Roman is important enough to chase to the ends of the earth.'

'You did when you gave the troops your *Winston Churchill* speech, and put a small fortune on his head.'

'If someone gets him, they get him,' replied Natty. He'd been furious at Roman and Keith for killing Carlton back then, but finishing Keith had mostly closed the book on that for him. 'Let me ask you a question, Clarke: is my uncle *ordering* me to prioritise going after Roman?'

'I'll speak to him and clarify,' said Clarke, sipping his drink. 'Lisa's still out there. She might get him, anyway.'

Natty nodded. That was certainly possible. Something else came to his mind that he'd lost track of lately.

'A while back, you said we could talk about my dad.'

Clarke chuckled, sliding to his feet and grabbing a glass, pouring a shot of brandy into it and handing it to Natty. 'You're right. I did.'

Natty's eyebrow rose. Clarke's demeanour was surprising, and he wondered what sort of conversation it would be. His intention, by asking, had been to see if Clarke would be reluctant to speak about him. Evidently, he wasn't.

'Your old man was a character,' said Clarke, draining his own glass, then pouring a shot of brandy of his own. 'I'm probably not telling you anything you haven't heard before, but he was well-liked, especially by the females.'

Clarke's last comment made Natty's stomach jolt, remembering the vicious words his mum had thrown at him about his dad's infidelity the last time they'd spoken.

'Your dad ran the streets and kept people in their place. Your uncle played the background and focused on the money. Rudy was there too,' Clarke's face soured for a moment, 'but he was closer to Mitch, though he and your old man were best friends. In fact, it was Ty that vouched for Rudy to Mitch.'

That comment was telling for Natty. His dad had vouched for Rudy, and Rudy had responded by sleeping with his wife and colluding with his brother.

'What about you?' He asked Clarke. 'Who were you closest to?'

'Mitch,' said Clarke. 'I worked with Ty from time to time, but he had his own crew that he trusted, and mostly rolled with them.'

'So, what changed?' Natty asked. Clarke hadn't told him much he didn't know, as he'd stated earlier, but he wasn't sure what to make of it. Based on everything Clarke had said, and his delivery whilst doing so, he hadn't known of Mitch and Rudy's machinations, but Natty couldn't be sure. He needed more information.

'Diverging agendas, I guess. The Yardies were on the scene. I mean, they were always around, but every now and then, they'd throw their weight around and start causing trouble. I'm sure you're old enough to remember that.'

Natty was. He'd just started high school, and at times, the tension in the streets spilled over into the school, with numerous fights and ambushes taking place before, during, but mostly after school.

'Anyway, the Yardies were a problem, and Ty and your uncle had different ideas on how they should handle them. Mitch wanted to focus on the business and let them fizzle out. Ty wanted to take them, and anyone else that stood in our way, out. They started clashing more, and if you ask me, Rudy drove a wedge between them.' Again, Clarke's expression was sour.

'Why do you think that?' Natty pressed, intrigued and eager to learn more. Clarke shrugged.

'He was the common denominator, and he was close to both.' Clarke sipped his drink, sighing. 'It all happened so long ago, but you know what . . . I still feel guilt.'

'From what?' Natty asked sharply. *Had he misinterpreted Clarke's involvement all along?*

'The Yardies shouldn't have even got close to your dad. If we'd stayed tight . . . if everyone had been on the same page, maybe they wouldn't have.' His expression darkened, then a grim smile appeared on his face. 'I tell you what, Nat . . . I made up for it, though. We all did. We took the fight to them, and put them down for good.' Clarke finished his drink. 'If you ask me, that might be why Mitch wants Roman dead . . .because he understands a key fact.'

'What fact is that?'

'When your enemies are down, finish them.'

Natty didn't refute the words. There was a lot he needed to unpack from the conversation. He didn't think Clarke had been dishonest, but he wondered about his instincts, especially as he'd never suspected Natty's uncle's duplicity in the past.

As the pair sipped their drinks in silence, the main factor Natty had thought about earlier, came back to him. Clarke would always put the crew first. He'd said so to Natty in the past, and that meant his loyalty would always be to Natty's uncle.

CHAPTER SIX

SPENCE YAWNED, his eyes burning with tiredness, but unable to sleep. He'd been trying for the past hour, keeping his movements to a minimum, not wanting to disturb Rosie.

Finally, he gave up, slipping from the bed as quietly as he could. Glancing back at Rosie in the bed, he had a view of her relaxed, sleeping face through a slit in curtains that allowed the moonlight to flitter through. For a moment, Spence was overcome by her beauty. Rosie was truly special, and Spence felt lucky that she was interested in him. Finally tearing his eyes away, he picked up his phone out of habit, noting a text message from Anika.

> Hey. I know you probably won't reply, but I hope you're okay, Spence.

Spence stared at the message, then locked his screen. After another glance at Rosie, he went downstairs, heading into the living room, able to navigate in the dark. Collapsing onto his sectional sofa, he sank into the cushions, again closing his eyes.

Spence wondered when Anika would stop messaging him. He'd

figured they wouldn't speak again after they'd met. After that, he figured she would get bored of messaging him, but she hadn't. Sometimes she would bring up random subjects and ask questions. Other times, she would tell him about her day, or ask about his. He didn't know what to make of it.

Lately, his instincts were all over the place. He didn't trust them.

He touched his shoulder through the grey t-shirt he'd worn to bed. Even now, he could still hear the loud bang, followed by the searing pain of the bullet. If Keith's aim had been just a little better, he wouldn't be here today.

Instead, Natty had killed Keith.

All his life, Spence had tried to make the right moves, but lately, things seemed blurred. He felt like he needed to redeem himself, but didn't know how.

No matter how much thought he gave the situation, he couldn't work out the answer.

Again, thoughts of strength came to his mind. He wondered if Anika was lying when she'd given her reasons for leaving him.

Could they have been saved if he'd just talked to her?

Unlocking his phone, Spence glanced at the message again. It had been sent hours ago. For a moment, he considered messaging back, sharing what was on his mind.

Instead, he deleted the message.

'Spence?'

The living room light was turned on. Spence blinked, allowing his eyes to adjust to the sudden light. Rosie walked towards him, wearing a lilac robe and matching slippers, her hair bedraggled in an endearing fashion.

'Hey, babe. Are you okay?'

Rosie frowned. 'Are you? I woke up, and you weren't in bed.'

Spence nodded.

'Sorry for waking you. I couldn't sleep.'

'I don't mind, Spence. Are you okay, though? Do you need me to get you anything?'

'I'm fine. Just need a moment,' said Spence, feigning a yawn. 'Let's try to get some sleep.'

'Okay,' Rosie said, following him out of the room, a deepening look of concern on her face.

————

THE NEXT DAY, Natty climbed from his car and hesitated outside Delores's place. For a long time, it was a familiar environment. He would meet Rudy there, and they would talk, and if there was one thing he could always count on, it was for Delores to baby him. Ever since he was little, she had doted on him, treating him like a grandson, and their bond only grew stronger as he got older.

Delores always seemed to be there for him, even when he didn't notice. After his dad died, when his mum grew distant, when the streets challenged every fibre of his being; he could always count on Delores to give him the reassurance he needed.

As he grew older, he realised what Delores provided him. She treated him with respect, love, and affection. Natty had lost his father, and, under the circumstances, it would have been easy to look at Natty with pity. Delores saw a young man who needed support, not sympathy, and that resonated with Natty.

Despite all that, Natty had forgotten about her, and he felt sick. There was no excuse for it. If she closed the door in his face, he would understand, but since she had dropped into his thoughts a few days ago, he couldn't shake the need to see her.

'Don't be a pussy . . .' he mumbled to himself, before taking a deep breath and willing his feet forward. He paused again, then knocked on the front door, the sound seeming louder than usual. As the seconds passed, his heart thudded harder against his chest. He considered leaving, but quashed it. No matter the outcome, he needed to do this.

Finally, he heard footsteps padding to the door. They were slow and laboured. Natty waited patiently, shifting in position. After several moments, the door clicked open.

Delores stared out at him. Natty stared right back, not trusting himself to speak. Delores shook her head, tears in her eyes, and he couldn't hold back anymore. He held the old woman tightly, feeling her cry against him, biting his lip to avoid following suit. It took almost a minute for them to compose themselves, but she led him into the living room, still sniffling.

Natty hadn't been in the room in years, but he was glad Delores hadn't led him to the kitchen. The kitchen was Rudy's domain. It was where Natty learned of his stepdad's nefarious plot to overthrow his uncle. He didn't know if Delores had sensed his reluctance, but it wouldn't surprise him. She was an insightful woman, and a fresh round of guilt infused him. He shouldn't have left her unattended.

'You silly, silly boy,' she murmured, shaking her head as she forced him to sit down on a burgundy sofa that notably groaned under his weight. The whole room had an old-fashioned vibe. There was no television, but there was a bookshelf and a mantlepiece with a few family photos. He knew Delores had once been married, and also knew she had a son who was in prison. There was a collection of antiques in another corner of the room, and a simple coffee table with potpourri and a selection of old newspapers.

The pale walls were host to several paintings that Natty assumed were parts of the West Indies. Above the fireplace, the Cathedral of St. John the Divine stood resolute, its white steeples standing out against the brilliant blue of the sky behind it. *Antigua.*

Natty didn't know if Delores had travelled back home since leaving, but she didn't strike him as much of a traveller. Overall, it seemed a lonely environment to Natty, and he felt sad for her, until he looked up, and saw the wide smile on her face.

'What are you drinking, child?' she asked. Natty smiled back at her.

'I'd love some peppermint tea,' he said. It was a lie. She'd given it to him when he was younger, and he'd hated the bitter taste, but he knew it would make her happy, and it warmed his heart when her face brightened, and she shuffled to the kitchen.

Natty took a deep breath. He hadn't expected to feel so overwhelmed. As disheartening as it had been when he'd gone to see Carlton's nana, he hadn't felt like this. He reasoned there was more of a bond with Delores.

Soon, he had a saucer in his lap, and was sipping his peppermint tea, trying to avoid making a face. He wished he'd asked for coffee, but he was trying to cut back on his caffeine intake. Besides cigarettes, it was one of the hardest things he'd ever given up.

'You look well, Nathaniel child. Better than you have for a long time.'

Natty smiled, feeling his cheeks burn. He never acted like this, but Delores always could make him feel young and shy.

'Thank you. I'm really sorry I—'

Delores held up a hand, cutting him off. She'd sat on the sofa next to him, holding a cup and saucer of her own. Her hair was wrapped up, and she wore a baggy jumper and old trousers. Natty had interrupted her cleaning, that much he knew without being told.

'Don't apologise for having a life, child. I know you've been busy.'

'Still . . . I could have made an effort, and I'm sorry.'

Delores shook her head, smiling again.

'Why don't you tell me what you've been doing?'

Natty did. He spoke about Jaden and Lorraine, and glossed over some of his business working for his uncle. He knew Delores knew what he did, but that didn't mean he would openly discuss it with her. Delores smiled all the way through his talk, nodding her head in approval.

'I'm glad you found someone, Nathaniel. I'm glad you took the chance on sharing yourself. I used to worry about you.'

'Why? I'm the last person you need to worry about.'

Delores shot him a knowing smile. It was warm, but penetrating. It made Natty feel like his mind had been downloaded; like she instantly knew Natty better than he knew himself.

'You always needed someone to worry about you. You were determined to grow too old, too fast, child. You didn't take the time to be young,' she said.

Natty couldn't argue. He'd wanted to walk a mile in his dad's shoes, and had done his best to replicate his journey. *The ending would be different*, he mused, as his mind drifted from Rudy, to his uncle Mitch, finally settling on his mum.

There was still a lot of work to do in that regard.

'I almost didn't take the chance,' Natty admitted. 'I did some dumb shi . . . stuff, and made people around me angry. I took the chance on speaking from the heart, and luckily Lorraine forgave me.'

Delores smiled.

'And this Jaden . . . her son; do you take care of him?'

Natty nodded. 'As far as I'm concerned, I'm his dad. It's not official or nothing, but I told him how I felt.'

'Do you show him?' Delores pressed. Natty nodded.

'I try to. At least, I hope I do.'

'Good.'

They finished their drinks in silence. Natty's phone vibrated, but he didn't take it out. He knew he had to leave, but didn't want to. He felt like he and Delores were reconnecting, and he didn't want to be rude and blow her off.

'You need to go, child. I can hear that phone of yours,' she said.

'I don't mind staying longer.'

'I do. I need to do my cleaning, and you're in my way,' she said teasingly. Natty laughed. He stood, leaving the cup and saucer on the table at her instruction, then followed her to the front door. He fumbled into his pockets for some money, but Delores put her hand on top of his.

'No. I don't need your money, child.'

'I . . .'

'I have my own money. I'm fine, Nathaniel. I promise.'

Natty nodded, accepting her response.

'I'm going to come and visit you soon, okay?'

Delores beamed.

'I hope you do, child. Bring that family of yours too. I want to meet the ones that are looking after my Nathaniel.'

'Count on it.'

When Delores closed the door on him, Natty stood there for a long moment, breathing in and out. He felt somehow lighter, and wondered if just being around Delores had made him feel better. Wiping his eyes, Natty made his way back to the car.

———

LORRAINE STIFLED a yawn as she entered her workplace. The offices they rented were situated near Great George Street in the city centre. Clutching her handbag and her laptop bag, she flashed her id at the security guard and took the lift to the 3rd floor.

The office was abuzz with chatter, as per usual. It was a spacious unit, with multiple long tables, desktop computers, and wide windows. Several of Lorraine's colleagues smiled at her, saying *good morning* as she walked by, with Lorraine returning the greetings.

Sliding into a seat, Lorraine booted up her MacBook — the same MacBook Natty had bought for her before they were together. The memory made her smile. She arranged her desk, connected the machine to the desktop monitors, and glanced at her to-do list. Before she could start, a figure loomed nearby.

'Hello, Lorraine. Could I have a word before you start?'

It was Angela, Lorraine's manager. She was a squat little woman, with curly auburn hair, a fleshy face, and pale blue eyes. As always, Angela's floral perfume was overwhelming, and Lorraine had to blink, clearing her eyes.

'Sure,' she replied, shooting the woman a small smile. She locked her MacBook and followed Angela into a meeting room, ignoring the whispers as she did so.

The meeting room was a cramped space, capable of sitting four people at a pause. It had light walls, a thin grey carpet, a small circular table, and two chairs. Against the far wall was a smart board with hastily rubbed-out notes from a previous meeting. It reeked of cleaning solution, causing Lorraine to rub her nose. The solution and Angela's perfume were a deadly combination.

Sitting at one end of the table, Angela motioned for Lorraine to sit down, a wide smile on her face.

'I know we haven't had a chance to speak in a while, Lorraine. How are you doing?'

'I'm okay,' Lorraine replied politely. 'I mean, I'm getting there.'

Angela had been Lorraine's manager for almost four months. She'd joined the company shortly before that, and was in her early forties. Lorraine knew she'd worked in higher tier positions for another company prior, but didn't know which one.

'That's good,' said Angela. 'I know Laurence thought the world of you. He believed you could go far.'

Laurence Blaine was Lorraine's former manager. He'd helped her when she joined the company, and had given her tips and guidance when she began working towards a role as a software engineer. He'd abruptly left the company months back, and Lorraine didn't know whether it was voluntary. The usual gossip that littered the office had been quiet on that front.

She suspected Angela was behind that.

'Laurence was great. I hope he's doing well,' said Lorraine.

'Yes, yes,' said Angela airily. When she spoke again, her tone had changed. 'I haven't seen that side of you yet, unfortunately. Under me, I've found you to be well-mannered and warm, but . . . something is missing. Numerous days off. Missed deadlines . . .' She met Lorraine's eyes. 'What is going on?'

The conversation startled Lorraine. Angela wasn't wrong. She'd had a lot of time off when Raider had attacked her both times, and that had led to work being pushed back. On a few occasions, her colleagues had picked up the work for her, but she suspected Angela was going to be less understanding.

'I've been through a lot. There were some challenges with the father of my son. He recently died, and it's been difficult for everyone,' she replied.

'Sorry to hear that,' Angela said, her tone unchanging. 'You can understand how consistent absences would hurt the company, yes?'

Lorraine nodded, knowing there was no other answer to give.

Angela sighed, giving Lorraine what she imagined was supposed to be a sympathetic look.

'I hope you're back on board. I really do. As you may be aware, the company is going through a challenging transitional period. That means we need everyone focused and moving in the same direction. Those that can't, will be left behind.' Angela's smile was chilling, and didn't meet her eyes. 'I want you focused on Linda's projections piece. I understand she's already briefed you.'

'Yes, she has.' Lorraine found her voice.

'Good. If you need anything, you know where I am.' Angela's eyes flickered to the door. Stomach churning, Lorraine nodded again, then left.

CHAPTER SEVEN

NATTY FINALLY LINKED up with Spence a few hours after visiting Delores. He hadn't eaten much, so he brought some chicken and dumplings from a local takeaway, and they ate in the kitchen of one of the safe houses. Loud laughter and shouting ensued from the living room. Spence chuckled.

'They're having a *Call of Duty* tournament in there,' he said.

'I know. I saw them when I came in. Bet Jaden could batter all of them if I brought him over.'

Spence laughed. 'Yeah, you've said before how good he is. Everything still cool?'

Natty nodded. 'Everything's fine.'

'Are you sure?'

'Natty glanced at Spence for a moment, thinking of his uncle; the score he needed to settle. He desperately wanted to tell his friend about it, but couldn't figure out how. He trusted Spence more than anyone. They had been through a lot together, and their friendship had survived.

Natty wasn't sure how Spence would take this, though. Natty's uncle was smart and cunning. He was sure his friend would remain loyal to him, but Spence had a lot to thank Mitch for. Reputation, opportunity and more money than Spence would likely spend in his lifetime. His uncle had bought his friend's loyalty.

'I'm sure. Just thinking about Roman. Clarke mentioned my unc wants me to move on him. He's worried.'

'Do you think he's got the manpower to go at us? We did a lot of damage.' Spence paused. 'Well, you lot did a lot of damage. I just flailed around and got myself hit,' he said darkly.

Natty shook his head. 'You still going on about that? Spence, it could have happened to anyone. You were a second too slow. That's it. The way I got Keith . . . that could have been me. Don't let it get you down.'

'I'll try,' said Spence. 'Like I was saying to you before, you've gone up in my dad's estimation. He's always talking about you, and how you *stepped up and saved his son.*'

Natty laughed. 'I've always got the impression your dad doesn't like me.'

'He doesn't,' Spence admitted. 'Well, he didn't. Not because of anything you did, but because of your family.'

'I get it,' said Natty. 'At least we're cool now. How have you been doing other than your arm? You and Rosie still good? You looked happy at the dinner.'

Spence hesitated, and Natty noticed.

'Has something happened?'

'Nah, nothing like that. We're cool,' said Spence, his tone unconvincing. Natty studied his friend, wondering what he was hiding. He wouldn't press it. If Spence needed him, he would tell him.

'Cool. I'm glad it's going well. She's good for you. Is she calmer around you now?' Rosie knew first-hand just how dangerous Spence's life could be. When she and Spence were ambushed in town, it changed her. She became attached, paranoid, nervous and clingy. When Spence was shot, those traits were embedded deeper. She was different to the girl Spence fell for.

Spence snorted.

'She's loosened up a bit since she saw the bloody bodyguard you're making me travel with, but I still let her know every once in a while that I'm alive and haven't been shot again.' Spence wiped his eyebrow.

'That's still crazy to say. I got shot, man. I don't think I'll ever get used to that fact.'

'Good. We're not gonna let it happen again either,' Natty vowed.

Spence looked down at the food, then back up at Natty.

'Listen, are you sure you're okay?'

Natty frowned. 'What do you mean?'

'I don't know. Guess I've just known you a long time, and I'd like to think I'm good at reading you. For a while now, it's seemed like you've got something else on your mind.'

Natty wasn't surprised that Spence had picked up on this. He'd done his best to hide his conflicting thoughts from everyone, but as Spence pointed out, he knew Natty. He circled back to his earlier thoughts. Spence was giving him a golden opportunity to share his change of heart towards his uncle, but he couldn't do it.

'I'm alright, Spence. Usual dramas. Nothing for you to worry about.'

Spence looked Natty in the eyes, then nodded, returning to his meal.

Both men finished their food, the comfortable silence punctuated by yelling and arguing, followed by cheers every now and then. After a while, the kitchen door banged open, and a young man burst through. He was tall and slim, with short hair, a large nose, and matching ears. He stopped short, freezing when he saw Natty.

'I'm s-sorry,' he stammered. 'Didn't mean to make noise. Just wanted a drink.'

'It's cool, Porter. Take the bottle with you,' said Spence gently. The kid nodded, shooting Natty another glance, then heading to the fridge. He grabbed two bottles of Lilt, a selection of paper cups from the cupboard, and disappeared, closing the door behind him, mumbling another apology.

'I'm shocked he could carry all of that without dropping them,' said Natty. He was shocked at the kid's reaction to him, but it wasn't an isolated incident. He'd always been looked at a certain way because of his surname. Over the years, he'd established a reputation for himself, too. Between his surname and the carefully cultivated air of authority he displayed, people had become increasingly cautious around him. Rumours about him ranged from the obvious to ridiculous, but Natty paid them little attention.

'I'm shocked he didn't wet himself when he saw the *great Natty Deeds*,' said Spence, chuckling.

'And the *great Spence* . . .' Natty retorted, making a face. 'We really need to get you a better street name, bro.'

Both friends laughed, enjoying the moment.

———

MITCH WAS all smiles as he left a five-star restaurant in the heart of the city centre. For once, he was dressed to the nines in a tailored grey suit with all the trimmings.

The dinner he'd just left had been an important business one. Mitch liked to keep his finger on the pulse of what was happening in Leeds. He'd grown up in Chapeltown and considered it his base of operations. It was vital to know the ins and outs of the city. It ensured he could react to profitable opportunities.

Good contacts and keen interest had aided him enormously over the years, especially where it pertained to development, and knowing where to invest his money.

One of Clarke's men shadowed him, and though Mitch disliked the practice, he accepted it was necessary, and wouldn't compromise his own safety.

They were heading to the car when Mitch's phone rang. He glanced around out of instinct before he answered, noting the withheld number.

'Yes?'

'I have bad news,' a muffled, foreign voice said after a moment. 'Sameer has passed.'

Mitch had known it was coming, but the words still buckled him. He summoned all his strength to recover, even as the bodyguard shot him a confused look.

'Thank you for letting me know,' he replied, glad his voice was under control. The person on the other end hesitated.

'Good luck.'

That was it. The person hung up. Mitch slipped his phone into his pocket, clenching his fists for a moment. There was a lot he now needed to do, and he hoped he was ready.

The drive home was uneventful. Mitch strode to his office, grabbing a glass and a bottle of gin. He poured a generous measure and downed it, then poured another, then a third, closing his eyes. Standing over his desk, he gripped the table, feeling his hands tremble. For the second time that night, he took a deep breath and composed himself.

Grabbing his phone, he called Clarke.

'Come to the house as soon as possible.'

As always, Clarke arrived promptly. Mitch had already cleared the glass and liquor. He'd also washed his face to freshen up and hoped he presented his usual image of power. If he didn't, Clarke's expression gave nothing away. Not that it ever did.

'Is everything okay?' Clarke asked. Mitch frowned.

'Why do you ask?'

'You look tense.'

Mitch waved his hand, leaning back in his chair for a moment.

'Not important. What's the situation with my nephew?'

'Hard to say,' said Clarke.

'What does that mean?'

'I mean, there's something there. Something I can't quite put my finger on. I spoke with him, and let him know what you'd said. He disagreed.'

'Is that so?' Mitch fought down his mounting fury. Lashing out at his nephew wasn't the move to make. He didn't know the things Mitch knew. Mitch had learned a long time ago that not everything was for everybody. Consequently, he told people only what he felt they needed to know. Nathaniel was no different.

'He said that he was focusing on the team, and growing profits rather than running after Roman. In a sense, he's right. The money is good. Better than it's been in a long time.'

'You think that's all down to Nathaniel?'

Clarke tilted his head. 'All of it? No. But there's no denying the positive effect he's had. The crew has grown, and he's liked and respected by most of the organisation. In his eyes, Roman isn't much of a threat at the moment.'

'Do you agree with him?' Mitch rubbed his forehead, careful to keep his voice level.

'To a degree. At the same time, I don't like the idea of leaving a dangerous enemy to grow stronger. Roman is no fool. Add to that, Natty took out Manson, and we know the sort of people Manson was connected to.'

'Has there been any contact?' Mitch asked, fully aware of Manson's dangerous connections.

'No. It's all part of the game, I suppose. That doesn't mean Roman isn't being schooled somewhere, and stepping up his level.'

Mitch scratched his wrist. He hadn't foreseen these sorts of issues when he'd elevated his nephew to the position of power he was in. For a moment, he wondered if they had another Tyrone on their hands. His brother had often bucked protocol, led by his emotions and feelings rather than logic. He didn't always see the big picture, and it had been down to Mitch to guide him down the right path.

At least, until that was no longer possible.

'Is that it?' He finally asked.

'Natty wanted to know if you were ordering him to go after Roman.'

Mitch wished his obstinate nephew was in the room so he could strike him. There were numerous other things he needed to consider, though. At this stage, every move was vital.

Shaking his head in exacerbation, he moved on.

'What did you learn about our other friends?'

Clarke rubbed his chin. Looking up at him from his chair, Mitch wished Clarke would take a seat. Years of meetings, and the only person ever to look down on him was his subordinate. He understood Clarke's reasoning. He liked to be in position to react to any situation. Still, it frustrated Mitch that they never seemed to meet one another at eye level.

'Roman is certainly their biggest client in Leeds. They've invested a lot in him, and that's likely why he developed the balls to attack us directly. Outside of Roman, there are a few other suppliers, but none to the level of Roman, and certainly none receiving such support.'

Mitch stared into space for a long moment. No matter how he analysed it, there was no easy way to proceed with his situation. Inwardly, he cursed Sameer for dying. It had been inevitable, but it had jeopardised everything. Mitch had slipped up. He'd thought he would have more time than he did, and now it was backfiring on him.

'I want an immediate reshuffle,' he finally said. 'From now on, Nathaniel reports directly to you, and you will keep me informed of all comings and goings, including direct profits being made from each area. I want regular reports on my nephew, and you can inform him I'm *officially* ordering him to track down and eliminate Roman.'

Clarke nodded, showing no reaction to the announcement, apart from a slight flash of the eyes. When Mitch blinked, he was back to normal.

'I'll put the word out.'

'Good. I have something else I'll need from you.'

'I'm listening.'

'The other major sellers for Jakkar's men. I want them eliminated.'

Whatever control Clarke had over his emotions broke. His eyes widened.

'Are you sure?'

Mitch just looked at him, and Clarke nodded, composing himself.

'I'll get right on it.'

CHAPTER EIGHT

NATTY BOTH DID and didn't regret his decision to let Jaden pick the music.

It was loud, with people rapping slowly, as if they were being electrocuted, but seeing Jaden nod along and rap a few of the words was cute, and made both Natty and Lorraine laugh.

They were driving back from Lorraine's mum's place, where they'd had dinner. It had been a nice, relaxing evening, and Natty was determined to enjoy the moment. As if sensing where his thoughts were, Lorraine squeezed his knee from her passenger seat, shooting him a sweet smile.

Natty liked the fact his relationship with Jaden had continued to improve after a rocky point a few months back. Evidently, Jaden had the same weakness for words from the heart that his mum had, because he and Natty were different now. They'd always been close, but there was a barrier there, with Natty being viewed almost like a big friend of Jaden's rather than someone who could date his mum.

Now, things had changed. Jaden knew about them and seemed to have accepted it. Alongside that, he and Jaden seemed to have their own rhythm now, which pleased him.

'Jay, is this what you want to do now?' He asked. 'You wanted to be a footballer before, but are you trying to be a rapper now?'

Jaden giggled, shaking his head.

'One of my friends wants to be one. He's making his mum get his piano lessons because he wants to be like *Dave.*'

Natty liked that, believing it was a strong ambition. Music had interested him when he was younger. He and his friends would rap at school, and sometimes on the corners in between shotting drugs when he hit his teens, but Natty never had much talent for it. He believed he would have made a solid hype man, though.

Even at an early age, he had the ability to keep people around him. He'd considered music production and had even made a few beats, but he never kept up with it.

It was hard regretting the past when there was so much about the present he loved, he mused.

Such as the woman sitting next to him.

'That's a solid ambition,' said Natty. 'He's your link to the Brits and the Mobos when you're older and banging in hat tricks in the premiership.'

'I might play abroad,' said Jaden, as the song finished. Natty turned down the music so he could hear Jaden, surprised at his words. He knew Jaden harboured a desire to be a footballer, and was definitely getting better, but he'd said nothing about playing in another country.

'Where did that come from?' Natty asked, sharing a quick look with Lorraine.

'I've just been thinking a lot. We watch the footy, and there are always lots of young kids going to play in America, or Germany, or France . . . places like that.'

'And?'

'Maybe they're doing it because it's too hard to play in the Premiership.'

Natty's heart plummeted. He didn't want Jaden to become disheartened with life while he was still a child. He wanted him to have fun and be happy, and make the choices he wanted to make, rather than choices he felt he had to.

'Jay, if you wanna play in the premiership, then make that your aim. I told you before, you can do it. You just need to work hard and don't let anyone tell you that you can't do it.'

'You stopped doing it, remember, Nat?'

Natty nodded as they turned the corner onto Lorraine's street.

'I did. Wasn't as good as you were, though. I was easily distracted. You're better than that. You just need to stick to it, and your mum and I will do whatever we can to support you. Cool?'

'Cool, Nat.'

Lorraine gave Natty another smile as they pulled up, one that told him he'd done well. All evening, she'd seemed in much better spirits. She didn't have the weight of the world on her shoulders for once, and Natty didn't know if it was because she was around her mum, or because he was there, but he hoped it was a sign she was moving past what she'd been forced to do to Raider.

Lorraine unlocked the front door and let them in. Natty quickly looked behind him, checking no one was watching them. It was a habit he'd picked up, determined to keep his family safe.

'Remind me I need to water those plants tomorrow, Nat,' Lorraine muttered, already distracted as she turned on the hallway light and began taking off her boots. 'Jay, straight upstairs to get ready for bed.'

'Okay.' Jaden had a face like thunder, but he still did as he was told without being asked twice. Natty kissed Lorraine on the cheek, then took off his trainers, arranging them neatly against the wall as Lorraine liked.

'You know that he's just going to play on his PlayStation all night, right?'

Lorraine giggled as they entered the living room.

'I'll check later. If he does, you're going to go in and tell him off, then you're gonna take his computer for a week. Maybe two.'

'I can't do that!' Natty was aghast, but Lorraine nodded as she plopped down on the sofa.

'Yes, you can, and you will. You can go without Jaden beating you on *Fifa* for a few weeks.'

'He doesn't win all the time,' Natty grumbled. If he was honest, Jaden had become far better than him on the computer. There was once a point where'd he would let Jaden win so he could make him smile, but Jaden was far beyond that now. Natty had to try his hardest, but he was lucky if he won a game out of five these days.

'Sure he doesn't, babe. Seeing as you're still standing up, you obviously want to make me a cup of tea.'

Natty opened his mouth, closed it, then went to the kitchen, flipping Lorraine a middle finger as she laughed at him.

———

LATER, they were lying in bed, holding each other.

'Nat?' Lorraine asked.

'Yeah, babe.'

'. . . You don't speak about your mum anymore. How is she?'

Natty stiffened without thinking. He'd avoided thinking about his mum since her revelation about his dad's murder. He was still furious at what she'd confessed, but he couldn't bring himself to act against her. Instead, he'd just cut her out of his life.

Telling Lorraine that would be too difficult, though. She didn't know his uncle had ordered his dad's murder. She didn't know what Natty would need to do to make things right, and he wanted her as far away from it as possible.

'Nat?' Lorraine said, when he didn't respond. Natty sighed, closing his eyes.

'We don't talk anymore,' he said, and underneath the anger, hurt lived, hurt that wouldn't go away. He'd always had a contentious relationship with his mum, but he'd loved her. He still did, even though he didn't want to. He'd promised he would always look after her, but had broken that promise after her confession.

'What?' Lorraine was stunned. She sat up, trying to look at Natty in the dark room. 'Since when?'

'A while now,' said Natty, gritting his teeth.

'Why? What happened?'

'Babe, I really don't want to talk about it. Please, just drop it.'

'Okay.'

Natty didn't like the hurt in her voice, so he pulled her close and kissed her.

'I'm sorry,' he murmured. 'It's not you, I promise. She's just not someone I want to think about anymore. When I've processed everything, I'll tell you the full story.'

'Okay, Nat. You know I'm always here if you need me, right?'

'I do. You know that goes both ways, right?'

'I do.'

They shared another, longer kiss.

———

ROMAN SAT in Danielle's living room, wondering — not for the first time – what he was doing there. Roman distrusted her deeply, and he wasn't sure that would ever go away. He fingered the glass of patron she'd given him. He wasn't a huge fan of tequila, and sipped it begrudgingly.

The situation was curious. He'd tried to will himself to stay away from Danielle, but it had become more and more difficult to do so. Roman firmly believed she was responsible for his friend's death. She had been there when Keith died, somehow escaping with her life. It seemed beyond coincidence.

Roman had planned to kill her for her part in it, but things quickly changed.

Roman remembered the night vividly. Having tracked her down, he stood outside her house, gun in hand, rain lashing at his face. When he knocked on the door, and Danielle answered, she flung herself onto him, embracing him as tears rolled down her face. Roman recalled looking down at her, taking pity on her. Realising the same sadness that he felt was mirrored in Danielle.

She invited him in, and they spoke at length, reminiscing about their lost companion. The pair drank together, toasting Keith and his memory. The next morning, Roman awoke. His head was fuzzy from the night before. The room was unfamiliar, as was the body nestled close to him in the bed. Roman would never forget that feeling of realisation. The betrayal they'd both committed.

The betrayal that he continued to commit.

Roman stared at nothing in particular, lost in his thoughts. As Danielle walked into the room, his eyes flicked up, tracing her movements as she stepped towards him, flashing a dazzling smile.

Danielle sat beside him, still beaming. She sipped her drink, looking at him over the rim of her glass.

'How have you been?' She asked.

'I've been good. Just doing what I need to do,' said Roman. Danielle nodded.

'I wasn't sure if you would come,' she admitted.

'Why not?'

'Because you get this look on your face sometimes when you're around me. It's like you resent me.'

Roman didn't respond. At times, he did resent her. Right now, he did. He resented her willingness to betray his friend, and loathed himself for doing the same. He sipped his tequila, wincing as he swallowed. Danielle giggled.

'You don't have to drink it if you don't want to. I don't have any other liquor, but I can make you a coffee or something if you want.'

'It's fine. You don't need to go out of your way for me.'

'I like it,' she admitted, almost shyly. 'I like looking after you.'

Roman felt a wave of dizziness. Her closeness made him heady, and the words were dangerously comforting. He didn't trust them. At least, he didn't want to trust them. Roman knew what Danielle was. What she did for a living. She was practised in making men feel good about themselves. When she reached over and took the glass from his hand, he flinched. Danielle's smile faltered.

'I'm not going to hurt you,' she said.

'I wouldn't let you,' Roman replied. Danielle placed both their glasses on the table, shaking her head as she stared deeply into his eyes. She leaned in and kissed him, and Roman kissed her back, lost in the feeling of her. Her closeness, the smell of jasmine in her hair, and the feel of her chest pressed against him, it was all too much.

The kiss deepened. He needed her. Needed this. They shed their clothes, and Danielle climbed on top of him. Her moans and whimpers grew louder, Roman's grip tightening around her. Their bodies tensed as Danielle rocked backwards and forwards, whispering Roman's name.

After a while, Danielle collapsed against Roman, sweaty and panting. Roman closed his eyes, guilt creeping over him. It was his friend's name that should have passed those soft lips. Roman closed his eyes tightly, cursing his weakness. He didn't know how long he'd laid there, but his eyes opened when a sharp prod in his side jolted him.

'I'm cramping up. I need to move.'

As they cleaned themselves up, Roman was ready to leave. He was thinking of his excuses when Danielle grabbed his hand, leading him up the stairs. Powerless to resist, he followed in tow.

———

'WHAT'S GOING THROUGH YOUR MIND?' Danielle asked him, an hour later. They were in her bed, and she was pressed up against him once more. Roman wasn't comfortable. Danielle's bed was smaller than his own, and the room felt cramped. A ridiculously large wardrobe spanned most of the room, towering over them. A large flat-screen TV dominated the feature wall. Roman felt stifled, like he was in a box, the walls closing in around him.

'Why do you have that thing?' Roman asked, motioning to the TV.

'What do you mean?'

'You never use it. What's the point?'

'I do when I'm not entertaining,' Danielle said.

Roman turned to look at her, but didn't speak. Resting his head on the pillow, his eyes focused on the ceiling.

'So, are you going to tell me?'

'Tell you what?' Roman replied.

'What's going on in that head of yours?'

'Nothing. I'm just chilling.'

'You must be thinking about something,' said Danielle, her finger trailing down his chest, her damp hair splayed against him.

'Nothing important,' said Roman, letting her play.

'What about the streets?'

'What about them?'

'Is everything going well?' Danielle pressed. Roman shook his head, his annoyance growing.

'I'm not talking to you about that.'

'Why not? Keith used to speak about what you lot were up to all the time.'

Roman's eyes darted to Danielle.

'What did you just say?'

'You're against the Dunns, right? I was there when Keith planned the attack on one of their spots. I was there when you came to the house, angry at what he'd done. Keith used to tell me a lot. He used to talk about me moving in with him when you'd taken them all out.' Her hand paused on his chest.

Roman's senses were going haywire. The conversation was unsettling, and he didn't like how much intel Danielle had inadvertently learned from Keith.

'He shouldn't have said anything to you,' Roman spewed.

'He trusted me, Roman. You can too. I didn't tell the police anything, did I?' Danielle softly pointed out.

'That's not the point,' said Roman brusquely. 'We don't talk business with anyone outside of the crew. You get fucked up doing that.'

Danielle let out an awkward laugh. 'Men always get chatty when you get them into bed.'

Roman's lip curled.

'You'd know,' he said, unable to stop himself. Danielle chuckled mirthlessly.

'I guess I would.' She shrugged. 'Even knowing that, you're still here; in my bed. Do you think you're any better than the ones that pay me for my company?'

Roman shrugged her off, climbing out of bed. Danielle sat up.

'Roman, come back. I was only playing around. Don't leave like this.'

Throwing on his clothes quickly, Roman exited through the bedroom door without a backward glance.

———

STEFON BLAKE SMOOTHED out his hooded top as he climbed from the taxi, grinning at the driver.

'Sayid, I'll see you on the other side, bro,' he said. 'Good luck with the kids.'

Sayid, the driver, grinned back, then drove away.

Stefon glanced around Sholebroke Avenue. He hadn't been around the area in years, but things still looked the same. An old woman limped up the street, giving him a look as she did.

Across the road, two teenagers clad in chains and designer gear strolled down the road. Both stared at Stefon, who stared back, daring them to make a move. Sensing the danger, they looked away, some of the swagger removed from their movements.

Stefon smirked, pleased to have won the small stand-off. Heading to a dark green door, he knocked twice, then walked in, hearing the patter of footsteps as the thin woman that had come hurrying to the door, stopped short. She had a few more lines around her face and a little grey, but she remained as beautiful as ever. When she saw Stefon, her mouth fell open, eyes shining.

'Stef! Is that really you?'

'Hey, ma.' Stefon grinned as she threw her arms around him. He hugged her tightly, enjoying the moment. 'It's so good to see you.'

'You too. I didn't know you were coming. Why didn't you say anything? How are the girls?'

'The girls are good, ma. They're with their mums, but I'll bring them to see you soon. They're always asking about you.'

'I can't wait to see them.' His mum smiled, then her eyes narrowed. 'Why are you here, though, Stef? Are you in trouble?'

'Nah, I just wanted to come back,' replied Stefon. 'I'll be around for a while too, so we can catch up.'

'You can stay here. No one is using your room. I know you don't like people touching your things.'

Stefon grinned again. He'd hoped she would volunteer without prompting. It would certainly make things easier for him.

His mum went off to prepare food, already talking a mile a minute about a party she wanted to throw for him. Stefon headed to his old room, marvelling at the fact nothing had changed, other than a thin layer of dust on several items.

He moved to the corner of the room, prying up a loose floorboard, grinning when he saw the money he'd wrapped several years ago, along with a gun and some ammunition. He grabbed everything and put the floorboard back in place. The money there, plus what he had on him, would last him a little while, but he would need to get his money up as soon as possible.

After a shower, he changed into fresh clothes and returned downstairs in a grey tracksuit and white trainers. He went to see his mum in the kitchen, giving her a smile when she looked at him.

'It's good to have you back, Stef . . . even if it's not forever,' she said. Stefon almost rolled his eyes. If it was up to his mum, he'd live with her his whole life. He wasn't against being pampered, but he needed his independence.

'I know. Listen, I'm gonna go out for a bit to check things out. You can reach me on my phone if you need me.'

'You only just got back. Can't that wait?' His mum frowned. Stepping into the kitchen, Stefon pulled her into a hug and kissed the top of her head.

'I'm not gonna get into any trouble, ma. I just want to see how things are. I'll be back later, and we can hang out and do whatever you want.'

Satisfied, his mum nodded her approval, and Stefon left. He was tempted to order another taxi, but decided to walk, wanting to see how everything looked.

The crisp air hit him, and he was glad he'd worn the hooded top, the gun resting in the folds. It was dangerous to carry, but he'd been caught without his gun in the past, and didn't intend for it to happen unless absolutely necessary. Despite having lived in Leicester for the past few years, he'd had a few scores he'd left unsettled in Leeds, and he'd found that when it came to beef, many in the Hood had long memories.

Stefon crossed Chapeltown Road and walked down Harehills Avenue, glancing at people jogging around Potternewton Park. It wasn't a particularly long course, but the uphill sprint could be punishing. He relished the idea, and planned to try it out soon.

Turning at the bottom of Harehills Avenue onto Spencer Place, he let his feet carry him along. He nodded at a few people as he walked by, his confident gait contrasting with his affable manner.

Before long, he reached a spot he'd been familiar with, noting two young men outside, passing a joint between them, listening to a drill song he didn't recognise on a phone. Both kids were bobbing their heads and didn't hear him enter the garden until he was right on top of them.

'Who the hell are you?' One of them asked. He was short and skinny, with a thin face, an upturned nose, and a patchy attempt at a beard. His partner had his back, and both glared at Stefon, who smiled at them.

'No disrespect, lads. Spence is waiting for me. He told me to walk right in.'

'He didn't say anything to us . . .' the skinny youth said, frowning. Stefon didn't hesitate.

'It was last minute. I got off the phone with him like ten minutes ago.' He held up his phone. 'Go in and check with him if you like, but you know how he gets.'

If one of them had questioned him on exactly how *Spence got*, Stefon would have been stumped. The youths glanced at the door behind them, then at Stefon, who was still smiling, his movements unthreatening. Finally, they nodded and stepped aside.

Stefon walked into the house. People moved around, some talking in loud voices. He considered going upstairs, but checked downstairs first. A man was talking on the phone in the living room. He glanced up at Stefon, assessing him with curiosity. His head snapped away as the person on the other end of the phone recaptured his attention.

Stefon pressed on, walking past the man with a short nod as his eyes flitted to him once more.

In the kitchen, a man was looking out of the window, but immediately turned when he heard Stefon enter. Stefon smiled, recognising Spence. He remained sharply dressed, his intelligent, calming demeanour palpable. Stefon had heard rumours, but was surprised to see the sling around Spence's arm.

'Stef?' What the hell?' said Spence. He moved forward, and the pair slapped hands, with Stefon careful not to aggravate Spence's injury.

'It's been a while, Spence. How have you been, man?'

'I've . . . been good. What are you doing here, though? I won't bother asking how you got inside.'

Stefon laughed. 'Yeah, your people are vigilant, but I'm not new to this,' he said.

Spence laughed.

'Sit down, bro. Do you want a drink, or are you hungry? I can send someone for some food.'

'I wouldn't say no, if you're planning on getting something.'

Spence left the room to give the order, and Stefon slid into a seat. Spence and the others had clearly done well for themselves over the years, just as he knew they would. Spence was a shot-caller, and early on, he'd always shown that spark of leadership. It pleased Stefon that he was thriving in the team.

He looked around the kitchen, the design similar to last time, though several of the products, such as the cupboards, kettle and microwave, had been updated. There were several energy drink cans on the counter, and a few dirty bowls and plates, but nothing over the top.

'So, what's going on?' Spence asked. Stefon shrugged.

'Same old. I thought I'd been away too long, and that I'd come and see what you lot were up to. Where's Natty at?'

'He's out and about. I was with him yesterday.'

Stefon grinned. 'I heard he's killing it out there. You all are.'

Spence smiled. 'You heard about us all the way down there in Leicester?'

'How did you know where I was?'

'Was it supposed to be a secret?'

'No, but still,' said Stefon. 'Anyway, I fancied a change, and like I said . . . I'd been away too long. I'm here to stay. For a while, anyway. I wanna get my weight up.'

'I'll talk with Natty, but he'll wanna help his cousin, no doubt about that,' said Spence, privately hoping he was right. He'd seen Stefon around the Hood, even before he and Natty started working together. They had always got along despite an undercurrent of tension existing between the pair.

Natty wouldn't be pleased Stefon was back around, especially if he was there to stay. As cool as Stefon was, he had a knack for attracting trouble, which was the last thing they needed.

Still, he sent Natty a text, and settled down to hear some of Stefon's patented stories, hoping that this would all work out for the best.

CHAPTER NINE

ROMAN COULDN'T SHAKE his annoyance with Danielle. She'd been right in what she said. Part of him respected the fact she owned it and made no excuses for her personality. He was furious at Keith. His friend should have known to keep his mouth shut.

Pillow talking had gotten a lot of people in their line of work in trouble in the past, and Roman didn't want it to happen to him.

Yet he hadn't cut it off.

Danielle hadn't reached out to him since he'd left. She didn't need to, and they both knew it. Whatever Roman was getting from being around her . . . it had tethered them to one another.

Brushing his teeth, he finished freshening up, choosing a simple outfit for the meeting: a dark grey long-sleeved top, a black jacket and jeans, with a pair of black shoes. He was making too much of an effort, and that irked him.

Everything irked him nowadays.

When Roman was ready, he drove to a restaurant on Roundhay Road. Parking outside, he entered the small establishment. It had one customer, sitting at the counter, eating a kebab. There were two seats to his left. Behind the counter, a balding Asian man with a potbelly nodded to Roman, signalling him to go through to the back.

Roman walked through the kitchen, comprising two middle-aged women shouting at one another whilst preparing food. The greasy, fried smell made his stomach turn, but he took a left, making his way through a door. Heading upstairs, he stopped in front of another, sturdier door. He knocked twice and, a few moments later, heard the locks being removed. A burly, shaven-headed man signalled for him to step in.

Ahmed waited, sitting on a faded grey sofa. He said nothing when he saw Roman, who sat nearby.

'Drink?' Ahmed finally said. Roman shook his head. 'To business, then. What is being done about the Dunns?'

'That's none of your business. Your only concern is that I pay on time for the work, which I do.'

'You're buying less from us,' Ahmed pointed out. 'That makes it our business. We supply you, and we are in a mutually beneficial partnership. The Dunns represent a threat to said partnership. The Dunns . . . Nathaniel Dunn in particular . . . killed your friend. Made you a laughing stock in the streets you hold so dear. You need to rectify this, or you risk being cut off completely.'

It wasn't just the words that bothered Roman; it was the completely toneless way in which Ahmed delivered them. Roman knew he wasn't wrong. The fact was, the Dunns had eliminated multiple people in his team, and he'd done little about it. Killing Carlton and poisoning a few testers wasn't enough. Roman knew what he needed to do, but disliked the way he was being spoken to.

Ahmed was sitting there, secure in the power, safe in his room, with his goon watching his back. Roman couldn't do anything about it now, but it didn't mean that he would swallow it forever.

'Is that all?' He said, resisting the urge to say worse. Ahmed shook his head.

'Don't view us as the enemy, Roman. I promise, we are the only people that care about your welfare. Continue to work with us, in the right fashion, and you will prosper.'

'Did your boss tell you to say that?' Roman retorted, all niceties gone.

Ahmed smiled for the first time.

'I'm paraphrasing slightly, but yes. Your lack of response has gone on long enough. Show us we were right to take a chance on you.'

————

NATTY WALKED with Jaden close to him, as they headed to the John Charles Centre for Sport, located in Belle Isle. The others were nearby, chattering excitedly about the fight and what to expect.

Earlier, he'd spoken with Clarke, who had confirmed Mitch's plans, which annoyed Natty. He had no issue regarding checking in with Clarke, but disliked being forced into a conflict that wasn't for the best of the crew.

As far as he was concerned, Roman had been broken. There was no threat from him, no matter who he was backed by.

For Natty, Mitch was the main threat, and over the past few months, he'd tried thinking of a strategy to get to the man so he could take him out. Going after Roman was counter-productive. He hoped Brown got back to him soon with something useable.

He thought back to the messages he'd exchanged with Spence earlier. His cousin Stefon was back in town, and Natty was curious as to why. He liked his older cousin, but he could be wild, and Natty would need to work to stop him from causing too much trouble.

'Are you a fan of boxing, Jaden?' Clarke asked, smiling at the young man's enthusiasm. Natty shook off his thoughts, focusing on their conversation.

'I've seen a few fights, and loads of highlights on YouTube. I wouldn't mind learning how to box,' he admitted.

'Maybe Natty can teach you. He's not bad with his hands,' said Clarke. Natty chuckled, rubbing the top of Jaden's head affectionately.

'Don't you two start,' Paula said, chuckling as Clarke and Natty began shadowboxing. 'Rachel is meeting us here. I said she could come with us, but she said she had a lift.'

Natty had heard them mention *Rachel*, and knew she was Danny's girlfriend. The four of them waited outside the centre. It wasn't cold, but it wasn't warm either, and Natty wished he'd bought some gloves with him.

After a few minutes, a car pulled to a stop, and a teenage girl climbed out. Natty felt Jaden straighten up next to him, grinning as he glanced at the girl that Jaden clearly liked the look of.

The smile left his face when he recognised the young girl. When her face paled when she saw him, it was clear she recognised him too. Months ago, Natty had raided one of Roman's stash houses. He'd found Rachel there, hanging out, and had warned her to stay away from the young thugs. He hoped she'd heeded his warning, but hadn't known she was involved with Danny.

Paula noticed nothing amiss, hugging the young girl and firing questions at her, asking how she was. Clarke, however, glanced from the girl to Natty, frowning. He said nothing, but Natty knew it was a conversation they would need to have soon.

Now that Rachel was with them, they entered the centre, showing their tickets as they were led to their seats. Rachel sat as far away from Natty as she could. He'd said hello, acting as if he'd met her for the first time. She'd done the same, but her delivery was shaky, and a little stilted. Jaden couldn't stop staring at her, and Natty thought it was adorable. To his knowledge, the young man had shown no interest in girls until now, but it wasn't an enormous shock that his first crush was one that was older.

Natty's had been too.

Settling in the seats, Natty lost himself in the events, with several fights taking place before Danny's. They each went the full distance, with each fight lasting three rounds. The boxers all fought well, but Natty found they were too cagey, not getting in there and taking advantage when they could.

'Danny is up next,' said Clarke, and Natty could hear the pride in his voice. As Danny came out, they roared. Danny was tall, gangly, with well-defined muscles in his arms and legs. His opponent was bigger and had a mean look about him. Natty rolled his eyes at the kid trying to act like *Mike Tyson*, attempting to stare down Danny, who seemed to take it in his stride.

After a few minutes, the fight began. Danny worked behind his jab while his opponent quickly tried to cut the ring off. He ate a few hits, but landed a few body shots that wobbled Danny.

'Shit, that one looked like it hurt,' said Natty, wincing. The opponent clearly hit hard. To his surprise, Clarke didn't look fazed. In the next round, Natty saw why. Danny's opponent had punched himself out in the first round, trying for the knockout, and Danny was all but hitting him at will, catching him with several neat combinations.

His opponent got desperate, throwing wild haymakers that would do massive damage if they landed, but they didn't get close, and on the last one, Danny caught him flush with a hook and knocked him down as the crowd went crazy. The kid got up, but was clearly wobbled. He beat the count, but Danny went on for the kill, and the kid's corner had seen enough, throwing in the towel.

The crowd were electric, and Natty loved the atmosphere, cheering for Danny as he held up his arm, before being taken backstage.

After the bouts finished, everyone waited for Danny to leave the changing rooms. Natty patted him on the back as everyone offered their congratulations.

'You looked great in there, Danny,' said Natty. He'd met the young man a few times at the house, and admired his quiet demeanour. 'I didn't know you were so polished.'

'I had some good teachers,' said Danny, glancing at Clarke, who smiled back warmly. A few people from rival gyms came up to Danny, offering their congratulations and shaking his hand. After that, Rachel gave him a hug and a kiss. Natty chuckled when he saw Jaden glaring at Danny, though the kid still congratulated Danny on the win.

'We're gonna get some pizza and celebrate,' said Paula. 'He deserves a treat after that performance. Do you and Jaden want to come, Nat?'

'I told his mum I'd have him home by now,' said Natty. 'Maybe next time.'

After saying their goodbyes, Natty and Jaden climbed into his car, and they drove away.

'You enjoy that?' Natty asked, as they pulled out of the centre.

'Yeah. It was great.' Jaden's tone lacked the earlier enthusiasm, though, and Natty knew why.

'You don't do things by half, do you, Jay . . .?'

'What do you mean?' Jaden's brow furrowed in confusion.

'Rachel.' He smirked as they stopped in traffic, Jaden's face almost as red as the light.

'What are you on about?'

'I'm talking about having an older girl as your first crush. I didn't think you were into girls like that.'

'I'm not. I don't know what you're talking about,' said Jaden, his voice growing more high-pitched. Natty laughed, but decided to hold off on the teasing. He wondered if Rachel was on the level. He'd warned her last time, and if it turned out she was messing around with Danny, he'd have to warn her again.

CHAPTER TEN

LORRAINE GRINNED as she sat at her corner table in the club, watching Rosie force their friend Poppy to have another drink. With Natty looking after Jaden, she'd spoken with her friends on WhatsApp, deciding to try to have some fun.

Lorraine held her glass of wine, her boys at the forefront of her mind. Jaden had been so excited to go out with Natty, which warmed her heart. There had been some tension between Jaden and Natty in recent times, but they seemed back on track. Staring off at nothing in particular, Lorraine's cheeks lifted, her smile widening.

She was thankful they seemed able to move on with their lives — particularly Jaden. His father's death had weighed heavily on him. Jaden and Natty spending time together was a surefire sign that things were healing. Lorraine couldn't help but wonder when she would feel that same relief. Looking down at the table, her smile faltered.

Closing her eyes, she inhaled deeply.

'Are you okay, Lo?' Rosie asked, noting her friend's pensive expression.

'Yeah.' Lorraine forced a smile. 'Just chilling.'

'You need to come up with a better excuse if you want to fool me.'

Rosie rolled her eyes, glancing around at Poppy, who was watching people dance. 'What is it?'

'Nothing you don't already know,' said Lorraine evasively. *What was there to say?* She was a killer. Lorraine desired what she knew she didn't deserve; peace of mind. She couldn't speak to a professional to help her. She could barely speak to anyone.

Lorraine had tried meditation, but was often disrupted by Jaden. Journalling she'd stopped when she found Natty *burning confession statements*. Lorraine had Natty and Rosie, and that was it. Both were there for her when she needed them, speaking to her about the situation and making sure she was ok, but it didn't make the situation any easier.

On top of that, she had Angela on her case. She didn't know what the woman's problem with her was, but there had been a weird energy since she had joined the company. For now, Lorraine planned to keep her head down and not give her any reason to make a stink.

'Do you want to get out of here and talk about it?' Rosie asked.

Lorraine shook her head, though the idea sounded appealing. She just wanted to enjoy her night out, or at least, not think about her issues.

'I'll be fine. Seriously. How are you, though? Is Spence's arm okay? Seemed better when you guys came over for dinner.'

Rosie nodded. 'He doesn't have to wear the sling as much anymore. It's coming off soon. He's getting full mobility back, but he overdid it at the gym the other day, so he needs to take time.'

'And you two? Everything still going well?' Lorraine asked, grateful for the change of subject. Spence and Rosie had looked happy when she'd seen them together, but she wanted to be sure.

'Mostly,' admitted Rosie.

'*Mostly?*'

Rosie nodded.

'He's a bit distant. I don't know what's causing it, but I thought everything on the streets was done. We haven't had anyone trying to kill us in public anymore, anyway,' she said, trying to make a joke, which fell flat.

'Natty hasn't said anything to me about it. He's been coming home at normal times, though, so I guess I just hoped everything was okay too. Have you tried speaking to Spence?'

Rosie nodded again.

'He just tells me everything is okay, but I can't help my instincts. If it was anyone else, I'd think they had another woman.'

'Spence is definitely not like that, Rosie. He really cares about you.'

'Do you think he loves me?' She quickly asked. Lorraine nodded.

'I do. His ex did a number on him, but he's been open with you about that. If you like, I can get Natty to have a word.'

'No, you don't need to do that.' Rosie vigorously shook her head. 'I don't want him thinking I'm chatting his business. I'll be fine. We'll be fine.'

Lorraine hoped so. She'd always hoped Rosie and Spence would get together, and thought the pair suited one another.

'Will you stop your little secret whispering,' slurred Poppy, her hand trembling as she held a half-full glass. Both women laughed at their friend, forgetting about their issues for a little while.

The night went on, and when the club became stale, they went to another on Call Lane.

Lorraine was nodding her head to an R&B song by the bar when she caught the eye of a man approaching. He was light-skinned, with neatly trimmed hair and a shaped-up beard. When he saw Lorraine, he froze.

Lorraine's eyes remained fixed on the man, whose eyes darted side-to-side. After a moment, Lorraine reached out to her friend Poppy, patting her on the shoulder and motioning to the man. Poppy smiled widely, squealing as she rushed into his arms. Embracing her awkwardly, his eyes flitted from Poppy to Lorraine.

'Curtis, babe! I didn't know you were heading here tonight. You should have said!' Poppy said, fluttering her eyelids.

Rosie's eyes shifted from Curtis, to Poppy, to Lorraine, and back again, confusion etched on her face.

'What's going on? Why is he looking at you like that?' she asked.

Lorraine's eyes narrowed as she continued to observe Curtis.

'I'm not sure. He's acting real shifty. Unless . . . ' Lorraine's eyes widened as she looked beyond Curtis.

'Unless what?' Rosie prompted, losing patience.

'Do you remember me telling you about Natty and me coming out before? How a guy was hitting on me, and Natty squashed it?'

'That was Curtis?' Rosie asked, her eyebrows raising. Lorraine nodded.

'Why does he keep looking at you like that, Lo? He looks terrified.'

'I'm not sure, but you're right. He does.'

Curtis ordered them some drinks, and though his friends kept staring at them, they kept their distance. Curtis didn't so much as look in their direction. Focusing on the back of his head, Lorraine wondered what could have prompted such a personality shift.

The common denominator was Natty. Curtis had oozed confidence before Natty intervened in their conversation the last time they met. After returning to his friends, his demeanour shifted immediately. Natty hadn't made any threats or advances, it was over.

Just like that.

Not for the first time, she wondered about Natty's reputation. He had all but inferred that he'd killed people, and had used that fact to try to make her feel better about herself.

Lorraine didn't know the circumstances, and didn't ask. She wasn't in the streets, but whenever she was around people, there was something extra there . . . often an odd look that suggested they were on guard around her.

Before long, Rosie was with Poppy, trying to get her to sober up outside the club. Their wayward friend had consumed too many drinks, too quickly, and now she could barely stand by herself. Lorraine was about to help, but Curtis was in her path.

'Listen, I know we've not spoken in a while, but I'm sorry how things went last time.'

'You mean when you made a move on me in front of my boyfriend, then wanted to fight him?' Lorraine wasn't going to make it easy on him.

Curtis rubbed the back of his neck. 'I'm sorry, like I said. It was a mad night, and I was with my boys. I got carried away, and they set me straight.'

'That shouldn't have needed to happen,' Lorraine pointed out. 'It shouldn't matter who I'm with. You should respect me enough not to move like that.'

Curtis nodded.

'I know. It won't happen again. I promise.' He glanced behind him at Poppy, who was being helped into a black cab by Rosie and several of Curtis's friends. 'How are you, though? Everything cool?'

Lorraine nodded.

'Everything's fine.'

Curtis sighed.

'It's probably not my place to say, but just be careful. Your man is into some big things.'

'Like what?' Lorraine asked.

'Like I said, not my place to say. Just be careful. His name is ringing out in the streets. That can be good, but it can be bad too. Can't really say any more than that.'

With a last look, Curtis went over to the group, leaving Lorraine staring after him.

CHAPTER ELEVEN

NATTY BOUNDED into the safe house.

'Where the hell is he?' He shouted, bursting into the kitchen. Stefon rose to his feet and hugged Natty tightly, as Spence looked on with an approving grin.

'Look at you!' Stefon boomed. 'I can tell you're still gymming it. Fucking hell.'

'I'm not the only one,' said Natty. He was a few inches taller than his cousin, but their builds were similar, and despite Stefon being five years older, you'd be hard-pressed to tell the difference between them.

'How long's it been?' Stefon asked. 'Feels like too many years, cuz. I can't believe what you're doing. I've heard big things.'

'I know, cuz. It's been mad. We need to have a proper catch-up, and I can tell you the story. What's been going on with you, though?'

'Life, fam. The kids are good. Their mums are cunts, but too late to do anything about that. I've been doing what I need to do, though. Legally and illegally, whatever makes money.'

'Are the girls still living in Manny?' Natty asked. He hadn't seen Stefon's girls since they were babies, but remembered the drama at the time. He'd impregnated two women within weeks of the other. They were in the same friendship group, and one had an older brother in the game.

There was a simplicity to Stefon that Natty both loved and loathed. He knew what he wanted and did what he needed to get it. Natty had lost contact with him over the years, but he was smart enough to realise there was a reason Stefon was here now.

'Nah, I didn't spend long in Manny. You're thinking of Leicester. They're gonna come and spend some time with me up here, once I'm established.'

'I didn't know you were planning on staying,' said Natty, keeping his voice neutral. He glanced at Spence, who gave him a short nod, showing he'd understood what Natty was thinking.

'Maybe for a little while. See how things are going; help out my little cuzzy!' Stefon boomed. 'I've heard you're top boy out here, man. You were always a little hothead; it's hard to believe.'

Natty smiled, knowing what Stefon was getting at. The pair had been *rivals* when they were younger, though it was somewhat one-sided. Stefon was five years older, was bigger, and established himself earlier. If he hadn't left Leeds, he could have easily formed his own crew, or risen highly within theirs.

Natty swallowed down a moment of frustration, imagining Stefon being in charge of their crew, ordering him, Spence and Cameron around. Then, he frowned, not wanting to think about Cameron.

'Like I said, it's one hell of a story. What about Leicester, though? Don't you have shit going on down there?'

Stefon took a step back, eyes narrowing.

'You're sounding like you don't want me here.'

'I'm just asking a question, Stef. You'd ask the same one if you were in my shoes, and you know it.'

The energy seemed to evaporate from the room. Spence slid to his feet, awkwardly watching the pair stare the other down.

Stefon finally smiled.

'You really have changed, cuz. You're a proper boss, man.'

That broke the tension, and everyone laughed.

'If you wanna hang around, then that's fine,' said Natty, resolving to keep an eye on Stefon, or to have Spence do it. 'You can work with Spence. He'll put you in play.'

Stefon nodded, his grin widening. 'Just remember, I'm a step above meeting sales on a corner, cuz. I'm a big man.'

'I know,' said Natty, already irritated with the conversation. 'Spence will take care of you, give you a few teams to run. He'll explain how it all goes, but Stef . . . don't step on any toes.'

Stefon waved a hand. 'You worry too much.'

'I'm serious. There's enough going on at the moment.'

'So I heard,' said Stefon. 'What's the deal with this Roman dude?'

'He got too close to the sun and got burnt,' said Natty. 'We're putting something together for him, to finish it once and for all.'

'Is that confirmed?' Spence asked, remembering he and Natty's discussion a while back.

'Yep,' said Natty. 'I'll sit down and properly run you through it, but I've gotta jet.' He slapped hands with both men, then turned to leave, his phone already to his ear.

———

'LOOK AT MY LITTLE CUZ,' said Stefon, watching after him. 'He really is proper big time now, isn't he?'

'He is,' said Spence, wondering about everything that was transpiring. He hoped Natty clued him in on the plan for Roman, recalling Natty's visible resentment over the move. With Stefon in the mix, he wondered how it would all go. It would take a supreme effort to keep everything on the level.

His phone buzzed, and his stomach lurched when he glanced at the screen and saw a message from Anika.

I miss you, Spence. I hope you're okay.

He sighed, tempted once again to block her, but unable to bring himself to do it.

'Everything good?' Stefon asked, noticing his mood shift.

'Yeah. Everything's fine. Come, let's go for a drive, and I'll give you the play.'

'Fine. I'll drive, though. Don't want your arm to fall off or anything.'

Both men laughed as they left the house.

———

NATTY WAS ALREADY in a bad mood as he drove to Clarke's. Stefon's return had thrown him for a loop. As much as he loved his cousin, it didn't stop him from being extra. If Natty let him, he would cause a heap of trouble that Natty would have to sort out.

Clarke waited for him, handing him a bottle of water without being asked. Natty expected to hear Paula moving around, but didn't.

'You look stressed.'

'It's been a long day. A family member is back around.'

'Stefon?'

Natty's brow furrowed. 'You knew?'

'I heard yesterday. I was surprised when you didn't mention it.'

'I wanted to speak with him and find out what was going on first,' admitted Natty.

'And? What's going on?'

'He's gonna be around for a while. I'll give him a few teams to run and see how he goes. He's a solid earner. He just needs watching.'

'Fine.'

'That's it?' Natty was surprised. He didn't think Clarke would overrule him, but he was surprised he hadn't put up any challenge. He was essentially taking Natty's word for it about Stefon. Natty wondered if Clarke had secretly had him checked out. Knowing how the older man operated, it wouldn't surprise him.

'You might need to check in with me, but you know your shit, Natty. You don't need to run hires by me. Just keep me in the loop and let me know what's happening with Roman.'

'Okay,' said Natty. He was done arguing about Roman, and still saw his moves against Mitch as the top priority.

For now, he needed a subject change.

'Danny, man . . . he's something special. I'd think he was older and more experienced than he is, the way he moves.'

Clarke grinned. 'He used to be a lairy little bastard. The boxing was a way to give him a bit of discipline, but none of us expected him to take to it the way he did. He has a knack for styles and soaks up stuff like a sponge. He could go all the way.'

'Yeah, definitely. If he sticks with it, and he looks like he will, there's no reason he can't,' agreed Natty.

'I was surprised that you knew Rachel,' said Clarke.

'You were?' Natty replied, keeping his tone noncommittal. He'd expected Clarke to bring this up at some point.

'Yeah. What gives? I thought she was gonna faint when she saw you, and you're not the kiddie fiddling type.' Clarke watched Natty intently.

'How long has Danny known her?'

'I don't know the exact date, but he's known her for a while, and said they only recently hit it off.'

Natty wondered if that coincided with him scaring her away from a drug spot.

'Do I need to be worried about her?' Clarke pressed.

Slowly, Natty shook his head.

'No. I don't think so, anyway.' He gave Clarke the story, telling him about seeing her at the stash spot and taking pity on her. Clarke whistled when he finished.

'No wonder she was so scared when she saw you. I'm surprised she kept it together after that.' Clarke scratched his chin. 'By all accounts, she's a good girl. Looks like you scared her straight, but if there's anything extra that needs to be done, rest assured, I'll handle it.'

That was all Natty needed to hear. He trusted Clarke to be vigilant. If Rachel was still hanging around the wrong crowd, it wouldn't take long for them to find out about it.

'Cool.'

'Other than that, everything good with you? Your unc doesn't say much, but he's worried. I am too.'

'I appreciate it, Clarke. It's just domestic stuff. Nothing I'm gonna bore you with.'

'Fair enough. How's your mum doing?'

Natty dipped his head, wetting suddenly dry lips.

'Fine.'

'Good. Keep an eye on her. Family is what it's all about.'

Natty didn't know if Clarke was implying anything in particular, but he nodded, wanting to leave the subject as quickly as possible.

'Roman. What's your plan?' Clarke asked after a long moment.

'Track him down and kill him.' Natty shrugged.

'You don't seem enthused about the task.'

'I said my piece, Clarke. I think it's a waste of time, but I'll put together a plan and get him. Might have to shake down some of his workers if I can find them, but he's probably communicating with them from a distance like he's bloody *Pablo Escobar* or something.' Clarke laughed at that. 'It might even be worth reaching out to his old bosses.'

Clarke shook his head. 'Mitch won't like that. Leave Teflon and the others out of it.'

Natty filed that reaction away for later.

'Fine. I'll have to get a feel for him again, and then I'll handle it. You can pass that back to my uncle when you see him.'

'Nat,' Clarke sighed. 'I'm not any happier about this than you are, but I've told you my feelings before. I respect the chain of command, and your unc gave me a directive to follow. If there's an issue, it might be worth you speaking to him directly.'

'Do you ever wonder why he's working through you?' Natty asked Clarke. 'Don't you find it strange that he's spoken directly to me in the past, and has given me directives, but now he's only speaking through you?'

'Natty, if you're trying to tell me something, then do it. Don't dance around it.' Clarke sounded rattled, and Natty decided to stop pushing it.

'It's cool, Clarke. I'll get the ball rolling on *Roman the conqueror.*'

'You do that.' Clarke smirked. 'You could even reach out to Lisa if you like . . . see if she's willing to help. Just make sure you keep your hands to yourself.'

Natty shook his head now, letting Clarke have his laugh. He had no intention of getting caught up with Lisa again.

CHAPTER TWELVE

'THIS IS THE LIFE,' said Natty, looking at Lorraine, who groaned.

'You're telling me,' she said, closing her eyes, enjoying the pleasure of Natty rubbing her feet. They were watching a true-crime documentary on Netflix, but Natty had tuned out ages ago. He didn't mind, simply happy to be spending time with Lorraine. Jaden was in his room, either sleeping or sneakily playing on his PlayStation.

Natty cherished the time he spent with Lorraine. Now, more than ever. He knew she and Jaden needed him, but he also knew that he needed them more. They were his safe space, a world away from the streets, and he cherished them for that.

Even as he said that, he thought about his cousin, still hoping he toed the line and didn't make waves. His thoughts shifted to his uncle, then to Roman, but when it came to Lisa, he shut off his brain, refusing to go there.

'Do you mind telling me why my son was begging me for boxing lessons earlier?' Lorraine suddenly said, her voice tinged with amusement.

'Let's just say he found his calling at the boxing event I took him to,' said Natty, smirking. Lorraine caught the expression and nudged him.

'What do you mean by that?'

'I mean that your son finally has an interest in girls.'

'What do you mean *finally*?' Lorraine laughed. 'He's only eleven. That's hardly a late bloomer.'

'I started earlier than that,' said Natty.

'Of course you did,' said Lorraine rolling her eyes. 'I suppose it's cute in a way. I thought he'd be happy doing the weights with you every now and then. I never thought he'd be into boxing, though. And as for the girls . . . I don't want my son growing up to be some sort of . . .'

'Some sort of what?' Natty pressed, enjoying the conversation. He found it amusing talking with Lorraine about Jaden, and knew she had certain expectations about how she wanted him to be when he was older. He still remembered the time she had flipped out on him when he'd jokingly called Jaden his *little soldier*. She lambasted him, telling him that Jaden was going to be better than that; that he wouldn't do what Natty did.

Natty agreed. He too wanted the best for Jaden, and would aid him in getting there, in any way he could.

'Don't worry, Lo. I'll teach him a few tricks when he's older . . . maybe thirteen.'

Lorraine laughed again, shaking her head.

'Absolutely not. That's what I'm concerned about. I don't need a *mini-Natty* running around charming all the girls.'

Natty guffawed, pulling Lorraine closer after he finished with her feet, and giving her a long kiss.

'I turned out okay in the end.'

'Yeah, you did,' replied Lorraine, eyes sparkling as she stared at him.

'How was your night out, by the way? I forgot to ask.'

'It was good. Poppy got herself in a state, but it was nice to be out, and to be around Rosie.'

Natty smiled, glad she'd had a good time. Lorraine sighed, her demeanour instantly shifting.

'I felt bad. I mean, I felt guilty, for not feeling guilty, if that makes sense.'

Natty didn't need to be told what she was referring to.

'It makes sense, but it's the last thing you should be feeling. Me and Rosie both told you the same thing. You defended yourself. It'll take some getting past, and that's totally normal, but the facts are the facts, babe.'

Lorraine snuggled against him, suddenly remembering her interaction with Curtis.

'I ran into one of your old friends too,' she said, moving on from the tired subject.

'Which friend is that?'

'The man who tried chatting me up in front of you. Curtis.'

'Is that right?' Natty instantly pictured the cocky man who'd started with him. He recalled how badly he wanted to fight him and his friends that night, and how frayed his emotions were at the time.

He felt like he'd made improvements since, but who really knew?

'Yeah. At first, he seemed terrified of even looking at me. His friends wouldn't come near me either. In the end, he apologised for the disrespect.'

'That's good,' said Natty offhandedly.

'Can I ask you something?' Lorraine said, her voice small.

'Of course.'

'How dangerous . . . are you?' She asked after a tense moment.

Natty found himself unsure how to answer. He didn't want to lie to Lorraine, yet he recognised it to be an incredibly loaded question. In the end, his conscience won out over his street instincts.

Sighing, he replied, 'I'm in the game deep, Lo. I won't lie to you. If I was to give you a straight answer, it'd be this: I'm probably one of the most powerful people on the streets of Leeds . . . especially around the Hood.'

Lorraine's heart sank. She wasn't entirely sure why. All she knew was that she didn't want Natty to be in any danger. She just wanted them to be happy.

'It's my uncle's power, though . . .' Natty added, as an afterthought, sounding distracted. Lorraine didn't know why he'd added it, and right now, she didn't care.

'Can you separate the streets from our life?'

Natty nodded. 'Yes,' he said quickly, hoping it was true.

Lorraine stared at Natty for a long time.

'Let's go to bed,' she said. 'I'm not even watching this anymore.'

They headed upstairs, and when they walked into the bedroom, Lorraine stopped short, pressing her curves against Natty. He squeezed tighter against her, inhaling the cherry scent of her hair spray, then kissed the back of her neck, making her shiver.

Spinning her around, Natty pressed her against the wall, kissing her thoroughly on the lips, then down the hollow of her throat, savouring her gasps and moans. They slowly stripped the other, feasting on the other's appearance as they stood naked in the middle of the room. Natty spread Lorraine on the bed. Before long, he was inside her, sliding slowly, just the way she liked, upping the tempo and the pressure until they crashed against one another, reaching mutually satisfying peaks.

Afterwards, Lorraine relaxed in Natty's arms, listening to the sounds of his breathing, feeling safe in his powerful arms.

Natty just needed to keep resisting the danger. If he did that, and she could get over her issues, Lorraine was sure they would be okay.

It was the last thought on her mind as she closed her eyes.

CHAPTER THIRTEEN

ROMAN SULKED for a while after his conversation with Ahmed. He hated the fact he was being told what to do. He understood it was a business, but there was something galling about bosses he'd never seen, giving him orders.

After leaving Ahmed, he'd stayed up all night, thinking of a plan. Roman had dealers to move product — albeit quietly to avoid detection — but had very little muscle. After thinking of people he could bring on board willing to go against the Dunns, a few names came to mind, but one popped up more than the others.

Roman met Maka in a restaurant in Bradford. He didn't trust moving around the Hood, and had travelled out of the way to avoid the spotlight of the Dunns.

Maka was already there, sipping a cup of coffee, seated in a spot that allowed him to see anyone coming through the door. He glanced at Roman, but said nothing as Roman sat down.

'Thanks for meeting me.'

'You reached out. Seemed no issue with me doing it,' said Maka, though his tone was carefully neutral.

'You're smart. You know why I'm here.'

'I do. You had a wasted trip. I'm not getting involved,' said Maka.

'Really? Even after everything?'

'Yes. After everything. What did you think you were going to do? Mention Manson and get me all up in a frenzy, screaming about revenge and *riding out*?'

'He was your best friend,' said Roman, his eyebrows contracting.

As the pair looked at one another, Roman thought about Keith. Things hadn't gone to plan in the war with the Dunns, and Keith was an important factor in establishing that fact.

Despite that, Roman would have given his life for his friend. Maka not being willing to do the same, confused and frustrated him.

'He was. He came to see me after he got out. Tried giving me this same pitch. I told him what I'm telling you; it's not happening.'

'They killed him,' Roman replied incredulously.

'They did. I gave him every opportunity to not involve himself. Tried bringing him in on what I was doing. A shot at the straight life. He didn't want it. He backed you and that fucking idiot, Keith. He paid for that with his life, and I'm not going to do the same.'

'Don't disrespect my friend,' said Roman coldly.

'Don't tell me what to do,' said Maka. 'I was in the streets before you. More importantly, I can use my hands. I'm not afraid of you and what you *think* you can do. If you want my advice, I'll tell you what I told Manson; leave the life behind. There's no winning.'

Roman's clenched teeth gradually relaxed, his hard eyes softening. He wasn't going to fight Maka. It was futile. He knew, deep down, that Maka was right.

Roman was envious of Maka's position; being able to assess the facts and decide whether to involve himself. It was a luxury he did not have. Roman sat up straighter in his chair, steeling himself. He'd come too far to go back now.

With or without Maka, he knew what he needed to do.

'Thanks for your time, Maka. I hope the family is well,' he said flatly, then slid to his feet.

'Roman?'

Roman glanced back at Maka, whose expression softened.

'Good luck, fam.'

Nodding back in acknowledgement, Roman left.

———

THE RED UBER pulled up to a house on Jackie Smart Court in the Hood, the bass from the music rocking the street. Natty climbed out first, followed by Spence and then Stefon, who was still bantering with the driver. The entire journey there, he'd made conversation with the old Asian man, asking about his family. Natty was impressed with his ability to get people to talk.

The trio were dressed up, kitted out in designer gear, with Stefon being the most ostentatious, wearing a white and gold t-shirt, with a thick diamond chain around his neck.

'Do we even know whose party this is?' Spence asked as they crossed the street, heading toward the house.

'Jermaine told me about it. Apparently, they begged him for me to show up. It's a good friend of his,' said Natty.

'I'm surprised that was enough to sway you. You don't even know Jermaine like that.'

Natty grinned. 'Maybe I just needed a break from everything,' he said. Stefon laughed next to him, already slapping hands with a few people as they entered, the drill tracks seeming to swell as he did so. Natty didn't know when playing these songs at parties became a thing, but he felt it sent a wild message to the partygoers.

Luckily, the crowd was predominantly older, and there were plenty of people around that Natty knew. Many of them knew Stefon from back in the day, so he didn't need to introduce him. He was pleased that Stefon had assimilated himself easily into the crew.

According to Spence, he'd taken control of the teams he was given, and so far, there had been no problems. Once again, he couldn't deny that Stefon had a way with people. If he stayed like this, there would be no reason that Natty couldn't bring him further into the fold.

For a moment, he wondered if Stefon was a potential ally against Mitch, but dismissed it. If he couldn't trust himself to tell Spence, he couldn't tell Stefon. There was too much at risk.

Pushing the thoughts from his mind, he headed into the living room, making his way through the crowds, inhaling several potent aftershaves and perfumes, mixed with weed smoke and strong alcohol.

Several cheap-looking black leather sofas had been pushed against the far wall. There was a rickety dark brown table underneath a window, with a selection of paper cups and several bottles of liquor.

Natty grabbed a cup and poured himself a glass of brandy, sipping it as he surveyed people. Spence had already situated himself in the corner, looking bored as a group of people tried talking to him. Stefon had grabbed a bottle and was dancing with two women, rapping along as they giggled and other people laughed at him. He grinned as a familiar face approached.

'Yes, Natty! Didn't expect to see you here,' said Sanjay, beaming as they slapped hands. He and Sanjay went way back, and Sanjay was his kind of drug dealer. He made good money and stayed low-key, and people always seemed to tell him things.

It was Sanjay who had given him the lowdown on Roman's manoeuvrings, and their association had only grown stronger over the years. Sanjay wore a cream shirt, grey ripped jeans and Air Jordan sneakers.

'I didn't expect to be here, to be honest, but I thought I'd give it a go. How's the family?'

'Everyone's good over my side. Everyone's eating,' said Sanjay. 'What about you? I'm hearing things?'

Natty's interest was piqued.

'What's the latest?' He asked.

'There's a lot of rumblings about your camp. Especially now that things are going well. People are jealous of the money flow.'

'People are always complaining about that. That's nothing new,' said Natty. Once upon a time, he had been one of those people. It had been a while since he had to worry about money.

He pondered that thought for a moment, vividly remembering the times he would sit and complain to Spence and Cameron. How he would list all the things he needed that he thought he would never get. Natty's life had changed dramatically in such a short space of time. He'd worked hard and, despite setbacks, had established himself as a real force.

He only hoped that it would continue, and that he could navigate through the next set of problems.

'Still, just watch yourself.'

'I wonder why I haven't heard anything,' Natty mused. Sanjay snorted.

'Look at you. In your position, no one is going to tell you anything. They're worried about what you might do.'

'Have you heard anything about Roman in your travels?'

Sanjay's eyes widened. 'Is that still a thing? I thought you lot wrecked him.'

Natty shrugged. He got along with Sanjay, but that didn't mean he needed to know everything he was doing. Sanjay chuckled.

'Fine. I'll look into what's going on. For now, I'm gonna get back out there and find someone to dance with.'

They slapped hands, and Sanjay left him to it. Natty watched after him. There was a lot in the air that he needed to navigate. He wondered how much the rumblings were connected to Roman. He would keep vigilant, and later speak to Spence and ensure he was aware.

If he knew his friend as he thought he did, he'd likely already heard about the rumblings, and would deal with them.

Thinking about the new chain of command, he decided he would speak to Clarke too. If anything, it would annoy him that Natty was running it by him. Sanjay was dancing now, his movements stiff and awkward, but nonetheless, he'd found someone to dance with.

———

SPENCE WAS ALREADY REGRETTING ATTENDING the Party. He tried not to think about Cameron often, but noted he'd been roped into attending fewer parties since Cameron had been gone.

On top of that, Spence had far more profile than he'd previously had. He was known as a high-ranking member of the Dunn organisation, and a close friend of Natty Deeds. This meant he had a host of people flocking to him, sucking up, or trying to talk him into snide investments.

Stefon was holding court, surrounded by a group of people, all of whom were laughing at a story he was telling. Spence liked that he'd settled in, and believed he would be a useful asset for their team.

Making his way through throngs of people, he fixed himself a drink in the kitchen, settling for vodka and lemonade. As he headed to another room, a woman crossed his path. Spence knew her from somewhere, but couldn't think where. Her eyes sparkled when she saw him, and she paused.

'Spence?'

'Sorry. Do I know you?'

'Claudette,' she said. 'I'm a friend of Anika's. She talks about you a lot.'

'Okay,' said Spence, not knowing what else to say. He had met several of Anika's friends, with Carmen being the first that sprang to mind. He hadn't spoken to her after Anika left, and wondered how she was doing. Claudette had light brown skin, several minor spots on her face, and dark brown eyes. Her hair was styled in Bantu Knots with braided sides, and she wore a short-sleeved red shirt and tight jeans.

'I know things went bad with you guys, but she loves you, Spence. She's been through a lot, but she regrets what happened.'

'I don't know what you want me to say,' said Spence, though it was making him wonder what exactly Anika had been through since she left. He assumed she'd had a bad time of it, but hearing it from a friend was different.

'I know, and I'm sorry. She's my friend, and I don't want her to hurt,' said Claudette. She gave Spence a soft smile, then left him. Spence's stomach twisted with guilt. He thought about the text messages he'd ignored, wondering how much it had taken to send them, even knowing he wouldn't reply.

Moving forward, he wasn't watching where he was going, bumping into a man. Spence almost apologised out of instinct, but when the man grunted and kept moving, he didn't.

'Excuse me?'

'You talking to me?' The man asked, frowning. He was similar in height to Spence, but slightly broader, with a lazy eye and a dark scar above his left eyebrow.

'You bumped into me. Least you can do is say sorry,' said Spence. They were drawing a crowd, but he didn't care.

'Chill. It happens. Don't turn it into a thing,' replied the man.

'It might already be a thing.' Spence shoved the man, people around them gasping. Before anything else could happen, Stefon got in between the pair.

'It's not going down. Step,' he ordered the man, who took one glance at Stefon and did just that. 'You good?' Stefon faced Spence.

'I'm fine. I'm just not gonna let dickheads like that take me for a fool,' said Spence, breathing hard. In the moment, he'd wanted the conflict, but with every passing moment, he felt sillier. He wasn't the type of guy to fight someone at a party. Normally, he was on the other side, maintaining calm.

'You sure? You wanna go outside and get some air or something?'

Spence shook his head. 'I'm good. The moment's passed. Cheers for having my back.'

'Anytime, fam. Shout me if you need me.' Stefon disappeared back into the crowd. Spence watched him. The moment had gone, but what stuck with him was the fact the man had been willing to fight Spence, but had backed down immediately when Stefon confronted him.

The more Spence considered this, the less he liked it.

———

THE PARTY WENT ON. Natty spoke with a few people, and even a few women made their way toward him, twirling their hair and flirting with him. He made conversation, but kept it moving. Natty found it easier, somehow. He loved Lorraine, and didn't want to hurt her.

Natty's eyes slammed shut as his mind skipped to Lisa. *Remembering the moment their lips met. His betrayal of Lorraine.*

His heart thumped in his chest as he opened his eyes.

Finishing a conversation with a hustler who'd been trying to do some business with him for a while, his eyes widened when he noted a familiar face. She had dark brown hair, greyish-blue eyes, round cheeks and alluring features.

Without hesitation, he made his way toward her. When she noticed him, she subtly beckoned to a corner. Natty glanced around, looking down at her.

'You know who I am, right?'

Natty nodded.

'Clara, right? Did you come here to see me?'

'I heard you might be coming, so I made myself available.'

'Looks like a few of the dudes around are hoping you're available.' Natty smirked. Three men were looking at Clara with hungry expressions on their faces. She all-but rolled her eyes, then frankly looked Natty up and down.

'What about you?'

'What about me?'

'Are you hoping I'm available?' Clara's tongue traced her upper lip. Natty tracked it, but didn't react. He was impressed, though. Clara was attractive and had a lot of sex appeal.

'I'm taken,' Natty said. Clara smirked.

'I know. Lisa doesn't like people playing with her toys . . . not unless she's there to observe, anyway.'

Natty pulled back. 'I'm not Lisa's toy. Say what you came to say.'

'Okay, *daddy*,' Clara said sarcastically. 'Lisa spoke with Clarke. She knows the plan, and she's working to bring the target into the light.'

Natty nodded. It was clear that Lisa was initiating the plan Natty had previously suggested. Lisa would use whatever means necessary to get close to Roman.

He stared beyond Clara, deep in contemplation. Lisa had paid a heavy price in her pursuit of Warren. She had given her body to get her man. Natty wasn't sure why, but his stomach ached when he thought about it. Lisa was always willing to pay the price for the sake of the crew, and Natty found himself wishing she wouldn't.

Roman would be no different, he mused, feeling increasingly uncomfortable.

Composing himself, his eyes focused on Clara once more.

'She knows to reach out if she needs any help.'

'She does. She also asked me to tell you something else . . .'

'Which is?'

'Protect yourself. There are a lot of—'

'*Grumblings*. I heard,' said Natty, recalling Sanjay's earlier warning. 'I can look after myself. Trust me on that. Anyone who tries me is going to regret it.'

Even as Natty said it, he became more alert of his surroundings, noting a man he didn't recognise. The man looked a few years older, with a double chin that even his beard couldn't hide, light brown eyes and fleshy cheeks.

'Oi, you fucking punk!' He shouted over the music. Natty recognised the tactic, and without thinking, he ducked, taking Clara with him as shots rang out.

Pandemonium ensued, people screaming and trying to leave the room as two more shots were fired. Natty fought his fear, grabbing a nearby bottle, gripping it tightly as the gunman, who wore a mask, approached. He pulled back his arm to throw it, still pinning Clara down.

Before he could let loose, he saw movement in his peripherals. Stefon had a gun, eyes blazing as he pulled the trigger and let off a shot, clipping the gunman, whose next shot went off course.

The spotter had already vanished in the crowd. Striding purposefully toward the injured gunman, Stefon kicked away his weapon. Hovering above him, he glowered down at the man, raising his arm and pointing his gun down at him. The man trembled as Stefon's finger tightened around the trigger.

'Stef!' Natty bellowed, getting his attention. 'Let him go. We need to get out of here.'

Stefon glared, but lowered his gun. Natty helped Clara to her feet. She shot him a thankful smile, then left.

'Come on. We need to jet,' Natty said to Spence and Stefon. They hurried from the house before the police could get there, and took off down the street.

CHAPTER FOURTEEN

'WHAT THE HELL WAS THAT?'

Natty paced the room, glaring at Stefon, who was sprawled on the sofa. Spence was on the phone, his eyes darting to the pair. Natty was beyond furious. Someone had dared to take a shot at him, and had done so publicly. Stupidly, Natty had figured his reputation would protect him from the worst of it, and it hadn't.

Now, he would have to deal with the situation.

Clarke had already called, just as they'd reached the safe house. Natty had told him he was being vigilant before the call ended, and he knew he needed to come up with a plan, but right now, he was far too wired.

'Why are you watching me?' Stefon asked, finally noticing Natty's attention.

'What the fuck were you playing at?' he snapped in return.

'I was saving your arse, wasn't I? That's what it looked like, anyway.'

'Saving me from what? Some two-bit shooter who I was about to take out? Who was dumb enough to fire wildly in the middle of the party? Did I look like I was about to get hit?' Natty said.

Stefon shook his head. 'Just keep talking shit, Natty. You should be thanking me. He had you dead to rights, and when you calm down, you'll recognise that.'

'You shouldn't be strapped at a damn party.'

'It's a good thing I was. You're the one who told me what you're into. Did you forget that this is the damn streets? It's play or get played in this game, and no one is playing me. I don't go anywhere without my burner.'

'Then you're a fucking idiot, Stefon. You talk about these streets like you know them, but you've been away years. Don't fucking lecture me about the streets you *chose* to leave. This isn't Leicester or wherever the fuck you were living. The feds here are just waiting for people like you to turn a corner with a strap on them.' Natty glowered at his cousin for a moment, then continued pacing the room.

Spence finished on the phone, warily watching the pair. Stefon stood, fury in his eyes, equally matched by Natty's.

'I don't like how you're coming at me, and I don't give a fuck what people think. Bottom line is, I saved you, and I'm not gonna have my little cousin thinking he can talk to me however he likes. That ain't gonna fly.'

Natty stepped forward, forcing himself not to react.

'You asked to be a part of what's going on here, and I'm cool with that. But you better recognise I'm your fucking boss first and your cousin second. I appreciate you having my back, but if you can't keep things low-key and do as I say, we're done here.'

The silence that followed seemed to stretch. Spence's mouth was dry, not knowing what to say to calm the atmosphere. It reminded him of the disagreements that Natty used to have with Cameron, dialled up to eleven.

Neither man was backing down, and Spence wondered if he could stop the pair from fighting if it popped off. He opened his mouth to speak, determined to calm the pair down, even if he didn't have the words to hand.

Before he could speak, Stefon nodded.

'Fine, cuz. I'll play it your way.' Stefon rubbed the back of his neck. 'I'm gonna get out of here and get my head down. I'll check you both tomorrow.' Slapping hands with Natty and then Spence, he left.

When the door closed, Spence blew out a breath. Natty still hadn't moved.

'Christ, Natty . . . I thought that was gonna get bad,' he admitted.

'You and me both,' said Natty quietly, still trying to calm down. He hoped Stefon learnt from the encounter. He had a lot on his mind, and the last thing he needed was to be wasting time reprimanding his cousin. 'Who were you speaking to?'

'Jermaine reached out. Seemed to think he needed to apologise for putting us onto the party. There are loads of rumours going around, but no one has any facts about what happened. Did you recognise them?'

Natty shook his head. 'I'd know the guy if I saw him again, but I didn't recognise him. The shooter was masked up, but they were definitely together.'

'Yeah, I heard the guy shout at you, but I figured it was because you were talking to his girl in the corner.'

Natty laughed, despite the situation. 'I'm not like that anymore.'

'I know, but that doesn't mean the whole world knows that. What did that woman want, anyway? I remember her from when we saw Lisa in town that time.'

'Funnily, she was warning me to stay safe, and telling me that Lisa was working on getting a line on Roman.'

Spence nodded.

'Do you think Roman was behind this?'

'It's plausible. He's my first guess, but apparently, we're attracting a lot of bad vibes. Clara mentioned it, and so did Sanjay.'

'Yeah, I saw Sanjay jamming down with a woman at the party. He's right, though. They both are. We're doing well, and things are quiet, but people are still complaining as they always do. Usual shit: they don't feel they're getting their fair share . . . they think we're pushing them out . . . so on and so forth. Still, a public hit attempt is a step too far.'

Natty let those words simmer. Spence was right. It was a step too far, and it was a sign of desperation. He glanced at his phone, then stifled a yawn, whatever adrenaline that had surged through his body after the shooting finally seeming to dissipate.

'It's a problem for tomorrow either way. I'm gonna get my head down and start afresh.'

'Look after yourself, Nat,' said Spence, slapping hands with his friend. 'People are after you, and they've shown they're not afraid to go at you publicly. Might be time to think about a bodyguard of your own.'

———

THE AFTERMATH of the party was telling. As per usual, word spread quickly around the Hood regarding what had transpired.

The common rumour was that a team of killers had tried shooting Natty Deeds, but had missed, hitting several innocents. The major addition to the story was that Natty and his team had fired back and murdered the shooters.

This was despite the fact that no one had died.

Natty was waiting for the police to come and see him. His name was out there, and he was the target, so it wouldn't be a leap that they would want to question him. He hoped no one had seen Stefon fire the shot. There had been a lot happening at once, but you just never knew what anyone was thinking.

Natty sat outside his regular safe house, wishing he could smoke a cigarette. His phone was ringing, but he was screening the calls. There weren't many people he needed to speak with.

Lorraine hadn't said anything about the shooting so far. She was happy he was okay, but he knew there was another deep conversation in their future.

Sighing, he clambered to his feet, stowing his phone back in his pocket and heading inside.

No good would come from overthinking.

CHAPTER FIFTEEN

'YOU COULD HAVE BEEN HURT.'

Spence and Rosie sat in his kitchen, eating breakfast. Over the past year, he'd been slowly changing to his kitchen in his spare time, and he liked the results. It had sleek surfaces, a neutral colour scheme, with smooth wood cabinets, and quartz countertops. The table they were sat around had clean lines, and was a light brown, oak design that had cost a pretty penny.

Realising Rosie was waiting for a response, Spence focused.

'I was nowhere near what happened,' he replied, tucking into his grapefruit. Rosie's lip curled as she surveyed him, not understanding how he could eat them. She could stomach them only as a last resort, and providing they had been coated in sugar.

'Someone fired shots at a party you were at, Spence.'

'They weren't after me. They were after Natty.' Spence fought to keep the exasperation out of his voice. He cared for Rosie, but it was exhausting going through this every time something happened.

Rosie folded her arms, frowning at Spence.

'Was that supposed to make me feel better, or worse?'

Spence grinned wryly. He hadn't expected it to work, but it was worth a shot.

'I know what you mean, and I'm not gonna say it wasn't scary, but it was a dumb move. Shooting at somebody, out in the open at a party? It's amateur. Believe me when I say, you don't have anything to worry about.'

'What did Natty say? I bet Lorraine is going spare.'

'Natty will be fine. Whatever's going on with him, it goes deeper than someone shooting at him.'

'What do you mean?' Rosie sat on Spence's lap, forcing him to abandon his messy fruit.

'Natty's distracted. I don't know what's causing it, but he's got something going on. He's really distant lately.'

'Have you tried talking to him about it?'

Spence shifted in place. Rosie meant well, but he didn't think she truly understood Natty. Spence did. It was part of the reason they made such good friends. He knew when to back off and give him space.

If you pressed Natty too much, he would usually get angry and end up hitting someone. He'd matured over the past few years, but the aggression was bubbling under the surface.

Natty was like a dormant volcano; the longer his temper remained checked, the more catastrophic it would be when it eventually blew.

'I tried, but he said he's fine. His cousin is here too, and he and Natty are clashing. It's like how Cameron used to be back in the day, but worse. I have to play peacemaker, while I'm dealing with my own shit . . .' he trailed off.

'What shit?'

Spence's mind flitted immediately to Anika, his stomach sinking. Glancing sidelong at Rosie, he composed himself. *Rosie would never know about Anika.*

'That whole shooting thing . . . I was just there, you know. I just stood there like a dick.' He settled on a suitable response.

'As opposed to what?'

'I should have stepped up. Time after time, these things are happening, and I'm just an afterthought. Natty is going from strength to strength. He's out there, doing whatever he needs to do. Do you know what happened? He looked like *Action Man*, dragging a woman to the floor and dodging bullets, and I was just there.' He hung his head, as some of the poison spewed out.

Rosie hugged him tightly, not knowing what to say. She hadn't realised Spence was going through so much. He just seemed to quietly deal with it.

'I know I don't have any place to say this, but I think you're being silly. There's a lot going on. I can't even begin to imagine quite how much, but Natty and everyone else relies on you, Spence. They rely on you to do what you do. Natty isn't asking for you to be Rambo. He just needs you to be you, Spence . . . that's enough.'

Spence smiled, despite himself, and hugged her back. He appreciated her trying to make him feel better. In a sense, she was right. Natty had never asked him to do anything but what he was doing. This was all him. It was all something he felt he needed to do. He didn't want to be the one letting the team down.

Once again, he wondered if he should tell Rosie about Anika. The longer it went on, the worse it would get. Claudette's words at the party had resonated with him. Even when they'd met, he hadn't considered Anika's position, or what she might be going through. Despite the fact she'd hurt him, he didn't want to reciprocate.

Kissing Rosie on the lips, he resolved to sort everything out, and soon. He couldn't let his issues overwhelm him.

————

'THEY TRIED TO KILL YOU, NAT.'

Natty nodded. He wasn't going to argue with Lorraine, and she had more than earned the right to worry about him. He didn't know why he wasn't more worried about it, and whether it was a sign he had become more desensitised to the goings on of the Hood.

He'd come close to dying. He'd been scared in the moment, but his instincts and training had kicked in. Natty had moved quickly, formulating a plan of attack and defending the vulnerable. He was proud of how he handled the situation.

Times like this, Natty questioned what his life had become.

Lorraine had been okay about it at first. He assumed she had heard on social media, but he still told her that there had been a shooting, and at first, she nodded, not saying anything. That hadn't lasted. By the night's end, when Jaden had gone to bed, she fixed them some drinks, and they sat on the sofa.

'Doesn't that scare you? Don't you think that's a sign that things are getting a little too dangerous? You were at a party, and they tried it.'

'I know, Lo. You're not gonna get an argument from me. They tried it, and I was lucky. I'm gonna be careful from now on, though. I promise.'

'Is that something you can promise?' Lorraine's voice rose, before she visibly calmed herself.

'Yes, I can. I'm gonna be out there, but I'm gonna find out who was behind it.'

'What are you going to do when you find them?'

The question hung in the air. Natty stared into Lorraine's eyes, but he couldn't say the words. The person who'd ordered his murder would die. Everyone knew it. Lorraine knew it.

Yet, she'd asked anyway.

'Why would someone shoot at you in public?' Lorraine moved on, fighting past her heart careening in her chest at the thought of someone killing Natty.

'I'm in an enviable position, and people don't like that. I've made enemies, but like I told you, I'm keeping that life away from this. From us. Whatever the reasons are, I'll find them out.'

Lorraine didn't know what to say. She wanted to scream at Natty to stop, to just slow down before he got himself hurt. She'd thrown up when she'd got a text message from an old friend, telling her that her boyfriend had been involved in a shooting. They'd also mentioned Natty had been talking to a woman, who he'd thrown to the floor, so they avoided the shots.

Natty hadn't mentioned the woman to her, and she felt it was too petty to bring up.

Natty had a past. A past she was well aware of. Even when they'd been uninvolved, she'd heard about the women Natty was involved with, some more serious than others. He'd never hidden it from her. He'd even slept with Ellie, someone she used to be friends with.

When Natty had stood on her doorstep and told her he loved her, she'd believed him. For the most part, she didn't believe Natty would ever step out on her.

Yet, he hadn't mentioned the woman he was with. He hadn't told her much about the night, except that he was going to do some obviously bad things to find out who had tried to kill him.

'Are you going to be okay?' Natty asked.

'If I said no, would you stop? Today?'

Natty hesitated. Lorraine didn't know about the deal he'd made to protect her; if he had his way, she never would. If he was honest, he doubted he would stop even if there wasn't a deal in place.

The sad fact was that he didn't have enough outside of the life he'd built for himself. Natty loved Lorraine and Jaden, and the life they had, but he also loved the game. He'd tried walking away from it, and had made a pretty decent attempt, but it hadn't lasted. He'd come back into the fold as quickly as he could, and was making more money than he had in his life.

'I can't, Lo. I don't expect you to fully get that, but I can't. I can't let people think they can take liberties either. If I do, then we're never safe.'

Lorraine nodded, her stomach plummeting. He'd given the answer she expected, but that didn't make it any easier. They finished their drinks, then sat in silence, both lost in their thoughts. Natty's jaw was tight as he looked down at his lap.

Lorraine closed her eyes but couldn't keep to it, opening them to look at Natty; to drink him in. He was an impressive man, and the worst part was, part of the life he led excited her, as much as it repulsed her.

CHAPTER SIXTEEN

LORRAINE TWISTED AND TURNED, unable to stop the scene in front of her. Raider, stalking towards her, hands stained with blood. She tried to get away, but her feet were stuck in place as the man's evil grin widened, watching her struggle, knowing she was going nowhere.

'I told you,' he said smoothly, his voice making the hairs on her arm and neck stand up. 'You're mine. No one else's. No one can save you.'

Lorraine screamed, still unable to move. She screamed for Natty, for Jaden, for anyone to come along, but it was futile. Just as Raider reached her, she was shaken awake.

'Lo! Lo, are you okay?' Natty leaned over Lorraine, and she reared back. Shoving past him, she hurried to the bathroom, just managing to get to the toilet before she threw up. She heard footsteps as Natty followed, holding back her hair and rubbing her back, murmuring nonsense words that, in any other circumstances, would have made her laugh.

'Was it the same dream?' Natty asked, minutes later, when she'd emptied her stomach and stopped retching. Lorraine nodded, not trusting herself to speak. She'd had similar dreams before. In the beginning, Natty was there. He would fight Raider off in the beginning, but somehow Raider would make it past him and get to Lorraine.

Lately, Natty wasn't in the dream. It was Lorraine, all by herself, just like she'd been the night she'd killed Raider. That moniker of being a killer hadn't grown any easier to accept. No matter what she was told, she didn't think it would ever be right. The dreams were proof of that.

They were a punishment for the sin she had committed.

'Do you want to speak to someone?' Natty asked. 'I mean . . . you can speak with me. Always. About anything, but maybe you need to speak to someone that can help you.'

Lorraine shook her head. 'That's too much of a risk, and you know it. Look, these dreams can't be helped. I'll understand if you want to stay at your place from now on.'

Helping her up, Natty held her close. If he minded the smell of vomit, it didn't show. Thankfully, he didn't try to kiss her.

'I'm here with you, Lo. I'm not going anywhere. I want to help you, and I will. I promise I will.'

Lorraine smiled, then lightly pushed him away.

'Let me freshen up, and I'll meet you back in bed.'

'I'm going to get a drink,' said Natty. 'I don't feel tired anymore. Do you want one?'

'Water, please,' replied Lorraine. 'I should have a fresh bottle in the fridge.'

'I know where you keep your good water.' Natty rolled his eyes and headed downstairs.

———

THE FOLLOWING DAY, Lorraine felt a little better. Her head was pounding, but she swallowed a few Anadin and drank plenty of water, beginning to feel better after a while.

Jaden was at school, and she was doing yoga in the front room, trying to get her mind right before she headed to work. She'd called to say she would be late, but hadn't explained why.

As she finished up her stretches and slid to her feet, Lorraine rolled her mat away, thinking about what Natty had said about her getting some help. No matter how much she considered it, she couldn't see a way past the issue. All she could do was keep doing what she was doing, and keep leaning on Rosie and Natty.

Sitting on the sofa, she closed her eyes and took several deep breaths, trying to lose herself in the moment, focusing on her breathing. By the time Natty stepped in, she hadn't made much progress.

'How are you feeling?' He asked, kissing her on the cheek, then rubbing his hands together. 'It's freezing out there. I keep leaving my gloves when I go out.'

'I can feel the cold. You're gonna make me put the heating on if you don't step back,' Lorraine joked.

'Don't try to change the subject. How are you feeling?'

'I'm not changing. You brought up the weather.' Lorraine stuck her tongue at Natty, and he flipped a middle finger at her, making her giggle. 'Honestly, these few seconds of conversation have made me feel a lot better than all the grunting and stretching I was doing before.'

'I'm sad I missed that,' teased Natty, winking at her. Lorraine shook her head. She wasn't supposed to be laughing and having a good time. Not with everything that had happened.

'What are you doing today?' she asked, noting him straightening, his eyes hardening. She'd noticed lately that he could switch his business side on and off, and in contradictory fashion, she found it incredibly appealing. He seemed like a new man, almost predatory, as his eyes took her in for a moment, his body instinctively angled to the side before he relaxed, and the moment dissipated.

'I need to speak to a few people,' said Natty. Brown had sent him a message while he was taking Jaden to school. They'd woken early to exercise at Jaden's insistence, and he definitely seemed to be taking to the regime a lot more.

Jaden hadn't mentioned Rachel since, but he'd asked a few questions about girls that Natty had tried to answer in a way that wouldn't infuriate Lorraine.

'Try not to hurt anyone, dear,' said Lorraine. Natty ruffled her hair.

'I'm promising nothing other than that I'll be careful.'

'That's all I can really ask for,' said Lorraine. 'I'm going to see my mum after work, but I'll cook dinner. I'll ring you later on.'

'Looking forward to it already,' said Natty. He headed upstairs, and she heard him moving about, before he bounded back down the stairs and then left.

Lorraine took another deep breath. Natty had promised he would be safe, but Lorraine knew that wasn't always possible in the streets. Thinking about Natty had been a refuge from her own issues for a while, but they were all connected. Raider had been a street guy too. Her brother Tommy had been a street guy. It was all around her, and she was still learning to navigate the murky waters after all this time.

Lorraine stepped into the shower, closing her eyes and letting the hot water cascade down her face and onto her body. She thought of Raider once more. He had status in the streets, but being with him was no preparation for what life with Natty was like now. He was on a whole different level.

Massaging her temples, her eyes still shut, Lorraine wondered when Natty's next near miss would be. Lorraine turned away from the shower, opening her eyes and sloshing a liberal amount of shampoo onto the palm of her hand. Rubbing it together in both hands, she slid the creamy liquid through her hair.

The last time was close enough, she mused. Natty needed to be more careful, or better protected.

As she washed the shampoo out of her hair, Lorraine's mind wandered to the woman Natty had saved. He still hadn't mentioned her, which Lorraine found strange. She wondered whether she was so unimportant to Natty that he didn't think to mention her, or if he was hiding something.

Closing her eyes once more, Lorraine took a deep breath and exhaled. Work was looming, and she needed to get herself in gear.

————

By THE TIME Lorraine made it into the office, it was after eleven. As she stepped on the office floor, all of the energy appeared to leave the room. A few people glanced her way, some giving her small smiles.

She didn't get a chance to sit down before Angela approached, motioning for her to go into the same meeting room as last time.

'You can sit,' said Angela, though she remained standing as she closed the door and leaned against it. There was no smile this time as she stared at Lorraine. Lorraine met her gaze, trying to ignore Angela's potent perfume. She rubbed her nose, which seemed to be the signal for Angela to start speaking.

'You're late.'

'I'm sorry about that,' said Lorraine. 'I spoke to Chloe when I called and told her I would be, though.'

Angela pursed her lips. 'We had a conversation a short while ago, and I thought we'd reached some understanding about the company, and our roles in driving the business forward?'

'We did. It wasn't intentional. I had a very bad night, and that affected how I started my day. I'll work the time back and I've apologised, but I'm not sure what else I could have done.'

Silence ensued, Angela's gaze boring into Lorraine's. Lorraine fought to keep her composure. Being late wasn't ideal, but she felt she had handled it in the best way. The office had a loose policy, but people tended to be at their desks between 9:30 and 10:00 — though it wasn't uncommon for people to arrive earlier. People were sometimes late, but it wasn't seen as a massive issue.

Until now.

'Are you still working on Linda's piece?'

Lorraine nodded. 'I have a progress meeting with her this afternoon.'

Angela's lips formed a thin line. She huffed.

'Fine. You can go back to your desk, but don't make a habit out of this, Lorraine.'

'Understood, Angela.' Lorraine slid to her feet and left the room, taking a deep breath and heading for her desk.

———

'Are you sure you're not hungry?'

'I'm fine, pops. I always eat before I come over.'

Wayne fixed his son with a look. 'That could be taken as you not liking my cooking.'

Spence almost rolled his eyes. 'I grew up on your cooking, and I don't remember ever leaving food on my plate.'

Wayne laughed.

'Fair enough. I'll give you that one. How's the arm?'

'It's fine. It gets a bit tight, but nothing I can't handle,' said Spence.

Wayne shook his head.

'It's still kinda shocking.'

'What is?'

'The fact you got shot,' said Wayne.

Spence didn't reply. It wasn't ever far from his thoughts. He was working past it, but it didn't change the facts.

'Are you still beating yourself up?' Wayne eventually realised he wasn't getting a response.

'I'm logically assessing the situation,' said Spence. 'That might involve a certain level of soul searching, still.'

'Fucking *soul searching*. What the hell is wrong with your generation, and why are you still going on like this?'

'Like what?'

'Like you did something wrong. Everyone under the sun is telling you that you didn't, but you're determined to act like a bloody martyr. I'm trying to understand why,' said Wayne.

'I'm not acting like anything. You said yourself that I needed to get involved in the war. You said I might *catch a body*.'

Wayne shrugged. 'I did, so what?'

'So, I persuaded my best friend to let me ride out on a dangerous mission, and I ended up getting taken out straight away.'

'Yes, because you didn't have training. Nat's a good kid, but he's lucky that he cleaned your plate, because if you'd died, I'd have killed him. He should have known better than take you into that zone.' Wayne's nostrils flared.

'How am I supposed to learn otherwise?'

'There are ways to learn to be in the game like that,' said Wayne. He paused, shovelling mouthfuls of food down his throat. He'd let it start to cool down, and regretted it. Plantain and eggs always tasted better hot. 'You can take your time training up, and that's the best way. Sometimes there's that other way, when the war gets dropped on your doorstep, and you need to react.'

'Every time that's happened, I've ducked down, out of the way, away from trouble.'

'Hang on. You were in town with your missus one of those times, and you smacked around the dude who tried stabbing you, right? Unless you lied to me.'

'No, that's true.' Spence was still shocked that a bigger deal hadn't been made of that incident. There were so many cameras in town that he was sure that the police would have followed up with him, or arrested someone for the act.

Spence was usually good with details, but couldn't recall what the attackers were wearing. He wondered if they had been taken out during the raids when Natty and the others crippled most of Roman's organisation.

'Well then. It happened. You weren't trained, and you got caught up. Just let it go. How's your boy doing? People popping shots at a party is wild. Especially when everyone knows everyone.'

'He's fine. Probably hunting for the people that did it. He was ace, pops. Shots fired, and he moved like he knew it was coming all along. Everyone else was frozen in place, before all the screaming started. I was just there, standing like a fool, waiting to get shot. Only Natty and Stefon represented.'

'This whole self-loathing shite you're doing . . . it's beneath you, Spence. What were you supposed to do? Jump in front of Natty like your secret service, and die? You both have your roles. If you wanna learn the other side, then ask if you can learn it, but you better be ready when you do.'

Neither man spoke for a few moments, Wayne taking advantage and polishing off the rest of his food. Without asking, he cleared the table, then made them both cups of coffee. Spence took it with thanks, the heat of the cup giving him a much-needed jolt.

'What's it like?'

'What's what like?'

'Killing someone.'

Wayne looked steadily into his son's eyes for a few more moments. Spence had no idea what he was searching for, when he nodded and spoke.

'It's awful. I'm not saying you can't get used to it, but it can fuck with your head if you let it. I've heard of people that go seriously around the bend after they do it.'

'How did you cope?'

Wayne shrugged. 'I coped because I had to. Simple as that. I had a job to do, and it was them or me. Just like your friend Natty knew that it was that Keith dickhead or him. He pulled the trigger and made that happen. I doubt he's skipping around, but I've seen him: he's coping well. Must be why everyone saw so much potential in him.'

Spence sipped his coffee, scalding his tongue, thinking of his dad's words. He knew they were from the heart and respected that. Natty hadn't glorified what he'd done. After he killed Rudy and Elijah, he'd been withdrawn. He'd admitted to Spence that he'd thrown up after he'd done it. He'd also struggled to sleep for a while.

Spence wasn't sure what to do. He didn't want to get left behind. He wanted to be an asset to the organisation.

'This Stefon dude . . . you said he's Natty's cousin?' Wayne said. He'd been silent for so long that his voice startled Spence.

'Yeah. He's a wildcard, but he's official. When shots got fired, he fired back. No hesitation or fear. I think he and Natty are gonna have problems, though. There's tension there.'

Wayne smiled. 'There's tension in every crew. Make sure you keep on top of things, son. That's more important now than ever.'

CHAPTER SEVENTEEN

'YOU DON'T KNOW HALF the trouble you've caused,' said Brown, as Natty climbed from his ride, leaning against his car door. Despite everything that was going on, it pleased Natty that Brown looked more ruffled than usual. His clothing was rumpled, as if he'd dressed in a hurry, and there were livid bags under his eyes.

'You need a haircut, bro,' said Natty, grinning at the state of the man. It made him feel better about everything going on.

For a few seconds, at least.

Natty shook those thoughts away. He needed to be in the moment here.

'Don't piss around, Deeds. Who the hell is trying to kill you in public?'

Natty shrugged. 'I hoped you could shed some light on that.'

'You know who you've pissed off more than I do. I've got people looking into it, but it's a ballsy move, going at the heir to the throne. Who was the one shooting at your side? One of the attackers got hit.'

'I don't know,' said Natty. 'I was too busy hiding like a normal civilian. Why would I know anything otherwise?'

'Is this how you think it's supposed to go?' Brown demanded. 'You think you get to ask for what you like, and I get nothing in return?'

'I think what you get in return is probably paying for your drugs and your lifestyle.'

'What drugs?' Brown said quickly. Too quickly. Natty chuckled. He'd had a hunch and gone with it, and it paid off. It was meaningless in the scheme of things. Brown being on drugs was minor, but it was a sign that Natty was on it; this would keep him in line, and more malleable to Natty's needs.

'Doesn't matter. I'm sure you'll do your best to find out who was firing shots at that party I happened to be at. In the meantime, what have you learned?'

Natty glanced around, noting that Brown did the same thing. The detective lipped his lips, then shook his head.

'Your uncle isn't an easy guy to look into, Deeds. He has friends in the force . . . ones that go higher than yours. That means I need to play this carefully.'

'So, keep playing it carefully, but give me what I asked you to find out,' said Natty harshly, tired of Brown mincing around. Brown glared at him.

'Don't rush me.' Again, he glanced around, then scratched his chin. 'Look, you probably know all of this. Your uncle has been doing his thing for decades. He's super-rich, lives in Moortown, and he's got more security than the pope. He's been linked to tons of events over the years, especially in the early 2000s, when he was a key component of all that Yardie bollocks going on back then.'

Natty's jaw tightened. Brown had been right; he knew most of this already.

'As interesting as this is, I hope it's not all you have.'

'Maybe you should tell me why you want to know. Do that, and I'll know what to look for,' said Brown. Natty stared at him, until Brown snorted. 'Fine. Shithead. Mitch Dunn has been seen meeting with an Asian man. He's not someone we recognise, but they've met a few times over the past few months.'

This piqued Natty's curiosity. His uncle hadn't mentioned any new contacts. Neither had Clarke. He recalled his conversation where they'd discussed Roman's supplier, who was Asian. That aside, Natty couldn't see how it would fit.

'I want to know who he was meeting. I want to know everything about them, Brown.'

Brown shook his head.

'You don't give orders around here, Deeds. We need to talk about the money.'

'No, we don't,' replied Natty. 'You've been content to take my money for ages. You said you would be an asset, so you're getting a chance to do that. The only difference is that you actually have to work for it. I expect results.'

'Are you fucking serious?' Brown exclaimed. His phone rang, and he snatched it up, staring at the number, making a face, and then ignoring it. 'Keeping your name off my bosses radar isn't easy work. You're a known face, Deeds. You're not some small-time pillock anymore. Watch your back, because it's clear someone wants to do you harm.'

'Tell me something I don't know.'

Brown smirked for the first time. 'How about this: we have a suspect in custody.'

That threw Natty for a loop. 'What the hell are you talking about? You said earlier that you were still looking.'

'We're still looking for means and motive. We haven't announced it yet because we don't have shit, but the guy we took in was trying to fix a bullet wound by himself. He fucked it up and had to go to LGI. We caught up with him there. Claims to have an alibi for the night in question, but it's bollocks.'

Natty took all of this in.

'I want a name.'

Brown smiled nastily.

'I want a pay increase, and I want some respect,' he replied. 'I'll be in touch, Deeds. Try to stay alive.'

Natty let Brown go without a word. He hadn't obtained much from him, but it was still information he could work with. He wondered what Mitch's game was. His uncle never mentioned any Asians in their business he was particularly close to. Natty considered reaching out to Sanjay, but decided to think about that some more. He needed to keep his cards close to his chest.

Finally, he climbed into the car and drove away, still eager to learn what Mitch was up to, and who was behind his attack.

He had a lot to do.

————

WHEN HE HEARD about the attack on Natty, Roman grinned to himself. He didn't know who was behind the attack, but he owed them a drink, regardless. After his conversations with Ahmed and Maka, he'd stewed for a while, weighing up his options. Maka had made some valid points, and a growing part of him liked the idea of getting out, and doing something different.

But his mind wouldn't allow it.

He didn't want to leave Leeds. He'd grown up there and loved it. The only way getting out would work, would mean a completely fresh start.

Putting those thoughts aside, Roman focused on business. Relighting his spliff, he leaned back in his chair, enjoying the potent haze as it spread through his chest. He needed to be war-ready. That meant allies. It irked Roman that he didn't have access to the same resources that K-Bar and Shorty had back in the day. Most of those had come from Teflon, but they had access to thoroughbreds; soldiers loyal to them, happy to spill blood, asking few questions.

Roman didn't know how he would inspire such loyalty, but he intended to try. He had the perfection to start with.

————

TRACKING down Jamal wasn't hard. He lived in Belle Isle, and some money to the right person led to Roman parked across the road from his home. It appeared to be a relatively new build, with a small, well-tended garden.

People were walking up and down the streets, and several neighbours were sitting in their gardens, or gardening. Several glanced at Roman as he climbed from his car, but he kept his eyes on Jamal's place.

There was a car parked outside — a black Audi — and he hoped that meant he was in. He'd gone over his words last night, and as he knocked on the door, he took a deep breath, forcing himself into the zone.

'Yes?' The door swung open, and a short blonde woman answered. She appeared to be in her mid-twenties, and had blue eyes and freckles. She eyeballed Roman, clad in her pink and grey exercise gear.

'Hello. Sorry to bother you. I'm looking for Jamal.'

The woman's eyes narrowed. 'What for?'

'I want to speak to him. Tell him that Roman is here for him.'

The woman stared at him for a second, then closed the door. Roman didn't move, hoping that she'd gone to do as he'd said. If she hadn't, he would knock on the door again until Jamal answered. It was potentially disrespectful, but he didn't have time to mess around.

Eventually, the door opened again, and Jamal loomed over Roman. He hadn't seen him in years. Jamal hadn't been caught in the same sweep that caused Roman to get locked up, and he looked well. His hair was cut short, and he was as ridiculously muscular as Roman recalled.

Roman was pleased when Jamal grinned and slapped his hand. He wore a grey vest and black shorts, and had a weightlifting belt around his waist. Evidently, Roman had interrupted their workout.

'Roman . . . Roman . . . didn't expect to see you again. Heard you were out, though.'

'I'm sure you did, fam. You look well. You definitely haven't been slacking on the training,' said Roman, grinning at the man's size. Jamal chuckled.

'I don't have fuck all better to do,' he admitted. 'Weight training's always been easy to me, innit. That and the street stuff.'

'That's why I'm here. I need to talk to you.'

'Now?'

'As soon as. I can wait, but I wouldn't mind getting you a drink later, and having a chat.'

Jamal flexed his left bicep, rubbing it with his right.

'Jenna will get pissed if I interrupt our session. She wanted me to tell you to fuck off. Listen, come back in two hours. We can have a drink here, and we can talk. Cool?'

'Cool.'

———

ROMAN DROVE around the corner and parked the car again, making a phone call to one of his street lieutenants, then messing around on his phone. He liked Jamal, but that didn't mean his old ally hadn't heard about the money on his head. If anyone was coming to set up on him, he wanted to see it. Thankfully, no one stopped outside Jamal's. When his time was up, Roman drove back onto the street, parked his car, and headed back to the house.

This time, Jamal answered when he knocked.

'Proper punctual, aren't you?' He said.

'Something like that.'

The house was cosy, and Roman immediately felt at home. The walls were a blend of cream and brown, and there were numerous photos on the walls, one of which appeared to be of Jamal and Jenna in another country. Roman didn't know which, but the sand looked golden, and the water behind them was so beautiful, it almost looked fake. As he walked into the living room and sat down, Roman looked out for Jenna, but didn't see her.

'She's upstairs,' said Jamal, guessing what Roman was thinking. 'She likes to stretch and relax after the workouts.'

'You lot take it seriously then?'

Jamal nodded. 'It's the one thing we've got most in common, so we don't wanna let that slide.' He flexed, cracking his neck. 'You want a drink or anything?'

'I'm good.'

Jamal slouched against the wall.

'Okay, what's up then?'

'Do you still keep up with the street stuff?'

'If you're asking if I know about you and the Dunns, then course I do. I'm inactive. Not dead.'

'Fair enough. I wasn't trying to disrespect you. I was just checking.'

'Look. You know what I am, and you know what I do. So, get to the point.'

Jamal was a little more direct than Roman remembered, not that he recalled having many conversations with him. They'd spent time around one another, but there were usually barriers, and conversation starters, people that seemed to control the discussions and topics. Roman was quiet, and he'd partaken in parties and hung out with Shorty and the others, but he didn't have the same bond some of them had.

'Fine. Why aren't you working for them?'

Jamal didn't blink. 'They never asked.'

'If they did, would you?'

Jamal tilted his head. 'These really the questions you want to ask?'

'No, but that doesn't mean I'm not curious. I want you to come and soldier for me.'

Jamal grinned. 'You're not in a good position.'

'I'm not. Neither was Teflon when you lot came on board, but you won.'

'You comparing yourself to Teflon now?' The grin widened.

'No. Just making a point. With people like you on my side, it's a different story. I have a plan. I need good people to execute it, and I'm paying well.'

'Paying how? You've been run out of the Hood.'

'Not completely,' said Roman, wondering who was keeping Jamal abreast of street news. 'I've still got people working for me, but not enough soldiers to make my moves. I've also got the plug.'

'Which plug? The same connect Teflon and them had?'

Roman nodded, smiling.

'The same one. Same pristine product. Same prices. You ever want to put the gun down, you could make serious money. You wouldn't even have to touch the stuff.'

Jamal waved him off. 'Let's stick to the point. I'm gonna get us both a drink, and we're gonna talk about this plan of yours. If I like what I hear, I'm in. If I don't, you're gonna go, and I'll never see you again. Cool?'

Roman weighed it up, but he didn't have a choice. Jamal was his best bet at making a stand, and he couldn't afford to alienate him. He hadn't intended to tell him the entire plan unless he had to. If he did, and Jamal still said no, it would leave him in a precarious position.

There was nothing else he could do. He'd banked a lot on this discussion, and he would need to let it play out.

'What do you have to drink then?' He asked, smiling again.

CHAPTER EIGHTEEN

A FEW DAYS after his talk with Brown, Natty was still constructing a plan for dealing with Mitch. He had something in mind, and was starting to believe that a direct attack might be the best move. Mitch was well protected, but Natty doubted anyone would expect it. He would need to position himself in a way that allowed him to escape, but still, he was growing more fond of the idea.

The rumour of a man being arrested for the attempted shooting grew. Natty assumed Brown was keeping his name out of it, because the police hadn't bothered him.

A man named Simon Denny was the one who had been arrested. Natty didn't know him, but apparently, he was a small-time dealer. The man who had spotted for him was in the wind, but that didn't matter. Natty remembered his face vividly. If he resurfaced, Natty would recognise him.

Natty had made a few calls, describing the man, but was still waiting for word to come back. Even Sanjay had been quiet.

On this particular day, Natty finished at the gym, sticking his sports bag in the back of the car. He had a car following his, a directive of Mitch and Clarke. One of Clarke's men was watching him. He'd not complained, expecting it to be a temporary measure.

He was about to drive away, when his phone rang. Natty glanced at the number, blowing out a breath.

Natty pulled up at the meeting spot, and left his guard outside. He walked straight in as arranged, taking another deep breath before walking into the living room.

'Natty Deeds . . . good to see you as always.'

Lisa sat there, cross-legged, on the sofa. She wore a pair of yoga pants and a sleeveless vest, and looked like she had been training. Natty tried not to notice, but she effortlessly seemed more beautiful than ever. He pushed away those thoughts, nodding at her and taking a seat.

'We're not hugging then . . .' she said in her melodic voice.

'We don't need to hug,' Natty said.

'You look good. Clara said you did, but she's a little loose, so I assumed she was exaggerating.'

'Thanks. Glad you're satisfied,' said Natty.

'If you wanted me satisfied . . . surely you'd want to help satisfy me?' Lisa's mouth curled into a sultry smile. It was still hard for Natty to connect this flirty, flighty woman to the cold-blooded killer he knew she could be.

'Is this why you called me? I got the message from your girlfriend.'

'Why are you so nervous about being around me? I thought we got past this. Is that why you've done your best to stay away from me? Scared you'll stray?' Lisa's eyes met his.

'It's purely coincidental,' said Natty dryly, refusing to let her get to him.

'Clearly, the kiss meant something to you. You'd have continued dealing with me like normal if it didn't.'

Natty shook his head. He couldn't deal with this. Not right now, at least. He needed to keep her on point.

'Stay professional, Lisa. I'm glad you're here, because I need to ask you something. I'll cut right to it: did you know I was going to be shot at?'

Lisa's expression shifted, her face becoming blank.

'I'm loyal.'

'You're loyal to the crew, not to me,' Natty snapped. Again, Lisa's expression shifted.

'Do you want my loyalty?' She asked softly. They stared one another down. Natty's heart raced. He was doing it again, and getting sucked into her game. He wiped his eyes.

'I don't want to play games, Lisa. I want to know if you knew.'

'I didn't know. I suspected people would try something, but I didn't expect something so audacious. Clara was amazed, by the way. I think she just thought you were a muscle guy. She didn't know you could move like that. Clarke has done well.'

'How do you know it was Clarke?'

Lisa simply raised an eyebrow, and Natty chuckled, despite himself. He suspected Clarke had trained Lisa, and that response told him all he needed to know. For a moment, Natty wondered where he would stack up against her in a battle. He doubted he was there yet. If anything, Lisa had more of an edge, and definitely had the experience.

'Fine. How are things going with your target?' He brought it back to work. He expected Lisa to keep flirting, but she surprised him.

'I'm keeping my eye on Danielle.'

'Which Danielle? The girl from Keith's?' Natty had let her go, warning her to stay quiet.

'Yeah. She's hooking up with Roman.'

'Really?' That was news to Natty. 'I thought she was banging Keith before he died? That's how we tracked him.'

'She's been doing Roman too. I don't know how serious they are, but her friends have big mouths.'

Natty grinned. If it worked to get Keith, then it could work again to get Roman.

'Keep me posted. I want to know as soon as you hear something.' Natty slid to his feet. Lisa's eyes stalked his every move. 'Look after yourself.'

'You too, Natty Deeds.'

Natty left quickly. The energy was still strange. Being around Lisa was extremely difficult, and he didn't want to make it more of a thing than it needed to be.

———————

'WANT ME TO MAKE THE CALL?'

Clarke stared at the body at his feet. The blood from the man's head wounds was already seeping into the plastic they had covered the cellar floor with.

'Yes,' he said after a moment. Tony already had his phone out, making the call to their cleaners, who would tidy up the mess. The situation still made little sense to him, but he hadn't questioned the orders, and neither had his team.

'They're en route,' said Tony, stowing his phone. He too looked at the dead man. 'That's the second person this week that we've dropped. Two in two days is mad. Even for us.'

Clarke nodded. Tony wasn't wrong. There was a lot more to this situation than he was privy to. He had worked for Mitch for many years, and he was many things, but he wasn't impulsive. Everything was calculated and well thought out, but this felt erratic. It felt like they were inviting something to happen, and Clarke hoped they would be ready if they brought the storm.

It brought him back to what Natty said about Mitch's motives. He'd ordered them to start tearing through the dealers that were connected to Jakkar. It had been easy enough to keep track of them. They weren't hiding, feeling unconnected to the on-and-off conflict between the Dunns.

The man they had murdered was a well-liked dealer named Darnell. They had caught him leaving his house, bundling him into the car, before Tony knocked him out.

Once they had him out of sight, they hadn't prolonged it. Clarke had shot him twice in the head, ignoring Darnell's pleas for mercy.

There would be blowback for this, though. That he was sure of. Darnell had connections. Landell, the man they'd shot and killed yesterday, also had connections.

Clarke didn't know how deep the relationship was between them and the suppliers, but even with the precautions they were taking, there was a chance their murders could be linked to the Dunns.

'They won't be the last ones we do. Make sure you're on standby in case I need you. I have a lead on the next one.'

'Got it,' said Tony. 'Why are we doing this, chief? Darnell was alright. Is this connected to Roman?'

'Not important,' said Clarke, his voice brokering no argument. 'We don't need to wait around for the team. They know what to do. Keep your head down as we leave.'

———

SPENCE AND STEFON were hanging out, waiting for a delivery. A contact was dropping off some money Spence had loaned them. Stefon had turned up with a cigarette in his mouth, planting himself at the kitchen table.

'It's baking out there,' he said. 'Police are hunting for whoever is picking off those dealers. Two in a week is crazy!'

Spence sniggered, letting Stefon talk. He was growing used to having him around again. He was a character; an older version of Natty, who was world-wise and told the funniest stories.

Spence had told Natty that Stefon was settling in well, but there was an edge to it. He had heard Stefon raising his voice and losing his temper with some of his workers. He was the sort who ruled by fear, and didn't like his decisions being questioned.

Natty was the leader who didn't hesitate to check someone if they messed up, but was respected. Spence knew that there were jealous members of the organisation kicking dirt on Natty's name, but they were few and far between.

Still, Spence was worried about the cousins. There was a clash brewing, and he hoped he was around to defuse it.

'Are you worried that you're next?'

Stefon took out a gun and put it on the table.

'I stay ready. If they come for me, they're gonna be in the cemetery,' he said.

'I thought Natty warned you about carrying?' Spence said delicately.

'Natty isn't around. I have the right to protect myself. It's dangerous out there. In fact, what's going on with you?'

'What do you mean?' Spence asked.

'You need to be protecting yourself too. I know Natty can. You need to too.'

'What are you talking about? I'm not soft,' said Spence, offended. He didn't want anyone thinking he was weak, least of all Stefon.

'Chill out. I never said you were soft. I saw you at that party . . . you were ready to fight that prick that got in your face. You need to be able to put a man down if he's coming for you, though. You're in the jungle. No one is playing games. I heard you nearly got caught slipping a few times. You ended up getting shot. If you want me to help train you up, I'm down.'

'How did you learn?' Spence was curious about Stefon. Even back in the day, he'd always seemed to know what he was doing. Stefon had the reputation, and was tough. Often that meant he needed to back it up, and he always did.

'I learned to fight because I had to,' Stefon said. 'My dad wasn't around much, and people were trying me. I got my arse kicked more than once, but I couldn't go to my mum. I had to learn to navigate. So, I kept getting beaten up, but the beatings made me tougher. I started working out, started fighting back, and then I started carrying a weapon. I got caught slipping in Leicester a few years ago. I was doing a deal with people I trusted, and they tried to set me up. Six guys, all with weapons, all tried rushing me. I had my strap and shot one in the leg. The rest scrambled.'

'What happened after that?' Spence asked, already forgetting his initial question.

'They begged for peace. The dude I shot kept his mouth shut, we went our separate ways, and I didn't do business with them again. They lost a lot of face around the blocks, and I stepped up.' Stefon made himself a drink, abandoning the cigarette he'd only partly smoked. 'To answer your question, though. I got my gun, and I practised. I got a connection that could give me ammo, and I found a shitty target practice. I'm not a marksman or anything, but I do alright.'

Spence agreed. Stefon had shown composure at the party, when the gunman had gone for Natty. He'd hit him with a single shot, and probably could have done more damage if Natty hadn't stopped him from going after him.

'And you can show me?'

'I think I should. You might never need to use it, but it's better to know. I'm surprised Natty hasn't shown you. He's definitely got some moves. He moved quickly when that prick started bussing at the party.'

'We never got around to doing it,' said Spence, thinking of the things he'd seen Natty do since rejoining the crew.

'Well, I'll sort you out then. Riddle me this for now. What's the proper story on this Roman character? Tell me what's gone down.'

CHAPTER NINETEEN

LORRAINE SIPPED a glass of water at the kitchen table, holding it against her forehead. She was home alone. Natty was out, and Jaden was at school. Her head was pounding, and she felt nauseous. It had started the previous night, but she had hoped she would feel better after sleeping. Instead, she felt worse.

Glancing at her phone, Lorraine took a deep breath. She couldn't face going into work today. Normally, she would try to power through, but in her current state, she wouldn't last the full day. Sipping some more water, she finally sent a text message to Chloe, a woman who often acted as a Duty Manager in the office, saying that she wasn't feeling well and wouldn't be coming in.

She was still sat in the kitchen when her phone rang. She recognised Angela's number and after a second's hesitation, answered.

'Hello, Angela.'

'Lorraine . . . Chloe passed on your message. I thought I'd call and see how you were feeling.'

'Thank you. That's really nice of you,' said Lorraine. 'I've felt terrible since yesterday. I'm nauseous and I have a headache I can't shift.'

'That's awful,' said Angela, her tone unchanged. 'Do you think you could make it in this afternoon? I know you had a productive talk with Linda, and she's ready to push ahead with some new implementations.'

Lorraine closed her eyes. Angela didn't care about her welfare. She hadn't expected support, but it was still irritating to deal with.

'I don't think that's possible. I just want to rest and see how I feel. I wouldn't be able to manage the afternoon.'

'With your record, you understand that means we can't pay you for the day, right?'

Lorraine's jaw tightened. She was sure she was still under on her sick days, and by all rights, should be paid for any more time off she had, but she didn't want to fight. Her throat felt tight, and her churning stomach seemed to be get worse.

'That's the last thing on my mind, Angela. I just want to get better. Why don't I give you an update later on today or tomorrow, and see how I'm feeling?'

Angela paused. Lorraine could practically hear the gears in her brain turning. Her stomach gave a lurch, and she put her spare hand to her mouth, swallowing down saliva.

'I'd rather get this resolved now, Lorraine. I'm sympathetic, but—'

'Angela, I'm really sorry, but I can't deal with this right now. As I said, I'll ring you later.' Lorraine ended the call. Leaping to her feet, she ran for the bathroom, narrowly making it as she threw up. After several seconds, she groaned, throat burning, sweat beading her forehead. Lurching, she threw up again.

———

STEFON LAY IN BED, wide awake and deep in thought. The woman next to him clung to him, and he frowned down at her, regretting agreeing to stay the night. Reaching out for his phone, he checked the time, seeing it was just after 8 am. He didn't have anywhere urgent to be, but that didn't mean he was going to stay here all day.

It had been over a week since his talk with Spence, and they had trained together twice. He didn't need to teach Spence anything about working out. It was clear he took his fitness seriously and ate well —

as well as anyone that spent most of their time in the Hood did, anyway. They trained with guns and paper targets, using a cellar that Stefon had quickly learned a few of the soldiers used — namely Clarke's men. Stefon had learned Natty used a different one, and worked with Clarke exclusively.

Stefon found his thoughts shifting to his younger cousin as he lay there. He was pleased with how he conducted himself, and his cousin's leadership abilities, but they definitely clashed with his own. At times, Stefon thought Natty leaned into his nickname a little too much. He was nice to the people around him, always willing to do favours, and while it resulted in a lot of goodwill, Stefon believed it was over the top.

Moving back to Leeds had been the right move. Not just because he needed to move from his old life, but because his family needed him. He wasn't a Dunn by surname, but he still respected what they had built, and wanted to do his bit to preserve it.

To Stefon, that meant ensuring this Roman character, and any other pretenders, stayed firmly in line. He intended to speak with Natty about this but found every time he did, they couldn't see eye-to-eye. He hoped it resolved itself in the future, but couldn't see how.

In general, though, he was happy with Leeds. There was a lot of money to be made if you were willing to go out and get it, and Stefon definitely was.

Unlocking his phone, he skipped to the video he had received from one of his daughters. It wasn't long — only forty-five seconds, but he could see Ashlee playing, and she told him she loved him, which made him smile. He intended to bring them to Leeds in the future, once he was fully set up.

Natty had set him up with a nice spot on the outskirts of the Hood. He had a car, a solid wage, and whatever else he needed. Now, he just needed to save his money. There were things he needed to pay for back in Leicester, which meant stockpiling cash and accruing the necessary resource.

Stefon had just laid back down when another phone rang, the vibration jolting the woman awake. She shot Stefon a sleepy smile, which faded when she saw the caller id on the screen. 'Shit.'

'What's up?' Stefon asked.

'It's my man.' Sighing, she answered the phone. 'Hey, baby . . . No, I was in bed asleep . . . It's still early. I can come to you . . . fine, ill see you soon . . . yes, of course, I want to see you . . . I love you too.' She hung up, sighing again, and then faced Stefon. 'You need to leave. Quickly. Johnny's on his way.'

Stefon shot her an insolent look. He didn't want to stay, but that didn't mean some two-bit wannabe like Johnny Bean would force him out. Johnny was a so-so dealer who'd managed to keep his head down and avoid the storm of the Dunn's conflict with Roman and his people. He earned decent money and was well-thought-of, but Stefon didn't like him.

Despite only having been back a short time, he had already clashed with a few people, and Johnny was one of them. He couldn't see his time was up, and was making things more complicated than they needed to be.

'I'm getting a shower,' said Stefon, sliding from the bed, still naked. He felt Bailey's gaze burning into him. She'd had her hands all over his body the night before, and he assumed it was bringing back some memories for her. 'You can join me if you like.'

'Are you serious? Get a shower at home!' she hissed. 'He's coming now, and I doubt he's that far away.'

'Why did he call you?' Stefon did a few stretches, then grabbed his clothes and strode towards the bathroom, Bailey hurrying after him to keep up.

'It doesn't matter why he called me. You can't get a shower here. He can't know that you're here. Trust me, you don't want to get on his bad side.'

'It must matter. Either he's very considerate, or he thinks you're stepping out on him, and wants to check. Who did you tell about us?'

'No one,' Bailey protested. Stefon stopped and looked back at her, slightly raising an eyebrow. Bailey's face reddened, and she dropped her head. 'I told a few of my girls, but they'd never betray me.'

'Of course not,' said Stefon dryly, resuming his walk. He stepped inside the bathroom. It was smaller than he would have liked, with reams of female products everywhere. The shower was also on the smaller side, but looked clean and well-kept, which he appreciated. There was some men's shower gel he decided to use, along with a few other skincare products. 'Get me a towel, please, darling.'

'Towel? Stefon, you need to go. I can't protect you from him. If he catches you, he's going to flip.'

'Let me worry about that. Get me a towel and a clean flannel, please. I don't suppose you have a spare toothbrush.'

'Stefon, you're not listening to me—' Bailey said, her voice growing louder.

'Hey.' Stefon's booming voice silenced her. She stared at him, wide-eyed. 'Get me what I asked for, please. Don't worry about Johnny. If you really cared, you wouldn't have been fucking me for weeks on end. Don't worry about him.'

Bailey looked like she wanted to protest, but didn't. She went out and returned a few moments later with the items he'd requested.

'Thank you,' said Stefon, giving her a dazzling smile that she responded to. 'I'd love a cup of coffee. Black, no sugar. I won't be long.'

Dumbly shaking her head, Bailey traipsed downstairs. Stefon hopped in the shower, setting the temperature to the hottest. After cleaning himself and drying off. He put his clothes back on, then creamed his face and body, before heading out, leaving the flannel and towel on the bathroom floor. He headed downstairs and took the coffee from Bailey with thanks. She kept glancing at the kitchen door, her hands trembling.

Stefon sipped his drink and watched her. Bailey was a decent girl, but she had got into a situation she couldn't control. She shouldn't have made him stay the night, and she should have told Johnny not to come over. She'd failed, and now she would have to deal with the consequences.

Stefon had almost finished his coffee when he heard a knock at the door. Bailey gave Stefon one last pleading look that he ignored. There was another, louder knock at the door, and she finally headed to answer, as if walking to her death.

Stefon leaned against the kitchen counter, completely calm. He could hear Johnny's voice, interrogating her about what took so long, ignoring her requests to go upstairs, or to go into the living room and chill. He wanted breakfast.

'I was gonna get some porridge, but Dutch P—' Johnny stopped speaking when he saw Stefon, his eyes widening, then narrowing. 'What the hell is this?'

'Just visiting my friend Bailey,' said Stefon, shooting Johnny a shit-eating gun. 'Nice to see you, pal. How's your crew?'

'Are you mad?' Johnny stormed over to Stefon, fists clenched, but Stefon had already planned his move. The remaining contents of his coffee mug splashed against Johnny's face, then he cut off the man's yell of pain when he clocked him in the side of the head with the cup.

Before Johnny could fall, Stefon kicked him in the stomach, then stomped on his chest several times when he toppled to the ground, until Bailey's screams brought him back to reality.

He stared down at Johnny, savouring the man's whimpers.

'Right, you little prick. I told you how it's gonna go, and you wanted to ignore me. Now, I'll tell you again. You and your team work for us now. You know who I'm with. Fifty-fifty split, straight down the middle. I'll be at your place later to lock it down. Don't piss me around.' Blowing a kiss at Bailey, who was in the corner, watching the scene in horror, he grabbed his stuff and left.

CHAPTER TWENTY

NATTY HELD Lorraine's hand as they entered the gambling spot on Nassau Avenue. Natty had intended to go alone, needing to discuss a small bit of business with an acquaintance, but Lorraine had asked if she could come with him, and he hadn't been against it.

Jaden was staying at his friend Robert's house, so they didn't have to look for a babysitter. Lorraine had felt rough for a few days after her conversation with Angela. She hadn't returned to work yet, nor had she spoken to her manager since. She was at a crossroads regarding what to do. Lorraine enjoyed her job, but at times, she wondered if she was on the right path.

As she followed Natty, Lorraine took everything in, immediately noticing how people were with him. A few guys had stood outside, talking loudly about something. When they saw Natty, they stopped their conversation, taking turns to greet him.

Like he was the king.

Natty had taken it in his stride and introduced Lorraine to them, and they had been respectful to her. As they'd entered, she'd heard their conversation start up again, as if they had never been interrupted. The gambling spot was a three-bedroomed house. She could smell fried food as soon as they entered the hallway.

Natty stopped in a room, slapping hands with the people there. Most of them were crowded around a pool table, watching two men play. A television hung above them, playing highlights of a football match that had taken place earlier.

There was a steady buzz of conversation, and the stench of cigarettes, weed, and liquor. In another room, people were sat at various tables, playing cards or dominoes, the loud slamming of the dominoes making Lorraine squeeze Natty's hand tighter. He approached the bar.

A black woman was serving a drink to an older man, who appeared to be arguing about the price. He finally paid and limped away, grumbling. When the woman saw Natty, her eyes brightened.

'Natty Deeds!' She said, touching his free hand. 'How are you doing? What are you doing with this beautiful woman? She's way too good for you.'

Natty laughed good-naturedly. 'I agree, Mrs Price.'

'No. You call me Mandy, or you call me Amanda. I've told you this before.'

'Sorry, *Mandy*. It won't happen again. This is my woman, Lorraine. Lorraine, this is Mandy. She runs this spot.'

The women made conversation for a few moments. Mandy, it turned out, was a good friend of her mum's, and had seen Lorraine a few times over the years. She was friendly and clearly had a lot of love for Natty, the feeling definitely mutual. Natty ordered their drinks and tried to pay, but a nearby man shook his head, and handed Mandy a twenty-pound note.

'No, let me pay, Natty. You did right by my cousin. I won't forget that.'

'Cheers, Mr Moe. Tell Jordan I said safe.'

'What was all that about?' Lorraine murmured. Despite Natty's presence, she found it hard to fully relax. These were her people; she'd grown up around them, but after things had imploded with Raider, she'd spent less time in the heart of the Hood, and more time setting up her career. Consequently, she felt there wasn't much she had in common with them.

She was glad Natty was with her. The way people reacted to him reminded her of the conversation she'd had with Curtis and what he'd alluded to about Natty.

'Amanda runs this spot for her husband. He's in prison, doing a long stretch. She's a good woman, and she's respected, so no one really tries anything. I had to have a word with someone who wanted to take over his business, though. A while back. He wasn't taking no for an answer, but I sorted it.'

Lorraine didn't bother asking how he'd *sorted it*. She didn't think she wanted to know. An argument started around the ramshackle dominoes table, though she didn't understand what it was about. Four men were shouting in each other's faces, while others milled around, laughing and watching with amusement. Even Natty had a smile on his face. Lorraine wondered if a fight was going to break out.

'What about the man . . . *Mr Moe*. He said you helped his cousin,' she said, to distract herself.

'Yeah. His cousin was fresh out of school. He was hanging around the ends, but didn't have any proper support. Mr Moe's respected, but too old to properly regulate. He ended up in debt to a vicious man, who threatened to kill him. I stepped in, had a word, and got the debt sorted.'

Lorraine was open-mouthed as she stared at Natty, listening to him speak. He sipped his drink, lazily taking in the surroundings. Despite how relaxed he looked, something in his eyes told Lorraine that he was ready in case anything popped off.

Another man approached Natty, offering to buy him a drink. Natty agreed, but Lorraine said no, deciding to settle for one.

'You might have to drive home,' Natty murmured in her ear, the feel of his breath against her turning her insides to molten liquid. She was glad Jaden was out tonight, because she planned on taking full advantage when they got back.

Thirty minutes passed. They checked out a few other rooms, and Natty almost got roped into playing a game of dominoes. Finally, a man approached him. Natty asked Lorraine to give him a minute and went to talk to him.

Once Natty went, Lorraine glanced around the room, not keeping her eyes on anyone. She instantly felt on guard. Seeing Amanda making herself a drink, Lorraine headed back over, hoping Natty would return soon.

'Everything alright?' Amanda asked, her eyes on Lorraine. Hurriedly, Lorraine nodded.

'Yeah. I guess I'm just not used to this anymore. Being around people.'

Amanda smiled. 'Yeah. Your mum was telling me how proud she is of you. Said you do something with computers, and that you work hard.'

Lorraine was amused that her mum had condensed her role and made it sound so dull, but her heart soared at the idea of her mum being proud of her. She'd said she was on more than one occasion, but hearing she'd said it to others seemed to reinforce the fact.

'I do my best. You and Natty seem to get along,' she said, trying to make conversation. Amanda shot her an amused grin.

'I'm not interested in your man,' she said, another loud bang and voices from the corner distracting the pair for a moment. 'He's a little younger than I like them.'

'I w-wasn't . . .' Lorraine spluttered. Amanda's grin widened.

'You're so cute. I'm playing with you, don't worry. Natty is a champion. He's a good man, and he's done a lot for people around here over the years. Myself included. I used to worry about him, though. I still do, in a way.'

'Why?' Lorraine asked, curious, but enjoying the warmness in Amanda's voice as she spoke about Natty.

'Because I used to think his parents had fucked him up,' she said, surprising Lorraine with her bluntness. 'Have you met his mum?'

Lorraine shook her head. She'd seen her around, and had seen his dad before he died, but never spoke to either. Even when she'd visited Natty's house when she was younger, she'd never had a conversation with his mum. The one time Lorraine had recently brought her up, Natty hadn't wanted to discuss her. She still wondered why.

'Tia is a tough woman . . . some women shouldn't have children. I can't tell you the particulars, but their relationship changed without Natty's dad around to balance it out. Ty was a prince, but he was a hothead. For a while, I thought Natty would be the same way; shagging everything in sight and getting into brawls until he ended up dead or in prison.'

Lorraine was engrossed in Amanda's words, and knew she was right. There was a strong possibility all of those things could have happened to Natty. It struck her, not for the first time, but never with such clarity, just how much Natty had matured over the past few years, compared to the arrogant, thoughtless, sometimes sweet man she'd known.

'Now, he seems much more focused, and I reckon a lot of that is down to you, so thank you. You're good for him.'

'Thank you, Amanda,' said Lorraine, smiling at the older woman. Despite the words, she wondered about the situation. It felt like Natty had a separate life. He had this secondary world, where people looked at him like a king, and he did favours like he was *Michael Corleone*. They called him *Natty Deeds* for a reason, she mused, wondering how much she truly knew about the man she loved.

When Natty returned, he had one more drink, then the pair said their goodbyes to Amanda and left.

'What did you two talk about?' said Natty, as he unlocked the car and handed the keys to Lorraine. She noted his eyes surveying the road as he spoke.

'Nothing,' said Lorraine, wanting to keep the conversation to herself. 'Just small talk.'

———

STEFON CLIMBED FROM HIS CAR, walking around the corner to a selection of houses on Hares Avenue. Finding the place he was looking for, he knocked, getting into character. It was opened by a mixed-raced girl in an ill-fitting wig. She had an attractive face, but the ridiculously long false eyelashes put Stefon off.

'Do I know you?' She asked. Stefon smirked.

'Do you?'

'Why are you playing around on my doorstep?' She asked, unamused by his response. Stefon nodded.

'Sorry. It's been a long night,' he said. 'Johnny told me to stop by and pick up the stuff from Roe Milly.'

'Johnny said that? He never told me. Roe didn't say anything either,' she said.

Stefon shrugged.

'I don't know what you want me to say. I'm only here because Johnny told me to be.'

The woman frowned. 'I'll give Roe a ring and check. He'll be pissed otherwise.'

Rather than panic, Stefon nodded again. 'Good idea. Do you mind if I step inside while you do that? It's hot out here, and I don't wanna bring drama to your spot.'

The woman nodded and let him in, locking the door behind him. Stefon didn't think that was a smart move. If he overpowered her, she'd be hard-pressed to escape him. He watched her reach for her phone, still frowning.

'How long have you and Roe been engaged?'

'What?' She nearly dropped her phone. 'We're not engaged. Who told you that?'

'I just assumed,' said Stefon, rubbing the back of his neck and shooting her a bashful look. 'You're so beautiful. I just assumed he'd locked you down before some lucky guy scooped you up.'

The woman blushed. 'We work together, that's it. My ex works for him, and I wanted to earn some extra money.'

'He told me you lot worked together, but not the details. His loss, I suppose.' Stefon's eyes bore into the woman, who looked ever more flustered. 'I'm Stefon, by the way.'

'Ella,' she replied. 'Do you want something to drink?'

'Please. I can have one before I go, but I'll need to get that thing and jet. I'm meeting Johnny at Krad's place.'

Ella visibly relaxed. Stefon was using names she recognised, and he had been so nice to her. She would check with Roe or Johnny later, but if this was someone they trusted, they wouldn't appreciate the show of disrespect by not trusting him. She poured Stefon a glass of red wine, then one for herself.

They made steady conversation, and Ella giggled whenever Stefon flirted with her. He was utterly shameless, but he was smooth, and she looked forward to getting to know him more.

When he'd finished his drink, he followed her upstairs and waited as she rummaged around in her room, finally returning with a carrier bag.

Stefon opened it, looking at the drugs inside, nodding.

'Thanks, darling. I'm gonna come back and see you soon, okay?'

Ella beamed, her eyes sparkling.

'You'd better.'

Stefon left the spot, steadily heading to his car, hiding the drugs under his seat and driving away at a moderate pace, laughing to himself. It was almost too easy. Johnny had been a trove of information since Stefon had forced him onto their team. Johnny was cool with Roe Milly, but hadn't hesitated to give up his location. They'd been partners once upon a time, but had gone their separate ways.

Their business didn't matter to Stefon. He was about making as much money as possible, and with the power of the Dunns behind him, he was unstoppable.

CHAPTER TWENTY-ONE

NATTY AND SPENCE sat in their regular spot. Spence stared into his cup of coffee, while Natty tapped the table, waiting for the third man to show up. He glanced at Spence, but said nothing, visibly growing more annoyed by the second.

Finally, the door opened, and Stefon bounded in, grinning at the pair. He wore a black and grey bomber jacket, jeans and boots, with a designer pouch around his neck. He touched fists with Spence, then Natty, heading to the kettle.

'Do you mind if I get a drink before we get started?' He said, already grabbing a cup and making his coffee.

Spence glanced at Natty this time. If it were a cartoon, he'd have had steam coming out of his ears. He took a deep breath, ready to play peacemaker, the tension in the room thick.

'What the hell were you playing at?' said Natty, unwilling to wait.

'You'll need to be more specific,' said Stefon.

'No, I don't. Don't fuck around. I want to know.'

'I'm regulating. Why do you think I'm here?' said Stefon, stirring his coffee and leaving the spoon in the cup before he faced Natty.

'Believe me, I'm still trying to work that out,' said Natty. 'What the hell is going on? How is *regulating* helping?'

'It helps two-fold. It gets our money up, by getting more people into the crew. Here you go, by the way. My cut is a little bigger this week.' Stefon reached into his pouch, tossing a stack of money onto the table. Neither man sitting reached for it.

Spence's eyes flitted from the funds, to Natty's furious face, then to Stefon, who seemed unconcerned with the response.

'You had no reason to smack Johnny around and force him to work with us. It draws unnecessary attention . . . not to mention this nonsense with Roe-whatever-his-name-is,' said Natty, his voice thick with anger.

'Do you want me to finish him? His team will probably still be on board. They're willing to get their product from us and give us fifty percent of the profits. I'd say that's a bargain,' said Stefon. Furiously, Natty shook his head.

'Don't you have enough going on with the teams I gave you to run? I didn't tell you to go on a recruitment drive. I didn't tell you to grind Johnny's woman, or rob one of Roe's spots. I just told you to run the teams, didn't I?'

'Hang on,' Stefon scowled, 'when the hell did you start telling me anything?'

'Probably around the time you came looking for a job, and I put you on. I looked after you because you're family, and because you looked out for me when I was younger, but don't start fucking up all of that goodwill and rocking the boat.'

Stefon shook his head. 'I think you need to remember who the hell I am, and watch how you talk to me.'

'I know you who are. You're my older cuz, and like I said, you did a lot for me growing up, and I'm grateful. I'm also the guy running this shit. If you don't like it, then fuck off back to Leicester.'

'Guys . . .' Spence started, the palpable tension making him uneasy. He needed to head this off before they started fighting. Neither man paid him any attention.

'What are you trying to tell me then?' Stefon said, his voice rising.

'Slow the fuck down. You're moving way too fast. I don't need you to do any of the things you're doing. Keep it low, keep getting your money up, and we'll be straight,' said Natty.

'There's a major problem with that, little cuz.'

'What's that? And don't call me *little cuz*,' warned Natty.

'You've gone soft. That's why people are trying you. That's why I'm out there, enforcing and laying it down for the team. For your family name. Why do you think people are taking shots at you in public? You haven't even sorted that out yet, and it's making you look damn weak. That I can promise you,' snapped Stefon.

'That's not your problem. It's above your pay grade. The second I need something handling, *I'll* handle it. If I need you for anything other than what I asked you to do, I'll let you know. Do you have a problem with that?'

The silence seemed to stretch on. Spence again shifted his attention between the pair. It wasn't the first time this had happened, but the tension now was far worse than it had been the night of the shooting attempt. Stefon's face was almost bloodless with rage. His drink had been forgotten, hands balled into fists. Natty's eyes were hard, boring into his cousin's. He too, looked seconds away from leaping to his feet and fighting Stefon.

Spence opened his mouth, searching for the words to defuse the conflict. To his surprise, though, Stefon nodded.

'Fine. You're in charge, like you said. Do you need anything else?' He shrugged.

Natty shook his head.

'Stef, I wanna see you win. I promise you, that. Work with me, not against me, though. I know how you get down, but trust that I know what I'm doing, and the sky is the limit for us. Cool?'

'Cool.'

The cousins slapped hands and began an unrelated conversation. Spence's heart raced as he studied the pair, unconvinced by the show of peace. Things were calm for now, but he knew it wouldn't be the last time the pair had words. He only hoped he would be around to mitigate the disaster when that time came.

———

CLARKE STOOD IMPASSIVELY and watched Mitch, knowing his boss was pissed off. They were in Mitch's office, and the rare autumn sunshine from outside leaked through the windows, shining across Mitch's face. Mitch glared up at his subordinate, choosing his words.

'Why haven't you done as I asked?'

'You asked us to eliminate dealers that were linked to Jakkar. That's what I'm doing,' said Clarke, confused by the vitriol.

'I also asked for reports on Nathaniel's actions. Is he prioritising going after Roman?'

'Yes, he is. What is it you're not satisfied with?'

'I want Nathaniel front and centre. He reports to you, and you then report to me. That's the way I wanted it,' said Mitch through gritted teeth.

Clarke nodded.

'I'll speak with Natty again and ensure nothing has been overlooked. I'll get those reports to you as well. You didn't specify a frequency when we last spoke.'

Mitch's eyes narrowed.

'Do you have an issue with what I've said? Speak your mind if you do.'

'I just think there are a lot of steps for a situation I don't fully understand. But, it's not my job to understand. It's my job to act.'

Mitch nodded. He understood Clarke's irritation, but he didn't care. He would show Jakkar that he wasn't to be trifled with.

'What's this I'm hearing about Nathaniel's cousin?'

'Stefon? He's cool. He's a soldier. Natty has him running a few crews. He's making his money, and he backed Natty when those dudes tried to shoot him.'

'Have we sorted that, by the way? There's a lot getting past Nathaniel at the minute. When things happen, and we don't respond in the right way, it makes us look weak. Is he handling his responsibilities? Do you think he's in over his head?'

'Natty is solid. He'll sort these things out, but like I said, I'll have a word with him.'

'See that you do,' said Mitch. 'His cousin too . . . Stefon.'

Clarke waited, still standing at attention.

'I want him watched. He's a loose cannon. There's a chance he could be an asset for Nathaniel, but if he looks shaky, I want him gone.'

'Got it,' said Clarke. He nodded to Mitch and then left. Mitch watched him go, shaking his head. There was a lot going on at present, and he needed his pillars to be on point and ready for it. He wondered if it was a mistake to promote Nathaniel. He had so much potential, and had done well, but he needed more from him, and hoped that he wouldn't crumble under the pressure.

Great leaders were formed in times of strife, and he wanted Nathaniel to prove his mettle, just like Mitch had himself.

As Mitch rose through the ranks, he had to make tough decisions; about the crew, their business, and their personnel. Those decisions defined and shaped the person Mitch became.

He was sure Nathaniel's moment would come in time. The path to greatness stretched far behind him, and Nathaniel was following in his steps.

———

DANIELLE SAT in the nail salon, watching a bony Vietnamese woman spreading acrylic onto her nail. Her eyes followed the intricate brush strokes as the mound of acrylic gradually smoothed out, replaced by a glossy sheen.

Danielle checked her phone with her free hand, navigating to her message conversation with Roman. Placing her thumb on the screen and scrolling slowly, she shook her head as the conversations came into view and disappeared again.

Things had changed since their altercation. They'd met up a few times and slept together, but the connection that was there seemed to have gone. There was no spark or edge. They would meet, have sex and leave, neither saying much to the other.

Danielle's thumb paused as she reached a barrage of lengthier text messages. Flicking through them slowly, a small smile curled the corners of her mouth as she focused on one in particular.

I really like you, you know…

Opening the keyboard, Danielle typed out a message asking to see Roman. When she had finished, she locked the screen and placed the phone on the nail desk. Still beaming, she looked across the nail technician at the selection of colours. Squinting slightly, her eyes traced along the rows, unable to decide.

'Pick red,' a voice sounded, so close to her ear it made her jump.

Turning around slowly, careful to keep her hand still, Danielle drank in the figure standing before her. The woman wore a Canada Goose coat, yoga pants and trainers, with a neat designer clutch on her arm.

Danielle's eyes bulged as they passed across the woman's striking features. Her face looked sculpted by skilful hands-on fine rock. Long black hair cascaded down her back like a waterfall. Her exotic skin seemed to glow in the bright light of the nail salon.

'Why red?' Danielle responded, keeping her tone neutral.

'Most men like it.' The woman shrugged, stepping back and taking a seat at the desk next to her. Danielle's eyes focused on the spot where the woman had vacated, wishing she was still close to her.

'How do you know it's for a guy?' she asked, looking down as the acrylic was smoothed onto the last of her nails.

'Because nobody who's choosing a colour for themselves looks at the options for that long.'

'Doesn't necessarily mean it's for a guy,' said Danielle.

'I suppose it doesn't,' the woman replied, arching an eyebrow and returning the smile.

Danielle turned to face the nail technician, whose eyebrows had contorted with impatience. Giving one more cursory glance to the colours, she finally responded.

'Red, please.'

'Good choice,' said the woman, glancing at Danielle out of the corner of her eye.

'Thank you. I'm Danielle, by the way,' she said, her eyes an invitation.

'Stephanie,' the woman replied, 'but you can call me *Steph* . . . if I can call you *Danni*.'

Danielle's shoulders shook as she chuckled.

'Deal. Nice to meet you, Steph.'

A short while later, Danielle extended her long slender fingers, admiring her nails. Reaching into her purse, she took out two twenty-pound notes and handed them to the technician.

'What do you think?' Danielle asked Steph, holding out her hands. Steph delicately took Danielle's hand in her own, moving it around to inspect each nail.

'Beautiful,' she responded. 'Just like you.'

Danielle visibly flushed, turning her face slightly to hide her embarrassment. She had all but forgotten about Roman and the text she'd sent.

'Do you want me to stay for a bit? Make sure you don't get bored?'

Steph smiled and nodded, turning her attention back to her nails.

The nail technician filed vigorously, ensuring the shape of the nails was consistent. When she was suitably happy, she paused, looking at Steph expectantly. After a cursory glance at the colours, she responded.

'I think I'll have red.'

Danielle's eyebrows rose.

'Trying to impress a guy?' she asked, repeating Steph's earlier assumption.

Steph looked across at her, smiling.

'Yeah, something like that. I hear Orientals like the colour red. Think it's lucky or something. I like good omens.'

Danielle's heart was beating quickly as Steph's look lingered. She wasn't used to the feeling of not being in control. Her job allowed her to choose who she wanted to spend time with, how long for, and how much they would pay her for the privilege.

Yet, here she was, volunteering her time to a woman she had just met.

'We do. We both have red,' she said, flashing her nails to Steph. 'Maybe we'll both get lucky.'

With that, she rose to her feet and made her way to the door, Steph's eyes following her as she moved. Opening the door a crack, she turned around and smiled.

'It was nice meeting you, Steph. I hope I see you again real soon.'

———

LISA WATCHED from her chair as Danielle rounded the shop front and disappeared out of sight. Looking down at the table, she noticed a slip of paper. Written on it was a telephone number and the name *Danni.*

Lisa smiled down at the paper. Shifting it slightly on the table, she pulled out her phone and added the number to her contacts.

'You done,' said the nail technician simply.

Nodding, Lisa rose to her feet. Extracting money from her purse, she dropped it on the table. Pulling her Canada Goose coat back on and zipping it all the way up, she gathered her things and left the shop.

———

'IS THIS THE PLACE?'

Jamal nodded in answer to Roman's question. They were parked down the road from a house on Monet Gardens, just off Beck Hill Grove. The house they were surveying had a white Audi A4 parked outside, tinged with dried mud, desperately in need of a cleaning.

'Yeah. Stern works out of there. Lives with his mum, but keeps her well out of his business.'

'How do you know about him?' Roman cut his eyes to Jamal. He was sitting in the back, Jamal alongside him. One of his men, a shaven-headed middle-aged man named Ralph, was driving.

'Did some work for him a few months back. Someone took a package and didn't want to pay for it. I made sure they collected.'

'Who's his supplier?'

Jamal glared at Roman. 'I don't fucking know. What does it matter? You're bringing him on board with you, right?'

Roman ignored Jamal's anger. In the time they'd been working together, he'd learned that the man had a temper he could switch on and off, also learning not to take it seriously. There was no denying his skills were an asset.

After bringing Jamal on board and explaining his plan, they'd got to work. Roman kept a small squad of people as close to Chapeltown as he dared. They sold where they could, giving the impression that Roman was still weak.

Elsewhere, Jamal had hooked into some capable soldiers from all over Leeds. They didn't ask too many questions and were happy to crack heads for him as long as the money was good.

The next step for Roman was to slowly step up his profit, moving weight through different people, whilst not directly engaging the Dunns. He'd learned from the moves Keith had made, and would strike against them when he was ready.

Thinking of the Dunns, made Roman think of Ahmed, and he scowled. They seemed divided. Ahmed had told Roman to recommence his war against the Dunns, but Ahmed's partner, Mustafir had apparently been behind the attempt on Natty's life at a party a while back.

It made no sense to Roman, but it was a sign he needed to box clever. He would only rely on Jamal and those he kept close, and would ensure that he continued paying well, so they didn't look elsewhere.

'Fine,' he said to Jamal. 'I like details. You should know that by now.'

Jamal continued to glare at Roman. When he realised he wasn't getting a reaction, he grinned.

'C'mon, then. Let's go introduce ourselves.'

They climbed from the car and moved towards the house. Other than not having much of a garden out front, it was pleasant. Until today, Roman had never even heard of the road. Somewhere down the line, it would make a good spot to live in, he mused.

Jamal led the way, with Roman and their driver a step behind. They were armed, but kept their weapons concealed. Roman surveyed the quiet area as they grow closer. It was dark, and there was a chill in the air, so the road was clear. Jamal knocked on the front door. A well-built blond man with a square jaw and beady eyes answered. He eyeballed Jamal, then looked past him at Roman and the driver.

'What?' He barked.

'Tell Stern that Jamal wants to talk to him.'

The blond man continued staring, then grunted and shut the door.

Less than a minute later, it was opened by another man. He was slightly smaller than his blond associate, and had thick black hair and dark blue eyes. When he saw Jamal, he grinned.

'Mal, it's been a minute. How are you doing?'

'Doing good, Stern brother. Need to talk some business with you.'

Stern nodded, his grin widening.

'Come in.'

Stern led them into a cramped front room. The man who'd answered the door was sitting in an armchair, a thunderous expression on his face.

'Take a seat, anywhere you like. Ignore Leslie. He's on some silly bodybuilder diet that makes him miserable as fuck.'

Jamal took a seat on a hideous orange sofa. Roman and the driver remained standing as Stern sat alongside him. The television was on, and there was a football match playing, but Roman didn't recognise the teams. It had been a long time since he'd followed football, and it didn't hold his attention.

Other than the TV that took up most of the wall, there was the orange sofa, a mustard yellow armchair, and an ottoman that had seen better days. The ramshackle coffee table was covered with old newspapers, a paperback novel with a missing front cover, and a chunky ashtray with the word *Marbella* emblazoned on it in fading orange letters. Everything seemed thrown together, and there was no theme to the decor.

'So, what's this business, Mal? Didn't even know you were still active,' said Stern, stretching and putting his hands behind his head.

'My man here,' Jamal motioned to Roman, 'he's got a plug that's giving him the best shit on the street. For the right price, we're gonna hook you up, and you're gonna buy from us directly.'

Stern's eyebrows rose. Reaching for a pack of cigarettes next to the ashtray, he lit one, closing his eyes as he exhaled, letting out the smoke after a second and sighing.

'Fucking amazing. Shouldn't be smoking, but there's nothing else like it, is there?' Without waiting for a response, Stern continued. 'I already have a connect. Been with him a few years, and he looks after me. There's no reason for me to switch, especially to some dude I don't know.'

Jamal looked to Roman, and he knew that was his cue.

'Get to know me, Stern. Jamal has told me good things about you, and I want to work with you. What do you wanna know?'

'Your name, for fucking starters, would help.'

Leslie chuckled in the corner, liking Stern's response. It annoyed Roman, but he forced away the feeling, remaining focused.

'I go by Roman. Like Jamal said, I have the best plug in Yorkshire, and I wanna share him with you.'

'Why me?' If Stern knew who Roman was, he wasn't showing it.

'Because you're a tidy worker, and I enjoy working with tidy people. I have goals, and my intention is to run Leeds completely. I have the backing to do it, but I need the right team around me. I want you on board.'

'Oh yeah?' Stern smirked. 'I like Jamal. He's a loyal dude, and he's done a lot for me in the past, but you have fuck all but words. Why would I burn my connect over that?'

'Because this is business. That means making the most money possible, with as little fuss. If your connect is a real businessman, he'll understand that,' said Roman. 'There's no reason you should just take my word for it. I'm willing to give you a box on credit. I know you're big into coke and spice, but you can have any drug you want. If it's not everything I say it is, I'll move on, and you can stay loyal to your people.'

Stern didn't immediately respond, which Roman took as a good thing. It wasn't the first time he'd given someone the spiel. He'd swayed a few small-time dealers into seeing his vision, but Stern was a definite step up.

Finally, he opened his mouth, but before he could speak, Leslie burped, then leant forward.

'You can't seriously be buying this shit, Stern. He's probably an undercover Fed.'

'Look, Leslie or whatever your name is. You don't know me, so keep that shit to yourself. I'm official. I don't need to set up Stern, or anyone else. I've done my time in pen, and I kept my mouth shut. Keep watching TV, and let us talk.'

'What?' Leslie stood. Jamal did the same, daring Leslie to make a move. The two behemoths stared one another down, before Stern stopped it.

'Knock it off, Leslie. This is a win-win situation.' Wetting his lips, Stern continued. 'Get me a kilo of white. You do that, and we'll talk.'

Roman nodded.

'Consider it done.'

They hung out for a few minutes longer, namely so Jamal and Stern could finish their conversation.

Soon, Stern led them to the door, shaking their hands.

'One last thing before you go . . . I recognise your name from some-where. You're Chapeltown, right?'

'I've got a few links there,' said Roman delicately, wondering where Stern was going with it.

'You know that Mitch Dunn and his people have Chapeltown locked down, right?'

'I do.'

'You're willing to go up against that?'

'I'm willing to make millions. That's where it ends for me,' said Roman. 'I'm not afraid of the Dunns, and when I'm ready, they'll understand why.'

Stern grinned. 'Fair enough. I'm not a fan. They're greedy fuckers, and they don't know when to back off.' He patted Roman on the shoulder. 'I think you and me can do some good business together.'

'Me too. I'll see you soon,' said Roman, and they left. When they were in the car, Roman again got in the back, but Jamal decided to sit in the front.

'What do you think?' Jamal asked as they drove down the road.

'He's in. He just doesn't know it yet,' said Roman, chuckling.

CHAPTER TWENTY-TWO

SPENCE STEPPED INTO HIS HOUSE, locking the front door behind him. Stifling a yawn, he walked into the living room after taking off his shoes and jacket. He'd had a long day. In the morning, he'd worked out and gone for a run with Stefon, then he'd spent most of his day running around sorting out minor disputes within the team.

Mostly, it was different factions of the crew growing annoyed over one reason or another and clashing. There was no violence, and Spence resolved everything without involving Natty, but it was still draining. He was glad he'd got his workout in beforehand, or he doubted he would have had the energy.

On top of the street stuff, Spence couldn't shake his thoughts about Anika. She'd only messaged him once more since the last time, but Claudette's words were still resonating. Resisting the urge to at least speak to her and have a proper conversation, was growing tougher.

'Where've you been?'

Spence blinked. Deep in his thoughts, he hadn't noticed Rosie standing in the middle of the room, with her arms folded. Her expression was mutinous, and without thinking, Spence straightened.

'Hey, babe. I've been out working. What do you mean?' He said distractedly.

'I rang you twice and sent you a text. How come you weren't reply-ing?' Rosie demanded. Spence grabbed his phone, glancing at the screen and seeing multiple notifications. He'd missed her calls by acci-dent. It hadn't occurred to him to check his phone in the past few hours, which was surprising.

Rosie reached out for his phone, but Spence pulled it out of her reach.

'What are you doing?'

'What are *you* doing?' She replied. 'Why are you being so funny about your phone?' Her eyes narrowed.

Spence sighed. He didn't want Rosie looking at his phone and seeing evidence Anika had contacted him. He hadn't replied, but that didn't matter. Rosie's reaction surprised him, though. She had never made such a move before, and he needed to take control of the situation.

'Let's just take a deep breath and calm down,' said Spence, still holding his phone. 'I missed your calls, and I'm sorry. I haven't checked it in a few hours, because I was dealing with some business. A lot of business. Thankfully, no one was shot at this time,' he finished, trying to make a joke. Rosie didn't look convinced.

'Are you sure there's nothing else going on?'

'I'm sure,' said Spence. 'It's been one of those days, and I'm a little drained. I was gonna order us some food and maybe curl up in front of the telly.'

Rosie surveyed Spence for a long moment, and then nodded.

'What do you fancy eating?'

'It's up to you,' said Spence, unlocking his phone and missing the suspicious look Rosie was giving him.

———

LISA STOOD in front of the mirror, concentrating as she traced her lipstick along the outline of her mouth. Pressing her lips together firmly, she stood up, moving her head side-to-side, inspecting all the angles. Nodding to herself, she grabbed her clutch bag and made her way to the door. Her taxi was waiting for her, and she didn't want to be late.

Lisa arrived at a bar in Chapel Allerton a short while later. It wasn't a favourite of hers, but it was quiet, and would give her an opportunity to observe and learn. Lisa strolled through the glass door purposefully, embracing the warm inviting air. As she took in her surroundings, looking for Danielle, her eyes met with the barman, who nodded. Returning it lazily, she moved past the bar.

Rounding the corner, she saw Danielle sitting at the far side of the bar in a booth. Danielle's eyes were flitting left and right, and she was drinking her cocktail quickly. Finally, Lisa decided to put her out of her misery and approach the table.

'Hey, Steph,' said Danielle. 'You're late.'

'Only just. Have I missed much?'

'Me, I guess,' Danielle responded, winking. Lisa smirked back at Danielle.

'How many have you had, Danni? I'm only fifteen minutes late.'

'Well, I bought two cocktails. One for me and one for you. When you didn't show up, I drank them both.' She shrugged, motioning to the empty glasses.

'I guess the next round's on me then,' said Lisa, turning and making her way to the bar.

After procuring drinks, Lisa returned, placing them on the table and sliding a fresh cocktail to Danielle.

'What are you drinking?' Danielle asked, eyeing Lisa's glass suspiciously.

'Vodka and orange. Single. Can't have a heavy one tonight. I've got a busy day tomorrow.'

'Guess it's a good job I finished that cocktail for you then, isn't it?'

'Yes. I will forever be in your debt,' Lisa replied, placing her hands on her chest, feigning sincerity. Danielle laughed, stirring the neon-coloured liquid around in her glass, unable to take her eyes from Lisa.

'You're cool, you know, Steph. I don't usually connect with people this quickly, but you're different.'

Lisa waited a moment before responding.

'How come? What makes you so guarded?'

Danielle looked from her drink to Lisa and back again. Moving the straw to the side, she threw her head back and finished the drink.

'Get me another drink and I'll tell you.'

Lisa nodded, rising to her feet and returning to the bar. Moments later, she returned, handing the drink to Danielle. Stooping down, Danielle sniffed the drink, making a face and coughing.

'Christ, Steph. What's that?'

'Same as you were drinking,' Lisa responded, shrugging. 'Just double the alcohol.'

Danielle placed her mouth around the straw, sucking liberally and wincing.

'So… I got you something strong. Now tell me about you. Tell me why I'm so special that you absolutely had to befriend me,' said Lisa, smiling.

Danielle observed Lisa for a moment, taking a deep breath and another drink.

'I'm an escort,' she said.

Lisa's eyes widened, an invitation for Danielle to expand. When she didn't, Lisa spoke.

'So? What? Wouldn't that line of work mean you have to be good at talking to people?'

Danielle took a deep breath, composing herself. She was frightened that her new friend would judge her. The fact she didn't was a sign that she had invested her time in somebody who was worth it.

'It's not so much the career, but the circumstances that brought me to it,' she said earnestly.

'Go on,' Lisa said, reaching out and taking Danielle's hand.

'I had a . . . tough upbringing,' Danielle said, stroking Lisa's hand with her thumb. 'When I was fourteen, I ran away from home.

'I had this stepdad, you see. Loved my mum to bits, apparently, but not enough to keep his hands off her daughter. I tried telling her, but he called me a liar. A trouble causer. Said I was trying to come between them.' She shrugged, looking up at Lisa, tears in her eyes.

'What an absolute scumbag,' Lisa said, her mouth agape.

'I know. When mum chose to believe him, I couldn't live there anymore. I tried for a while, but it didn't last. Whenever she went out, he would *punish me*. It was *our little secret,* and I'd *betrayed him.'* Danielle made air quotes with her fingers.

'So you left?'

Danielle nodded.

'So I left. It was fine at first. I had my boyfriend. First love and all that. Went to live with him and his parents for a little while. When I explained why I'd moved out and why I couldn't go back, he left me. Kicked me out. Told me I'd cheated on him and that he couldn't look at me the same way.'

A single tear traced down Danielle's cheek. Leaning across the table, Lisa wiped it away with her free hand.

'I'm so sorry, Danni. That's absolutely awful.'

'I know,' she replied, smiling now. 'From that day, I vowed never to let a man hold power over me. I do what I do, so I hold the cards. I decide who I spend time with. How much time I spend with them. I control every aspect of my life.'

'You remain distant. Build up your walls to help you deal with your past. Forgo relationships to ensure you never land in the same spot,' said Lisa, looking away from Danielle. She needed a moment to compose herself. She was a professional, but Danielle had caught her off guard. A damaged individual doing what she needed to survive the horrors of her past.

Heading to the bar, Lisa ordered another cocktail for Danielle and an orange juice for herself.

'So, enough about me,' Danielle said, sipping her drink, 'tell me more about you.'

'There's not much to tell, honestly,' said Lisa. Danielle frowned in response.

'It's awkward, Danni. You've just sat here and told me about what a terrible life you've had. I've not had any of that. I don't want to rub it in your face that I had two supportive parents that loved and respected me,' Lisa lied.

'You asked me earlier what made you so special,' Danielle said, her eyes burning into Lisa's. 'You've just shown why. Besides your good taste in nail colour, you're empathetic. It's clear how much you care.'

Lisa watched as Danielle's face moved closer, her eyes closed, and her lips parted. When Danielle's lips met hers, she didn't pull back. Placing her hand on Danielle's cheek, Lisa deepened the kiss, pulling her close, placing her tongue in Danielle's mouth. A few moments later, they parted, smiling at one another.

'I'm drunk,' Danielle said, placing her hands on her cheeks and shaking her head. 'I should get a taxi.'

Lisa watched as Danielle struggled to navigate her phone. Reaching across the table, she pulled the phone out of her hand.

'Here, I'll do it for you,' she said.

Lisa opened WhatsApp, searching for Roman's name and opening their conversation. After scrolling a few times and reading messages, she accessed his number, consigned it to memory, and closed the application. She opened the Uber app, ordering a taxi before passing the phone back across to Danielle.

'I just need to order one for myself too,' said Lisa, opening her phone, punching Roman's number in and saving it.

'Thanks for helping me, Steph. You're a real friend.'

Lisa didn't respond, watching as Danielle placed her head on the table and closed her eyes.

―――――

SPENCE SLOUCHED ON HIS SOFA, eyes barely following the mindless action film he'd put on. Since his conversation with Rosie, she'd been staying at her house. Despite claiming nothing was wrong, he assumed it was her way of showing she wasn't pleased with him.

He didn't blame her. Spence didn't enjoy making someone he cared about suspicious, but he was still trying to work out how to handle everything.

He chuckled, thinking that the selling drugs part of his life was the easiest. Everything else was clouded. Natty seemed to be operating on a different level, and Spence seemed to have lost the key to how to pull his friend back; how to give him perspective. Roman was still out there. There were rumours of power plays, and Natty being usurped. People were shooting at them at parties. Stefon was settling in nicely, but Spence knew enough about him to know that could instantly switch.

And then there was Anika.

Spence looked at his phone. The message she'd sent an hour ago was still on the screen when he unlocked it:

I'm sorry.

Sitting up, Spence grabbed the glass of red wine he'd placed there, draining it. Before he could think, his phone was in his hand, and he was calling Anika.

'Spence?'

He closed his eyes for a moment, her voice instantly conjuring up memories he'd tried his hardest to suppress.

'Why?' he finally asked.

'Why what?' she sounded confused.

'Why do you keep contacting me? Why are you back here? Why are you making things so complicated?' The questions burst out before he could stop them.

It took a few moments for Anika to gather her words.

'I'm sorry. I can't help it. None of this is good . . . I know.' Her voice shook. 'You were good for me. I ruined that, but I can't stop myself from trying. From hoping that you might give me a second chance.'

'If your life was in a better position, you wouldn't care, though, right? You wouldn't give a shit because you left me. After cheating on me.'

Anika sighed.

'I wish it was that simple. I wish I could just leave you alone, the way I did for months, but I can't. I'm not denying that I messed up, but I can't help what's going on right now.'

'Why didn't you speak to me before leaving?'

Again, Anika took a second.

'Because . . .' the words seemed to catch in her throat. 'I didn't plan it. I didn't plan to leave, but it happened, and before I knew it, I was on my way out of the city, destroying the life I'd built. The life *we* built.'

Spence sighed. There were so many more things he wanted to throw at her. He wanted to tell her how disgusting she was. He wanted the name of the man she'd cheated with, so he could kill them. Again, his eyes closed.

'Spence?'

'I . . . feel like I'm changing,' he said after another second.

'Changing how?'

'I'm angrier. I hide it well, but I feel it bubbling. I almost got into a fight at a party a while back—'

'Claudia . . . she told me.'

Spence nodded, despite knowing she couldn't see it.

'She seems to really care about you.'

'She's an angel. I'd be in an even worse position without her,' said Anika.

'What happened to Carmen?'

Anika blew out a breath. 'She won't speak to me. Hasn't done since I left.'

'I'm sorry about that,' said Spence. Some of the anger he'd felt earlier had bled out, and he found he felt a lot calmer.

'I earned it. Hopefully, one day I can talk her around. Let's focus on you. You called for a reason, so you must have needed it. Is there something going on that you can't speak to Natty about?'

Spence chuckled. Despite everything she had put him through, Anika had pinpointed his anxiety.

'I don't know how to. We're cool, but it's like we're in two different places right now. He's hiding something, and I'm feeling . . . I don't know. Insecure.'

'You? *Insecure?* You're the most secure person I know.'

'Once,' said Spence, laughing darkly. 'Now, I'm trying to make everything make sense. I need the game I'm in to make sense. It did for a long time, and now I'm not sure.'

'You don't know what your position is?'

'I do, and I think that's the problem,' admitted Spence. 'I'm the weak link. Everyone around me has stepped their game up, and I feel like I'm a hindrance, holding people back.'

'Spence, I doubt any of them really think that,' said Anika. She hesitated. 'Do you . . . want to meet up, discuss it some more in person?'

Spence straightened, blinking.

'I need to go.'

'Spence, I'm sorry. I didn't mean to push, I just—'

'Thanks for listening, Nika. I hope you have a good night.'

'Spence—'

He hung up, taking a deep breath and letting the phone fall onto the sofa next to him. A small smile crept onto his face, and he shook his head.

Spence wasn't sure of the intent behind speaking to Anika, but he couldn't deny how good it had felt to get things off his chest. Sliding to his feet, he grabbed his empty glass and traipsed to the kitchen.

CHAPTER TWENTY-THREE

LISA SIPPED A DRINK, watching Danielle speak with her friends. They had hung out twice in the past few days, and Lisa found it interesting, because, despite the people Danielle kept around her, she seemed lonely. She seemed to keep her friends at a distance, clearly bored with being the queen bee of her little clique.

Lisa couldn't have planned it any better. Danielle was already confiding in her about her friends, and Lisa was providing just the right amount of enthusiasm to keep Danielle primed. They texted and FaceTimed often, and Lisa kept her disdain hidden.

When Danielle turned to her to bring her into a conversation, Lisa smiled and rattled off some inane small talk. It seemed to work, and the women went back to speaking among themselves.

After an hour, Lisa struck gold when Roman entered, flanked by two other men Lisa knew to be members of his team. She tempered her excitement, trying not to look too eager as Danielle giddily approached Roman.

———

ROMAN REGRETTED TELLING Danielle he would stop by. He didn't owe her anything, yet here he was, showing out, spending more time with her and getting in deeper than he intended. Roman didn't know what it was. He was attracted to Danielle, but that had never been an issue before. He had always detached from women before it became too serious, but seemed unable to do that now.

As Danielle flung her arms around Roman and kissed him on the cheek, he felt his men staring at him. He moved his head back as Danielle stepped backwards, smiling up at him. Roman's eyes moved from Danielle, to her friends, to his guards. He didn't intend on sticking around long, and planned to use his people as an excuse to leave.

'Good to see you, babe. Let's get you a drink, then I'll introduce you to people.'

'Okay. You two, do what you're doing for a bit. I'll come and find you in a little while.'

The men nodded and wandered off to work the room.

'Why did you bring them?' Danielle asked, throwing the pair a dirty look.

'Business, Danni. You know what it's like,' said Roman. He glanced around Danielle's living room, seeing a few people recognised.

There was a woman stood nearby who caught his eye. She was attractive, potentially younger than him, wearing a tight-fitting white top and a grey skirt. Roman didn't know what it was about her, but there was something strange. Something that didn't fit. He met her eyes for a moment, and she smiled, then entered into conversation with another woman.

'Who's that?'

'Who? Steph? She's really nice. I met her a while ago.' Danielle turned to see who he was referring to.

'You haven't known her long then?' Roman asked, frowning. Danielle elbowed him.

'Stop staring at her like that. You're so shameless. You're here to see me,' said Danielle, pouting. Roman grinned.

'You're right. Come, let's go get me that drink you promised me,' said Roman. He allowed Danielle to lead him away, but glanced back at Steph one last time. His instincts were right on this one: he was sure of it. He resolved to do some digging when he had a spare moment.

––––––

NATTY GLANCED to the side as Lisa climbed into the passenger seat. She shot him a quick smile as she shut the door.

'Do you want to drive, or do you want us to talk like this?' She asked, staring at him.

'We can stay here. It's cool,' said Natty. 'What's going on?'

'How's Lorraine doing?' Lisa asked. Natty shook his head.

'Don't start,' he warned. 'I'm assuming you have something, or you wouldn't have reached out.'

'I do. I got eyes on Roman.'

'How?'

'I'm best friends with Danielle. She had a little drink-up at her house. Roman turned up with two heavies. I was going to follow him, but I figured *Danni* would notice her friend going AWOL.'

Natty grinned. He'd yet to pin down Roman, but was tracking several of his associates, waiting for him to pop his head out.

'That's excellent. I'll get surveillance put on Danielle, and she can lead us right to him.'

'You can try that. I don't think it will work, though. Roman is a lot more cautious than Keith. Something tells me he might even plan for that, and try to use it against us.'

Natty considered that. Lisa was right. Roman was definitely the cautious type, and his actions were always well thought through. He'd proven this in the past.

Natty thought back to the bodies of the testers who had overdosed on Roman's tainted stock, his brow furrowing. Lisa was closing in, and it made sense to defer to her expertise.

'Do what you need to do then. You know the numbers if you need any backup, but if you get the chance to finish him, I'm confident you'll take it.'

'I'm confident I'll take it too,' said Lisa. 'Now that business is out of the way, tell me about Miss Richards . . . any intention to make an honest woman out of her?'

'You can't really believe I'm going to have a conversation with you about her.'

'You might do. Maybe you'll answer whether kissing her felt the same as when you kissed me?'

Natty licked his suddenly dry lips. The last thing he needed was to think about the kiss he'd shared with Lisa all over again.

'All you need to know is that I'm happy in my relationship, and that won't change.'

'Were you happy when we kissed?'

'Drop it, Lisa.'

'I will for now,' she said, smirking. 'If there's nothing else, I need to see a man about a dog.'

'Okay.' Natty was relieved that the conversation was over. 'Do you need a lift anywhere?'

'I won't say no,' said Lisa. Natty snorted, starting the engine and driving away. He and Lisa were so distracted by one another, that they didn't see the car parked nearby. The driver reached for his phone and dialled a number.

'Roman, it's me. Yeah. She's with Deeds. They just pulled off. Want me to follow them?'

'No,' said Roman, leaning back on his sofa in his living room, beaming. 'I'll get her soon enough. Don't risk spooking them. There's a bonus on its way to you for fantastic work.'

———

'GET UP.'

Spence stood. Stefon had just put him down on the ground. They had been boxing for over an hour, taking brief breaks in between. Stefon was a handy fighter, and Spence was decent, but he couldn't get close to Stefon.

'Can you continue?' Stefon asked. Spence nodded. He put up his hands, ready to go again.

Later, they finished up, and Stefon tossed Spence a bottle of water.

'You did well, bro. You're coming along nicely.'

'Do you think I need to know how to box?' Spence asked. Stefon nodded.

'Course. It's important to have hands, just in case someone tries you.'

'People don't try me,' said Spence, conveniently forgetting his argument at the party. 'I'm the one that stays calm, while you and Natty flip out. That's always been my role.'

Stefon sniggered. 'My cuz is a bit of a hothead. He used to be, anyway. Seems to have calmed down now. It's only me that seems to bring it out in him.'

Spence agreed. Every time Stefon and Natty were around one another, their interactions were laced with tension. Neither aimed to cause it, but they brought it out in the other.

'I mean well, though, Spence. You lot are letting me get my money up, and I'm grateful. Like I said, I just wanna make sure no one fucks around.'

Spence nodded, checking his phone, seeing a message from Rosie. He called her, stepping away from Stefon.

'Hey, baby,' he said when she answered. 'Sorry I missed your call.'

'I just wanted to see if you were coming home for dinner?'

'I'll be there soon,' said Spence. 'Just training with Stef.'

'Okay,' said Rosie. 'See you soon. Love you.'

'Love you too.'

Spence hung up, sipping his water.

'How long have you been with your girl?'

'Less than a year,' said Spence. 'It took us a while to get together.'

'Cool. It's tough having women in this game. I could never make it work with any of my women, so I keep it casual.'

'Natty used to be like that. He was all about keeping his numbers high, and not ending up in sticky situations.'

'What changed?'

Spence thought that over. The changes in Natty had been coming for a while, but there had been a moment where he had stopped lying to himself, and realised what he wanted. He'd almost messed things up with Lorraine, but he had taken a chance and let her in on what he was feeling, which had worked.

'I can't put it down to a specific thing. He just started looking at life differently, and realised what was important.'

'Cool. I get that. Good on him. Both of you. If you've found women that make you want to be with them, I say keep going. Just don't fuck it up.'

Spence's stomach lurched. Stefon's words made him think of Anika, who was still out there. He'd replied to a few of her messages after their call, but little else.

'What's next then?'

'We'll do some more shooting training. I'll see if I can put together a scenario to give us some practice. I might get some paintball guns or something. Regardless, you're coming along nicely. In crunch time, just remember one thing above all . . .'

'What's that?' Spence asked, still holding his empty water bottle.

'If it pops off, it's them or you. Shoot and ask questions later. It might just save your life.'

———

LISA WAS AT HOME, drinking water. She'd finished a tough workout, liking the way it made her muscles feel. The pain was good for her. It kept her switched on, ensuring she didn't slacken, and for that reason, she continued to push herself.

Her phone rang, and she grinned when she saw Danielle, answering.

'Hey, girl.'

'Hey, Steph. What are you up to?'

'Nothing. Watching some terrible show on Netflix. What about you? Have you got anything going on?'

'I don't know about you, but I fancy some pampering,' said Danielle excitedly. 'I know a nice place we can go to. Are you up for it?'

Lisa didn't know what it was, but her instincts were going haywire. She'd spent a lot of time with Danielle, yet she'd felt her pulling away since Lisa had met Roman at her drink-up. She'd assumed Danielle was jealous, incorrectly believing Lisa and Roman were into one another, but she wasn't sure. This sudden spa trip was definitely a red flag.

She decided to push.

'I'm not sure . . . my gas and electric bills left my account, and it was a nightmare. I don't have much money right now. What about next month instead?'

'No, it has to be now!'

'Why?' Lisa asked, drawing Danielle further in. She could practically hear her thinking.

'Because . . . I've got a friend who can get us half-price access, but it won't last until next month. If you're having money problems, I can pay for you. That's not a problem.'

'That man of yours must be taking care of you if you can floss money like that,' said Lisa, needling her. She knew how Danielle felt about her independence.

'I don't need him to take care of me, Steph. I told you, I make my money, and I run my own life. Me and Roman . . . balance each other out.'

'You're right,' said Lisa. 'I didn't mean to assume.'

'Don't worry about it. I know you didn't mean anything by it. Look, let's make it happen today. We can get massages and facials. There's loads of stuff we can do. I'll send you a link, and you can check it out for yourself.'

'Okay. What time do you want me there?'

'We'll set off at two. I'll drive us, so you don't need to worry.'

'That's cool,' said Lisa. 'See you soon, babe.' Hanging up, Lisa rushed to her feet, grabbed her jacket, slipped her feet into some boots, and left the house. She drove her car to a private garage in Chapel Allerton, where she had another car parked: a black Toyota Supra.

Lisa drove to Danielle's place and parked down the road, her position giving her a view of Danielle's place.

She was hidden between two vehicles, so she hoped her car would blend in. It was after twelve now. She had two hours to kill, and settled in to wait. She kept her eyes on Danielle's place.

An hour passed, and a car rumbled into view. Roman climbed out, followed by the same two men from the party. A fourth man, who was driving, pulled up, then he too got out and followed Roman and the duo into Danielle's house.

Lisa shook her head. Danielle had overplayed her hand, and Lisa planned to make her pay. She pressed a button and opened the stash spot under her glove compartment, taking out a pistol: it was a SIG Sauer that she'd had for a few years. It held sixteen shots and fired well, but Lisa didn't use it too often, other than for practising and keeping her skills sharp.

Lisa took a moment to assess her situation. She was outnumbered, and if Roman and his team were planning on setting her up, they were likely to have weapons too. She called Clarke, but he didn't answer. Natty didn't either.

Lisa cursed, wishing she'd had the foresight to ring them before she set off. After thirty minutes, Roman, Danielle, and his men left the house. She could see the angry expression on Roman's face as he and his men drove away, whereas Danielle looked resigned.

Lisa's phone rang as she was driving away. It was Natty.

'Lis? Everything okay?'

'Everything is fine. I have something to do, but I'll explain what's going on later,' said Lisa curtly. She hung up and headed home, already planning her next step.

CHAPTER TWENTY-FOUR

NATTY DROVE to Meanwood with his bodyguard in tow. He had been working behind the scenes to learn more about who shot at him, content with leaving Lisa in charge of the Roman hunt. Mitch wouldn't like it, but Natty didn't care. People wouldn't get away with shooting at him.

He'd learned through Brown that the man they'd arrested had been released without being charged, as they didn't have enough evidence. He had also given Natty some details about him, which had led Natty to his current journey.

As he drove along, Natty considered Brown's angle. He seemed more willing to work with Natty since he stood up for himself. Natty presumed he must have some intel for him, as Brown seemed eager to meet up. He'd given little consideration to the task he had allocated Brown, but it was important. Having little time to dig himself, Natty hoped Brown would help identify the mysterious contingent his uncle was working with.

'Right, watch my back,' Natty told the bodyguard, as he arrived at the destination. Four men were stood in a ramshackle garden, arguing loudly. One of them had a spliff in his mouth, another had a cigarette, and a third was vaping off to the side.

Natty glanced at the man he'd come to see. Brown had given him a description of a rat-faced man with a thin nose, crooked teeth and lank brown hair. Natty zeroed in on him as the guard murmured his assent.

Climbing from the car, Natty didn't break stride, hurrying into the garden toward the quartet.

'Oi,' said the man with the spliff, 'who the fuck are—'

Natty swung a short right hook into the man's solar plexus, stepping over the man as he hit the ground hard. Two more men moved towards him, but stopped when the guard pulled a gun.

With them taken care of, Natty grabbed the fourth man, dragging him out of the garden. Opening the car boot, he stuffed him in and closed it. He and the bodyguard then drove away.

———

NATTY STARED down at the man who had tried to kill him. He was naked, tied to a chair and trembling. So far, he'd given Natty no resistance, more of a snivelling wretch than a cold-hearted killer.

'What do you have to tell me?' Natty said. He knew that the man was called Barry and that he was thirty-three years old, but little more than that.

'I'm sorry,' Barry mumbled. Natty shook his head.

'Save the apologies. You tried to kill me, and I need to know why you were dumb enough to think that would fly.'

'I . . . they paid me . . . and—'

'Who paid you?' Natty interrupted. 'Forget that. First, do you know who I am?'

Barry nodded.

'Who am I?'

'N-Natty D-Deeds.'

'Do you know what I'm about?'

Barry's shaking was almost uncontrollable now. He thrashed in his seat, tears streaming down his face and snot running from his nose. Natty curled his lip in disgust as Barry nodded.

'So, knowing that, you still thought it would be smart to go against me?'

Barry wisely stayed silent. Natty let the silence stretch for several long moments, before he spoke again.

'It was silly, Barry. You should have planned it better, left nothing to chance. Maybe my guy wouldn't have put a bullet in your arm then. What did you tell the police?'

'I told them someone shot at me when I was going home one night, and that I d-didn't know who. I didn't mention nothing about you. Swear down.'

Natty knew this to be true. Brown had the interview notes, and he'd confirmed that Barry had *no-commented* most of the questions given to him by the arresting officers. The officers had tried painting Natty as a dangerous criminal, offering to protect Barry if he worked with them, but Barry had remained firm.

'You're from Moortown, right?' Natty asked.

Barry nodded.

'Which means you're probably part of Kirk's crew. Kirk is an annoying shit, but he's not stupid.' said Natty, pacing the room. 'No. Setting a dog on somebody in public, now that takes some balls. Kirk wasn't the man who put the battery in your back. Am I right?'

Again, Barry nodded.

'Why did you do it then? Now you can answer.'

Barry took a deep breath. He was no longer crying, and when he spoke, it was in an oddly muted voice, resigned to his fate.

'They paid me to do it. I got my cousin to keep an eye on you at that party. I'd heard you were gonna be there, so his job was to send me a text message when you were in a decent position, then distract you. He did his job, and I moved in, but it went to shit.'

Natty's eyes narrowed. 'Someone paid you to shoot at me, then . . . who?'

Barry wet his lips, not meeting Natty's eyes. Irritated, Natty stepped forward and gripped his chin, forcing Barry's eyes upward.

'I asked you a fucking question. Who was it?'

'I don't know him. I promise. H-He found me one night and told me what he wanted. At first, I said no. I knew what your people would do to me, but he offered me twenty-five grand. I couldn't turn down that sort of money.'

'Why did he go to you?'

'I've done it a few times before. I'm not a master assassin or noth-ing, but I've killed a few people. They didn't want it linked back to them,' said Barry.

Natty nodded.

'Ok, so if you don't know the name of the person who hired you or who they roll with, what do you know? What did they look like? Sound like? Did they have a distinctive smell?' he pressed.

'He's Asian. Well-spoken; clearly had some cash behind him. He dressed smart. I swear, though, I don't know his name. One of his people said something beginning with M - Mus something — but he went crazy when he did. It was clear he didn't want me knowing it. Backhanded the guy right across the face.'

Natty frowned. He remembered speaking with Mitch a while back about Roman's suppliers. One of them was a man named Mustafir.

Why would Mustafir want him dead? Did it involve Roman?

'What about Roman? Do you know Roman?'

'Yeah . . . we're not friends or nothing, but I know who he is.'

'Was he there when Mustafir tracked you down?'

Barry shook his head.

Natty would need to dig further into it, and make sure it was the same person. He didn't know any other Mustafir's, so chances were it was. He needed to be sure, though. The situation was only growing more complicated, and he needed to know everything.

'Let him go,' Natty said to the bodyguard, who immediately did as he was told. 'I'd suggest lying low for a while, or getting out of the business completely. If you ever in breathe in my direction again, it'll be me hunting you, and I promise I won't miss. Get me?'

Barry nearly broke his neck nodding.

'Get the fuck out of here then.'

———

LISA WAS on her way back to Danielle's. This time, she didn't hesitate, revenge on her mind.

Breaking into Danielle's place was child's play. Stepping inside, she had her knife by her side, keeping it low. Pushing open the door to Danielle's living room, she heard a slight creak, and stepped out of the doorway just as several bullets narrowly missed her.

Lisa rolled out of sight, then popped up, firing blindly into the darkness, and hearing a yell of pain. There were more bodies, though, and they were still firing.

Lisa needed to get out of there, before they attempted to flank her. Lunging for the front door, another bullet slipped by her, and she felt her heart almost stop. That had been too close for comfort.

Wrenching open the front door, she dived down the stairs, already rolling and halfway out of the garden as Roman and his men fired at her, none of the shots coming close this time.

Lisa reached her car, which she had smartly left unlocked, starting the engine and flooring it down the road, as more gunshots thundered by her.

Lisa was furious. Not only had Danielle tried to set her up, Roman had almost got the drop on her. She'd come far too close to dying, and had no intention of letting it slide.

Once she had recuperated and got things back in order, she would be back, she vowed.

———

NATTY SPENT the next day making phone calls, gathering more information about Mustafir. He knew he worked alongside a man named Ahmed, and as he'd suspected, they supplied Roman, along with a few other suppliers. When digging, Natty also linked them to several dead drug dealers who had recently turned up.

No one had claimed the deeds, and the police were barely investigating, as always.

Natty found the entire event strange. If they were backing Roman, he could understand financial support, but paying someone to shoot him seemed shortsighted. Natty was sure that they had access to their own killers if they needed them.

Could Barry have lied?

Natty didn't see it. Barry hadn't tried to hide. He'd got away without being charged, going back to his life. It had taken little effort for Natty to break him down. Barry had nothing to gain from lying to him.

Unless that was all part of it?

Natty rubbed his head, drinking the remaining mouthful of his coffee, which had gone cold. It was foolish to drink coffee before he went to bed, but he hadn't been thinking. It was after midnight now. Picking up his phone, Natty ignored the swath of messages and notifications and dialled Sanjay's number.

'Bro, do you know what time it is?'

'I need to talk to you. Are you about now?'

'I'm in bed, Nat. It's late, and I've had a long day. Can we do it tomorrow?'

'I'll drop you a text in the morning. Breakfast is on me.'

Natty went to the bathroom after hanging up. He regretted not staying with Lorraine, but he hadn't wanted to wake her up, and when they'd spoken earlier, he hadn't known what time he would finish.

———

SANJAY SLID into a seat opposite Natty the next morning. They were at a cafe on Chapeltown Road. Parking was tricky, so Natty had parked on Oak Road, then walked down onto Chapeltown Road to the spot. He didn't know where Sanjay had parked, but he instantly got the whiff of cigarettes from his associate, and it made him crave one. He shovelled a forkful of beans into his mouth to distract himself.

'Get what you're getting,' he said to Sanjay, when he'd chewed and swallowed. 'It's on me.'

'So it should be. My girl is pissed at you for waking us up.'

'I'll buy her some flowers,' said Natty, smirking.

'Forget that. She might think you're propositioning her and leave me. I'm already punching above my weight as it is.'

They laughed, then Natty carried on eating while Sanjay placed his order.

'What did you want, anyway?'

'Mustafir and Ahmed. Those names mean anything to you?'

Sanjay's eyes widened. 'You're talking about major levels there, Nat . . .'

'I'm guessing by that you mean *Jakkar*, right?'

Sanjay grinned, impressed by Natty's knowledge.

'People don't know that name. Jakkar is serious, Nat. If you have a problem with him, I'd suggest resolving it diplomatically. He's not the sort of person you want to get on the wrong side of.'

'I think I might already be on his wrong side.' Natty gave Sanjay an overview of the conversation he'd had with Barry, and the information he'd gleaned from him.

'That's dodgy,' said Sanjay. His food arrived, and he thanked the cook before tucking in, talking between mouthfuls. 'I mean . . . these lot are deep. If they really wanted to take you out, I bet they know people you'd never see coming.'

'That was my thinking. I thought they might be doing it on Roman's behalf, but I couldn't make it make sense, so I'm not sure. Do you have anything I can use?'

'I could ask, but I'd need to be really discreet about it. I don't want them getting onto my tail because they think I'm after them. What are you going to do?'

'Keep analysing the situation,' said Natty. 'Not much else I can do for now. Did you hear about their dealers?'

Sanjay nodded. 'Everyone did. Was it you?'

Natty shook his head. 'I've got nothing against them. There's something I'm missing, though. Just can't figure it out.'

'I'll see what I can find out, but don't get your hopes up. These guys are insulated.'

Natty wouldn't. He had done his research, but there was little information available. He would focus on his uncle for now, and hoped Brown had something he could use.

After assessing the terrain, he would look into the assassination attempt.

CHAPTER TWENTY-FIVE

ROMAN LEFT the spot he was staying at, walking to the car that was parked in the driveway. Jamal was behind the wheel, nodding along to a *Wretch 32* track. Ralph was in the passenger seat, smoking a cigarette, giving Roman a cursory glance and a sharp nod.

'What's new?' Roman asked. He slapped hands with Jamal, then reached across to dap Ralph.

'Nothing. I don't know what that bitch's game is, but she's gonna pay for killing my guy,' vowed Jamal. He'd been saying the same thing since they'd attempted to ambush Steph at Danielle's, intending to settle up with her.

Roman had underestimated Steph. He hadn't liked the look of her, and learning she was working with Natty, had figured Natty's men would be the ones to come to Danielle's. Instead, a single woman had killed one of their men.

Danielle hadn't known much about her, saying they'd met at a nail shop and become fast friends. He'd put pressure on her to set Steph up, after explaining that she was working with the enemy. Roman had hoped Jamal would gather some new intel, but they were apparently out of luck.

'I asked around. No one knows of anyone called Steph, either affiliated with the Dunns or anyone else,' he said.

'I thought we'd agreed she was probably using a fake name?' Jamal
reminded him.

'Still, we don't know her fucking name, so we have to try
something.'

Jamal shrugged, half listening to his music.

'What now then?'

'Put a team on her. Have a couple guys out there, hunting her
down. I don't have a picture or anything, but she's very good-looking.
I'll give you the description, and we'll see what happens.'

'A description?' Jamal wrinkled his nose. 'What the fuck am I
supposed to do with that?'

'Use it, plus what we know. Get as close to the Dunns as we can.
We know she's affiliated with them, so use it. Other than that, we're
fully on track. Stern's people are working out for us. We just need to
keep moving as we are for a little longer, and keep gathering string.'

'Hope so,' replied Jamal, stifling a yawn. 'I need action, bro. I'm
gonna get out of here, anyway. You need anything else?'

'Nope. Get the people after that woman, and let's finish her off.'

———

Brown seemed in a far more chipper mood when he climbed into
Natty's car.

'Deeds, how's it going?'

'Can't complain,' said Natty politely, matching the attitude of the
detective.

'My day has been long,' said Brown. 'Running around doing stuff
for you, on top of my day-to-day. I'm looking forward to the rest.' He
stifled a yawn. It was early evening, but people were still walking
about. As Natty watched, an older black man held the hand of a
woman as they traipsed up the path, deep in conversation.

'Do you know anything about these dealers getting slotted?' Brown
continued. Natty shook his head.

'I thought I was coming to you for information?'

'Helping me, means helping you. It's a competitive business. If I'm out there catching criminals and solving cases, I get promoted. If I get promoted, you've got more chance of gaining those same internal connections that your uncle has.'

'Speaking of him . . . what do you know? I hope you've got more than last time.'

'I hope you've got some money for me,' Brown retorted. 'Look, I told you last time. It ain't easy getting stuff on Mitch. I had a youngster watching him from a distance, but even that was hard. He doesn't go out much, and he's got cameras covering his house, so it was tricky, but we did it. Planted himself further down the street, where he could observe your unc coming and going.'

'And . . . ?'

'And, like I said. There isn't much. Especially when I don't even know why you're asking for information on your own family member. Every Tuesday, he leaves the house to go running. From what I can tell, he doesn't like a lot of people around him when he runs, but that's the only actual break from routine we noticed. He had a few dinners in the city centre last week at some exclusive spots, meeting a few bigwigs, but that appeared to be about business, rather than any dirty business. What the hell do I know, though? Not much difference between the two, if you ask me.'

Natty tuned out Brown. He knew his uncle liked to stay fit, and he'd seen him train on more than one occasion in his makeshift gym in the garage.

For a moment, it reminded Natty of his own training with his dad when he was younger. He'd wanted desperately to be like him, and when his dad wasn't around, he would work with the heavier weights, wanting to gain bigger muscles so his dad would be proud of him.

Thinking back, he was lucky he didn't do permanent damage to his body, but it was worth it.

'Thanks,' he said to Brown.

'Is that it?' Brown's tone was incredulous. Natty handed him a bundle of notes.

'That's a bonus. Don't spend it all at once.'

'I still wouldn't mind knowing what's going on. What are you planning?'

'Who said I'm planning anything?' said Natty. 'Go home and get some rest. Like you said, it's been a long day.'

———

Lorraine sat in the doctor's office, watching as the doctor read through her history. The office didn't stand out from any previous doctors' offices Lorraine had been in. There was a painting of an old building that looked like a lighthouse, surrounded by sea. Other than the desk and computer, there were numerous files, and a large potted plant in the corner of the room.

Dr Beck had light brown hair tied in a ponytail, thin facial features, and warm hazel eyes. After a few moments, she faced Lorraine and smiled.

'Hello, Lorraine. Do you want to give me an overview of how you're feeling?'

Lorraine knew she couldn't tell the doctor everything that was going through her mind. A lot of it, she didn't understand herself. She hadn't even contemplated going back to work, and had no desire to face Angela. It felt like there was a reckoning coming between them, and Lorraine wasn't sure what to do next. She'd yet to speak to Natty about her work problems. He knew she'd taken time off but didn't think much of it. Lorraine doubted he ever needed to arrange to take time off in his line of work.

'I've felt unwell lately. I've had a few personal issues. I'm not sure if they've had a negative effect on my health, though.'

'When you made your appointment, you mentioned feeling nauseous, getting headaches, and that you'd vomited several times, correct?'

Lorraine nodded. 'That's correct.'

'When did you last vomit?'

'The day before yesterday.'

Dr Beck nodded, typing on her keyboard as Lorraine spoke.

'How's your appetite?'

'Up and down, but I've been able to eat mostly without issue.'

'You mentioned personal issues. What's been going on?'

Lorraine hesitated, eyes darting around the room for a moment. Finally composing herself, she responded.

'I had some issues with the father of my son. He was in and out of our lives, negatively affecting us. He . . . died recently.'

'I'm sorry to hear that,' said the doctor. 'Do you think this could be the cause?'

'I don't know. He wasn't a very good man, but still. It was someone I knew.' Lorraine had a flashback to Raider looming over her. Her stomach tightened, and she coughed into her hand, shaking her head.

'Are you okay, Lorraine?'

'I'm fine. I've also been having some issues at work. I'm clashing with my manager, and they haven't been particularly supportive during this process.'

'Stress can affect your body in a multitude of different ways, Lorraine. Based on what you've said so far, it sounds like this could be the case.'

They spoke for a while longer. Doctor Beck asked more questions about Lorraine's sleep patterns, gently probing more into her state of mind. Lorraine answered as honestly as she could, and by the end, she had a sick note and was signed off work for the foreseeable future.

As she left the doctor's, her phone was buzzing with several emails, with signposts to literature regarding stress and anxiety. She would need to make another appointment in the next two weeks for an update, but for now, she was free.

As she walked to the taxi she'd ordered, Lorraine pulled her coat tighter around her, conscious of a lingering chill in the air. When she'd settled in the back of the taxi and put on her seatbelt, she looked over one of the links Dr beck had sent, sighing.

One way or another, she needed to make sense of everything going on, and get back to normal.

———

On Monday night, Natty again spent the night away from Lorraine, staying at his house. He'd yet to move out of his home in Chapel Allerton, and though he liked his space, he missed Lorraine and Jaden. They'd become such a huge part of his life, that being in his own space felt foreign.

The house had a large flat-screen TV mounted on the wall, along with a high-quality sound system. Along with a light brown sofa, he had a leather recliner chair he was currently sitting in. The room also contained a PlayStation console — though he didn't have as many games as Jaden — along with a sleek, modern coffee table serving as a centrepiece for the room, and an area rug adding a final touch. The walls were a mix of cream and beige, and Natty had wide windows that offered a nice view.

Despite all the effort he'd put into his place, it wasn't home.

Natty shook his head, focusing. He'd come up with a makeshift plan for taking out his uncle, but he remained more conflicted than he'd imagined.

Natty loved his family. He loved his surname and the doors it opened. Ever since his mum had blurted out the truth of what happened to his dad, Natty had tried to go over it in his mind. From his conversations with his mum, and what Clarke had told him about his dad, something had gone wrong on the business end.

Natty remembered the tensions with numerous West Indian gangs when he was younger, and Clarke's assertions that he'd gained revenge by taking out a Yardie crew seemed to fit that narrative.

The more he thought about it, the more he wanted to know the ins and outs of the situation. He'd tried talking with Mitch about his dad before, but somehow he suspected it wouldn't be as simple this time. There was a disconnect between them, and part of Natty wondered if Mitch knew what he was up to, though he dismissed it.

He needed to ensure he was in place way before 10 am the next morning. He couldn't set up or get into place just before; there was too much chance of his uncle seeing him closer to the time. For that reason, he got an early night, surprised when he actually fell asleep straight away.

Natty readied himself early the next morning, and by 8 am, he had left the house. He drove to Moortown, parking two streets away. It was risky, but he didn't want anyone to connect him to the event. As Natty climbed from the car, he made sure he had everything. He had two guns — one of which was strapped to his body — a pair of latex gloves to avoid detection, and a bland outfit that would blend in: a grey hooded top underneath a black jacket.

He kept his hands in his pocket and his head low as he turned onto his uncle's street, looking all around him as he slipped into a nearby garden. It afforded him a superb view of his uncle's place, and he suspected it was where Brown's lackey had conducted their surveillance.

By now, it was eight thirty, and he settled in to wait. He monitored the house behind him as he hovered in the garden, but there was no movement from inside, and the curtains remained closed.

Natty distracted himself by going over the plan in his head. He would shoot his uncle three times to be sure, then he would make his getaway. After making sure Jaden and Lorraine were safe, he would link up with Clarke and let the chips fall where they lay. If Clarke was on board, he would tell him what he had done, and the full story behind it.

This wasn't the time to get ahead of himself, though.

As he waited, Natty felt his legs beginning to ache from his crouched position. He fought through it, keeping his mind focused on the task at hand. He had a silencer on his main gun. It wouldn't completely prevent sound, but it would be better than disturbing the quiet street with louder gunshots.

Around Natty, the day came alive, with people leaving their houses to go to work, and two separate people walking their dogs. Natty checked the time, his heart racing when he realised it was nine fifty-five am.

This was it.

He was in place, and he was ready.

He rose to his feet, heart careening against his chest as the time hit ten o'clock. His breathing intensified as he noted Mitch leaving the house with only a single bodyguard in tow.

Mitch did some stretches in place, happy to ignore his bodyguard.

He wore a dark grey warmup tracksuit and cheap running shoes, and had a focused look on his face, with not an ounce of fatigue in his demeanour. Mitch was about to start running in Natty's direction.

Natty ensured his balaclava was covering his face, then positioned himself.

Mitch began jogging, starting slowly, allowing his muscles to stretch and warm up. Natty slipped out of the garden, raising the gun, his finger on the trigger.

'Mr Dunn!' a friendly voice called.

Mitch stopped running just as a bullet cracked, hitting a hedge next to him. Mitch looked around in alarm. Natty glanced at the neighbour who had called to Mitch. The man had caused him to shoot early, and now Mitch knew what was happening. Mitch turned on his heel and ran for the house. The neighbour also ran away screaming.

Natty fired at Mitch's retreating back, but the shot narrowly missed. He went to fire again as Mitch hurried back into his garden, but the bodyguard returned fire, shouting instructions into an earpiece.

Natty didn't have time to play with him.

He aimed low, catching the guard in the thigh. As the man fell with a scream, Natty dropped the gun and took off running just as he heard loud voices from behind, assuming Mitch's bodyguards had mobilised. He had a decent lead on them, though, running past a street and keeping his head down, making it to his car in record time.

He jumped in and drove away, pulling off the balaclava and hitting the steering wheel, letting out a furious yell.

'Fuck!'

The neighbour had ruined it for him. He'd come so close to finishing his uncle, but he had failed, and now he would need to go back to the drawing board.

First things first, he needed to ditch the car and get home, then he needed to find out what had transpired.

CHAPTER TWENTY-SIX

NATTY WAS with Lorraine later that evening, stewing over the failed attempt on Mitch.

Word had already leaked, and the streets were buzzing with news of the attempt on Mitch Dunn's life. Everyone had a story about who was behind it, but most people believed Roman was responsible, as he had the means and motive.

It was an audacious attack that rocked the perception. Mitch had been deemed untouchable, yet if the rumours were to be believed, he had come close to being killed. With his shooting attempt taking place not long after Natty's, questions were being asked.

Natty was furious at what had transpired, cursing his hesitation. The neighbour had thrown off his shot and made him miss, and his follow-up shots were panicked and off-target. It shouldn't have happened. His training with Clarke had readied him for these situations. His uncle would be on his guard now. Natty would never get another shot like that, and it galled him.

'Are you okay, Natty?' Lorraine asked, pressed against him. Something had made Natty tense, and she wasn't sure what it was. She had cooked for him and Jaden earlier, and Natty had made conversation, but was quieter and less animated than normal.

Lorraine wondered what had transpired in the streets today, wondering if Natty was in danger. She'd noted he'd spent a few nights at his place. Whatever was going on likely affected that, but she would only ask if it became impossible to ignore.

'Yeah, I'm fine. Probably just tired,' said Natty listlessly. 'It's been a long day.'

'I'm here if you need to talk. Okay?'

Smiling, Natty kissed the top of Lorraine's head. 'I appreciate that. Thanks.'

They kept watching television, but now and then, Lorraine would glance at Natty, his pensive expression worrying her more each time. When his phone vibrated, she nearly jumped out of the chair.

'Sorry about that,' Natty said to her, glancing at the screen and cursing under his breath. 'Yeah? Right, I'll see you there.' Natty hung up and clambered to his feet. 'Sorry, babe. I've gotta go out for a bit. It's business.'

'Do you know how long you'll be?' Lorraine asked. She didn't want Natty to go out, but couldn't tell him that. Lorraine was being irrational. She knew what he did, and knew that it involved late hours sometimes. Something about the current situation just made her uneasy, and she couldn't shake it.

'I'll try to be back as quickly as possible. I just need to speak to a few people. Do you mind if I still stay?'

Lorraine frowned. 'You don't have to ask, Nat. I've told you that before. I want you here all the time. You make me feel safe.' She bit her bottom lip as her words spilled out.

Natty was out of harm's way if he was with her, she reasoned.

'I love you.' Natty gave her another smile. After a quick kiss, he hurried out. Lorraine watched the door, blowing out a breath. Heading to the kitchen, she went to make another cup of coffee, determined to stay up and wait for him.

———

NATTY CLIMBED FROM HIS CAR, noting Brown already waiting for him, a wide smile on his face.

'What's up?' Natty bluntly asked. He had no time for the niceties right now.

'You tell me, *killer*,' said Brown, laughing.

'Don't fuck me about. I was in the middle of something. If we're not talking business, I've got things to do.'

'I bet you do.' Brown smirked at Natty, surveying him. 'I wondered what your angle was, but I didn't think you'd have the balls to try a takeover. That's some audacious shit, Deeds.'

'What are you talking about?' Natty's stomach lurched. It appeared Brown had already put the pieces together. It wasn't a hard puzzle, but it was still worrying.

'I'm talking about me telling you a little titbit about your uncle, and you going out there all guns blazing and trying to kill him on his morning run.' Brown shook his head, laughing again. 'You've got balls, Deeds. Massive balls.'

'I don't know what you're talking about.'

'Don't mug me off. I'm better at this than you are. You pepper me for info about your unc. Days later, someone tries to kill him, taking advantage of a blip in security. You're not gonna convince me you weren't involved.'

'I don't need to convince you of anything,' said Natty. Brown had put the pieces together, but he knew enough about the detective's personality to know that he would want more details at this stage. Natty had proved that last time when he'd dismissed the minuscule information he'd received from Brown about his uncle, causing the man to go out and find more.

Still, this was the last conversation he needed right now.

'Once again, I don't know what you're talking about. I don't give a shit whether you believe that.' Sliding a hand into his pocket, he handed Brown a fat wad of notes. 'This is double your usual amount.' As Brown reached for it, Natty pulled back. 'If you take it, it comes with strings.'

'What strings?'

'Roman.'

Brown's brow furrowed. 'What about him?'

'I want him. You're gonna help, so if you learn anything about him around the office, or from one of your little snitches, I wanna hear about it.'

'You can become one of my snitches too if you like, Deeds. Just say the word, and I'll get you the paperwork.' Brown's eyes were on the money as he took it.

'Remember what I said. Don't ring me again unless it's important.' Natty headed back into his car and drove away. He would have to keep Brown in line, and stop him from talking to people about Natty's involvement in Mitch's shooting attempt. It was likely to cost some big money too, but he'd figured it was a possibility when he put his plan together.

As he turned left onto a main road, his phone rang again. It was Clarke.

'Hey, boss,' said Natty.

'You're needed. I'll give you the address. Get over there right now. Cool?'

'Cool,' said Natty, pleased his voice sounded normal as he hung up. The address came through in a text message. Natty glanced at it, swallowing down a lump of fear. There was a possibility he was walking into an ambush, but he didn't have a choice. He took a deep breath and kept driving, trying to keep his thoughts in check.

———

MITCH PACED the room at a safe house. It was in Pudsey, with half a dozen armed men downstairs, and another outside in a car, watching the property. He was taking no chances.

Complacency had nearly cost him his life.

Mitch hadn't even seen the shooter coming. If his neighbour Tim hadn't hailed him, Mitch would be a goner. To add insult to injury, the shooter had clipped one of his bodyguards. They had taken the man to a private doctor. Mitch would pay for his recovery, but right now, it was the least of his problems.

Clarke entered the room, followed by Nathaniel, grave expressions on both of their faces. Mitch assessed his nephew. They hadn't spoken in a while, but right now, he needed to surround himself with his most capable soldiers. As Mitch glanced at Nathaniel, he definitely looked capable. His nephew cut an impressive figure. Tall, powerfully built, with an air of confidence that seemed to grow over time.

If he could stay on course, Mitch knew Nathaniel would be the next great leader.

'What do we know?' He asked, addressing Clarke. There were several chairs in the room, along with satisfying hardwood floors that were good for pacing.

Despite the seats, both Nathaniel and Clarke remained on their feet. Nathaniel had his arms folded, leaning against the wall. Clarke had his hands clasped behind his back, almost at attention as he stood.

'Nothing so far. The shooter got in and out without a trace. He had it well-scouted. He appears to have lain in wait, then attempted to shoot at you.'

Mitch's jaw tensed.

'How do you think he set it up?'

'Professionally. I'm guessing he had his getaway vehicle set up on another street. He analysed the best time to get at you, and it was dumb luck that he missed. We have to assume somebody as methodical as the shooter is trained with weaponry.'

Pausing, Mitch considered Clarke's words.

'You think he'll try again then?'

Clarke nodded.

'I'm not pleased,' said Mitch, feeling his anger growing, furious that someone had tried him, and so publicly. 'No one should have got that close to me. The fact we don't know who, and that they are still breathing, is pathetic. You are my key men,' he continued, his voice rising. 'You don't know who tried to kill me. What are you good for? Well?'

'We'll find them,' Nathaniel spoke for the first time. 'Roman is the most likely guess. How he found out where you were, I have no idea.'

'*Roman* . . . remind me nephew, who was it I tasked with eliminating Roman?'

Nathaniel didn't respond, his gaze fixed on his uncle.

'You really think he would have the balls to come for me?' Mitch continued.

Nathaniel shrugged.

'He wants to win. Best way to do that is by going straight to the top.'

Mitch scratched his chin, his nostrils flaring. Nathaniel had floated a good theory. It was a solid place to start.

'Something big needs to happen. Plan amongst yourselves what that is. I cannot have people thinking I'm accessible, and that I can be touched. I want to be kept in the loop.'

Nodding, the men went to leave.

'Nathaniel?'

His nephew paused, then turned to face him.

'I want Roman finished. No more messing around. Clarke, stay.'

Nathaniel nodded and made his way to the door. As he moved, Mitch's eyes traced every step. When the door closed behind him, Mitch paused for a moment, before turning his attention to Clarke.

'You've continued to train my nephew, correct?'

'That's right.'

'Discontinue that immediately.'

Clarke's brow furrowed, confusion etched on his face.

'A capable Natty is good for the crew, Mitch. Now more than ever.'

'Are you second-guessing me?' Mitch's voice was dangerously low.

Clarke shook his head.

'No. I just don't understand.'

Mitch scratched his chin, focusing on the door Nathaniel had just exited through.

'I'm not asking you to understand. I'm ordering you to do as I say.'

Clarke nodded.

'I want your full concentration on finding out who attempted my life. I'm counting on you, Clarke. Don't let me down.'

'I won't.'

CHAPTER TWENTY-SEVEN

STEFON PULLED up outside his Aunt's house on Hares Avenue. He'd stopped in earlier to see his mum, and she had mentioned her sister. Stefon realised he hadn't been to see her since he was back, deciding to rectify that.

He'd forgotten how easy it was to get sucked back into the street life. It hadn't taken long for Stefon's money to increase. Whatever his issues with Natty, his cousin paid him fairly, and Stefon did his thing on the side. His business with Johnny had opened up several lucrative doors for him, and he was taking full advantage.

In general, Stefon wasn't sure what to make of the situation in the streets. Natty was doing his best, but everything was up in the air, and with two separate attacks on Natty and Mitch in the past few weeks, people were wary of their roles in the organisation. They needed to take out Roman, and it needed to happen soon.

Spence was a surprise. Stefon remembered him back in the day, but he always seemed to be in the background. Nowadays, he seemed a lot more assertive. During their training, Stefon had seen his determination to get better, and there was a definite improvement.

If things worked out as Stefon expected, Spence would get the opportunity to put it to the test soon enough.

Knocking at the door, Stefon glanced up and down the quiet street. Other than a few older people walking up and down, and some Asian boys standing on the corner, dressed in parkas and woolly hats, talking animatedly to one another, there was nothing to see.

Stefon gave the boys one more look, then turned back to the door as it opened. He hadn't seen his Aunt Tia in years, but she looked the same. She gave him a piercing look, then her eyes softened as she realised who it was.

'Stefon? That can't be you. When did you get so big?'

'Auntie Tia, it's lovely to see you.' Stefon beamed at her.

'Come in, come in. People are nosy. You don't need to stay on the doorstep like a stranger.'

Stefon followed Tia inside. He didn't have many memories of being in the house, but it was cosy and extremely clean. As he sat in the living room, he couldn't see a speck of dust anywhere. There was a television that was turned off, and an old-school HIFI that was playing music at a low volume. There was a magazine half-opened on the coffee table, next to a half-drunk cup of tea.

'What can I get you? Are you hungry?' Aunt Tia asked. Stefon shook his head.

'I'm good, thanks, Auntie. I ate before I came out.'

'What about a drink? You must be thirsty.'

'I'm cool. Seriously. I'll let you know If I change my mind,' he assured her.

'Good. We've got a lot to talk about. Sit down. Where is it you're staying again? Leicester?'

'Yeah,' said Stefon, surprised that she'd remembered. 'I've been back in Leeds for a few weeks.'

'And you're only just getting around to seeing me?' Tia arched a delicate eyebrow, re-taking her seat and picking up her drink. She closed the magazine with her spare hand, then fixed her eyes on her nephew.

'Sorry, I got carried away. You know how it can get out there. Some-times you forget to take a minute and breathe.'

'Hmmm.' Tia pursed her lips. 'I hope you're staying out of trouble.'

'I'm trying,' said Stefon. He'd received a few angry phone calls after his moves against Roe-Milly. If his people came for Stefon, he would be ready.

'Good. Keep trying. How's your mum? I keep meaning to see her, but I don't leave the house very often, if I'm honest. Health issues.' She coughed, reaching for some tissue.

'Are you okay?' Stefon leaned forward. His mum hadn't said anything, but Tia was getting older, and probably more susceptible to illness.

'I'm fine, Stefon. I promise. Just some stomach issues, along with slowing down in general. I'll have to go see my sister, though. See what she has to say. How are your kids?'

Stefon spoke for a few minutes about his children, and his plans for bringing them to Leeds. Tia smiled, her eyes twinkling as she listened.

'You're such a wonderful dad. I always knew you'd turn out well,' she said. 'Have you seen any other family since you came back to Leeds?'

'Other than Natty, not really. Everyone's out there doing their own thing. It'd be nice to have a proper family get-together, though. I might put something on.' Stefon noticed Tia's eyes tighten when he mentioned her son.

'Don't bother,' she replied.

Stefon paused before responding.

'Don't you think it would be nice for us all to get together? You can see mum and catch up.'

'I'll make some time to see her. Don't worry yourself.'

Stefon wanted to enquire further, but there was a clear finality in his aunt's expression.

They spoke for a while longer about family members. For a woman out of the loop, Tia seemed to know a lot about them, and what they were doing. He ended up staying for dinner, ignoring his phone and watching television with his aunt, enjoying it more than he'd thought he would.

By the evening, he went for it, and asked what he'd wanted to ask all along.

'What's the deal with my cousin? I go away, and Natty is this little kid running around after the hustlers. I come back, and he's a boss. He's come a long way. You must be proud.'

Tia snorted, her expression disdainful.

'He's not right in the head, that boy. Worst of all, he's forgotten where he came from.'

'What do you mean?'

Tia sniffed, pursing her lips.

'Just watch your back, that's all I'm saying. You might think Natty is cool, but he's a bad seed, just like his dad, and just like his uncle.'

This confused Stefon. He'd expected a bit of gossip when he brought up the subject, but not the barely contained vitriol he was getting.

'What do you mean, though? What's he done? I've noticed he's bossier now, and he always seems stressed.'

'He never could handle the pressure. His dad was the same way. Natty . . . he abandoned me,' said Tia.

'Abandoned you how? I heard you two were on the outs, but I didn't know it was that deep.'

'He's cut me out of his life. He'd rather play house with his little slut and her son. Can you believe that? He's raising some other man's kid, giving to them and not me.' She hung her head, sighing. 'I'm not even after his money. I know how that sounds. It just hurts that he resents me. We haven't spoken in months, and I don't know if we ever will again.'

Stefon's head was reeling from the information he'd been given. None of it made any sense. Tia could be shrewish, and he recalled her snapping at Natty when he was younger, but he didn't understand what could have made Natty treat his mum the way he had.

Reaching into his pocket, he pulled out a stack of money, and counted out a significant portion, before offering it to her. Tia shook her head.

'You don't have to do that, Stefon. I'm not destitute.'

It was Stefon's turn to shake his head.

'No, I want you to take it,' he said softly. 'I don't forget, and neither does my mum. We'll always be grateful for you looking out for us. As long as I'm around, I'll do the same. Make sure you take my number before I go, and reach out to me if you ever need anything. Day or night.'

Tia's smile encompassed her entire face now. She took the money.

'Thank you, Stefon. You were always a good boy. Don't let your cousin drag you into his mess. You're strong. You always were. Keep him in line, and make sure he's telling you the truth about everything. Okay?'

Stefon nodded.

'Good. Let's have another drink before you go. I'm sure you've got more stories to tell me.'

———

Natty arrived at the usual training spot, warmed up and ready to go. Knocking on the door, it opened a crack, two piercing blue eyes peering out at him. Nodding slightly, the door swung open, the muscular man stepping aside and letting him in.

Natty made his way through the kitchen, opening the cellar door and jogging down the concrete stairs, dust kicking up with each step.

As he rounded the corner, his eyes met Clarke's sat on a fold-up metal chair, fingers laced and elbows resting on his knees.

'You left your gym bag in the car?' Natty asked, smiling.

Clarke's expression remained neutral. Natty's smile faltered.

'Are you sick of me kicking your arse now? Is that it?'

Clarke rose to his feet, stepping across to Natty and standing in front of him.

'What's going on, Nat?' Clarke asked.

Natty's heartbeat increased.

'What do you mean, what's going on?'

'Your uncle's told me I'm not to train you anymore. I don't understand why and he wouldn't tell me. I'm hoping you can shed some light on the decision.'

Natty's eyes searched Clarke's. He could feel his pulse hammering in his throat. Fighting to keep his face neutral, he responded.

'Unc told you not to train me?' Clarke nodded. Natty looked

beyond Clarke at the firing range, scratching his chin. 'What the fuck's that about?'

'I don't know, Nat. That's why I'm asking you. Has something happened between you and your uncle that I'm not aware of?'

Natty shook his head.

'No, nothing. He cut me out ages ago, remember? Told me to report to you. I don't know what he's trying to do. I'm only back in this life because he couldn't let me go. Why did he hook me back in just to limit my effectiveness?' Natty was breathing slowly, trying to regulate his heart rate.

Clarke's eyes examined Natty's, flicking from left eye to right.

'I don't know, Nat,' he finally responded. 'But he's serious. He told me we're done, and I take his word seriously. You know that.'

Natty nodded.

'So now what?'

Clarke blew out a breath.

'Now you do what you need to do to sharpen your skills. I've given you the tools to improve. You can do that with or without me.'

Natty shook his head.

'None of this makes any sense. With Roman making moves and taking shots, we all need to be sharp. This is the worst possible time to be pulling back,' he said.

'I thought the same.'

Clarke stepped beside Natty, clapping him on the shoulder. Nodding once, he stepped past him, scaled the stairs, and left.

When he heard the cellar door close, Natty shut his eyes, inhaling deeply through his nose. Stepping to the table in front of the range, he picked up the handgun and emptied the clip into the target, his face contorted with rage.

———

LATER, Natty was with Lorraine. They were curled up on the sofa, the film they'd watched just finishing. He'd left the training spot early, wanting to spend some time with Lorraine before it was too late. He was trying his hardest to avoid thinking about his mounting issues. By being too overzealous, he'd messed up, and now he needed to box clever.

Brown was breathing down his neck. Clarke had stopped their training, and Mitch was on the warpath.

Add to that, the Asians that supplied his enemy were funding people to kill him.

It was a lot to deal with, and he was working hard to avoid becoming overwhelmed.

Lorraine had been quiet all evening. They'd sat together cuddling for most of the evening, but something seemed off. She was fidgety and seemed uncomfortable. Every now and then, Natty caught her looking at him out of the corner of her eye.

He wondered what could be bothering her. Her dreams seemed to be a little better lately, but it was clear the events with Raider still haunted her.

On several occasions, she had woken up in the middle of the night, looking pallid and feeling sick. When she did, she often struggled to keep it down. She had woken up and thrown up at least once since the last time. He knew she'd taken more time off work, but she hadn't said much to him.

'Are you okay, babe?' He asked, stroking her temple, smiling as she shifted herself so he could continue.

'Just thinking,' she said, her voice quiet.

'Anything you want some help with?'

Lorraine sighed. 'We've been through it all before. I don't want to bore you by repeating myself.'

Natty tilted her head, so she was facing him, brushing his lips against hers.

'Tell me,' he said. It took a while for her to speak, and he didn't rush her.

'How long did it take you?'

'Take me to what?'

Lorraine hesitated.

'To get over it.'

Natty frowned, but quickly gathered himself. His instincts were correct regarding Raider. He knew she'd struggled to get past her issues, and cursed himself that he hadn't been there for her in the way she needed. After inwardly going over it, he decided to be as honest as possible.

'The first time it happened, I threw up. I was in a room full of people, and it got on top of me. The smell. The sight of the blood . . . it plagued me afterwards for a long time. You were a big factor in me learning to push past it.'

'How?'

'I love you. You've constantly been good for my life. You made me want to be better, and the vibes were good. That helped me, even without me realising. Being able to admit that to myself, and to have you forgive me after that bullshit with Raider that time, it was big for me.'

Lorraine smiled at him, but as quickly as it came, the smile vanished.

'I don't know how I could do that.'

'You focus on the important facts: Raider was a horrible man. He had no redeeming qualities. He wasn't trying to do right. Instead, he wanted to do wrong to everyone, you more than the rest. Even his son couldn't make him fix up. It could have easily been you that died.' Natty held Lorraine's hand. 'You did what you had to do . . . just like I said to you last time. The fact you're reacting as you have, it's just a sign that you're a good person.'

They sat in silence for a moment.

'What about you?' Lorraine delicately asked. Natty scratched his cheek with his free hand, staring at the *Netflix* screen, caught up in the advert for a film.

'I've never done it for fun. Every time I've done it, I had to. It's business. That's what I'm in. It's kill or be killed, and I count on you, Jaden, and the people I keep close, to get me through it.'

'What about the morality line?' Lorraine asked, absorbing what Natty had said.

'I don't really know what to say to you,' said Natty. 'All I know is that the people that I did it to get little of my sympathy. Raider should get none of yours. He wanted to kill you. Do what you need to do, but don't get any deeper than that.'

Lorraine sighed.

'I guess I just need time,' she said. 'My manager isn't helping either.'

Natty frowned, glancing at her.

'What do you mean? What are they saying?'

'It's nothing major, Nat. They're just . . . I don't know. The things we've been speaking about, I'm trying to deal with that along with focusing on my day-to-day at work. My manager . . . Angela . . . she's fairly new to the business. I don't think she likes me.'

'Lo,' said Natty. 'If anyone at work is troubling you —'

'It's not that. I'm just trying to cope. I went to my doctor recently.'

'Is everything okay?' Natty's frown deepened.

'I'm stressed. I need to keep working through things, and work isn't the best place to do that, so the doctor signed me off.'

Natty nodded.

'Why don't you quit?'

Lorraine glanced at Natty, tilting her head.

'I like my job, Nat. It's just a bad time.'

'You could still work. You're the smartest person I know. Work for yourself if you need to. At least that way, you can do everything on your terms. The money isn't a problem. I've more than got you covered.'

Before Lorraine could respond, there was a knock at the door. They looked at one another, both startled.

'Are you expecting someone?' Lorraine asked. Natty chuckled.

'This is your place, remember?'

Lorraine smiled, then stood.

'I'll see who it is. It might be my mum, but she normally rings rather than just show up.'

Lorraine went to the door, and Natty glanced through the options on the screen, wondering if they could make it through another film. None of the tv shows appealed to him. He considered turning it off and putting on some music instead.

'Nat?' Lorraine's voice sounded strange. He glanced up and jumped to his feet without thinking.

Lisa was next to Lorraine, glancing at him, her eyes twinkling in amusement. Natty stared dumbly at the pair, not understanding what was happening. Lorraine shot him a strange look.

'She said she knows you,' she said, her eyes searching Natty's.

'Yeah . . .' Natty found his voice, 'she works for me . . . for my uncle.'

Lorraine and Lisa shook hands, Lisa smiling. Natty knew the smile was fake. His mind was still trying to catch up and make sense of what was happening. *What the hell was Lisa playing at?*

'You have a beautiful home,' Lisa gushed, looking around the room. 'It's really… homely. Perfect for a happy family.'

'Thank you,' replied Lorraine, still looking confused.

'I'm jealous. I hope someday I can find a man to share a home like this with.'

Natty stared at Lisa, alarmed. Lorraine's eyes flicked between the pair of them.

'Lisa, did you say? Can I grab you a drink or anything?'

'She doesn't need a drink,' Natty interrupted, not liking Lisa's disingenuous approach. 'I'll be back in a minute,' he said to Lorraine, leading Lisa outside.

Lorraine frowned at the pair as Natty pulled Lisa away.

'What the fuck are you playing at?' Natty hissed as he stood outside with Lisa. The nonchalant expression on her face only annoyed him further.

'I wanted to speak to you.'

'That could have been arranged without you fucking ambushing me. How the hell did you know I was here?'

'Where else would you be? You're always here,' said Lisa simply. 'What are you so worried about?'

'Cut the shit,' Natty snapped. 'You knew exactly what you were doing, showing up like that.'

Lisa's expression turned sultry, eyes boring into Natty's as she shot him a lascivious look. Instantly, her expression changed, and she was all business.

'My plan failed. I thought you should know.'

'That probably doesn't happen to you very often,' Natty remarked. Lisa shrugged.

'Danielle tried to set me up. I don't know how she got onto me, but I met Roman at a party she had. They're definitely close, but he must have said something.'

'What happened?'

'She tried to invite me to a spa, but her tone . . . everything about it was off. She offered to pay, and she was desperate to get me out in public the same day.'

'So, you went? You're supposed to be smarter than that,' Natty chided.

Lisa rolled her eyes. 'Of course, I didn't go. I went to Danielle's later to show her how I felt. Roman was waiting for me with some men. I got away, but it was tough.'

'Are you okay?' Natty asked softly. He knew Lisa's skill set, but it was still a lot to go through.

'You don't need to worry about me,' said Lisa curtly, her tone surprising Natty.

'Fair enough.'

'I'll speak with Clarke and let him know what's gone down. I'll go to ground for a while. A lot of what I do relies on secrecy, so some time out is best for everyone.'

'Look after yourself, Lis,' said Natty. 'Either check in with me or Clarke regularly. Just announce yourself if you need me,' he joked.

'Got it, boss.' Lisa's eyes searched Natty's again, and their stare-down lasted almost a minute, before she nodded and left. Natty watched her slip into the darkness.

Roman had played it well, luring Lisa to him. Natty didn't know how he'd suspected her, but it said a lot about his instincts.

Natty needed to take him out for good. He couldn't rely on Lisa as much now if Roman had made her.

Heading back inside, the television was turned off, the space where they'd been sitting cleared. Lorraine was in the kitchen washing up. Natty stood in the doorway, surveying her. If she heard him, she said nothing.

'Are you okay?'

'Yeah, just tidying up,' said Lorraine. 'Did you sort out your business?' Her tone was neutral.

'Yeah,' said Natty, not knowing what else to say.

'Lisa seems nice . . .' *Same tone.* Natty hoped it wouldn't turn awkward.

'She's quirky, but she's alright.'

'She looks like a supermodel . . .' Lorraine sounded incredulous now. 'How can she be involved in your business? Look at her.'

'Looks can be deceiving. She's not to be taken lightly. She's dangerous.'

Lorraine nodded, continuing her washing up. Natty stepped into the room and helped her, standing alongside her in silence. Despite his words, Lorraine wasn't assured. She'd never seen Natty react in the way he had. He'd leapt to his feet when Lisa came in, and he'd seemed nervous when he saw her. Add to that the fact he immediately took her outside . . . Lorraine wasn't sure.

Deciding she would think about what she'd witnessed, she filed it away for future pondering.

CHAPTER TWENTY-EIGHT

TWO DAYS after Lisa's visit, Natty linked up with Clarke. They met at a new safe house just off Roundhay Road, behind Tescos.

Natty sat at the kitchen table, sipping a hot drink. As was his custom, Clarke remained upright.

'Why do you always do that?' Natty asked.

'Do what?'

'Stand up. You're old. You should be off your feet.'

'I'm old, but I'm not dead,' said Clarke. 'I like to stay upright where I can.'

'Fair enough. Have you spoken with Lisa?'

'Yesterday. She told me about her plan. I think it's the right move.'

'I need to move against Roman. Clearly, he's back in the thick of it. It's looking more likely he was the one who targeted Mitch.'

'Maybe,' said Clarke, frowning. 'Something about it seems off. If Roman had the drop on Mitch, you'd expect him to send more people, rather than a single man. That's the sort of thing you'd do if you wanted to hide your involvement.'

Natty's stomach dropped, trying to maintain a neutral expression. Clarke was perceptive, and extremely good at what he did. Natty needed to be careful and to ensure he let nothing slip.

'Roman can be crafty. He's shown it before, like when he poisoned our testers. I'll get him, regardless. Maybe that will calm Mitch down.'

'He's behind those other murders.'

'What murders?' asked Natty.

'The other dealers that died recently. We did that,' explained Clarke.

'Why?' Natty was surprised. The fact he hadn't been aware was another sign that Mitch was distancing himself from him.

'Mitch's orders. He told us to eliminate any major dealers linked to Roman's suppliers. There's a chance that spurred Roman to attack, but it doesn't fit.'

Natty mulled it over. He recalled the Asian man Brown had mentioned Mitch meeting with, wondering once again if it was all connected.

'Does Mitch have many Asians that he's close with?'

Again, Clarke frowned.

'He's made a lot of connections during his career. Remember just how long he's been in the game, Nat.'

'I know. I just think it's strange that he's randomly getting you to target dealers that are linked to an Asian supplier. The man that shot at me . . . I caught him and made him talk. A man named Mustafir paid him . Mustafir and his partner Ahmed are linked to Jakkar . . . the man Mitch warned us about when we had that meeting that time.'

Clarke leaned against the wall, closing his eyes for a moment, clasping his hands together.

'It seems there's a lot going on, but it's too early to speculate,' he said. 'It's suspicious, though. I'll give you that.'

Natty didn't follow up on what he'd said. Hopefully, he'd planted a seed within Clarke, and Clarke could use that to find more information for him. It had the additional benefit of keeping Clarke from getting close and unearthing his attempt on his uncle's life.

'Do you want another drink?' He asked the older man. 'I'm kinda thirsty now.'

———

ROMAN GLANCED BEHIND HIM, seeing nothing in the darkness before he climbed into the back of the blacked-out 4x4. Jamal waited for him, Ralph driving as per usual. Roman closed his door, giving Jamal an expectant look. Jamal nodded.

'We've looked at those spots we spoke about. Two of them have been bolstered. Rotating different men around the properties. They have cameras watching the surrounding areas.'

'What about the third?'

Jamal shook his head. 'Nothing so far. It would probably be our best shot if we were attacking, but they could be expecting it. Like we said, those are the main spots, though. We could do a lot of damage with the right sort of move.'

Roman scratched his chin, evaluating what he'd been told. None of it surprised him. He recalled how deeply the Dunns operated from when he'd been planning attacks with Keith. With the months that had passed, it was possible that the Dunns were growing complacent — despite the fact they were rotating at least two of their major spots.

'Keep it up, and keep out of sight. What about that other thing?'

Again, Jamal shook his head.

'No sign of her. She might have left the city, or she might be waiting us out. My boys have been asking about her discretely, but nothing. Has she tried to contact your bird?'

Roman scowled at him. 'She's not my bird. We're just cool,' he said, though the words sounded unconvincing even to him. Jamal smirked.

'Okay, bro. Has she?'

'No. She's not gonna contact her if she thinks she's trying to set her up. What do we do here? Keep up the hunt?'

'Seems pointless. Whoever this Steph bird is, she's small time. She lucked into a friendship with your bird, and then she came at us and got scared off. I say we let it go, and focus on the big fish.'

Roman didn't bother correcting Jamal this time.

———

DANIELLE WAS on her way to meet a client, nodding along to the *Lizzo* track playing through her AirPods. She was in the back of an Uber, mentally preparing herself for the night ahead. Usually, she met her clients in hotel rooms, but she travelled when needed, adding it to her fee.

As she listened to her music, Roman was on her mind. More often than not nowadays, that seemed to be the case, and she wasn't sure what to make of it.

Getting involved with him likely wasn't smart. She'd thought he was cute when they first met, and after Keith's murder, she'd wanted protection from Natty Deeds.

Keith's murder had stunned her. The act itself had been terrifying, but it was the detached manner in which Natty Deeds spoke to her that was the real horror. She wanted no part of that. She wasn't silly enough to go to the police. That never worked out. They couldn't protect her.

Roman could protect her. He was sharp and had a get-shit-done attitude. They'd hooked up, and she enjoyed the set and companion-ship, but Danielle had survived on her own for so long by remaining loose and unattached.

Now, she was complicit in setting people up.

She wondered if Roman had taken care of Steph like he'd planned. Under Roman's orders, she hadn't been back to her place since her attempt to set up her fake friend.

Danielle felt hurt and betrayed when Roman explained her connec-tion to Natty Deeds. Part of her didn't want to believe it, but she had no choice. Roman was clear that if they didn't get to Steph first, she would get to Danielle.

Still, she felt a pang of sadness at losing someone she seemed to get on with so well.

Danielle never suspected Steph was playing her. *Had she been so desperate for a friend — a genuine friend — that she'd turned off her brain?*

Danielle watched a few TikTok videos until she arrived. Climbing out, she took three quick breaths, getting into work mode. Her hips swayed as she approached, entering the house without knocking. As arranged.

The house was a roomy, three-bedroomed, richly furnished prop-erty. John was a generous tipper and passable lover. He would have champagne ready for her. Heading up the stairs, she heard music already playing. She recognised the *Ella Mai* song as one they'd played together before.

Danielle planted a sultry smile on her face and entered John's bedroom.

Stepping through the doorframe, she froze, her eyes widening as she forced down the instinct to scream.

John was slumped face-down on the bedroom floor, blood pooling around his body. On the bed sat Steph. Her gun was pointed at Danielle, and she had a bland expression on her face.

'I . . .' Danielle trembled, her throat constricting, 'It w-wasn't my fault.'

Steph smiled, her hand unwavering.

'Lisa,' she said.

Despite her terror, Danielle blinked.

'What?'

'I figured you deserved to know my real name.'

'No, I—'

The bang startled her, but the burning in her stomach was a pain she'd never experienced before. Her body felt weightless. She couldn't speak, blood billowing from her throat. Lisa pointed the gun at her head just as her eyes dimmed, and everything went dark.

Lisa watched Danielle's eyes close. She pulled the trigger again, the bullet slamming into Danielle's forehead. Gazing at her for a moment, Lisa stepped over her body, left the house, and disappeared down the street.

———

MITCH DUNN ADJUSTED the cuffs of his custom-made suit, heading into an exclusive restaurant. He'd eaten there many times, entertaining various potential partners and discussing ventures. He sauntered through the venue with a confidence he didn't truly feel, though he understood the facade was necessary.

His nerves had been shot since someone attempted to kill him. It was a reminder of the dangerous times back in the early 2000s, when watching his back had been a necessity every time he left the house. He'd fought hard to leave those days behind, but he'd grown soft, and nearly paid the price.

Jakkar waited, as he'd expected, knowing he would arrive first. Like Mitch, he'd dressed well in his tailored dark suit. He looked the same as he had the last time Mitch had seen him, nearly five years ago. Jakkar acknowledged Mitch with a nod.

Subtle jazz music played in the background of the establishment, creating a relaxed ambience. On the walls were various oil paintings of classic English portraits, complemented by decorative wall sconces. The tables were elegant, dressed in crisp, high-quality white linen. Mitch adjusted himself in the comfortable leather seating, giving a cursory glance around the room.

They ordered food, Mitch picking red wine and Jakkar water. It was as tense as Mitch expected. Despite the fact he'd called for the meeting, he understood that there would be a long silence; a war of wills on both sides. Mitch was speaking to a man of means and great power. As galling as it was, it wasn't often he spoke to people on his level.

Or above.

'You missed a wonderful service,' said Jakkar. He startled Mitch, though Mitch hid it well, refusing to show his confusion.

'Sameer's funeral,' Jakkar continued. 'It was a lovely service. Warm. Moving.'

Mitch saw straight through the subtext. This was Jakkar's way of mentioning the link between Sameer and Mitch.

'How long have you known?'

'Of your *business relationship* with Sameer?'

Mitch nodded.

'It became clear when Sameer began vetoing any attempt to move against you in Chapeltown.' Jakkar smiled. 'You're more resourceful than I gave you credit for.'

'I see,' said Mitch. 'What I don't understand is why you would overplay your hand, Jakkar.'

Jakkar's brow furrowed, clearly confused by the question. Mitch wasn't convinced.

'You didn't make it to his level unless you were skilled in all fields.

Including acting. The attempt on my life. The wounding of my body-guard.' Mitch locked eyes with Jakkar. 'Funding Roman and the others is one thing. A direct attack is another.'

Jakkar chuckled, holding his reply until their food arrived, and the server had dispersed.

'I'd wondered why you wanted to meet . . . It's amusing to know that you have enemies other than me. Let me point something out . . . Your killers are eliminating numerous mid-level dealers. Maybe one of their subordinates could be behind your misfortune.'

Mitch swallowed a mouthful of food. 'That's the sort of thing you would say if you wanted to hide your involvement.'

Jakkar grinned, his smug demeanour aggravating Mitch.

'I don't need to. My people wouldn't miss. Had I deemed it necessary, you would already be dead.'

'Mine don't either,' said Mitch venomously.

Jakkar put down his knife and fork, using his napkin to wipe his mouth. 'You played the game, Mitch. This time, you lost.'

Bristling with rage, Mitch said nothing as Jakkar dropped a stack of money on the table for the bill, then left.

CHAPTER TWENTY-NINE

ROMAN GLANCED AT JAMAL, trying to rein in his anger.

'Are you sure?'

Jamal nodded.

'A few different people are reporting it. She was found dead at some dude's house. The dude got it too. Multiple gunshots. If you've got a link in the station, let me know.'

Roman could see the pity on Jamal's face, though the soldier's tone was respectful. Roman had been linked to Danielle. He wondered if the police would want to speak with him.

It was a stress for another time, though. He'd received a phone call from Ahmed that morning, insisting they needed progress. He would have to make his move against the Dunns, and soon.

When Jamal left, Roman lit a spliff, Danielle remaining on his mind. She had agreed to help, but guilt over getting her involved in the situation swirled around his body. The potent weed helped, but couldn't fully take his mind off things.

Roman liked Danielle, that much was clear. He didn't like what she did for a living, and was repulsed by the fact she'd had a thing with his friend, but he'd liked her company, and always admired that she simply owned everything she did. She didn't back away from it. She never backed down from him.

There was a chance the police would see it as a crime of passion, attempting to paint him as a jealous suitor, but Roman knew differently. *Steph* was behind it. He'd sensed there was something strange about her from the first time they'd met. She'd taken out one of his guys, and now she had taken out Danielle.

All because Roman hadn't properly protected her.

He'd looked further into Steph's background, but still couldn't find anything.

Ultimately, it didn't matter. She would die along with the rest of them.

———

Despite her conversation with Natty, Lorraine couldn't stop thinking about Lisa and the way Natty reacted to her. Lorraine trusted him, but she couldn't deny his womanising past.

Lorraine knew he liked his life with her and Jaden, but now she wondered if he was bored with them. Based on his status, he no doubt had his share of women trying to get with him.

Lorraine recalled the period when Natty was furious at her about Raider seeing Jaden, and wasn't talking to her. For over a month, he'd maintained his distance, and only the circumstances of Raider's death brought them back together. She'd never heard Natty mention Lisa and wondered if something had happened between them then.

Lorraine wasn't sure what to think. She'd never seen Natty react as he did, and when he'd leapt to his feet, he looked unnerved. She couldn't shake her gut feeling that there was more to the situation than met the eye.

———

'It's possible,' said Rosie. A day had passed. She, Lorraine, and Lorraine's mum sat in Lorraine's living room drinking. She'd filled them in on Natty and Lisa, wanting their opinions.

'You think he did something with her then?'

Rosie shook her head. 'It's possible, but I can't see Natty straying. That man adores you, and even before you became a couple, he loved you and Jaden. He wouldn't do anything to jeopardise that.'

'Mum? What do you think?'

'Natty would never step out on you. Ever. I agree with everything Rosie said, but there's another factor you're not acknowledging,' her mum said.

'Which is?'

'With you and Natty, what is the one consistent factor between you?'

'I don't know, mum,' said Lorraine. 'You're going to have to spell it out for me.'

'All of your problems stem from miscommunication. Things between you don't get resolved, because you don't share everything, and you fall out. Sit down, talk with him properly, and let him know how you're feeling.'

Lorraine considered the words for a moment. It was true. Often, when they fell out, it was because somebody was hiding something. Most of the time, it was to protect the other, but it didn't stop tempers flaring. Lorraine resolved to speak to Natty.

Taking a deep breath, she smiled back at her mum and Rosie.

'Thanks for the advice. I'll speak to him.'

———

SPENCE COVERTLY STUDIED Rosie as she ate. They were sitting at his kitchen table, making general conversation. Spence had cooked earlier, the guilt over speaking with Anika hanging heavily over him. Despite how relaxed he'd felt after the phone conversation, he was doing Rosie a disservice, yet he couldn't help it. Anika was a good sounding board, and he was reminded of the woman she had once been, as they spoke.

'Did you train today?' Rosie suddenly asked. Spence blinked. He'd grown too caught up in his thoughts and hadn't realised she was watching him.

'I did earlier,' said Spence. He and Stefon had done some shooting practice in the morning, and he'd done a short upper-body workout at the gym.

'You can tell. Lately, you've put on some muscle.'

'I'm enjoying it. Just trying to stay healthy,' said Spence. There was something about Rosie's expression and her words that unnerved him. For a moment, he wondered if she knew about Anika, but dismissed it. The idea of telling her that he'd been speaking with his ex, of sharing his thoughts and feelings, struck him, but again, he dismissed it.

Rosie had been through a lot during her association with him. Spence didn't want to make it worse.

'Can I ask you something?' Rosie suddenly asked, again taking Spence by surprise.

'Of course,' he replied, bracing himself for the worst.

'Do you think Natty would ever cheat on Lorraine?'

Immediately, Spence shook his head.

'Definitely not. Where did that come from?'

'I spoke with Lorraine. She and Natty were at home, and a woman came to the door. Natty knew her. It was about business, but Lorraine said Natty reacted like he was under attack. Apparently, it looked really weird.'

Spence could only think of one woman who would show up without a word and cause Natty to react in such a fashion. He wondered what Lisa's game was, and what she'd wanted to happen.

'We deal with some characters, but Natty wouldn't ever do that.'

'How can you be so sure? I mean, Natty's a good-looking guy. He's popular, and he has money. Why wouldn't some woman want to get that?'

Spence read between the lines. Rosie wasn't just referring to Natty.

'It doesn't matter what they'd want. Only what Natty wants. He loves Lorraine. Honestly, she's likely the only woman he's ever loved.'

Rosie gazed at Spence for a moment.

'If he ever did cheat, would you tell me?'

'Rosie, he wouldn't do that.'

'That's not what I asked you. Would you tell me?'

Looking Rosie in the eye, Spence told his first lie of their relationship.

'Yes. Yes, I would.'

———————

'EVERYTHING'S STILL on the up then?'

Spence nodded. It was the following day, and he and Natty had been sat together for over an hour, talking business. There were the usual rumblings of discontent, but on a whole, things were running as usual.

'I figured we'd take a dip, but we're still smashing it on all levels. Roman's people have been out a bit more, but people seem reluctant to work with them.'

'What about those dealers that were killed? Anyone saying anything?' Natty asked, his tone listless.

Spence shook his head, trying not to over-analyse his friend. Natty seemed less energetic than usual, as if he was just going through the motions. He'd noticed it immediately, but wasn't sure how to bring it into the conversation.

'Just rumours about who's behind it. There's talk about new gangs wading in trying to take over, but it doesn't have much steam.'

'It's Mitch,' said Natty. Spence tilted his head, his expression quizzical.

'What?'

'Mitch is behind the hits. Our people did them,' Natty explained.

'You?'

'Not me. I've been kept out of it, but I was told it was us.'

Spence rubbed the knuckles on his left hand.

'What the hell could have caused that? I mean, your uncle can throw down, but he usually likes things quiet, or things done quickly and efficiently. The dudes who were killed weren't a threat. They made money, but they weren't infringing on our territory or any shit like that, so what's the point?'

Natty took a moment to appreciate his friend. Spence had a solid way of grasping an issue and cutting past the babble to get to the point.

'I have no proof, but I think Mitch has an ongoing agenda with the Asians.'

'Which Asians?' Spence frowned.

'The ones that supply Roman. Ahmed and Mustafir. I have a feeling it could spell trouble for the entire team.'

'How? You think they'll come after us all?' Spence asked.

'I'm not sure. I'm still putting it all together.'

'What about the shooting attempt on Mitch? People are talking about that,' Spence said.

Natty had heard some chatter too. People had continued to speculate about who was after Mitch, and the fact no one had been confirmed as having been behind it only added further credence that they didn't know.

So far, no one suspected him, and he only hoped he could keep it going, and keep diverting any attention he might receive.

Evidently, he wasn't doing a good job, because Spence was staring at him.

'What's going on?'

'What do you mean?'

'You look funny. Do you know something about Mitch that you're not saying?'

'No. Me and my unc aren't really clicking at the moment. If they have a theory on what went down, no one's telling me. I'm reporting to Clarke now. You could almost call it a demotion.'

Spence continued looking at Natty, who wondered if Spence knew he was lying. He definitely suspected something.

'What's going on with Lisa?'

Natty looked up at the ceiling, letting out an awkward laugh.

'She and Lorraine met.'

Spence chuckled.

'Rosie mentioned that. I'd have given my right foot to be a fly on the wall for that meeting. What the hell happened?'

'Let's see . . . she turned up at Lorraine's. Fuck knows how she got the address. Lorraine let her in, and I jumped in the air like it was fucking cartoon.'

Spence was howling with laughter now, slapping the table.

'Absolutely brilliant!'

'It was anything but brilliant. I don't know what she was playing at, but Lorraine's been dodgy ever since.'

'That was what Lisa wanted, I'd imagine. She could have contacted you a dozen different ways, but she has an agenda where you're concerned.'

'She came to tell me that Roman made her. She learned Roman and Keith's ex were getting close. They nearly set her up, but she got free.' Natty blew out a breath. 'I shouldn't have kissed her.'

Spence watched Natty, a sudden urge to mention Anika coming over him. It was the perfect time. Natty was in a funk over a mistake with another woman, and Spence could relate.

For a moment, Natty looked back at him, and both men looked like they had something to say. The moment passed, though, and they moved on.

CHAPTER THIRTY

MITCH REMAINED at his safe house the day after his meeting with Jakkar. He had yet to return home, and was considering moving to a new location. At the moment, he had more pressing matters.

Namely Jakkar.

He hadn't admitted to being behind the attack, but he remained Mitch's prime suspect. Nothing about the situation filled him with any joy, and the idea that Jakkar could humble him was galling. Mitch had worked too hard. Sacrificed too much. He would not allow it to end like this.

There was a knock at the door. Clarke was led to him by one of his guards, followed by Lisa. Mitch looked at his best soldiers. He hadn't seen Lisa in a while, but she appeared as beautiful and dangerous as ever.

'Do you need anything?' Clarke asked. Lisa had slouched on a loveseat, and he'd taken up his usual position.

'I need progress,' said Mitch. 'What is going on out there?'

'Same as last time,' replied Clarke.

'That's not good enough,' thundered Mitch. 'We should have had this all sorted by now. You know the play. Eliminate everyone, and keep it contained. I'll ask again: what is going on out there?'

'A lot of targets have gone to ground. They're scared, and they know the score. We could probably get them, but it'll take a while, and it will take significant resources.'

'You should have taken them out in one fell swoop,' said Mitch. He knew he was being unreasonable, but he didn't care. This was his team. If he wanted to take out his mood on them, that was his prerogative.

'That's not practical. You said we have a way of working, and that's not it. Doing too much, too quickly would lead to mistakes. We took out the biggest targets first,' said Clarke.

'I don't want to hear that. Just get it done,' said Mitch. 'Spend what you need to, but I want any links to those suppliers eliminated.'

Clarke and Lisa left a short while after. Mitch poured himself a drink, still bristling with anger. Jakkar was a big problem, especially now that he had no leverage.

For now, Mitch needed to keep shining a light on him. If there was one thing he was sure of, it was that Jakkar was more powerful from the shadows.

———

'HE'S TWEAKING.'

Clarke shook his head. He didn't use the same language as Lisa, but that didn't mean she was wrong. Mitch was keeping things from him. It wasn't Clarke's place to question orders, but without the full picture, he was firing blind, and that was dangerous for their people.

They climbed into the car. Clarke drove, and Lisa sat in the passenger seat, connecting her phone to the aux cable. A song began playing, but Clarke didn't have a clue what it was. He turned it down a little as he drove.

'He's under a lot of pressure. Things like this don't happen on his watch.'

'That's more than pressure. He looks half-pissed, half-terrified. I can't see a couple of gunmen putting that kinda fear in him, which means there's something else going on,' said Lisa.

'Whatever it is, we'll need to rely on Mitch finishing it. He's told us what to do.'

'He has,' said Lisa. 'What's Natty saying about it?'

Clarke shot her a quick look. 'We talked about this.'

'I'm just asking a question. He's the guy on the streets, so he must have something to say about it.' Lisa's innocent act would have fooled anyone other than him. Clarke shook his head.

'He's pissed off. He can't hide that temper of his . . . not from me,' he said as they drove down a long road. 'There's something going on with him and his uncle. I don't know what, but there's tension.'

'Maybe you should speak with him and find out what's on his mind? I mean, this all feels like it's escalating,' said Lisa.

'I'll take that under consideration. For now, you need to get back to wherever you've been staying. That job you did on the girl was risky. She's a civilian.'

'*Was* a civilian. And she should have thought about that before she set me up.' There was a bite to Lisa's tone.

'Still, it was risky,' said Clarke. 'What you do relies on smoke and mirrors for maximum effect. Roman shouldn't have got close to you.'

'He won't again. Danielle was a liability. Natty should have killed her when he dropped Keith,' replied Lisa.

Clarke didn't bother replying. He loved Lisa, but at times, there was no talking to her.

———

Stefon strolled into Natty's favourite safe house, pleased that his cousin was there. As Stefon stepped into the kitchen, he was in the middle of a conversation with two workers, standing by the back door. Spence sat nearby with a cup of coffee. Stefon nodded at him, then took a seat at the table.

'Everything good?' Spence asked.

'Yeah. Why wouldn't it be?'

'You've got a look in your eye. I know how you two get around each other,' said Spence. Stefon chuckled. He enjoyed how perceptive Spence was. It always made for interesting conversation.

Truth was, Stefon didn't know what to expect from speaking with Natty. Ever since he'd spoken to Tia, the thought of Natty dismissing her had gnawed at him. Stefon had done a lot wrong in his life, but he always did right by his mum. It was how he'd been brought up. Natty's actions were disrespectful, and someone needed to call him out on it.

Someone was about to.

'We're just gonna talk. That's all,' he said.

'That's not as convincing as you want it to be,' said Spence, shaking his head.

'You don't have to be involved. This is on me.'

'Involved in what?'

Both men glanced up. They hadn't realised Natty had finished his conversation, and was now watching them.

The two workers shared a look and quickly left the room, sensing it was going to get bad.

'We need to talk,' said Stefon, standing.

Natty's jaw tightened as he eyeballed his older cousin.

'Okay. Let's talk.'

'I want to know what's going on,' said Stefon.

'With what?'

'With you. I was gonna keep this to myself, but you've changed, cuz. The money changed you. All these people kissing your arse has changed you. You've forgotten where you came from.'

'You don't know anything about it,' spat Natty. 'I don't know what's got you twitching and talking shit, and honestly, I don't really care. There are real things going on right now.'

'When was the last time you saw your mum?'

Natty scowled. Stefon's anger made more sense now. He could only imagine what his mum had filled Stefon's head with.

'I've got nothing to say to her,' he replied, fingers twitching as he tried to control his mounting annoyance.

'Yeah, she told me. What the fuck is going on? No matter what happens, cuz . . . you always take care of family, especially your mum. You know better than that.'

'You've obviously spoken to her. Did she tell you why we're not speaking?' Natty's tone was deceptively calm.

'It doesn't matter why,' said Stefon.

'You can't say that. Look at you . . . charging in here, all emotional, when you don't have a fucking clue what's going on. You don't know the facts, so you need to back the fuck up and stay out of it.'

'You two need to calm down,' said Spence, speaking for the first time. The tension between the two cousins was beyond palpable, and he didn't want to ignite it further.

Stefon stepped towards Natty, ignoring Spence's words.

'I think you need to remember that you're the little cousin,' he said.

'I think *you* need to remember that I'm not a punk,' replied Natty, nose-to-nose with Stefon, waiting for him to make the first move. Stefon's eyes narrowed.

'Guys! Fucking listen.'

Both men looked to Spence. He got between them, forcing them apart.

'You're family. There's a lot going on, and you're stressed, but fighting isn't gonna fix things. You need to bury this, and you know I'm right.'

Natty nodded, fighting against the part of him that wanted to tear Stefon limb from limb.

'I'm the one in charge,' he finally said to his cousin. 'You better decide whether you can work for me. If you can't . . . then leave.'

Stefon nodded to Spence, then went to leave the room. At the door, he paused.

'You're not in charge yet.'

With that, he left. Natty watched him go, nostrils flaring.

'Nat, what the hell was that?' Spence asked after a few seconds. He couldn't believe how quickly that had escalated, and how close the cousins were to fighting.

The news about Natty and his mum was surprising. They'd always had a contentious relationship, but he knew Natty always made an effort to spend time with her. The fact was he wasn't speaking to her anymore was huge.

'Nothing.'

'I'm not trying to be nosy. You know that, fam, but what's going on with your mum? Why wouldn't you—'

'I said it's nothing, Spence. Just fucking leave it alone,' thundered Natty. He rubbed his forehead and took a deep breath. 'I'm sorry, bro. I didn't mean to snap at you, but it's not worth talking about. I've gotta go, but I'll check you later.'

Natty touched his fist and left the room. Spence stared at the door. The mystery surrounding Natty just kept growing. It felt like there were layers of family politics involved, and Spence couldn't make sense of any of it.

Natty and his uncle seemed tense. His uncle was making Natty report to Clarke only a few months after putting him in charge. Natty was having problems with his mum.

It didn't fit.

Glancing around one more time, Spence took out his phone and called Anika.

'Hey,' he said when she answered. 'Are you okay?'

'Yeah. Are you? You sound stressed,' she replied.

'I don't know. I was just with Natty, and he's in a bad way, but I can't get him to talk about it.'

'What do you mean?'

'I tried, and he snapped at me. I didn't want to push,' admitted Spence. Somehow, admitting it to Anika felt less shameful.

'If you think something's wrong with your friend, you have to try again . . . right?'

'I suppose.' Spence blew out a breath. 'Sorry. I don't even know why I rang you. You were just the first person I thought of.'

'You can speak to me anytime, Spence. Even if it's just for a few minutes.' Anika hesitated. 'Do you . . . we could go out for dinner sometime, and talk some more?'

The word *no* was on the tip of Spence's tongue, but he stopped himself.

'Okay. Dinner sounds good,' he said.

CHAPTER THIRTY-ONE

WHEN NATTY RETURNED to Lorraine's, he was still furious about his blowup with Stefon. If Spence hadn't been there once again, he knew that they would have come to blows. Long-term, he couldn't allow it to continue. If his cousin wouldn't respect him as a boss, he would need to take decisive action. Spence might object, but he would ultimately go along with Natty. Clarke and the others wouldn't care.

So, why didn't he?

Stefon was a terrific earner, and he was tough, adding further credibility to the organisation. Natty didn't want to move him over a personal issue, but he couldn't perceive the idea of potentially backing down from him. If other people in the organisation saw Stefon talking to Natty as he was, they'd think it was open season.

He should have warned Stefon about his mum, that much was clear. Natty knew how manipulative she could be, and he also knew that Stefon had a close relationship with his own mum. It was inevitable that he would learn they weren't talking.

So, why didn't he?

Natty couldn't understand why he felt so strongly about holding things back from Stefon and Spence. He'd had the opportunity to tell them about his mum and her knowledge of his dad's murder, but he didn't.

Natty considered why. At first, he wanted to keep low-key, but things changed. Natty wanted to share with Spence, but it was clear that Spence was holding something back too. It made Natty wary of sharing his own secrets.

Natty blew out a breath, sinking further into Lorraine's comfortable sofa. There was so much he needed to sort out, and he needed to do it quickly.

It had been months since he'd spoken with his mum, yet here she was, still in his business.

Natty played video games with Jaden after dinner. They were picking new teams on *Fifa*, when Jaden turned to him.

'Natty, can I ask you something?'

'Of course,' replied Natty, picking the away kit for his team.

'How old were you when you properly started liking girls?'

Natty hid his smile. 'Is this about Rachel?'

'Yeah,' said Jaden, then he paused. 'No. Kinda. She's too old for me, and she goes out with your friend's son.'

'Okay, so what brought this on?'

'I just . . . dunno. I think I like a girl at school, but I don't want my friends to laugh at me. I think she likes me too, but she's really nice to everyone.'

'I was about your age, maybe younger, but I wish I'd waited sometimes,' said Natty.

'Why?' The pair had started the game, but Jaden paused it before they could kick off, the PlayStation controller still in his hand.

'Because I had my whole life to get used to girls, and I rushed it. I rushed a lot of the key aspects about women, and honestly, I didn't really get it right until I met your mum.'

That made Jaden smile.

'I'm glad you two are together.' Jaden unpaused the game, then instantly paused it again. 'I wish you were my dad, Natty.'

Natty was floored, unable to believe what Jaden had just said. He felt tears springing to his eyes, trying to process one of the nicest things anyone had ever said to him.

'I am your dad, Jay. I loved you from the moment you were born, and I promise you, I will always be there for you.'

Jaden nodded.

'I know.'

That was it. They went back to playing their game, but there was a new level of comfort between them, and they played the rest of their games with wide smiles on their faces.

Natty left Jaden's room, telling him to brush his teeth and wash his face. He headed downstairs, noting Lorraine was still on her MacBook, a serious expression on her face. She had been in a weird mood all evening, but he hadn't had the chance to speak with her about it, having been in a funk of his own.

'Your son is definitely on the lookout for a girlfriend,' he joked. 'I tried to avoid giving him too many *Natty Deeds* answers, but it'll be interesting to see what kind of girl he ends up liking.'

Lorraine smiled, but didn't respond. Natty studied her, noticing that her face looked a little drawn. He frowned.

'Are you okay, babe? You look a little peaky.'

'I'm fine.' She closed the MacBook and put it on the coffee table. 'Can I ask you something? It's treading old ground, but I can't let it go.'

'Course,' replied Natty. It was shaping up to be one of those evenings, where his answers were in demand, by the looks of things.

'Lisa.'

Natty held his reaction better this time.

'What about her?'

'Why did you jump to your feet when she came in?'

'Because I was surprised to see her,' admitted Natty. He couldn't give Lorraine the full story, but that part at least was true. 'I didn't expect to see her.'

'So?'

'So, she works for the crew,' said Natty. 'I associate her with badness, and when I'm with you and Jaden, you're my sanctuary. I don't want business brought around you.'

Lorraine nodded, before continuing.

'Have you slept with her?'

'No, I haven't. You're the only woman I want to sleep with, Lo . . . right now if you're up for it.'

Lorraine ignored his attempt to lighten the mood.

'We were apart for over a month, Nat. When that thing with Raider happened, we weren't seeing each other.'

'We weren't talking, but we were still a couple, Lo. At least, I hope we were.' Natty raised his eyebrows, his face a question.

'You might have thought otherwise,' said Lorraine.

'Did you?' Natty countered, his voice low, bracing himself for the answer. 'You were around Raider. Did you sleep with him when we weren't talking?'

'Are you serious?' Lorraine's voice rose, her eyes flashing dangerously.

Natty took a deep breath.

'No. I don't think you would do that, but we need to trust one another. I love you, and I don't want to sleep with anyone else.'

Natty held out his arms, relieved when Lorraine fell into them. He hugged her tightly, his expression tight, uncomfortable with the conversation they'd had.

The same expression was on Lorraine's face, but he couldn't see it.

————

STEFON STOOD in front of Mitch Dunn, just about keeping his composure. He'd reached out to request a meeting, having previously made the acquaintance of Clarke. He hadn't known if Mitch would agree, but he was pleased he had. It had taken two days to set up.

Stefon didn't know what was going to happen with Natty, but if he had Mitch on his side, it would make getting rid of him much harder. He'd grown accustomed to the Leeds life again, and didn't intend on giving it up.

Stefon knew little about Mitch, but if there was one thing he was fully aware of, it was that Mitch was all about family. He knew that Mitch still gave money to Tia, and he had given Natty a top-tier position in the organisation. Stefon doubted he knew about Natty and his mum, and intended to find out if he was right.

Stefon was picked up at his house, blindfolded, then driven to the spot. It was over the top, but he understood the risk. They still hadn't learned who was responsible for the shooting, after all.

Mitch sat in a living room, signalling for Stefon to sit down when he was shown in. Mitch looked older than he had the last time Stefon saw him, but still good for his advanced years. He went to shake Mitch's hand, then thought better of it and sat down.

'Thanks for seeing me,' said Stefon. Mitch shook his head.

'Don't mention it. You're a good kid. I remember what you were like back in the day. Ty always liked you.'

'Thank you,' said Stefon, wondering if Mitch was implying he hadn't liked him. It was hard to tell with the cagey man. Pushing past it, he continued. 'Uncle Ty was a top guy. I learned a lot about how to move when I watched him way back when.'

Mitch nodded, keeping his expression neutral. It was tough talking about his brother. The good memories they had were overshadowed by the night he'd been forced to order his death. Though he maintained he'd done the right thing, it was still his family, and at times, the guilt ate away at him.

At least he'd done well by his son.

'My brother was a special guy. Nathaniel . . . he's an advanced version of Ty. Uses his brain a bit more, but he's got Ty's fire.'

Stefon snorted, unable to control it. Mitch looked at him quizzically. It wasn't the reaction he was expecting.

'What does that mean?'

'Natty's cool. He seems to be doing well, but I dunno . . . maybe he's in over his head. He's got a lot going on at the moment. One thing I'll say about Uncle Ty . . . he was always about family. I don't think his son inherited that.'

'What does that mean?' Mitch straightened in his seat, eyes bulging. *What had Nathaniel been planning?*

'Did you know he hasn't talked to his mum in months?'

Mitch visibly relaxed, relieved, but curious.

'What?' Mitch had continued sending money to Tia, but hadn't spoken to her since before Rudy died. He knew she held him responsible for Rudy's death, and he hadn't wanted to face her rage.

Her and Nathaniel not speaking was a shock, however. Nathaniel had said nothing to him about it.

'Yeah. She told me, and he confirmed it,' said Stefon.

'Why aren't they speaking?'

'I don't know,' said Stefon. 'She says it's all his fault, and he didn't really deny it when I confronted him.'

'You confronted him?' Mitch tilted his head.

'Course I did,' said Stefon, forgetting he was talking to the boss for a moment. 'That's family. Family always comes first, especially with mums.'

Mitch smiled.

'You're a good kid, Stef. I need you to keep an eye on things. You're right, Natty is under a lot of pressure, and this is a pivotal time for the team. I need you to step up when it's needed, and to stay on top of things. Can you do that for me?'

'Of course,' said Stefon, buoyed to be so well thought of by Mitch. He left soon after, leaving Mitch in the living room, deep in thought.

Mitch made himself a drink, mulling over the fresh development. It was possible that Natty's issues with his mum were the reason he didn't seem so invested in their organisation as of late.

Sipping his drink, he continued pondering this new puzzle, pleased by the distraction from his tension with Jakkar.

CHAPTER THIRTY-TWO

CLARKE AND LISA had kept themselves busy after their latest conversation with Mitch. Knowing he expected results, they had been on any of Roman's men they could find, whilst also trawling for any dealers connected to Roman's suppliers.

The suppliers were in the wind, though. There were rumours that at least two had seen the writing on the wall and left town.

No one knew the Dunns were involved, but there was a clear pattern. Someone was picking off dealers connected to Ahmed and Mustafir, and that was enough for them to take flight.

Using street talk, along with Lisa using her feminine charms to subtly gain information from several other sources, they finally made some progress.

Lisa and Clarke had tracked Roman to a safe house in Halton Moor. Posted down the street, they could see that Roman was taking no chances with his personal security. In the twenty minutes they'd been there, they'd spotted almost a dozen soldiers.

'That's Jamal,' said Clarke, handing his binoculars to Lisa. 'He's an old-school killer with a solid reputation. Vicious, but he's got a brain. He's worked all around Leeds, and even worked for Teflon. Spent a bit of time out of town too. That could be bad if he had the connections to bring more people in.'

'We could sort that now,' said Lisa, staring at the stocky man through the binoculars. 'Call backup, block off the street, ambush them both.'

'That's too risky,' said Clarke. 'They have a lot of men, they're ready for war, and look at their discipline. Look at how they're moving around, checking up on one another, and staying sharp. They could even have people in the surrounding houses, keeping a lookout.'

'We'd outnumber them,' Lisa pointed out. 'We could make a call now and have fifty people down here in fifteen minutes.'

'Agreed, but we have to pick the right battlefield. We're at war, and these guys know they're at war,' said Clarke. 'Even if we ambush them, it would likely lead to a protracted bloodbath. No one will like that result, least of all Mitch.'

Lisa shrugged, still not pleased with Mitch's attitude as of late. He was the boss, but there was something deep going on with him, and it irked her that she didn't know. If Clarke knew, he wasn't telling her, but Lisa was a good judge of character where her mentor was concerned. If Clarke knew anything, he'd have told her, she was sure of it.

'From the sounds of things, Mitch just wants it over. I think he would welcome any way of efficiently doing that.'

'It wouldn't be efficient,' said Clarke. He understood where Lisa was coming from, but he refused to work untidily.

'Okay,' said Lisa, not arguing the point. 'What do we do then?'

Clarke snapped some photographs of the soldiers milled around the property.

'We're going to leave. I'll call someone to relieve us, and they'll follow Roman wherever he goes. The rest of the soldiers, we'll look for opportunities to take out. I'll speak to Natty. Mitch wants him involved in this, but I haven't been checking in with him.'

'How's he supposed to be in the trenches with us, and also be running the team at the same time?' Lisa knew Natty had skills, but it seemed silly to pull him in both directions, especially at a critical time like this.

'That's a discussion for another time. Let's go. Keeping looking straight ahead as we drive by these lot.'

———

'THIS BETTER BE IMPORTANT,' said Natty, climbing out of his car. Brown had requested a meeting as soon as possible, and Natty had accommodated him. Brown was annoying, but easy enough to handle, and it was a nice distraction from everything else he had going on, namely Lorraine. She had surprised him when she'd confronted him about Lisa, and he found the drama tiresome.

Natty was equally annoyed with Lisa. She'd made the move purposefully, turning up to unsettle him and force a reaction. It had worked.

For Natty, that was the most annoying thing of all. He was supposed to be better than that, yet at every opportunity, he let Lisa get under his skin. Now, Lorraine was distrusting, and he had to placate a dangerous woman.

To Natty's surprise, Brown hadn't come alone. He had two other men with him. One was a youngish-looking black man with a cocky demeanour and an inflated build. The other was a burly, scowling white man with closely cropped dirty blond hair.

'I wouldn't contact you if it wasn't,' said Brown, scowling. 'Watch your tone too. I'm here for your benefit.'

'Sorry, darling, I forgot how sensitive you are,' said Natty mockingly. The two men with Brown glared at Natty, but he wasn't fazed. 'Who are these two?' He motioned to the pair.

'Friends of mine. They're on the level, so you don't have to watch what you say around them.'

'Am I supposed to be moved by that?' Natty locked eyes with Brown. He didn't care if the pair were offended. He wouldn't discuss business around them.

'Fine. Wait over there, lads. This won't take long.'

Neither man liked it, both shooting Natty death glares as they went to stand by the car Brown had driven in. Natty moved back a few paces, and Brown followed, rolling his eyes.

'Mate, if I wanted to bust you, I wouldn't need them to do it.'

'Whatever, chief. Just tell me what's on your mind,' said Natty.

'I want some reassurances.'

'About what? Seriously, what the fuck is this?' Natty couldn't believe Brown was bothering him over nothing.

'Bodies are dropping all over the place. That complicates things. I've told you in the past that my position is contingent on me actually arresting people once in a while. Seeing as you refuse to help me with that, throw me a bone and stop the shooting. End this bloody gang war now.'

'I don't know what war you're talking about, and I really don't have time for this nonsense.'

Brown looked at his men, then back at Natty, shaking his head, his eyes blazing with anger.

'I don't think you realise exactly what I've done for you, because you keep insisting on treating me like a mug. I suggest you fix up and sort it, before it's too late.'

Natty took a step towards Brown, doing a better job of hiding his anger.

'You can try to threaten me, but it won't get you anywhere. Fuck off if you don't want to be involved, but don't cry to me because you can't do your job.'

Brown's eyes widened, shocked by Natty's audacity. 'I think you need to remember what I've done for you.'

'And I think you need to remember that you came crawling to me,' Natty countered. 'It wasn't the other way around.'

'Don't get smart,' snapped Brown. 'Remember what I have over you, and show some manners.'

'What exactly do you have over me,' said Natty. Part of him wished he'd just called Brown's bluff earlier when the detective had confronted him. Maybe if he hadn't been in the middle of the Raider drama with Lorraine, he would have.

'I know what you did to Raider.'

'Oh?' Again, Natty stepped closer. 'Prove it then.'

Brown's expression was murderous. His two cronies straightened up, both aware of the growing tension.

'I warned you once, and I'm, going to warn you again, Deeds. You don't want me as an enemy, and you definitely don't want me digging into your background, dragging all your little dirty deeds into the light. You must have a short memory.' Brown let out a short, harsh laugh. 'You even tried offing your uncle, for fuck's sake.'

Natty laughed, refusing to let Brown know he'd got to him.

'Where did you get that one from?'

Brown grinned evilly. 'I'm not an idiot. Why else would you want information on him? Also, conveniently after I tell you about his routine, someone just happens to try to kill him? Pull the other one, Deeds.'

Natty snorted, inwardly cursing himself for not covering his tracks better. It had been an ill-thought-out plan, with too many holes and issues. Still, he would maintain his poker face around Brown, and keep him off-balance.

'You need more than, mate. You can try to run with it and see where it gets you, but I think you're smarter than that.'

'How much longer do we have to put up with this joker?' The black officer said, moving from the car and getting into Natty's face. 'He talks a lot for a scumbag. I say we use him and send a message to his shitty team.'

'Yeah?' said Natty, eyes gleaming. 'How do you plan on doing that?'

'Easy. We take you somewhere, finish you, and leave you for the other shitheads to fi—'

Natty stepped back and levelled him with a corker of a short right, knocking the man off his feet and to the ground, where he didn't move.

'Fucker!' The second man charged forward, but Brown blocked his path.

'No! We're not doing this. This isn't how it's going down,' he hissed, struggling to hold the man back as his colleague stirred on the ground.

Natty's fists clenched, ready to take them on if needed. Hitting the black officer had been stupid, but he was tired of people taking liberties with him.

When Brown had his friend under control, he turned back to Natty, panting with exertion.

'Deeds, this isn't the way. We can still do business, and we can play nice, but you need to give me summat. I want a good faith payment of fifteen grand. You give me that, I'll see it as a commitment to you making the right move going forward. Gimme that, and you'll learn everything I know about Roman, and the tidy little gang he's gathering around him.'

Natty said nothing. He already knew that Roman was reaching out to solid soldiers, including a hitter from back in the day named Jamal. He'd had a rushed conversation with Clarke in which this had been relayed to him, but he was in charge for a reason. If there was a chance to find out information they didn't already know, fifteen thousand would be a drop in the ocean to get that done.

'Think about it, Deeds. Don't think for too long, though. The walls are closing in, and I'm the best friend you've got.'

Brown and his colleague helped the man Natty had knocked out to his feet, leading him toward the car. Before he climbed in, he shot Natty a hateful glare, which Natty returned in kind.

As the trio drove away, he took a deep breath. Losing his temper and potentially giving Brown leverage had been a foolish move; the sort of move he'd have made a few years ago. Natty had left that side of him behind, and this was crunch time. He needed to be better; no two ways about it.

Climbing back into his car, he reversed and drove away.

CHAPTER THIRTY-THREE

SPENCE LAUGHED, shaking his head at something Anika had said. They were having dinner in Guiseley, at a small, out-of-the-way restaurant. It had a medley of different wooden furnishings of various shades, and each table had a small candle as a centrepiece.

So far, Spence was enjoying the night. When Anika was happy and engaged, she was like a different woman. During the evening, she had been congenial and charming, and she'd had him in stitches remembering stories from back in the day.

'I'd forgotten about that,' he admitted. 'It wasn't even the fact the dude fell over that was the funny part. It was the fact he got back up and tried chasing down that kid, and then fell again. His belly protected him.'

'I know,' said Anika, giggling. 'I can still see it all in my head. That was hilarious.'

Spence sipped his drink, wincing as he moved too quickly.

'What's wrong? Are you okay?' Anika asked, noticing the movement.

'I'm good. I came straight here from a workout, and I don't think I stretched properly,' he said.

'I noticed you looked bigger, but I didn't want to make it weird by pointing it out,' Anika replied.

Spence scratched the back of his neck. Rosie had recently said the same. His workouts with Stefon had done wonders for his physique. Best of all, he seemed to have more energy. He didn't know what kind of witchcraft Stefon was working with, but he knew his stuff, and knew how to target various body parts for maximum effect.

'Yeah, I've just been trying new things.'

'What does Rosie think?' Anika suddenly asked. Spence was flummoxed for a second. Anika hadn't brought up Rosie since the first time they'd spoken, when Spence had told her they were in a relationship.

'She likes it. I mean, she noticed, but we don't really talk about it,' said Spence.

'Why not?'

Spence shrugged. 'No reason. It's not a big deal, it's just something I wanted to do.'

'After you got shot.'

'Yes. After I got shot,' said Spence. Anika reached out and touched his hand, pulling away a second later as though scalded. A moment was enough. There had been a shooting pulse of electricity that surged up Spence's hand, and he knew she'd felt it too. He coughed, trying to avoid the moment growing more awkward.

'Sorry,' said Anika a second later. 'I didn't mean to . . . It's just, I can't get my head around you getting shot. I forgot myself for a second.'

'No harm done,' said Spence, not wanting to harp on it. They'd finished their meals a while ago, and Anika had ordered some ice cream for dessert, Spence declining. He'd indulged in a glass of wine, though, but wasn't impressed with the white wine they'd picked.

Neither spoke for a moment, but it didn't take long for Anika to break the silence.

'Does Rosie know?'

'Know what?'

'About us.'

'Us?' Spence said sharply. Anika blanched, hanging her head.

'Sorry, I didn't mean for that to come out as it did,' he added, feeling guilty.

'Don't worry about it.' Anika wiped her left eye. 'I probably deserve worse. I just wondered if she knew we were speaking.'

'She doesn't,' Spence admitted. 'I don't even know why I kept it from her. I just didn't say anything at first, and then it never seemed to get easier. Truth be told, I haven't told anyone.'

'Not even Natty? Still?'

Spence shook his head. 'Not even him.'

'It's not like you lot to keep things from each other.'

'There's been a bit of that lately,' admitted Spence. 'I mean . . . he's my brother, but there's something between us. There's a gulf, and it's growing. I don't know how to stop it. I tried talking to him, but he didn't want to hear it.'

'Is this when he snapped at you?'

Spence nodded, taking a deep breath.

'He apologised, but I can't get him to talk to me. And I can't talk to him about the shit I'm going through. Some of it he's heard before.'

Anika eyed him. 'We can talk about something else if you'd prefer.'

'Sure,' said Spence, shrugging. 'Let's talk about you.'

Anika's expression seemed to grow more intense before she spoke.

'I've been thinking about something for a while. In fact, it's one of the reasons I wanted to do this,' she started.

Spence's stomach lurched. The meal was feeling like a mistake. He'd enjoyed the night, and that was the main issue. He'd enjoyed it more than expected. Anika was his past. She had cheated on him and left him in the lurch with nothing more than a note, and yet here he was. Indulging her, speaking about the past, liking her company.

So much was up in the air at the moment, and it wasn't easy talking to Rosie about it. She was so unnerved and worked up from the ambushes and attacks of the last year that she didn't want to discuss it. When she did, she was often overwrought.

It wasn't her fault. Spence understood why she'd responded how she had, but there was something about being able to speak with Anika, someone he saw as fully removed from everything going down in the Hood.

'What's on your mind?' He asked. Anika gathered herself, sipping her drink before she spoke.

'I'm leaving. I don't know when, or where I'm going to go, but coming back to Leeds was a mistake.'

'Why?' Spence asked, before he could stop himself. When she'd first contacted him, he would have welcomed the news, but now he wasn't sure.

'I thought I could rebuild my life here, but it's hard. My family are distant, and it's harder than I thought to be around you. You're a great guy, Spence, and there are all these regrets, and what-ifs. I just wish I'd spoken to you. If I'd shared what was on my mind, maybe I wouldn't have lost the best thing that ever happened to me.'

'Anika . . .' Spence started, though he had no idea what he was going to say. She shook her head, stopping him.

'Don't. I'm sorry for making it awkward. I just wanted you to know how I felt.'

The waitress came over with the bill, which Spence quickly paid, sending her on her way with a generous tip.

'I said this was my treat,' Anika protested. Spence shook his head now.

'It's fine. I wouldn't have ever let you pay for me, but I appreciate the attempt.' He sighed. 'I wish things were easier. Despite everything, this has been a really enjoyable night. Maybe if we'd had a few more of them, things would be different.'

They gathered their things and left the restaurant.

'Do you want a lift?' Spence asked, signalling to his ride. His body-guard had waited outside the restaurant in the car the entire time, and still appeared alert and ready. Anika shook her head.

'My Uber is already on the way. They should be here in a minute.' She stepped closer to Spence. 'Thank you for keeping me company, Spence. You didn't have to. You could have told me where to go, but I'm glad you didn't.'

Spence's throat was tight. He inched closer, and the pair hugged, neither pulling away.

'I'll contact you soon. When I know more about my plans.'

Spence nodded, tightening the hug, inhaling her fresh scent, and loving the feel. Being back in Leeds had done her wonders. Despite what Anika said, she seemed far more alive than she had when he'd met her after her return. He wondered if there could ever be a life for her in Leeds.

A bright light startled him, as Anika's Uber, a blue Toyota Yaris, eased into the car park. Spence released the hug and stepped back. He turned and walked to his car.

'Spence?'

Spence faced Anika, who had a wistful look on her face.

'You could always come with me. We could leave together.'

Before Spence could respond, Anika climbed into the back of the Uber, which drove away, leaving him slack-jawed, standing in the middle of the car park.

SPENCE FOUND himself out of sorts after Anika's words. He'd allowed himself to get carried away in the evening's magic, and now he regretted it. He had no intention of leaving with Anika, but the night they'd shared had been a blast from the past for him. It was a reminder of how things between them could be, and he'd missed that more than he thought.

The day after the dinner, he drove to see his dad, needing a second opinion. When he entered, his dad was in the living room, lifting dumbbells while an old Western blared on the screen.

'Why's it so loud, dad?' Spence asked, grabbing the remote and turning down the television. His dad lowered the dumbbells, panting. He wore an old Leeds United shirt, tight around the arms and stomach, and a pair of shorts.

'I like it loud,' said Wayne. 'It keeps me in the zone. What are you doing over here, other than messing up my workout?'

'I cut out early. I'm gonna check on people later, but I needed a change of scenery,' said Spence. 'What's with the working out? You trying to get fit for a woman or something?' He joked. He wouldn't mind if that was the case, but his dad had been funny about being around other women since Spence's mum had died.

'Come out of here with that nonsense,' said Wayne. 'The doctors suggested I get fit. I went for a checkup, and they were concerned about some things.'

'*Concerned* how? And what things?' Spence asked quickly.

Wayne waved him off. 'Nothing major. Like I said, they suggested I get fit, and I've definitely been slacking off a bit, so here I am. Don't read too much into it. Now, let's stop going on about me. What's going on, and why do you look like that?'

'Look like what?'

'Thoughtful. More than you normally do. Summat is on your mind, so let me in.'

'Okay, but don't give me any shit for this,' said Spence. 'I've been seeing my ex.'

Wayne's eyebrows rose. He muted the television completely, giving his son his full attention.

'Anika?'

Spence nodded.

'What the hell brought that on? I thought she was gone?'

'She came back,' said Spence glibly. He sat down, telling his dad the full story of Anika getting in touch, all the way until their dinner the night before.

Wayne stared at him the whole time, his exercise forgotten.

'Why did you do it?' He finally asked. His tone wasn't judgemental as Natty expected. Instead, he sounded more curious.

'I don't know.'

'Yeah, you do. We'll come back to that. Ultimately, you can't help your feelings, son. Especially with women. You haven't made things easy for yourself.'

'You're right. I'm not even considering what she said, but it definitely knocked me for a loop. I don't understand why I couldn't tell her it would never happen. I mean, she knows about Rosie. She knows how I feel, but she asked anyway.'

'Maybe she sees what I see.' Wayne lowered himself to the floor, completing a slow set of press-ups.

'What's that?'

'A man that's conflicted about his decisions. Ask yourself Spence, why are you helping her? More than that, is it being done out of love?'

'No,' said Spence quickly. 'I . . . I guess it's based around proving that I'm better. She cheated on me, pops. I never thought she would, but she did. I wanted to prove that I could forgive her, because she means less to me now.' Spence sighed, shaking his head. 'It's all a mess.'

Wayne leaned over his son, gripping his shoulder firmly.

'If that was the case, you'd be able to tell Rosie about it. She doesn't know about you and your ex, does she?'

Spence shook his head. 'She wouldn't understand.'

'Wouldn't she? Because I think you're the one that doesn't understand, Spence. You picked a good woman. She's sensible . . . or at least she appears to be.'

'You thought Anika was sensible too,' Spence started, but Wayne let out a harsh laugh.

'No, I didn't. I never said anything of the sort.'

'I'm sure you did . . .' the more Spence thought about it, though, he wasn't sure. In fact, he couldn't recall his dad saying much at all about Anika. He'd been polite to her when they were around one another, but he never asked about her.

'I didn't. Sort it out, Spence, before it goes too far. Now, what's going on in the streets?'

'I can't call it.' Spence gratefully seized the subject change. 'I was going through some stuff. I spoke to you about it that time. How I felt after what happened with Keith; needing Natty to defend me again. It's been hard to shake that feeling of inadequacy, but I'm pushing through it. I'm training, and I've been doing street drills with Natty's cousin.'

'Which cousin? That Steven kid?'

'*Stefon*,' Spence corrected. 'I told you he was back in Leeds. He's cool, and he's quick on the trigger. He's been helping me.'

'Just be careful. Everyone has an agenda. Make sure you know what his is.'

'I will, pops. Right now, I'm more concerned with preventing him and Natty from killing each other. There's some bad blood there.'

'You'll be fine, Spence. Leave them to it, and they'll get over their own problems. Regarding you . . . cut the chord with your ex, and do it quickly. That's my advice. As for the streets, you need to let what happened with that Keith shithead go. He had the drop on you, but you were still there, riding out with your team.'

'I asked to be there, and I couldn't match up.'

'Fuck that!' Wayne snapped, startling Spence. 'The game is the game. It's rarely straightforward, but you do what you can. If you forget everything else I've taught you, remember this: sometimes, it comes down to that split-second decision where it's you or the other guy. Do you know what you do in that situation?'

Spence waited, unnerved by the serious expression on his dad's face.

'Make sure it's the other person, son. That's all you need to do.'

CHAPTER THIRTY-FOUR

ROMAN FOUND it harder than expected to stop thinking about Danielle. He struggled against his resentment, both because of her profession, and because of the role he felt she had in Keith's death.

That being said, her dying had hurt him, and it had only increased over time. He wondered if they ever had a chance, and felt guilty for not protecting her. It made him think of Maka and the life he'd built for himself. Maka flatly refused to consider going back to the streets, and in his current state, sitting in a safe house chain-smoking cigarettes, Roman again wondered if he could have made such a decision. He heard footsteps approaching the room and straightening, sitting up in his chair as Jamal bounded in, his eyes gleaming.

'We've got them,' he said. 'We're ready.'

'Are you sure?' Roman leaned over and stubbed out his cigarette in a nearby ashtray.

'I'm sure. I've double-checked everything. We've got the line to Natty Deeds.'

Roman felt a surge of warmth spread throughout his body. *They finally had him.*

'Are we ready to move?'

Jamal nodded. 'We've had eyes on his girl all day. We saw her at the chemist's and followed her. Natty's in there. We just need to go and get him.'

Roman stood, grinning.

'And the other thing?'

'We've picked the spots, and everyone is in place. We're just waiting on you.'

'Lead the way, bro,' said Roman, pushing his thoughts about Danielle to one side. 'Let's get them.'

———

NATTY SEEMED to be spending a lot of time, sitting around and thinking about things. When he'd sat back in his younger days and imagined running things, he never thought it would go like this. He'd assumed it would be easier, and that everyone would just fall in line. Right now, he felt like a puppet on a string, forced to serve his uncle's agenda.

The same uncle he wanted to kill. The same uncle he had failed to kill.

It was all a mess, and it wasn't growing any easier. Natty's list of enemies seemed to grow. His list of allies seemed to shrink, or were being subverted from him. Even Stefon seemed determined to be against him.

Natty kept thinking of a future where he could breathe, where these issues would be removed for good, but implementing that future was a struggle. He needed Mitch out of the way. He needed Roman eliminated, and he needed the room to continue his work.

Natty thought of Brown and the threats that had been made. He grinned for a second. Despite knowing he'd made a mistake, hitting Brown's man had been satisfying to think back on. In his younger days, hitting people had always felt like that.

It was only the aftermath that caused issues.

Brown was an irritant, but easily placated with money. Mitch and Roman were the key factors. Then, he could look to the Asians who had hired a sloppy shooter to end him. He wasn't sure how he could make a successful move against his uncle now. He'd been lucky he hadn't been found out after his assassination attempt.

Outside hitters were a possibility. They were all about the money and less likely to be subverted by politics, but it was still a risk. His uncle had a lot of connections, and if they learned Natty was planning a hit against him, he'd be stopped before it could begin.

Natty refused to let himself be brought down by a whistleblower.

As he leaned back and closed his eyes, memories of his dad flooded his mind. He wondered how his dad would have handled these problems, remembering the old mantra about not backing down. Smiling, he breathed deeply, then sat up, determined to push ahead, alone if needed.

Natty remained deep in thought, distracted by his vibrating phone.

'Yeah?'

'It's me.'

'Lisa? What's up?'

'I need to speak to you.'

'I swear if I look out of the window and you're at the fucking door...'

Lisa chuckled.

'I learned my lesson, Nat. It was an innocent mistake,' she said.

Natty rolled his eyes. He could imagine Lisa, phone in hand, twirling her hair and batting her eyelids.

'So what's the problem?'

'Figured you could do with an update, and there are some things with the big boss I could use a second opinion on.'

Natty sat up. This could be perfect. Lisa was close to Clarke, who was close to Mitch. There was a chance she knew more about Mitch's agenda. He would have to box clever with her, but he could do that.

'Okay. I'll see you soon. Text me the address.'

———

Spence was at home, deep in thought after speaking with his dad. He was surprised at the strength of the advice his dad had given him. It was sensitive and well-thought-out.

The more Spence thought about it, the more he realised that was a common factor of his dad's advice. He was blunt and always spoke his mind, but he was rarely wrong. He'd said that Spence would need to bloody himself in a war, and Spence was starting to believe that was true. It was why he had subjected himself to the punishing training Stefon had put him through.

He sighed deeply, determined to resolve how to remove the mounting stress weighing down his shoulders. There was a lot going on in the organisation that he didn't understand. He and Natty were keeping secrets from one another, and there were multiple threats converging, bodies dropping and assassination attempts. It had been relentless for the past few years, yet now it was more serious than ever. Spence needed to keep up.

He needed to speak with Anika, and get her out of his space once and for all. Attacking his problems one by one was the logical thing to do.

Calling Anika, he shook his head when she didn't answer. Ending the call, he typed a quick text message, stating he would contact her later. Sniffing under his arms, he wrinkled his nose. He'd done some exercise after leaving his dad, but hadn't freshened up. Standing and stretching, he shouted to Rosie, who was in the kitchen, that he was going to take a shower.

'What did you say?' Rosie asked, walking into the living room just as Spence had gone upstairs. She heard the shower turning on and smiled to herself, considering joining him.

Spence had been distant lately, and it would be a good way to reconnect. She was about to head back into the kitchen when Spence's phone vibrated. Rosie glanced at the screen and was about to walk away, but picked up the phone on impulse. Before she could convince herself it was a bad idea, she answered the call.

'Hello?'

The person at the other end said nothing.

'Hello?' Rosie repeated.

'. . . Is this Rosie?'

'It is. Who's this?'

'I was looking for Spence . . .'

Rosie's stomach lurched. She saw spots, sitting on the sofa, phone pressed to her ear.

'Anika?'

'I . . . think this is the wrong number. I don't know who that is,' the woman said, but her voice faltered.

'Stop lying. Why are you ringing Spence? You have some nerve calling him.'

'I . . .'

'What the hell do you want?' Rosie barked.

'Look, it's not what you think. I just . . .'

'Just what? What the hell would Spence want to speak to you about?' snapped Rosie. Spence had been distant for a while, and she'd thought it was down to the current conflicts in the streets, but she was wrong, it was deeper than that. He was still dealing with his ex-girl-friend; the same ex-girlfriend that had broken his heart and left him a mess.

'It's not so deep. Honest. I just needed to speak to him.'

Anika's attempts to remain polite only served to make Rosie more furious.

'You have no right to ring him. Stay the hell away, and don't contact him again.' She hung up, breathing hard, her hands trembling. She stared ahead, feeling tears spill down her cheeks, furiously wiping them away. Rosie wouldn't cry. She'd already lost her composure with Anika, and that was beneath her.

There was only one person she needed to speak with.

She stormed up the stairs and into the bedroom. Spence was on the bed in his boxers, creaming himself. He looked up at her and smiled, though it quickly vanished when he saw the look on her face.

'What's wrong?'

'Do you really want to know?' Rosie asked, her voice low.

'Of course,' said Spence, standing. He reached out for Rosie, but she stepped back.

'Anika,' she said the name, wanting to illicit a reaction. Spence's eyes widened, and he flinched, but he composed himself quicker than expected.

'I was going to . . .'

'Why didn't you? You thought you could dip your ex on the side and keep it from me? Are you really that weak?'

'I haven't done anything with Anika,' said Spence in a tired voice.

'I'm sorry I didn't tell you. I promised that I was going to, but it was something I wanted to sort out on my own. Work got in the way, and I'm sorry.'

'Why are you in contact with her if you're not sleeping with her?' Rosie demanded.

'She contacted me a few months ago. She was in a bad way, and she wanted to get back together. I said no, but I still wanted to help her. Once upon a time, I loved her, and I didn't want to see her go out like that.'

'Fuck her!' Rosie screamed. 'She cheated on you and left you. When someone does that, you don't owe them a thing. You don't help them get their life together, ring them late at night, and keep it all from your girlfriend.'

'I know,' said Spence. He hung his head, still awkwardly standing in the middle of the bedroom.

'You can't even be honest either. You did all of this because you liked the attention. I bet it really appealed to have your ex crawling back to you . . . bet that was great for your ego.'

'It wasn't like that. It wasn't about that.'

'That's exactly what it was about,' roared Rosie. 'Everything you've said has been nonsense. I waited for you, Spence . . . for months, I waited for you to let me in. I cared about you, but you never felt the same way. You've never put me first, and I'm sick of it.'

'Rosie. Rosie, just listen to me,' said Spence. She shook her head, but she stopped talking, her level of fury almost overwhelming. All the deep breathing in the world would not calm her down.

'I don't have any feelings for Anika. That's the truth.' He blew out a breath. 'I just didn't want to kick her while I was down, and I wanted to prove I was the better person.'

Rosie looked at him in disgust, and Spence instantly knew he'd gone too far.

'When you were working on trying to prove to the ex that stomped on your heart that you were the better man, you should have been thinking about me.' Rosie turned to leave the room. Spence followed.

'Rosie, please don't go. Let's talk about this.'

'No. Let's not. You had your chance to speak to me, and you've proven I will never matter,' said Rosie. She grabbed her jacket and her handbag, and left, slamming the door behind her.

'Fuck!' snarled Spence, resisting the urge to punch the wall. Breathing hard, he considered going after Rosie. Calling Anika back and giving her a piece of his mind was another plan he was leaning toward, but his phone, still on the sofa where Rosie had left, lit up.

Spence glanced at the screen, expecting to see Anika's number. When he saw Clarke's number, though, he shook off the drama and answered.

'Hey.'

'I need to see you. ASAP. Meet me at the main spot.'

'I'll be there shortly,' said Spence. Hanging up, he hurried upstairs to throw on some clothes.

CHAPTER THIRTY-FIVE

LORRAINE HAD DROPPED Jaden at her mum's earlier. She'd felt drained for the past few days, and wanted to sit down with Natty and hopefully spend some quality time with him.

Lorraine worried she was relying on her mum too much, but she loved spending time with her grandson, and equally, he loved spending time with his nana. They had a great relationship and had their own inside jokes, which she found amusing.

Jaden was growing too quickly for her. The fact he was now interested in girls was something she had expected when he was older, and Lorraine wasn't looking forward to it.

For a moment, she'd wondered if the fact Natty was around had somehow propelled her son's development, though she quickly dismissed it.

Lorraine pulled up at the house, just in time to see Natty leave. With brief consideration, she followed him. Lorraine wasn't skilled at tracking people, and had never tailed someone in her life. She had expected Natty to notice her immediately. Surprised when he didn't, she continued her pursuit, concocting excuses in her mind to explain her actions should Natty make her, following as he turned onto a street in Harehills.

She drove past him as he parked. Pulling in further up the road, Lorraine looked into her mirror as a black 4x4 parked behind her. She climbed from her car just as Natty walked into a house.

Taking a deep breath, she followed, unable to dismiss the shaky feeling that had taken over her.

———

ROMAN STILL COULDN'T BELIEVE it had worked. They'd followed Lorraine and Natty to what appeared to be a safe house. He didn't know who was inside, but he was ready. His men were all armed, and for the first time, it appeared he was going to get the jump on the younger Dunn. Grinning, Roman made a phone call.

———

WHEN NATTY ENTERED the safe house, Lisa sat on the sofa, drinking. Natty spotted a bottle of Ciroc on the table. He considered pouring a glass, but didn't. Lisa looked as good as ever, but when she glanced up at him, he noted the circles around her eyes. Clearly, she'd had more than a few late nights.

The sight affected him more than he expected. Natty had begun to see Lisa as invulnerable. She seemed to be a constant. Always deadly, a serrated blade beneath a gorgeous body. Always snarky and ready to counter.

Right now, she just looked like a tired little girl.

'Are you okay?' He asked softly. Lisa frowned.

'Why wouldn't I be?'

'I don't know. You just look sad.'

'I'm thoughtful, not sad,' Lisa corrected. 'Are you going to make me drink alone?'

'I don't feel like drinking at the moment,' said Natty. 'What's on your mind?'

'Do you ever get the feeling that you have no clue what's really going on?'

'More often than ever lately,' said Natty. 'What don't I know?'

'I haven't been lying low. I've been working with Clarke, Tony and the others. We've been going around, killing the drug dealers. Not sure if you know about it, but Mitch ordered it to be done.'

'Clarke told me, but didn't say why. I don't know what my uncle is playing at, but he has some vendetta against the Asians.'

'What vendetta?'

'You already know that the people being killed are connected to Jakkar . . . the big bad Asian supplier who's giving Roman and his people all the drugs they need. The guy that shot at me and Clara. They sent him after me.'

'How do you know that?' Lisa drained her drink. Her voice was calm, but there was emotion in her eyes that she couldn't hide. He hadn't seen the emotion since the time she had kissed him.

'I went after the shooter, and he told me.'

'Do you think he was lying?'

'I don't. I think my fucking uncle is playing a dangerous game and has roped us all in without letting us know the rules.'

'That's his position,' said Lisa. 'He points the finger, and we execute. That's the way it's always been.'

'Is that enough for you?' Natty asked heatedly. Lisa didn't reply straight away.

'That's the job,' she said after a while.

'That's not enough. That's not the way for anyone to work. All he has done is fuck everything up. Look at what we're dealing with, and how many fronts we're dealing with issues on. We were good, Lisa. For a while, we were on point. We took out Keith and Manson, and there was no blowback. I was half-expecting Teflon and Shorty to get involved and come after us, but nothing happened. We were making money. Everyone was happy, then suddenly, Roman is back on the agenda. You lot are out, dropping dealers that have done nothing to us, making shit hot again. I thought this was all about money. I thought we made the money, fed our families and lived well . . . not all this other shit.'

Lisa arched an eyebrow. 'You're angry.'

'What gave that away?' Natty rolled his eyes, finally taking a seat.

'I don't enjoy seeing you angry,' said Lisa quietly. Her eyes were on his as she reached out and took his hand.

Just as the door burst open, and Lorraine entered.

The pair reacted instantly. Natty pulled out a gun and aimed it. Lisa moved quickly, reaching for a weapon of her own. Natty's heart raced as he realised it was Lorraine. He cursed himself for not locking the door, knowing Clarke would crucify him when he learned of it.

Thoughts of Clarke evaporated when Natty realised how the situation would look to Lorraine. As it was, her face was pale, eyes blazing with fury as she looked at Natty with disgust.

'I can't believe you,' she said, seemingly not noticing he'd pointed a weapon at her. Natty lowered the gun, taking a step towards her, stopping when Lorraine shook her head. When he saw the tears, it tore him apart inside.

'Lo, listen, there's not—'

'Don't even try it, Nat. I've caught you. Sitting on the sofa, holding hands with the woman you told me I didn't need to worry about.'

'You don't,' said Natty hurriedly. 'This is business. I swear, there's nothing else going on other than that.'

'This couldn't be less of a business setting if you tried,' said Lorraine. She turned her attention to Lisa. 'I should rip your eyes out of your head, you little sket. Who the hell do you think you are?'

'Listen to your man,' said Lisa, smiling now. 'Stop being emotional.'

'Don't tell me what to do.' Lorraine stepped to Lisa, but Natty blocked her path. Lisa was being nice now, but he didn't want to know what she would do if she began seeing Lorraine as a threat.

'Lo, don't.'

Pausing, Lorraine stared at him in utter shock.

'You're defending her?'

Natty's eyebrows pinched together in anger.

'Defending her? I'm defending *you!*'

Lisa bit her top lip behind Natty, failing to hide her smile.

'Oh, you think it's fucking funny, do you?' snapped Lorraine, looking past Natty.

'Kinda.' Lisa shrugged.

Natty turned, impaling Lisa with a glare. Returning his focus to Lorraine, he spoke.

'Lo, I've told you, this is a business meeting. Don't torture yourself over something that isn't true.'

Lorraine stepped back slowly, shaking her head.

'I have more respect for myself than to stand here and listen to you lying to me. I'll leave you to your little tryst,' she said, almost sweetly. 'When you're done here, please get your fucking things out of my home.' She faced Lisa, giving her rival a scornful look. 'He's all yours, darling.'

As Lorraine turned to leave, gunfire ensued. She screamed as Natty ran forward, pulling her out of the way as a man barrelled into the room, gun raised.

———

SPENCE HURRIED into the safe house. Clarke and Tony were in the meeting room. Both looked up when they saw him. Clarke looked more serious than usual, while Tony looked equally surly and tired, stifling a yawn.

'What's going on? This looks serious,' said Spence, reading the room.

'Roman,' said Clarke. 'He finally made a move. Sent a three-man team to raid one of our bigger stash spots. The one near Spencers.'

'Shit,' said Spence, happy to have a distraction from his female drama. 'What's the damage?'

'We ran them off. I dunno why they sent such a small team after such a well-protected spot. One of the men was wounded, but nothing serious. We've reinforced it, along with our other big spots.'

'That makes no sense,' said Spence. 'Why would he make such a daft move? He's basically done nothing for months. Surely, he'd want to take out soldiers, rather than going after product?'

'What are you getting at?' said Clarke.

'I'm saying, Roman is supposed to be smart. That's the sort of move his partner would have made. Unless he was testing . . . shit.' Spence didn't get the time to say anything further. They heard yells and cracks of gunfire.

Clarke and Tony went for their guns, but the attackers were quicker. Tony was riddled with bullets and fell before he could get a shot off. Clarke was on point, taking out two gunmen with precision aim. Spence crouched in the corner, frozen at the sight in front of him. He stared at Tony, shocked to see the man he'd been speaking with a few seconds ago, now dead.

'Call for backup!' Clarke shouted at Spence, kicking over the table and gingerly using it for cover. A fourth man ran into the room before Spence could act. Clarke put him down, but it was a ruse. Another man shot him, and Clarke fell back with a grunt, landing hard on his back. The shooter sauntered closer, grinning at Clarke.

'I'll get a delightful bonus for this, Clarkie,' he said in a deceptively soft voice.

'Get it over with, Jamal,' replied Clarke, breathing hard, his face tense. Jamal aimed the gun. Spence fought down his fear. He couldn't allow this to happen. Tony's gun was next to his body.

Spence reached for it, forgetting everything that Stefon had drilled into him, instead remembering his dad's words. He wouldn't hesitate. He pulled the trigger, watching with stunned horror as his bullet slammed into the side of Jamal's head. The killer slid to the floor, blood spurting from the wound.

Silence ensued, immediately broken by Clarke's heavy breathing.

'Call backup . . . Spence . . . then get out of here.'

'I'm not leaving you,' Spence shouted. He took out his phone and called Natty, receiving no answer.

'Call this number,' said Clarke, clearly in a lot of pain. He hadn't moved since Jamal had shot him. He relayed the number, and Spence called. 'Tell them that there's been a *code black*. They're to secure Mitch, and send five men over here, along with some cleaners.'

Spence did everything he had been told, then hurried over to Clarke, helping the man sit up. Blood poured from a wound on Clarke's side.

'I'll be fine when I've seen a doctor. Help me to my feet,' said

Clarke, immediately lurching. Spence helped him, and they moved out of the safe house.

Spence still had the gun, holding it in his left hand, working to secure Clarke with the right. He expected to be gunned down immediately, but the men out front had done their job. The path was littered with bodies, and Spence fought the urge to throw up. This wasn't the time.

More than ever, he needed to be strong.

Finally, the pair made it to Spence's car. He helped secure Clarke, then climbed in the driver's seat, started the engine and drove.

'I'll . . . direct you,' gasped Clarke. 'I know a doctor that will sort me.'

After Clarke gave him the address, Spence headed in that direction, his thoughts all over the place. Roman had played them. Spence had no idea how he'd learned of the safe house, but it wasn't exactly a classified location. Like the stash spot Roman attacked, it was out in the open and had people coming and going. It was well protected, and that was deemed to be enough. Seemingly, Roman had taken advantage of the traffic.

Another, more terrifying thought came to Spence's mind.

What had happened to Natty? Why hadn't he answered the phone?

CHAPTER THIRTY-SIX

LORRAINE SCREAMED as the man raised his gun, but a deafening bang made her tumble away, staggering back. She looked at Natty in shock. He held his smoking gun, a grim expression on his face.

'Keep moving,' Lisa called, and Natty reached out and grabbed Lorraine, shoving her into a corner as several men entered. Lisa shot one of them in the head, but the other got two shots off, seeing her as the target. Natty put a bullet in his head.

———

ROMAN STOOD OUTSIDE THE HOUSE, eyes fixed on the flashes of light escaping through the window.

'More,' he snarled, looking to his left and motioning for a new group to enter. A black car pulled up beside Roman, who glanced at it briefly, before turning his attention back to the house. Four men rushed to his side, watching Roman and waiting for their orders.

'Go,' he said, without so much as looking at them. Without hesitation, the group ran, hurtling through the door and into the action.

LORRAINE WATCHED in stunned silence as Lisa and Natty worked. Natty had called the woman dangerous, and now she understood it. They'd killed five people between them. The acrid gun smoke hurt her throat, and she could barely hear between the various loud bangs.

More men poured in. One aimed at Natty, who slid his body to the side, barely avoiding the bullet that crashed into the wall behind him. He fired back at the man, his jaw tight, eyes focused. Lisa had forgone her gun and had a knife, sliding by Natty, cutting down two men so quickly, Lorraine wasn't quite sure how she'd done it.

Another man entered and aimed his gun at Lorraine. She took a deep breath, unable to move or make a noise. Until she saw the man's throat explode. He slid to the floor, choking on his blood, trying to talk. Natty stood over him, a cold, dark look on his face. His finger tightened on the trigger, and he shot the man twice in the chest.

Lorraine finally lost her composure and threw up on the floor. Natty went to her.

'Lo, are you okay?' he asked, his voice full of concern.

'Get her out of here,' ordered Lisa. 'I'll clean up.'

'This was Roman,' said Natty, facing her. 'He did this.'

'Probably. Doesn't matter for now.' Lisa grabbed a gun and cautiously looked out the front. 'If he was here, he's gone. Take a car and get out of here.'

Natty gave Lisa a quick look, then he gathered Lorraine to him, keeping their heads down and rushing to his car. Lorraine's car was there. Taking that would be smarter. His car had no links to him. He secured Lisa in the passenger seat, pleased she'd left the key in the ignition.

Starting the engine, he floored it, motoring down the road, wondering precisely how Lisa would clean up before the authorities arrived.

LISA LEFT THE HOUSE, pleased to see the fire had taken up quickly, swiftly spreading through the front room. Rather than take a car, she crossed the road and walked at a steady pace up the street.

There were people coming out of their homes to survey the damage. A few had their phones out, but none were paying any attention to Lisa.

Turning a corner, she walked another two streets down to a grey, nondescript Nissan she'd stored there. Starting the engine, she drove away, already planning to check in with Clarke and get the lay of the land.

———

THE DAYS after the attacks on the Dunns were messy, charged with rumours and misinformation. People had died, arrests were made. Police counted on their informants to lead them to the people responsible.

In a single night, over a dozen people had died, and something needed to be done. The police had set up shop in and around the Hood, and they were letting nothing go. Anyone they saw that looked suspicious was subject to intense questioning, either on the spot at the police station.

Things had gone too far. The arrests weren't enough. People wanted faces. They wanted the people above the street level. Reports of the attacks had made the national news, and the streets were buzzing.

Mitch ordered everything shut down. The streets slowed to a crawl, with little product moving. Only the truly brave — or stupid — were still trying to sell drugs in the current climate. They didn't fear the police or the possibility of being gunned down. All they cared about was the greater profits they could make.

Spence paced the room, waiting to be allowed in to see Clarke. The doctor had said he wasn't in any immediate danger, but that hadn't stopped Spence from worrying.

Days had passed, but he was unable to properly process what had happened. The war had well and truly come for them. Roman had wanted to end them all and had nearly succeeded.

Spence had spoken with Natty sparingly, but had yet to speak with him face to face. He'd had days to think about everything. Anika still needed dealing with.

Rosie hadn't responded to his messages. He'd asked her for forgiveness, and had told her he was safe, not knowing if she'd heard about what had happened in the Hood.

For now, he was heavily focused on the streets. He'd thrown up multiple times, seeing the man he'd shot every time he closed his eyes. He often thought about the conversation he'd had with Natty. About how Natty felt after the first time. Spence couldn't believe his friend had felt what he was feeling and decided to kill again. Nor Clarke. Nor his dad. They were all killers.

He was a killer.

Spence wiped his face, regulating his breathing. He would not throw up on himself again. He focused on Clarke, hoping he could see the man soon. He'd lost a lot of blood from the bullet to his side, but he was recovering, though the last time the doctor had spoken to Spence, he'd told him Clarke was still weak.

What felt like seconds later, Spence was awoken with a jolt, as the doctor shook his shoulders.

'Are you ok, son?' the doctor asked.

Spence nodded.

'You can see him now. He's asking for you.'

Spence took a moment to wipe his eyes, stifling a yawn, stretching as he stood, feeling his tense muscles popping, almost welcoming the pain. He followed the doctor into the bedroom. Clarke was in bed, his surprisingly toned upper body on show, his lower half covered by the quilt. Slowly, he turned his head towards Spence, smiling.

'How are you doing?' He croaked. Spence leaned in and forced a glass of water to his lips, removing it after Clarke took several sips. 'Thank you.'

'Don't worry about me. The most important question is, how are you? You're the one that was shot.'

'It's not the first time.' Clarke grimaced, clearly racked with pain. 'You saved my life, Spence.'

Spence numbly nodded. He didn't like to think about it. The man — Jamal — had made an error. He should have killed Spence first, but he was more focused on Clarke. Spence had got very lucky, and saw little to celebrate. He'd taken part. All because he couldn't control his emotions; seemingly jealous of Natty and the others for being real men, while he'd been left back.

'Spence.'

Spence blinked, focusing on Clarke, who was still watching him.

'I know what you're going through. Trust me on that. It will get easier, but you're gonna need to weather it. Now, what's going on out there?'

'I got word to your woman. She knows you're safe. Everyone's on standby. Mitch ordered everything shut down until the heat dies down. Natty and Lisa got attacked, but they got away. Roman went for them in force, but they held off his people.'

Clarke nodded, satisfied.

'Get out of here, Spence. I'm in no danger.' Clarke's eyes fluttered. 'I'm just tired. Come back and see me soon, but for now, go see that woman of yours. She must be worried sick.'

Spence stood, gently gripping Clarke's shoulder. He wasn't going to tell him what had happened with Rosie. It was foolish, with every-thing going on at the moment.

'I'll be back,' he said.

———

ROMAN ANALYSED THE DAMAGE. In the past two days, he'd moved spots four times, just in case. He'd blown the streets wide open, catching the arrogant Dunns with their trousers down. He'd missed his primary targets, but he was pleased with the damage he'd caused.

To the people that mattered, his name was ringing out. They knew what had happened, and that he had been the architect. Despite this, the cost of executing the play had been heavy, and he'd lost key personnel, namely Jamal. He had sent Jamal after Spence and the others, and they'd taken out several soldiers, but ultimately, they'd perished.

Roman fixed himself a drink. This was the time to finish things. He just needed to work out the best way to take advantage of his chaos.

———

SPENCE KNOCKED AT THE DOOR. He still had a key, but he didn't want to startle Rosie. She opened the door, eyes narrowing when she saw him, but to his surprise, she let him in, locking the door behind him.

'Drink?' she asked. Spence blinked, stunned. She sounded almost . . . nice. For a moment, he wondered if it could be so easy.

'No thanks. Are you okay?'

'I heard about what's been happening. I got your messages, and people are talking. Sounds like things got very messy.'

'They did,' agreed Spence.

'I'm glad you're okay. I know a lot of people died.'

Spence said nothing at first. This wasn't the conversation he wanted to have.

'Rosie . . .'

'Spence, we're over.'

It was like getting hit in the stomach. For a moment, his head swam. Spence opened his mouth, closed it, then opened it again.

'No . . .' he finally said.

'I can't trust you, Spence. I don't know what to believe,' said Rosie calmly.

'Nothing happened with Anika. I swear, Rosie. I didn't do anything with her.'

'You kept her from me. Whatever you did or didn't do, if nothing was going on, you would have told me, and you didn't.' Rosie choked down a sob, her composure crumbling.

'Rosie . . . I'm sorry. I really am. I can't explain it. I thought I was doing the right thing by helping her, but I don't want her. I want you. You're all I want. Please, just give me another chance, and I'll never give you another reason to doubt me.'

Tears ran freely down Rosie's cheeks. For a moment, Spence thought she was going to forgive him, but she went she opened her mouth to speak again, he just knew.

'I can't do it, Spence.' She shook her head, gaining strength from the action. 'I won't do it.'

CHAPTER THIRTY-SEVEN

NATTY HAD COUNTED on the ongoing drama to keep his mind off Lorraine. She'd been half-catatonic when he'd dropped her at her mum's, warning her not to go home yet. He'd sent men to guard the house, under orders to protect the occupants with their lives. He would need to have a tense conversation with her, but now wasn't the time.

He'd heard his uncle's edict, and had been in contact with multiple higher-ups, painstakingly working over the past two days to keep things in order and shoot down rumours and twisted tales of what had transpired.

When Spence called him, he drove to meet him, meeting well away from Chapeltown. They were in Middleton. Spence climbed from his car and got into Natty's. Glancing at his friend, he saw the same fatigue he knew was mirrored in his own demeanour.

'How are you?' Natty asked.

'I'm a mess,' admitted Spence. 'Everything that's happened . . . it's a lot. I guess I'm still trying to process things.'

'You and me both. I heard what you did, though. I'm proud of you, Spence. What you did . . . I've been there. The circumstances weren't the same, but you saved Clarke's life.'

Spence gave his friend a tired smile.

'I appreciate it, but I'm not sure I'm in the right mindset to hear compliments for taking a life. I've kept a lot from you, Nat. How I've been feeling. Things that I've done. I'm sorry for that, but I couldn't help it. For a while, I've just felt . . . less. I've felt inadequate. *Soft.* When you're feeling like that, talking about relationship issues feels weak. You're out there, running the streets and holding shit down for the crew. Protecting our people. How can I come to you crying about shit in those circumstances?'

'Spence . . .'

'No, Nat. Let me say what I'm saying. I had to prove myself. Now that I have, I don't know if I can ever go back.'

Natty waited a few moments to make sure Spence had finished before he spoke.

'You never needed to prove yourself. To me or to anyone else. But, when it was needed, you proved you will always do the right thing. You might have taken a life, but like I said, you protected Clarke.'

'You're wrong, fam. I don't always do the right thing,' Spence said, his watery eyes focusing on Natty.

'What do you mean?' said Natty, confused.

'Anika.'

Natty's confusion deepened.

'What about her?'

'I've been seeing her.'

'What?' Natty spluttered, almost breaking his neck to look at his friend.

'Not like that. Nothing happened, but she reached out a while back. She needed help, so I helped her.'

Natty's first reaction was anger. After everything Anika had done, Spence should have spat in her face and told her where to go. He calmed himself down. Spence needed to get it all out.

On top of that, he had his own secrets he was keeping.

'Does Rosie know?' He finally asked.

Spence hung his head. 'She does now. She dumped me.'

'I'm sorry, Spence. I know what she means to you. Is there no way back?'

Spence shrugged. 'I don't know. I mean, I don't think so. She sounded pretty certain.'

Natty didn't know what to say to Spence. He hated the fact his friend was going through it over Anika again.

'What are you gonna do now?'

'I need to speak with Anika.'

'Okay,' said Natty. He didn't want to do what he was going to say next, but he had to. 'Ring her.'

'What?'

'Ring her. Find out where she is, and we'll go to her. I'm not letting you go alone. That war of ours isn't over.'

MITCH COULDN'T BELIEVE the state of things. He stared out the window as he was driven through the Hood. Police were everywhere. As they turned a corner and drove down Spencer Place, he noted several cars with flashing lights, accosting and searching a group of sullen youths.

Mitch didn't care about their plight. He was furious that his carefully cultivated organisation had taken so many hits. He'd told Nathaniel to take out Roman, and he hadn't, and that allowed their enemy to do damage, injuring Clarke and killing scores of their men.

Because of the current circumstances, he'd planned this trip well. As the car pulled onto Hares Avenue, two cars packed with soldiers were already in place. Mitch climbed from the car, flanked by his men. He doubted there would be any trouble, but he had recently learned the hard way about compromising his safety.

The money Mitch had lost in the past few days was monumental. He had other streams of income that didn't involve drugs, but drugs were the most profitable, and it was hurting him.

Mitch knocked at the door. Tia answered, her eyes narrowing when she saw him, immediately looking past her brother-in-law to the men he'd brought with him.

'They're not coming into my house,' she said shortly, as if she had expected him to come. Mitch turned to his men.

'One of you stand outside. The others can go back to the car.' He left it to them to decide, and followed Tia, closing the front door and locking it.

Tia's house remained the same as it had the last time he'd visited. Mitch couldn't remember the occasion, but Rudy had been there too. There was a foreboding feel about the home. It once housed two men that Mitch held dear. Men whom Mitch had ordered the murders of. Mitch felt the hairs on the back of his neck stand up as his eyes swept across the place.

Steeling himself, he walked forward, entering the living room.

Mitch sat down. Tia busied herself in the kitchen, returning with a cup of coffee, which she handed to him. She hadn't asked how he wanted it, and either hadn't cared, or wanted to be spiteful. Still, Mitch took a sip of the watery drink, avoiding making a face. This was definitely a snub, but he wouldn't give her what she wanted by commenting.

'Thanks.'

Tia didn't react. She sat nearby, crossing her legs and staring at him. She looked well. Her eyes in particular, were as alert as he remembered. He smiled, but she still didn't react.

'You look well.'

'Thanks,' Tia replied.

'I know it's been a while. I'm sorry for that, but things haven't been easy—'

'Have you come to admit what you did to Rudy?'

Mitch's eyebrows rose. He'd expected more small talk, but she seemed content to dive right into the meaty subjects.

'Is that important to you?'

'I loved him.'

The corners of Mitch's mouth upturned. 'Is that really true? Have you ever loved anyone?'

'I could ask you the same thing, Mitch.'

Mitch smiled, already enjoying the conversation. There wasn't enough of this nowadays. It was like speaking with Jakkar. A multilayered conversation that kept him on his toes.

'I realised a long time ago that women were a drain I couldn't afford. I loved my brother, though. We built an empire together, and I've kept it alive in order to protect his legacy. Our family's legacy.'

'Why did you have your dear brother killed then?'

It was Mitch's turn not to react, though inwardly, her words had stumped him.

He snorted a moment later.

'Where did you get that fascinating idea from?' he asked.

'It's more than an idea,' said Tia. 'I all but cleaned the blood from Rudy's hands, after you made him do what you didn't have the balls to do.'

Mitch studied Tia carefully, weighing up his words.

'You'd never have remained with Rudy if you thought he had your husband killed. You certainly wouldn't have continued taking my money.'

'Tyrone Dunn was a dad. He wasn't a husband.'

'I seem to recall you two being married.'

'Doesn't matter,' said Tia.

'It does to me. My brother provided for you and Nathaniel,' said Mitch.

'I could have provided for myself. Sometimes money isn't enough.'

Mitch shook his head. 'You're too clever to believe the nonsense you're spewing. I know you are. Did you know about Rudy's ambitions?' As he asked, he wondered where it would lead the conversation. It was a probing question that established motive on Mitch's behalf. It was clear that Tia had been playing a game for some time. She was more involved with their business than Mitch ever realised. A threat, unchecked and unchallenged.

'You're focusing on the wrong areas,' Tia said. 'Rudy isn't your big problem. He never was.'

'I'm waiting for you to stop dancing around and say what's really on your mind.' Mitch took a sip of the abysmal drink, then put the almost-full cup on the coffee table, tired of the pretence.

'How do you think Nathaniel would react if you knew you'd ordered the death of his beloved dad?'

Mitch blanched, carefully and efficiently sifting through her words.

His mouth tightened, trying to impale the woman with his gaze as an unfortunate truth came to light.

'You told him, didn't you?'

Tia nodded.

'I didn't mean to, but he got under my skin.' She scowled, her eyes burning with anger. 'He always gets under my skin.'

It took a few moments for Mitch to find his voice.

'Do you have any idea what you've done?' He asked, voice thick with barely repressed rage.

'I did nothing,' said Tia, unafraid of his demeanour. 'This is all you. You're the one responsible for this mess. No one else. You can spout all the nonsense about family that you like, but you did all of this for yourself. It's all about you and your ego. Ty saw it. Rudy saw it. Now, it's Nathaniel's turn. We both know that he's Ty's son through and through. There's not a chance in hell that he will forgive you.' She smiled at him, showing her teeth. 'Can I get you another drink?'

CHAPTER THIRTY-EIGHT

SPENCE STOOD on the doorstep of a redbrick terraced house, Natty remaining in the car. Anika had been staying with friends since returning to Leeds. She'd looked for her own place for a while, but stopped when she decided to leave.

Spence glanced back at the car, wondering what was going through Natty's head. He knew full well what Natty thought of Anika, and it was hard to turn off the part of his brain that felt ashamed of how he'd allowed Anika back into his life.

'Spence? Are you okay?' Anika flung her arms around him. Spence stiffened in her arms, but tentatively returned the hug, releasing her quickly.

'I'm fine,' he said.

'I've heard a lot of stuff. People were dying, and I know you were out in the mix, and . . .'

'What did you say to Rosie?'

Anika froze, her mouth falling open. She wet her lips, closing the door behind her. The weather was warm enough for them to stand outside, and she didn't bother going for a jacket.

'I just tried returning your call. She got angry at me, but I kept calm. I didn't really know what to say to her.'

Spence nodded, sighing.

'I should have told her we were speaking.' He rubbed his forehead. 'I fucked up. I've been doing it a lot lately.'

'Why do you think you didn't?' Anika asked. Spence's brow furrowed.

'What do you mean?'

Anika took a deep breath. 'Maybe . . . it's a sign. If Rosie knows about us, then we don't need to hide. We can be together. You can leave Leeds with me, or we can stay here if that's what you want to do. All I want is to be with you, Spence.'

Spence let the words wash over them. They had been delivered with passion. He had to give her that.

'You had your chance, Anika. You could have been with me, but you squandered that. All I wanted was to help you get on your feet. I fucked up . . . I let you back in, and I lost the best woman I ever had because of it.'

'That's not true.' Anika's lips quivered. 'Don't you see? This is it. Nothing is holding us back.'

'There's nothing to hold back,' said Spence. He reached into the folds of his jacket and pulled out a thick envelope, which he handed to Anika. She took it with a startled look on her face.

'What's this?'

'It's your second chance. There's enough there to get you set up. Whether you stay is up to you, but you and I will never happen.' Spence turned to leave, ignoring Anika's calling of his name. He breathed deeply as he climbed into the car, feeling lighter.

'Didn't even look back,' said Natty. 'I'm proud of you, bro.'

'Let's just go. No reason to stick around here anymore.'

Chuckling, Natty drove away.

———

Lorraine handed Rosie her drink, which her friend took with thanks. Jaden was at school, and her mum was working.

When she learned Rosie was off work, she invited her over. She knew Natty had men watching her. She'd seen them outside, but didn't have the energy to insist they leave.

Deep down, she wasn't sure they'd listen to her, regardless.

Rosie looked as pale and drawn as she did, and they sat and sipped their drinks in silence for a while.

'Do you want to go first?' Rosie finally asked.

'You're the guest,' said Lorraine with a wry smirk. 'You go first. My treat.'

'Okay. I answered Spence's phone the other night, and Anika was on the other end.'

'What?' Lorraine was stunned.

'Yeah. That's what I was thinking. I was furious, Lo. I don't even really remember what she said, but I hung up on her . . . I remember that part.'

Lorraine was slack-jawed, still trying to comprehend the words.

'I need the full story. Now.'

Rosie told her everything, and Lorraine's eyes widened, her mouth still open. She couldn't believe it.

'Spence was still talking to her after everything?'

'Yeah. He wanted to help her, apparently. He swears they weren't sleeping together, but what am I supposed to think?' Rosie sniffed, wiping her eyes. 'I had to break up with him.'

'Have you spoken to him since?' Lorraine reached out and squeezed her hand.

Rosie shook her head. 'I ignored his calls. He's probably with Anika,' she said darkly.

'Maybe. Honestly, I doubt it, though.'

'Why? Why would he be speaking to her if he wasn't sleeping with her?' Rosie demanded.

'If I can play devil's advocate . . . maybe for the reasons he said. Hear me out,' said Lorraine hurriedly, as Rosie opened her mouth to retort. 'No matter what, Spence did wrong. He shouldn't have been dealing with her, and he definitely shouldn't have hidden it from you, but Spence is a genuinely nice guy. If there's one person I could believe had wanted to help their ex with no ulterior motive, it would be him.'

'You think I should forgive him then?'

Lorraine shook her head.

'I'm not saying that. One way or another, I can't tell you what to do. I can only tell you to go with your instincts.' Before she could add any more, she felt nausea in her stomach, surging quickly. She leapt from her seat, startling Rosie, and hurried to the bathroom, getting there in time, throwing up the food she'd eaten earlier.

Dimly, she heard Rosie calling out, asking if she was okay. She closed her eyes, sucking in deep breaths, not daring to move. . After a few minutes, she climbed to her feet, brushing her teeth and washing out her mouth.

Leaving the bathroom, she nearly collided with a concerned-looking Rosie.

'Are you okay?'

Lorraine nodded.

'I think it's just a bug or something. I've been on and off for a while.'

'Come on. Let's get you some water.'

Rosie and Lorraine sat at the kitchen table. Lorraine sipped the cold water and felt a lot better, pressing the cool glass against her forehead for a moment.

'Now that we're up to speed with my problems, what's got you camped out at your mums?'

Lorraine rubbed her chin, then pinched the bridge of her nose, before addressing Rosie.

'The woman I told you about. The one that I told you came to the house to see Natty. I followed Natty to a house, where she was waiting.'

'Lo . . .' said Rosie, stifling a gasp. When she went to speak, Lorraine shook her head.

'Let me get it all out. I walked in, and they were sitting on the sofa. There was a bottle of vodka, and I think Lisa was reaching out for him when I walked in. I didn't actually see them doing anything, but they seemed close, and I just lost it. I didn't really get the chance to say my piece, though. People with guns attacked the house. I don't know if they followed me, or Natty, or if they were already there, but there were lots of them. They just kept on coming.'

'I don't believe it,' said Rosie, seconds later, when she found her voice. 'How did you escape?'

'Natty and his . . . associate. They killed everyone, Rosie. They were ruthless, and in sync, and I saw a side to the man I love I suspected, but never truly believed existed. He was remorseless. They both were . . .' Lorraine trailed off.

Rosie swallowed, still struggling to comprehend what Lorraine had said. She'd thought her story was shocking, but Lorraine had easily pipped her.

'They protected you.'

'Yes. Natty kept me out of the way. The one time one of the men tried shooting at me, Natty shot him in the throat, then stood over him and shot him again.' She closed her eyes for a moment. 'I still see it.'

'I don't even know what to say . . .' said Rosie, her mouth opening and closing.

'Same. I love Natty, and he saved me. They both did. No two ways about that. He was still meeting with her and secret, and I don't know . . . he's dangerous. Seriously dangerous. He's never shown that side to me or Jaden, but it exists now, and I'm having to come to terms with that.'

'Have you spoken to him since you've been over here?'

'We've sent a few texts, but I've not taken any of his calls. He has men guarding me. I know we need to talk, but I'm honestly not sure what to say.'

Rosie stood over her friend and hugged her tightly, letting her cry. Looking after Lorraine allowed her to bury her own grief over the breakup with Spence. She didn't know if Lorraine would tread the same path, but they'd both had a rude awakening lately about the men they loved, and the other women in their lives. Stroking Lorraine's hair, Rosie fought back tears, forcing thoughts of Spence from her mind.

CHAPTER THIRTY-NINE

AFTER DROPPING OFF SPENCE, Natty returned home. He knew Lorraine was still at her mum's, and though he had a key to her house, it didn't seem right to be there without her.

He'd gone back to his own place, opening all the windows and airing the place out. Collapsing onto the sofa, he closed his eyes.

For days, he'd allowed the street drama to dominate him. He didn't want to think about the mess he'd made with Lorraine, or what she had seen him do. He'd hinted at it. When he'd spoken with her about Raider, and the fact she'd killed him, Natty had made it clear that he could relate.

He knew it wasn't the same, though. Lorraine had seen him murder multiple people. He'd defended her, just like Lorraine had defended herself from Raider, but he'd willingly gone beyond that. When one of the shooters had dared fire in Lorraine's direction, Natty had put him down, shooting him again even when it was clear the man was already dying.

He'd managed to get Lorraine to her mum's and in the car, the whole way there, Lorraine hadn't said a word, staring ahead wide-eyed, overwhelmed by the events.

Natty needed to speak with her. He needed to do a lot of things.

Taking out Roman, for one. He'd not taken the task particularly seriously, and Roman had surprised him once again.

Natty's phone rang, and he opened his eyes, cursing. Tempted to ignore it, he answered anyway, not caring who it was.

'What?'

'We need to talk. I'm at the place we met last time. Don't be long.'

Brown hung up. Natty closed his eyes again. Brown was the last person he wanted to speak with right now, but he still stood up, went to wash his face, and then left the house after throwing on a hooded top.

Natty could have taken his time to assemble some backup, but so far, he'd kept his visits with Brown discreet, and saw no reason to upend that now. He drove steadily, foregoing any music, trying to keep his head in the zone, wondering if when he finally went to lie down, he would be able to sleep without issue.

Brown was again with the troops. As Natty climbed out of the car, he was pleased that the man he'd hit last time was nursing a wicked black eye. He glowered at Natty, who ignored him and focused on Brown. Brown had his arms folded, shaking his head as he studied Natty.

'What the hell have you been up to lately? After our last conversation, I thought you'd take heed, but instead, you've been out there causing even more trouble. What gives?'

'Are you here to arrest me?' Natty asked, already bored with the conversation. Roman had escalated the conflict, not Natty.

'I should, but I'm here to get the money that I'm owed. You can kick that up to twenty bags now too, after all the additional havoc you've caused.'

Natty mockingly patted his pockets, unsure why he was so hellbent on taunting the detective.

'Whoops, sorry. Must have left your money in my other trousers. Easy mistake to make.'

'Do you think we're fucking about?' The man he'd hit last time snapped.

'Dawkins, relax. I've got this,' said Brown. His colleague bristled, but heeded the order. 'Deeds, we've given you a lot of chances, but you're still not taking us seriously. This gang war of yours has caused a lot of shit, and we need to solve it ASAP. That's gonna require some more cooperation from you.'

'Oh?' Natty didn't like where this was going.

'You know the players that are involved. We need some names. If You're not gonna take the hit, we need people who can. Give us four or five names, and we'll do the rest.'

Natty let the words sink in, raising his eyebrows at Brown's expectant face.

'You want me to snitch . . .'

'Don't look at it as snitching. Look at it as doing a service; one that will ensure you and your band of murderous thugs can keep on exploiting people and making money.'

'You must be out of your mind if you think I'm gonna help you.'

Brown rubbed his forehead, then looked up at the sky.

'Deeds . . . fucking hell, man. I don't know what else I'm supposed to do. I've tried everything, but you're too stubborn. You believe your own hype, thinking you're some sort of Chapeltown Don. I've been patient, but frankly, I'm sick of it. You need a little lesson in manners.'

Dawkins had been slowly sneaking up on Natty. When Brown finished talking, he swung, but Natty had already moved, dodging his sloppy hit and cracking him in the face, knocking him back. The third guy had counted on this, and made his own hit count, smashing his fist into Natty's liver. Natty, off balance, couldn't stop it. A wave of nausea cascaded through him.

Dawkins recovered, taking a run-up and kicking Natty in the chest. He fell to the floor and tried to cover up, but his body was sluggish now, and slow to respond. He took multiple punches and kicks, struggling to defend himself.

Before long, Brown called off the troops, Natty unable to even raise his arms.

'You're lucky you're still needed,' he growled, standing over Natty, flanked by his men. 'I tried to be nice, Deeds. You fucked that right up. By all rights, I should kill you right here, but I'm gonna let you get yourself fixed up. You're gonna get me one hundred bags now. Twenty grand isn't enough, so you're gonna pay more. If you don't, then maybe Roman's side is the one I need to be on . . . he'd probably fucking appreciate me more. Get his arms.'

The troops held his arms, Natty trying to struggle, but too weak to put up a fight. Brown grinned, then slammed his fist twice into Natty's stomach, driving the wind from him.

'Let him go.'

Natty was dropped back to the ground, writhing in pain, struggling to breathe. Brown and his men walked to their car. Dawkins stopped, turned back around, and kicked Natty twice more. Once in the back, then in the head.

'Dawkins. We need him alive for now,' said Brown.

'See you later, Deeds,' sneered Dawkins. He climbed in the car, and they drove away, leaving a bloodied Natty in their wake.

CHAPTER FORTY

NATTY HEADED HOME and cleaned himself up, popping several painkillers and easing onto his leather reclining, grimacing. Relaxing his guard around Brown and the other officers was foolish. He should have taken more precautions and kept his distance. Now, he'd been beaten badly, and had certainly made an enemy of the corrupt group. Brown's taunt about going to Roman stuck out in Natty's mind.

Groaning as he waited for the painkillers to kick in, Natty thought about the situation, and how he could take control. Going at his problems alone was failing him. There were severe ramifications to everything he was doing, but the fact was that his enemies were too powerful for him to take out by himself.

Spence had confessed about Anika, but Natty hadn't reciprocated. There was a risk of Mitch finding out about his intentions if he started telling people, but the alternative wasn't working out for him.

Eventually, Natty fell asleep. He woke up and trudged upstairs, checking out his face. He had some bruising, but nothing too serious. His ribs felt tender, though. He would need to be careful.

After a quick shower, Natty dressed in a dark grey tracksuit and black trainers. Grabbing his keys and wallet, he left the house. He glanced all around as he climbed into his car, feeling paranoid. He had a gun in a special compartment underneath the glove compartment that he could easily get to if needed.

Natty had called ahead and knew Spence was at an out-of-the-way spot near Bankside. He parked outside, a man immediately approaching. He was larger than Natty, shaven-headed and beady-eyed, but paused when he recognised him.

Natty gave him a nod, pleased he was doing his job, then headed inside. It was quiet. Natty wasn't sure if Spence had kicked everyone out, but there was no one in the kitchen, and he couldn't hear anyone upstairs.

In the living room, Spence sat on the sofa, his phone on his lap. Stefon stood in the far corner of the room, eating a container of corn-meal porridge. His eyes narrowed when he saw Natty, but he said nothing.

Natty ignored him, slapping hands with Spence and sitting next to his friend. The room was neater than their usual safe houses, with a medley of light brown furniture and magnolia-coloured walls. There was a television on the wall, currently turned off. Natty wondered what the pair had been speaking about before he went in.

'You good?' He asked Spence. Spence nodded.

'I needed a change of scenery. Rattling around the house by myself was getting to me. Ran into Stef when I got here.'

'Cool. Anything happening? Anyone saying anything?'

'Usual rumours. Roman has been seen once or twice, but nothing major. Our customers are getting twitchy. Might take a while to get them back if the shutdown continues much longer,' said Spence.

'We'll get them,' said Natty. He glanced to Stefon, who'd finished eating now, then back to Spence. He wanted to ask his cousin to leave, but resisted the urge, knowing it wouldn't go down well. 'I erm . . . I need to talk to you, bro.'

'Everything okay?' Spence straightened, his face serious. 'What happened to your face?'

'Don't worry about my face. I'll explain everything later.' Natty gathered himself. He hadn't gone over what he was going to say, deciding he would do what he often did in these situations, and speak from the heart. 'I've been keeping shit from you for a while now. Not because I didn't trust you personally, but more because the things I had going on . . . they're dangerous. People could get hurt behind the things I know, and I wasn't sure how to go about it.'

'Nat . . . you're not making any sense, bro.' Spence's brow furrowed.

'I know. You need to hear this, though. I've been blinded for a while, determined to do things in secret and go about things on my own, but I can't do it. This shit I'm doing . . . what I need to do. I can't do it alone. I need you.'

Spence stared at Natty, clearly trying to make sense of what he'd said. He opened his mouth to speak, but Stefon beat him to it.

'Finally admitting that you fucked up then?'

'What?' Natty glared at his cousin, seeing the same anger reflected.

'You heard me. All this shit that's going down . . . it's your fault.'

'That's not fair, Stef,' said Spence.

'Isn't it? Natty's supposed to be in charge. He's supposed to be the one people can turn to, but look at him.' Stefon glared at Natty. 'You folded, and now we're sitting here, unable to move, all because you couldn't do your job and just finish Roman. You not being able to put the crew first, fucked everything.'

Natty stood, ignoring Spence, who tried to pull him back down.

'As always, you don't have a clue what you're talking about,' he snapped. 'Look at me? Look at *you*. Why are you even here? You came crawling back to Leeds because whatever hustle you were running elsewhere probably flopped. I took you on with no hesitation, and this is how you wanna come at me?' He moved closer to Stefon. 'Fuck you.'

Stefon's face twisted with anger, and he hauled off and clocked Natty in the face. Natty stumbled back, but righted his position, dodging the second blow and hitting Stefon in the solar plexus. Growling, Stefon slammed into Natty, and they fell to the floor, Natty groaning in pain as his ribs were jolted.

They were strong, well-matched, even with Natty's injuries. They each landed a couple of shots, then scrambled back to their feet.

Breathing hard, Natty nodded, moving forward to attack again, but Spence got in between them.

'That's it!' He bellowed. 'This is not the time for this. You two are family. Family sticks together. They don't turn on one another, especially when you need them the most.'

Natty and Stefon were breathing hard, but Spence's words were doing the trick. Locking eyes with his cousin, Natty gave him a stiff nod.

'He's right,' he said a moment later. 'You were right about some things you said too, Stef. I don't wanna be fighting you. I want us to work together.'

Stefon sighed, nodding back in agreement and wiping his lip.

'I want that too, cuz. A big part of me was probably still seeing you as a yout, but we need to bury this.'

They shook hands. Spence grinned at the pair, patting them both on the back. They all sat down, and Spence fixed three glasses of brandy. They toasted and drank.

'What's on your mind, Nat?' He asked after a while.

'There's a lot going on, but we're gonna break things down one by one,' said Natty, feeling more confident than he had in a while. 'I have something big to share.'

'Cool. We're listening,' said Stefon. Natty gave him a grim smile.

'Not yet. Before we take that step, we've got some work to do. Roman needs to be dealt with, once and for all.'

'Okay,' said Spence. 'How do we get to him?'

'I've got a plan, but we're gonna need help to execute it.'

'Whose help?' Stefon asked, frowning. Natty laughed.

'A friendly detective mate of mine,' he said.

CHAPTER FORTY-ONE

BROWN WAS SPRAWLED on his sofa watching a football game when his phone rang. Sitting up, he groped around for the device, half in a stupor. When he saw the caller, he grinned before answering.

'Deeds.'

'I've got what you asked for.'

'Just like that?' Brown had expected more fight from Natty Deeds. He'd watched him for a while before he'd initially made his move, and had liked what he'd seen. Deeds had the bloodline and the force to go out and take the streets of Leeds.

All he needed was someone to give him the right leg up, and when Raider was murdered, Brown thought he had that. The aim was to slowly bring Deeds along, and make him dependent on what the police force could do for him.

As Deeds rose, Brown too would rise through the ranks, sitting pretty like the higher-ups he swore up and down were connected to Mitch Dunn.

Deeds was too stubborn, though. He felt he was the one making the rules, and it had forced Brown to show him who was really in charge.

Apparently, the beating had paid off.

'Yeah. The last thing I need is more trouble.' Deeds sounded troubled, and it caused the grin on Brown's face to rise. The money would help him and his compatriots massively. A nice cash injection before they moved on to the next phase of their plan.

'It's bad that it took a sharp lesson for you to learn that, but at least you learned,' said Brown, not attempting to keep the smugness out of his voice. He was surprised at how little effort it had taken to break the criminal down, and regretted not smacking him around from the start. Sometimes he tried too hard to be subtle when it wasn't needed. When Natty didn't respond, Brown continued. 'You shouldn't be so hard-headed, Deeds. Especially when people are trying to help you. It worked out for the best, though. Didn't it?'

'When do you want to meet?' For the first time, Deeds sounded annoyed, and that only made it sweeter for Brown. His team hadn't liked the idea of working with Deeds in the first place, but he'd shown them. He was the leader for a reason. He had vision the others didn't, and it was paying off handsomely. No matter how the conversation ended, Brown had already won. He was two moves ahead of everyone else, and this solidified it.

'I'll be in touch. Keep the goods close and be ready to bounce. It's hot at the moment, with all the mess you and your bandits caused. We'll discuss that too, face to face. Understand.'

Deeds paused, and Brown waited him out.

'I understand.'

Deeds hung up, and Brown laughed out loud. Standing up, the football match forgotten, he fixed himself a glass of Bacardi and lemonade, beaming. This was brilliant. He couldn't have planned it any better.

When he'd calmed down, he put the next stage of the plan into action. Scrolling through his phone, he stopped at the number he'd acquired a few weeks ago, but had yet to use. Calling it, his heart raced in anticipation. He was so close.

'Who's this?' A voice answered, clear but cautious.

'Don't piss around. I know you saved my number,' said Brown.

'Get to the point, or I'm hanging up.'

Brown's eyes narrowed. These criminals had major chips on their shoulders. He would look forward to breaking this one too.

'I'm meeting your competition tomorrow.'

There was a pause on the other end.

'Go on . . .'

Brown smirked, knowing he had Roman's full attention. Through his street contacts, he'd arranged a meeting with him to discuss doing some business after the Dunns had been eliminated. Brown had made tidy money from Natty Deeds over the past few months, but that run had come to an end.

'I'll provide the time and place for a one-off fee. After that, we're in business, and you pay me every week.'

'How much?'

'Five hundred bags up front.' Brown held his breath, unsurprised at the derisive snort on the other end.

'You must be on spice if you think I'm going for that.'

'I'm sure you've already had me checked out, Roman. You know my reputation, and you know I can deliver. Think about the benefits of having your rival on a platter, alone and vulnerable, then decide if it's worth it.'

More silence.

'One hundred bags up front. The rest after the deed is done. Take it or leave it.'

'Done,' said Brown. 'I'll lock down the spot. You get the money together.'

Roman hung up, and Brown grinned at his phone. The Dunns would be weakened by Deeds' death. He was their frontman. The advantage would go to Roman, and Brown would sit behind the throne, pulling strings, manipulating things to his advantage, as his star rose within the police department.

Success was so close, he could almost taste it.

———

AFTER SPEAKING WITH BROWN, Roman made a phone call, pleased when Ahmed promptly answered.

'Hello, Roman. How are we doing?' Ahmed's attitude had improved immensely since Roman had made his move. While being unable to freely operate in Chapeltown was a negative, that he'd caused the Dunns to backpedal was a plus factor, and put the advantage firmly with Roman. He was pleased to have them off his back for now, but there was still work to do.

'We're on. That bent Fed came through. The one I asked you lot to check out.'

'Excellent. Next steps?'

'We're meeting tomorrow. Deeds thinks he's meeting them, but my people will be waiting for him.'

'Wonderful. I look forward to the aftermath. Contact us when it's done.'

Roman hung up on Ahmed, nodding to himself. He dialled another number, ready to speak to his remaining team and let them know the play.

At this stage, getting Natty was almost as good as getting Mitch. He would focus on the chance he had, then consider what would come next. Taking out the Dunn's frontman so soon after attacking their crew directly, would turn the streets further against Mitch and his remaining people.

The money it would cost was huge, but the potential profits that he could garner with a smoother market were astronomical.

As the first subordinate answered, Roman put the thoughts to one side for now. He needed to get there first.

CHAPTER FORTY-TWO

THE MEETING SPOT was an abandoned house near Harehills. Brown was the first to arrive. He walked in by himself, unworried. His team was nearby. They would let him know when Roman and Natty arrived. He'd staggered it so Natty would arrive first. Brown would ensure he got paid twice, then he would get rid of both Natty and Roman, ultimately taking the credit for ending the gang war.

He allowed himself a smile. It was all so close. He had made the most of an unpleasant situation, and as he always did, he would profit. The gangsters had no idea what was coming to them. Brown's phone buzzed. He checked the screen, smile widening when he saw the number Natty always called from.

'I'm nearby,' said Natty.

'Good. Walk straight in. I'll be waiting for you.'

———

'THERE HE IS. We should take him now.'

Roman ignored the chatter of his men. His pulse throbbed, breathing intensifying when he saw Natty Deeds climb from the car. A bodyguard waited in the driver's seat. He was likely armed, but wouldn't be a problem. They would take him out along with his boss.

'It's a good thing we got here early,' said Roman. 'Get your guns ready. Brown said we're gonna give them a few minutes, then rush in and take Natty.'

'What about the copper?'

Roman allowed his grin to widen. In the slight light from their phone screens, it looked almost grotesque.

'Take him out too. I'm not paying him another penny.'

————

NATTY WALKED TO THE SPOT, glancing back at his bodyguard. He tried to remain in control, but his heart was smashing wildly against his chest. What he'd planned earlier now seemed silly. There were so many things that could go wrong. Righting himself, he calmed down. He needed to make it through, regardless of what happened.

He'd done the right thing.

Natty entered the house, floorboards immediately creaking underneath his weight. Brown had picked a suitable spot. No one would sneak up on him without him knowing it.

He headed into the barren room that was likely once a living room. A flickering, dim lightbulb was the only light in the place, just allowing him to see Detective Inspector Brown, watching him with a speculative look.

After a long moment, Brown smiled.

'Glad you could make it, Deeds. You look well . . . all things considered.'

Natty didn't rise to the bait. Instead, he yawned.

'It's been a rough few days.'

'That could all have been avoided, if you'd just played the game the right way.'

'Snitching isn't the right way,' said Natty. 'Neither is dealing with a bent Fed. Brown, you're nothing. You can't even do your job without a leg-up. Let's be honest, you don't help anyone but yourself.'

He'd got him. Brown's jovial demeanour vanished, and the ugly parasite Natty was more familiar with resurfaced.

'Don't you dare judge me, you piece of shit. How can you? You're here right now because you need me. You'll always need me, bro. You don't get to be a disgusting, drug-pedalling scumbag, and then try to judge the people on the side of good.' Brown spat on the floor. 'I'm not wasting my breath on you. Hand over the fucking bag.'

Natty tossed the bag on the floor. Brown shot him a dirty look, then knelt down, using the flashlight on his phone to check the money.

'Make sure you're all in place,' said Dawkins. He and the others had a selection of unmarked guns, along with masks and gloves, in case there were any witnesses. They stepped from the car, ready to take out Roman once he showed, along with any other loose ends.

'We know, Dawkins,' another man groused.

'You better know. If you fuck up, you won't make it back to your slag in Scott Hall.'

Guns ready, they moved forward. A sharp crack sounded, and one of Dawkins's men slid to the ground.

'Ambush!' Dawkins called out, but he was too late. They didn't even get their guns up, all four of them dropped where they stood. A slender female stood over Dawkins, winking, before pulling the trigger.

'What the fuck is this?' Brown asked, looking up at Natty. 'I wanted one hundred grand. There's ten here, tops.'

'Yeah. Ten's about right,' said Natty. He had his gun out, and he aimed it at Brown, enjoying the way the detective's eyes widened. 'I don't think you're gonna get to spend it, though.'

'You can't be serious . . . do you know who I am?' snapped Brown.

'Yeah. A greedy prick who thought he had me in his pocket.'

'Deeds, put the gun down and don't be silly. Don't do something you're gonna regret,' said Brown, his voice trembling slightly.

Gunshots rang out then. Brown internally rejoiced, expecting Natty to panic, to turn away and allow him to get the gun. Instead, Natty grinned.

'Right on time,' he said, pulling the trigger.

———

'FUCK THIS, LET'S GO IN,' said Roman. He and his team gathered their guns and stepped from the ride. They crossed the road to the house, only for all hell to break loose.

Roman saw two of his men fall before the others could shoot back. He had no idea where the enemy had come from, but he recognised two of them: Spence and Natty's cousin, Stefon. Rather than shoot back, he ran toward the house, narrowly dodging a bullet heading his way.

He heard yells and screams, but he didn't stop, bursting into the house.

———

ROMAN HAD HIS GUN READY, charging into the room, firing when he saw Natty, who ducked out of the way and returned fire. The pair traded shots, but the small room and lack of cover made it difficult to gain an advantage. A bullet narrowly whizzed by Natty's face, and he held his breath. That had been too close for comfort.

'This is better,' Roman yelled. 'I kill you, and I'm free. Don't even have to spend my money,' he said. 'Better make your shots count, pussy.'

Natty didn't respond, though he took Roman's advice, shooting out the light, bathing the pair in darkness. Roman fired blindly, his shot grazing Natty's neck. It burned, but he'd got what he wanted. Using the muzzle flash, Natty shot Roman in the chest.

Roman's gun went flying, the ramshackle room shaking when his body hit the floor. Gingerly touching his neck, Natty edged forward, barely able to make out Roman's features in the dark. He heard his wheezing, then fumbled for his phone, wanting to see his face.

Roman was bleeding heavily, choking on blood as he tried to speak. Natty didn't smile. He took no pleasure in what he needed to do.

'Tell Keith I said hello,' he uttered, then fired two more shots into Roman's chest.

———

Outside, Natty again touched his neck. There was a lot of blood, but the bullet had barely clipped him. He'd get it looked at once they were done.

Natty checked his pockets, ensuring he still had Brown's phone, planning to dispose of it later.

Lisa, Stefon, Spence, and several others stood there. They nodded to Natty, and he nodded back, letting them know it was done. Keeping their heads low, they quickly left the scene, leaving the dead bodies slumped in the streets.

CHAPTER FORTY-THREE

THE AFTERMATH of the *Harehills Massacre* was as chaotic as
expected. A medley of officers had arrived on the scene, stunned at
what they'd seen. The reports were sketchy, but Detective Inspector
Christopher Brown, a recipient of numerous commendations, but one
currently under investigation, was found alongside Roman Fielding, a
criminal not long released from prison, with high-level links to organ-
ised crime.

They had found money at the scene, but no one was saying how
much.

The investigation remained ongoing, but if the rumour mill was to
be believed, all those involved simply wanted to put the matter to bed.
Police officers being linked to turf wars and being found alongside
nearly a dozen bodies was damaging to their reputation.

THE STREETS KNEW DIFFERENTLY. No one could prove it, but The Dunns
stood tall in the end. They'd responded to Roman's attack on their
organisation, by wiping out his team, along with a few corrupt officers.

The incident enhanced Natty's already impressive reputation, and the customers that had scuttled away from the crew initially, returned in droves, once again wanting to do business.

———

NATTY DROVE to Lorraine's mum's place two days after the murders of Brown and Roman.

It had taken a while to get everything back in order. The pipeline was moving again. People were being served product, and those in the streets were breathing deeply, happy to be away from the drama that had plagued the Hood.

Natty had been front and centre, working through his problems until he could not avoid them. He felt nothing at the deaths of Brown and Roman. There was no sense of relief, just a dull reality.

Without thinking, he touched his neck as he climbed out of the ride. It was hard to believe he'd been shot. Looking back, Natty knew he should have had a better plan for dealing with Roman. Hubris had taken over, and he couldn't allow that to happen again. He had a bodyguard following in another car.

The war was done, but he wasn't ready to relax just yet.

Lorraine met him at the door. She looked pale and drawn, and nervous to be around him, which hurt. He gave her a small smile, crushed when she didn't return it.

'Can I come in?'

Lorraine sighed. 'I don't think that's a good idea, Natty. She glanced past him. Natty was unsure what she was looking for, but her fear and nervousness were palpable.

'It's over, Lo. That whole situation . . . the one you got caught up in, is done.'

'I know,' said Lorraine with a curt nod. 'I saw the news. You've been busy.'

The conversation was jarring for Natty. He wasn't used to Lorraine being fully part of his world, and wasn't sure how to take the cavalier statement.

'I'm sorry for what happened,' he said.

'Are you apologising for Lisa, or something else?'

Natty tensed. He didn't want to have the conversation at all, especially on a doorstep.

'Lo, Lisa is just someone I work with.'

'That's not true. I know what I walked in on, Nat. I saw you looked together. How close you were when I entered that room.' She took a deep breath. 'Worst of all, I saw you looked together when you were killing those men.'

Instinctively, Natty glanced over his shoulder. He didn't like this. He felt exposed. Lorraine was looking at him, but her eyes were devoid of their usual energy. He had done this to the woman he loved, and it didn't feel good.

'Lo . . .' he tried again, but she shook her head.

'I don't know if I can do it, Nat. Stand by your side like that.'

'You don't have to. I love you. I love Jaden. Having you both with me makes everything else easier. That's all I want from you. It's all I've ever wanted.'

'I can't see it like that, Nat. I wish I could, but I can't. When you were angry about Raider . . . you gave me time. Space. Now, I'm asking for the same thing.'

Natty stumbled, his legs suddenly weak. He didn't like this. This wasn't how it was supposed to go.

'What does that mean?' He asked dumbly.

'It means that you need to do what you're supposed to do . . .' she took another deep breath, '. . . and then we'll see.'

Heartbroken, Natty watched as the door was closed, wondering if they were done for good.

———

LORRAINE BURST into tears as she closed the door, glad that her mum and Jaden weren't around to see her like this. She went back to the bathroom, where she had been before Natty knocked. Looking on top of the sink, she hoped it had been a figment of her imagination, but it wasn't.

The positive pregnancy test remained where she'd left it.

———

Spence and Stefon were waiting in place as Natty met them at the lower entrance to Potternewton Park. They exchanged greetings, then walked up the hill. The autumn weather was warm enough to have people out, walking the trail, a few jogging. To the right, there was even a dreadlocked man in a vest and shorts, teaching yoga to a group of women.

The trio walked along in silence, waiting for Natty to speak.

'Mitch had my dad killed.'

The reaction was as expected. Both Spence and Stefon immediately stopped short, mouths open as they gawped at Natty. He nodded, confirming his words.

'That can't be true,' said Stefon, as Spence shook his head in shock. 'That's his brother. He wouldn't do that.'

'I know how you feel, cuz. I wanted to think that too. I've always been proud to be part of my family, but when I found out, it stunned me to my core,' said Natty.

'How did you find out?' Spence asked softly.

'My mum told me. Blurted it out, really. We were arguing, and she let some stuff go. Mitch had my dad killed. She knew about it.'

The pieces clicked for Spence. Natty saw it from the expression on his friend's face, the shock replaced with grim realisation.

'Rudy did it.'

Natty nodded.

'I'm sorry.'

To Natty's surprise, the words came from Stefon. He'd never seen such a desolate expression on his cousin's face.

'That's why you stopped talking to her. I let her manipulate me . . . I should have just asked you.'

'Nah, you did what you needed to do. I've been living with this shit for a while. I should have told you. Both of you, but I was worried.'

'You thought we might work against you,' said Spence, fully into business mode now.

'Mitch is our boss. He's powerful. Even more so now that I wiped out his main opposition. I'm taking a chance by telling you, but I trust you both. You're my blood and my family. Both of you. Whatever happens, you deserve to know the truth.'

Spence and Stefon shared a look, Natty unable to glean their expressions. They seemed to come to some unspoken arrangement, then Spence shrugged.

'Right. When are we going at your unc again?'

'Again?' Natty asked.

'It's obvious now that it was you the first time,' said Spence.

'You might have actually succeeded if you'd reached out,' added Stefon.

Natty's heart raced, unable to accept what was happening.

'You mean . . . you're with me?'

Spence snorted. Stefon shook his head.

'Like you said, we're family. No matter how powerful your uncle is, he doesn't get to corrupt that,' said Spence.

Natty hugged them both, overcome with emotion. Both men patted him on the shoulder as he let them go.

'Thank you,' he said, as sincere as he'd ever been in his life.

'You don't need to thank us,' said Stefon. 'I hope you've got a plan, because this shit won't be easy.'

'Let's finish getting our exercise in. After that, lunch is on me. We'll see what we can get into.'

————

Paula let Mitch in, giving him a hug, her expression tight. Mitch understood it. Paula was a good woman, and life had knocked her around a lot. She'd settled with a good one in Clarke, and she didn't want to lose him.

Mitch hoped she wouldn't.

'How are you getting on, darling?' Mitch asked. Paula sighed.

'Just taking it as it comes. Nothing else to do,' she said. Mitch patted her on the shoulder, though the gesture was awkward. 'Can I get you a drink?'

Minutes later, Mitch had a cup of coffee, and sat in the living room with Clarke. His right-hand man was lying on the sofa, wearing a thin t-shirt and cotton trousers. He looked tired, older than Mitch remembered seeing him. That made Mitch pause. He needed Clarke. He was one of his pillars, and had been there since the beginning.

No matter what happened, he needed to make sure his subordinate made it through this.

To Mitch's surprise, the house was quiet — except for the western playing on the television. He wondered where the kids were, and if Clarke and Paula had made them go out, because he was coming.

'How are you feeling?' He asked Clarke. Clarke scratched his chin.

'Not the first time I've been shot. Paula is pissed with me, though. Says I don't value my life.'

'Do any of us?'

The pair chuckled.

'I spoke with Lisa,' said Clarke. 'She told me about Roman and the bent copper. Nice little result there.'

'Yeah. They did well,' said Mitch. 'Took them longer than it needed to, though. A lot of people got hurt behind that, and now we need to build back up.'

Business had resumed for the Dunns, but there were still a few factors Mitch wasn't clear on. The corrupt team of officers were ones he was familiar with. They weren't on his payroll, but their bosses were, and they'd told him nothing about their involvement with his nephew.

It made him wonder how many other bits of information he wasn't privy to.

'We will,' said Clarke. 'I'll be back with you as soon as possible. I'm losing my mind sitting around here.'

'You're going to take your time. If you don't, I'm gonna tell Paula what you're saying, and she'll deal with you.'

Clarke grinned. 'Fair enough.'

Mitch sipped his drink, savouring the flavour. Paula could make one hell of a cup of coffee. It was a skill few people got right, he'd learned over the years.

'I've got other things to discuss with you.'

Clarke frowned. 'What's going on?'

'Nathaniel's cousin, Stefon.'

'What about him? I know you wanted him followed, but we found nothing concerning when we shadowed him.'

Mitch waved his hand. 'This isn't about that. He came to see me, after you vouched for him. He told me that Nathaniel and his mum aren't talking. In fact, they haven't been talking for a while. Did you know?'

Clarke shook his head, puzzled. 'I don't think Natty has ever mentioned his mum to me. Why aren't they talking?'

'She told him some things, and he believed them.'

'What things?' Clarke pressed, as Mitch expected.

'He thinks I had Ty killed.'

Clarke's eyes narrowed, mingled with the puzzlement on his face.

'Why would he think that?'

'Because his bitter mum, the one who I've always looked after, put the idea in his head. Nathaniel being Nathaniel, he believed her,' said Mitch.

'Is it true?' Clarke asked a moment later.

'He believes it is,' replied Mitch. He saw the doubt on Clarke's face, and he didn't like it. Mitch had done the right thing all those years ago, but Clarke valued loyalty. Mitch wasn't sure he could make a case for why he'd done it that Clarke would buy.

'Natty's intelligent, Mitch. I'm guessing he knows his mum better than anyone. He wouldn't blindly believe something so deep. Not without cause.'

'What are you asking?' Mitch snapped, all civility vanishing. Clarke stared back at him, taking his time before responding.

'I've already said it, Mitch. Even asking goes way beyond my pay grade, but I'll as once more. Did you have your brother killed?'

Mitch didn't hesitate.

'No. Of course I didn't.'

EPILOGUE

JAKKAR SAT in the main warehouse. Ahmed and Mustafir worked out of here, and he understood why. It was out of the way, and spacious enough for them to sprawl out. He listened to the sounds of people working, pondering the next steps.

Roman, the pawn, had failed. With him gone, the organisation was out a key distributor. Along with the dealers that Mitch had eliminated, this left them in a rough position in Leeds. They would need to act soon, or they would lose their foothold in the city. The cost to establish themselves would be huge, and it would force Jakkar to answer tough questions if that happened.

Jakkar had wanted to settle his score with Mitch Dunn for years, yet despite his power and resource, he'd underestimated the kingpin, and it had cost him momentum. Mitch had lorded over him for years, safe in his bubble, but now, the time had for him to pay his dues.

'They're here, sir,' a man poked his head around the office door after knocking.

'Show them in.'

The two men were unassuming, but hard-eyed. Zayan and Ghazan were casually dressed in black. Both stood in front of Jakkar, feet a yard or two apart, hands clasped behind their backs.

'Have you been briefed on the objective?' Jakkar asked.

'We have,' said Zayan promptly.

'Good,' said Jakkar. 'You'll have whatever you need. I believe the necessary contact numbers have already been provided.' He glanced from Zayan to Ghazan. 'I want all the Dunns eliminated. Once and for all.'

ALSO BY RICKY BLACK

The Target Series:

Origins: The Road To Power

Target

Target Part 2: The Takedown

Target Part 3: Absolute Power

The Complete Target Series Boxset

The Deeds Family Series:

Blood & Business

Good Deeds, Bad Deeds

Deeds to the City

Hustler's Ambition

No More Deeds

Other books by Ricky Black:

Homecoming

ABOUT RICKY BLACK

Ricky Black was born and raised in Chapeltown, Leeds.

In 2016, he published the first of his crime series, Target, and has published eleven more books since.

Visit https://rickyblackbooks.com for information regarding new releases and special offers, and promotions.

To MyMy

Because you made me promise to write this.

And because I love you.

Copyright © 2023 by Ricky Black

All rights reserved.

No part of this book may be reproduced in any form or by any electronic or mechanical means, including information storage and retrieval systems, without written permission from the author, except for the use of brief quotations in a book review.

Printed in Great Britain
by Amazon

23132344R00189